GW00771200

LEGION THAT WAS

BOOK I OF THE IRONBREAKERS

Vijay Hare

First paperback and eBook editions published in 2021 through Amazon.

Cover image by Book Beaver

Editorial services provided by John Rickards

ISBN: 9798522515089

The year is AD 12. A once-divided and riven Rome now prospers under the rule of its first Emperor, Caesar Augustus. But the Civil Wars have cast a long shadow, and men still remain who remember the Republic that came before the Empire.

Gaius Sertor Orbus, Praefector of the Emperor's XII Legion, is stripped of his rank following an act of cowardice too shameful to name. Expelled from his beloved Legion, Orbus is given a punishing chance to redeem himself. Taking command of a new Cohort of auxilia, benighted men with no citizenship, prospects or future, he vows to lead his charges to an honourable death. Or perhaps, more dauntingly, to an honest life.

When war calls, Orbus faces a foe who speaks to his own Republican sympathies. How many comrades will he sacrifice for victory? And just how much of his soul?

For Iulus Bond, Gaius Civilius Handa and Brauda Manfredi-Haylock.

PROLOGUE
NO BACKWARD STEP

DEATH HAS COME for me at last.

That, at least, is my hope. A swift and merciless death would be preferable to this. The shame of dishonour. The guilt of still drawing breath with my duty undone.

I swore oaths to stand shoulder to shoulder with my *milites*, to push my people's borders forward. To take no backward step defending Rome's Empire. I swore them out loud, crying them to the sky, and I have broken them.

I am bound to the whipping post, all the better to be punished. That, alone, demonstrates the severity of my sins. As if I did not know already.

Somewhere in the sky above me, a crow calls out. My eyes are closed, but my mouth twitches in a smile. It occurs to me, with a dose of irony, that I have inflicted this fate on countless unlucky souls in my many years with the XII.

Years back, Scipio and I put down a slave rebellion in Pamphylia. I had ten of the ringleaders leashed together before the town they'd failed to overturn, and personally flogged them to within an inch of their lives. One of them died, and I was later told that two others never recovered from the onslaught. None of that ever bothered me, and I never slept any lighter in the years that followed. Honourless men deserve honourless ends, and I have never once questioned my role in asserting that truth.

A small part of me wonders who was chosen to deliver sentence. I cannot turn my head, and whoever it is does not speak. Corporal punishment can only come from a man of officer rank, and that narrows the list considerably.

Thracian, perhaps. He would undoubtedly jump at the chance to humble me, and he certainly has the sadism for it. Or maybe Ardius. I doubt he would lack the professionalism to carry this out. He may not want to, but I cannot see him or Alvanus shying away from the burdens of duty.

Gates of Fire… it could even be Cascana. Has our glorious Legate ordered him to carry out the sentence, as a show of fortitude? That would only compound my shame, if young Cascana suffered for his loyalty to me.

No, I decide. It is not Cascana holding the *flagella* behind me. Legate Urbanus is a hard and unyielding man, but he is not without mercy.

Mercy for Cascana, of course. Not for me. I am beyond the reach of mercy now.

I hear the crack of unwound leather, and the tell-tale *whoosh* of displaced wind as my punisher gives the air a slash. Flagellation, then. Less than I feared, but no less than I deserve. Blood loss alone could finish me off, or maybe infection from my wounds, if the Halls of the Dead are that eager to claim me.

He slashes the air again, again, and again. Warming up his arms, perhaps. Or simply anticipating what is to come. *Whoosh. Whoosh. Whoosh.* I can picture him spinning it mid-air, ready to bring it cracking down between my shoulder-blades.

And then I hear him speak. His voice, oaken and earthy but as strong as a youth's. I recognise it at once, for it belongs to the man who rules my life.

'In the name of Jupiter the Almighty, to whom we cast our gaze up,' Urbanus solemnly intones, 'of Pluto the All-Claimer, to whom we cast our gaze down, and to our beneficent Emperor Augustus, to whom we owe all and cast our gaze askance—' The *flagella*-spinning reaches a fever-pitch. '—do I hold thee unequal before your oaths and duties to your legion.'

Down comes the whip, and my world goes red.

WINTER NIGHTS BITE hard in the Gallic hills and valleys. Not even the fires of Saturnalia can warm us here, but that won't stop the men of the XII from trying.

The torches have been lit. The ale is flowing. The time for feasting is over, the time for Saturn's droning rites further gone still. We are deep into the drinking, and all that follows. The air is hot and heavy and alive. Sound fills all the senses, in the form of singing, shouting and cheering as my milites *forget their Roman-ness for one day of the year, and simply get to be men again.*

Legionaries and officers shout at each other, to each other, with each other. It is the sound of a legion camp in full celebration. To an outsider, it doubtless sounds like hell itself.

To me, it is the sound of life.

'Io, Saturnalia! Io, Saturnalia! Io, Saturnalia!'

Many of them throng together, competing against each other to drink, dance and in some cases fight. Many more have quit our raucous castra *entirely, snatching whatever girls and wenches have caught their fancy for a little fun among the trees.*

Their whoring is not extended to the prisoners, and that at least is something. Lustful violence against the defenceless is not the way of the Fulminata. We hold ourselves to a higher standard, and leave such pursuits to lesser men, in other legions. Few of our captive men and girls are preyed upon by drunken legionaries, few that I can see anyway. The worst transgressors to that unwritten rule will find themselves punished by their officers tomorrow, as if their hangovers and injuries won't be brutal enough.

None of this occupies me. This is a night of feasting and merry hedonism. Hardly a time to worry about my duties.

I keep to the festival's outskirts, nursing my beer. Saturnalia can be a time of upheaval, where free men cook and serve their slaves, and centurions play second fiddle to their own soldiers. I have ignored the jeers and raucous jesting of my legionaries as I served them their meat and ale, taking them in the good spirit I hope they were given. But my part is over now. Some of my fellow officers will happily lead their men into debauchery tonight, but that is not something I particularly care for.

Salius shatters my reverie, crashing down beside me. He shines with glistening sweat, honestly earnt from his frolicking. It catches the light of the torches all around us.

'Good old Praeto,' he half-mumbles. 'He's getting his prick sucked by that girl from the baggage train. The one with the...' He cups his hands over his pecs, spilling drink over his tunic.

In more sober times, Salius is the picture of calm, reserved officiousness. The ale has turned my optio *inside out. His cheeks and brow are ruddy red with the alcohol. I can scarcely believe he hasn't passed out yet, and my incredulity must have shown on my face.*

'Oh, loosen up, Praefector,*' he slurs, clapping my shoulder in a not very professional manner. 'It's Saturnalia. Unscrew that bloody crest off your helmet, you miserable old sod. You'll love it.'*

My men are out of earshot. Salius is a good man in a fight, and an even better optio *off the battlefield. These things grant him the liberty to speak to me like that. If any of the rank and file tried the same, I would march them through snowfall in nothing but tunics and iron-shod boots. Even on Saturnalia.*

As it is, I smile knowingly at him, and take another sip from my flagon.

Something crashes behind us. A man in centurion's garb is wobbling on top of a wooden barrel, drink in hand. He is attempting a rather shaky recital of the Judgement of Paris, but he falls into the men around him before he can manage so much as a verse.

The men around him are evocati, *from their uniforms. Good men, through and through, who have completed their first tour of service. They fight in the legion because they want to, rather than simply having to. That selfless return to duty has a double edge, though. It brings with it a certain ego, and can sometimes render them beyond an officer's easy authority.*

'Bloody Alvanus,' Salius grumbles. 'And he wonders why the men don't respect him.'

But I am no longer listening. I am looking back at the clearing behind us, trying to pick out something – anything – through the trees. I have been looking at the torches for too long, and it has ruined my night vision.

Careless.

'Did you hear that?' I ask the open air.

I CRASH BACK from that first blow, but of course I cannot. I am still bound to the post, and I have nowhere to go. My arms and torso pull back, as taut as the bonds that hold me fast, and all I can do is bleed.

Again, with the *flagella*. Again. And again.

I realise that I am screaming. I cannot stop myself, and I do not want to. I sowed this harvest, after all.

I can barely even hear myself. I hear my heart thumping in my ears, and that is all I hear.

Something trickles down my back. The breeze breathes on my wounds, and that only makes them worse.

SALIUS CRASHES BACKWARD, dead in a moment. A brief but promising military career is ended with a single bronze arrow.

Suddenly, I am sober. The flagon falls from my hand. I am already backing away, stumbling over my feet without daring to turn my back. I find myself moving faster than I have in years. I cannot see them. Not yet. But I know what they are.

'Gauls,' I snarl as I reach the evocati. *A shaft sails past my head, knocking a lantern. 'Gauls! Ambush!'*

Alvanus, at first, is too drunk to comprehend me. I barge a drunken evocatus *aside and clap both of his cheeks, shaking his head with my hands. 'Wake up, man! Bugle! Now!'*

The enemy, the Gallic filth, have planned this ambush well. They'd avoided harrying our scouts and forays into the neutral wilderness, letting us dig in and set up camp unopposed. Then they'd let us be, until Saturnalia came.

That one night of the year when our guard is down. When our legionaries are intoxicated into uselessness. When the chain of command is upturned by commanders playing at being servants.

Stupid, stupid, stupid.

I snatch the horn from Alvanus' belt. Drunken fool. I am shouting at the top of my voice. The milites *all around me finally, finally sense something is wrong.*

I draw in a breath, and bring the bugle to my lips.

Another arrow takes Alvanus' shoulder as I blow. Around me I hear more shouts, some in Latin, some in the Gallic dialects.

And then the screaming starts.

BY THE FIFTH blow, I have no air left to scream. I still can barely hear, but I feel my lungs grow ragged and raw.

My back is now positively sodden. Rivulets of blood *pitter-patter*, worming their way down my shoulder blades. A small, detached part of my mind – the part still capable of conscious thought – wonders if the lashing has torn through to the bone. It is possible. I have seen it happen.

By the sixth and seventh, I feel my consciousness start to fail me.

By the tenth, I can no longer recall my own name.

'ORBUS!' SOMEBODY SHOUTS for me. 'Praefector! Is that you?'

I wheel on my heels. My sword is sheathed away in the command tent, practically half the world away, and this stolen gladius *is all I have. I hold it in my other hand as a pair of* principes *– the least drunk of their tentmates – rush past to wake the most inebriated of their fellows.*

Someone, somewhere, has knocked the torches over. Maybe one of our drunken legionaries by accident, maybe one of the bastard Gauls to smoke us out. But now flames are spreading through the castra, *every bit as quick and lethal as the enemy.*

I clutch Alvanus' bugle with my teeth as I drag him behind me, gladius *at ready.*

'Praefector,' the voice calls again. I know it this time. 'Well met.'

'And you, Nicanor,' I manage through occupied jaws. I spit the horn out, hauling Alvanus over to him. 'Get him to safety. The other centurions?'

'Dead. Gone. Either.' The standard bearer is ever a man of few words, but we are short on time. 'I've lost my signa.*'*

That would warrant a court martial on any other night. I let it pass.

Nicanor looks at me. 'Orders, sir?'

The enemy answers before I can. Something dark and robed and angry crashes into me head-on, bearing me to the ground. I land hard. The impact almost knocks my gladius *out of reach. Almost.*

I catch the oncoming blow. I headbutt. I twist.

I stab.

Nicanor helps drag the dying Gaul off me. I wrench my sword free as I rise. Five seconds, one death blow, and still enough blood to paint the three of us.

The standard bearer hauls Alvanus to his feet. 'He can still run,' he comments. 'What now, Praefector?'

SIXTY-FOUR LEGIONARIES dead. Almost twice that number injured or unable to see battle again for months. The gods only know how much of our armoury and supply train liberated, torched or ruined beyond recovery.

More lost in one night of ambush than in the last three months of campaigning put together. The XII hasn't taken such a mauling in years.

I am owed this. This is what I deserve.

For the first time today, I try to speak. My lips move. My jaws part.

'More,' I mouth to the morning air. 'More…'

WE FALL TOGETHER in a tangle of limbs.

Everything is on fire now. A group of us huddle, back-to-back, in the failing shadow of a burning mess-tent. Gallic blood carpets my face and brow.

Tactics become frivolous when your prey is in disarray. They fall upon their us like nightmares. We fight back, and they die. But we die faster.

My gladius' *pommel cracks a man's skull. He drags me down as he drops. The legionary beside me grabs my shoulder, trying to stop me falling. He fails.*

Someone, somewhere, is blowing a bugle. I recognise the pattern of toots. It is a rallying cry, a call to unity in the middle of our camp.

I fall over Nicanor's corpse as I grab a Gaul's neck. I hammer his head against the stony earth. He is dead. Or stunned. Either way I win.

Blood of Teucer… this is going to be a massacre. Alvanus is gone from my side, dead or fleeing. I haven't seen another centurion, and if Legate Urbanus is still alive, he is camped too far off to fight his way to us. Half of our men are barely even wearing armour, let alone sporting weapons. Beer has slowed the sharpest of us, and utterly ruined the drunkest of us.

I go for my gladius *as more Gauls hurl themselves forward. They bear us to the ground, hacking at us with flensing knives as we struggle for our lives. Proud legionaries with noble lineages – heroes of battle, each and every one of them – are ignobly slaughtered around me, falling to callous murder.*

And this is how it ends.

TIME HAS PASSED.

Urbanus flogs me again, and again. The *flagella* is no longer even sodden. The layer of blood around the knots has hardened. I jolt awake, and the agony is there for me when I do.

One of my fetters has broken. This is no source of relief – I still hang from the whipping post, only now I hang lopsided.

I can hardly complain. I am camp prefect of the XII Fulminata, and I am guilty of fleeing from battle.

I have broken a trust held sacred for nearly thirty years. A trust it is my place and burden to punish lesser men for breaking.

I am not fit to crawl before my legate, let alone hang before him.

I AM CRAWLING. I am choking.

I am crawling through the dead, Gaul and Roman together. I am choking from the blood in my throat, and the burning smoke that fills the air. My gladius *is gone, I don't know where.*

How long have I been down here? Who are these men around me? Are they my own? Should I recognise them?

The fires burn so bright I cannot see. The shadows in the air... they could be clouds of smog that crown the flames. Or maybe the silhouettes of our burning barracks, still somehow keeping their form.

Maybe the smoke is clouding my vision. Maybe it is the blood that fills my eyes.

Or maybe I am dead, and it is the dark halls of Erebus that I steal through now.

I pull my way through the souls of the fallen, somehow finding my feet. That is a mistake. The higher I rise, the less I can breathe. I splutter the burning smoke out from my lungs.

I turn.

I run through the flames, and do not stop.

Somewhere in the chaos behind me, a bugle cries out.

'DOES THIS SOOTHE your shame?' someone calls out. Is that Urbanus' voice? 'Does this scourging give you closure for your treason? For your lack of moral strength?'

The second fetter has broken. I am no longer bound; now I simply lie in the dirt where I undoubtedly belong. Urbanus does not care. The sentence has been carried out.

Something wet and viscous drips from my mouth, falling to earth beneath me. Maybe spit. Maybe blood. Most likely a mix of both.

Footsteps, receding into unconsciousness.

'Remove this honourless wretch from my camp,' Urbanus orders. 'Or simply leave him for the crows.'

PART I
LUSTRICUS

I

TONGUE OF SILVER

THREE KNOCKS ON the masonry outside broke Orbus from his reverie. He'd been thinking about the future, and the thoughts had been dark.

'Come in.' He kept the words neutral, tactfully hiding his eagerness. His would-be gaolers here in the *Castra Praetoria* had allowed him Puli for day-to-day use, but other than the slave, this would be Orbus' first actual visitor since his confinement.

He didn't have long to speculate. The crisp young man who strode inside wore a centurion's embroidered tunic of office, as well as the silver-plated leather belt worn by every soldier of Rome. It was fashioned to accommodate a sword-sheath, and quite tellingly that sheath wasn't empty.

The officer had come armed, and to openly bear arms inside the city walls required clearance not easily sought. That *gladius*, catching the afternoon light from the cell's one small porthole, was a statement all on its own. It had probably been Urbanus' idea, for the first visitor to be seen to make demands, rather than amends. Orbus' hopes for what lay ahead, already low, quietly plummeted.

'Praefector,' the Centurion said after a long moment, seemingly lost for words. This incarcerated meeting didn't come naturally to either of them. 'It is… good to see you. Even in these circumstances.'

Iulus Cascana had a youthful, unscarred face with a default expression of tentative hope. To a man who didn't know him well, that might come across as naïve and idealistic. But Orbus was not one of those people, and he knew Cascana was neither of those things.

'Iulus…' he began, and found himself at a similar loss. The first thing he said wasn't how he'd meant to start this. 'Do the others know you are here?'

Cascana half-smiled, more ironic than amused. 'The Legate granted me permission to see you, before we begin proceedings. It was a favour to me, not you.' His gaze briefly toured the metal sleeping rack, the small goblet and carafe of drinking water, and the cell's other spartan features before re-alighting on Orbus. 'Today is the day, Praefector. The officers have said their pieces. Urbanus' final judgement awaits.'

'It's happening, then.' Orbus snorted, and then suddenly winced. He'd moved his head too fast, which sent a jolt of pain down the scarring over his back. He was still getting used to that. 'I am to be court-martialled.' Of course he was. Else why bother bringing him back to Rome?

'Indeed,' was Cascana's neutral reply. 'I must admit, it has been a while since I last saw the other centurions so in lockstep, or so in touch with the feelings of the men. The scale of your transgression is not in question, nor was Urbanus' choice to flagellate you. All that needs deciding is the rest of the punishment. You have become a rather unpopular man, Praefector.'

Orbus had to supress a wry smile at the other man's politic response. Cascana was young for his rank, and had earnt his crest fair and square. But he was no longer the sallow, lanky youth Orbus had helped his father teach to fight. Years had passed, wars had tempered them both, and yet Orbus still sometimes found himself forgetting that.

He moved – or more accurately, hobbled – over to the washing basin at the foot of his sleeping rack, taking a moment to splash some water over his haggard features.

'I would hazard a guess,' he spoke as he washed his face, 'that once today is said and done, you will no longer be addressing me as Praefector.'

Cascana couldn't look him in the eye. For whatever it was worth, he didn't try to lie to him either.

'Come now, uncle. The Legate is waiting.'

IT WAS STARTING to get dark as they made their way through the fortress. Light came in the form of burning braziers set into the granite walls, or torches carried in the hands of passing Praetorians. Sound came from within and without, from the muffled murmuring of raised and lowered voices within the walls and from the distant song of cicadas and wind outside.

Cascana must have sensed Orbus' thoughts, for he chimed in as soon as the Guardsmen were out of earshot.

'I don't trust them, either.'

It was a sentiment shared by many among the legions, although few were tactless enough to speak it openly. Most outsiders would chalk it down to a soldier's simple grievance; the Praetorians rarely left the city borders, and rarely fought at the front lines without their emperor. It was in battle that the truest bonds of brotherhood were forged, and so the Praetorians simply couldn't forge those bonds of trust.

A soldier's grievance, then. Or maybe it was something more.

'Look sharp, Praefector,' Cascana warned him as they ducked under a stone lintel, entering another antechamber. 'We are almost there.'

'I didn't know if you'd survived,' said Orbus apropos of nothing. 'I knew nobody high up the chain could had died... but none of them would tell me anything. That was the worst part, even after everything else.'

That brought Cascana to a halt. He turned back to look at the Praefector almost twenty years his senior, a man he'd come to love like family who returned the feeling in kind.

Orbus fought back the instinct telling him to keep the silence, to not ruin the moment. For all he knew, this would be the last private word they'd share before Urbanus and the officers decided his fate.

'I know I've let you down, Iulus. Let you all down. But whatever is to come...' He trailed off. What in Pluto's depths was he even trying to ask for? Lenience in his sentencing? He hardly had any grounds for it. A reprieve for mercy? That would have been unforgivably craven, even privately to Cascana.

Orbus realised the younger officer was still watching him intently.

'Do you believe I deserve what is to come?' he eventually finished. It wasn't what he'd planned to say, but the words felt right as they left him. If

Urbanus and the others had made up their minds, nothing Cascana could say would sway them anyway.

The Centurion didn't reply for a moment. There was no malice or judgement in his expression. But nothing particularly forgiving, or reassuring, either. The little Iulus of yore had never been skilled at lying or delicacy, especially not with his nearest and dearest. But the prudent and ambitious Centurion had come a long way since then, no matter what his intentions were.

'I suppose,' Cascana neutrally replied, turning to stride up the stone walkway, 'that would depend on what is to come.'

'STATE YOUR NAME,' Urbanus calmly demanded, 'in its entirety, for the tablet.'

Orbus hadn't even noticed the scribe in the corner of the room, hunched wretchedly over his writing column. Such was the Legate's force of presence.

'Gaius Sertor Orbus, of the Emperor's XII Legion.'

'State your rank,' Urbanus replied just the same, beat for beat, 'in its entirety, for the tablet.'

'I hold the rank of *praefectus castrorum*. Camp prefect.'

'State your tribe,' the Legate continued to press him, 'for the tablet.'

Orbus swallowed. 'The Palatina.'

The clerk went on writing, the *scritch-scratch* of stylus on wax now the loudest sound in the chamber.

'Then we are ready to begin,' Urbanus replied.

Decius Octus Urbanus was a legate – and more precisely, a human being – of whetstone-honed precision. This was the first time Orbus had seen the old man since Saturnalia, over a month ago.

On the outside Urbanus appeared little different since then. His thick crown of silver hair, normally manicured in peacetime with stately care, had been simply slicked back and tied to obedience as was his preference on deployment. Urbanus' face was the picture of stentorian creases and furrows it always was. Orbus doubted few men in the XII could tell which of those lines had come with age, and which were from frowning.

'How fare your wounds, Praefector?' he suddenly asked, from nowhere.

Orbus swallowed. Was this an attempt to catch him off guard?

'They are healing, my *Legatus*.'

'Good.' Urbanus didn't seem inclined to delve into that any further. He looked at the six impromptu jurors around him, five of them centurions of the Legion's First Cohort. They bored into Orbus with their eyes, and though few of them could truly emulate Urbanus' exquisite self-control, they gave it their surest efforts nonetheless.

The chosen chamber of judgement was a large, circular hall that overlooked the Quirinal and Viminal Hills. A horizontal slit porthole dominated one half of the circular roof, allowing quite the commanding view.

It was also rather airier than the lattice of passages and walkways that led here, and that was a small mercy. Orbus had dressed in his full Praefector's panoply, minus arms – a court martial demanded no less – and the number of clustered torches in such claustrophobic confines had made him sweat through his tunic. At least in here he'd be able to breathe easily.

'You are aware of the magnitude of your transgressions, as well as the calamitous example you have set to the men under your command,' Urbanus began, dispassionately, as if simply reading from a manuscript or declaiming an ancient piece of rhetoric, 'and the charge, as you are no doubt equally aware, is of the highest magnitude.'

Urbanus paused for a moment, letting that sink in. No-one needed to say the word out loud, and Orbus clearly knew what he was in for. *Maiestas*. A treason charge.

In a lawcourt, that alone would see him half the way to the Tarpeian Rock. But the Roman army dealt with its own. Justice here was unlikely to be quite so swift and painless.

'I appreciate the seriousness of the charge,' Orbus gravely replied. 'As was impressed upon me by my return to Rome, and my confinement here in the *Castra Praetoria*.'

That actually made Sallus Thracian smirk, from his seat at Urbanus' side. He sat nearest the Legate, as was his right as *primus pilus*, the First Spear. Being the Cohort's premier centurion had its burdens and responsibilities, but as Orbus' gaze met Thracian's tanned, beady face, it was all too easy to appreciate the privileges too. Orbus wondered just what counsel he'd been pouring into Urbanus' ear before he'd got here.

He had a point, at any rate. Orbus had been kept in the officers' personal custody ever since his flight and recapture, and had journeyed back to Rome under guard. He'd been remanded in this fortress, as far away from the men of the XII as was possible.

If Orbus had been billeted in the XII's usual *Principia* with his men, he would have been lucky to survive a single night. A dagger in a dark corridor, ground glass or pottery in his morning mess; a callous murder would have come to him, one way or another, no matter what fate the Legion's officers decided for him. Assuming they would even try to collar their men.

'Will I be granted the chance to speak in my defence?' Orbus found himself asking. Only he knew, immediately, that he'd picked the wrong way to broach the subject. Urbanus' face remained impassive as ever, but he could almost sense the roiling emotion behind his eyes. The other officers – men that Orbus technically outranked – were less skilled at hiding their distaste. Knuckles tightened over armrests, and eyes narrowed. The only man who didn't appear on the edge of anger was Cascana.

'This is not a court of law, Praefector,' Urbanus finally replied. 'And you are not on trial. The degree of punishment has already been decided. Only the passing of the final sentence remains, once we decide whether or not there were any extenuating factors or circumstances to mitigate.' For a minute, he seemed to soften into the Legate Orbus had followed in happier days. Not that the man had been particularly soft on *any* day. 'You will get your chance to speak, Orbus, but do not count on changing our minds. And there are other, better men who will speak first.'

Orbus cast his gaze over the gathered centurions. 'Ask your questions, my comrades. I will answer what I can.'

Rufus Alvanus began to chuckle, drawing the others' attention. Before the Praefector's arrival, he and

Marcus Scipio had been hunched together, whispering conspiratorially. They'd put a stop to that as soon as Orbus had looked their way, pulling apart with an almost farcical lack of subtlety.

The two centurions had plenty in common – they commanded the two centuries of *triarii*, the most heavily-armed and elite veterans of the Cohort – but two more different men could seldom ever be found. Only today they were united in their gaze of malevolent suspicion, regarding Orbus as if his sins were somehow contagious.

'We talked of this a great deal,' Alvanus began, taking his cue to begin the inquisition. 'We talked of it on the march back to Rome. We talked of it in the barracks. And just now, in the hours you were pissing your dreams away in that cell.' He snorted. 'The oh-so-clever men around me see this as a matter of principle. As if how we deal with you will reflect on how we deal with problems in the Legion going forward.'

'Won't it?' Orbus asked him drily.

Alvanus glared daggers at him for a moment before pressing on. 'Maybe,' he decided. 'Maybe the opinions of *civilians* should matter to men of arms... but let's just cut to the meat of it, shall we?' He held up one hand, horizontal, palm down above his bench.

'The penalty for desertion, in the rank and file—' He waved his hand to mark that one point. '—is *fustuarium*. A painful death, but a quick one.' He then raised his hand a little higher. 'Desertion for a *decanus*, watchman or *optio*? *Fustuarium* again, with a considerable forfeiture of money and estate. Better, in my opinion, as the punishment affects more than the guilty party, just as the crime does.' Alvanus raised his hand higher still, almost level with his eyeline. 'But desertion of a centurion? *Fustuarium*, forfeiture of every *sesterce* to your name, and your family's barring from temples and religious rites for twelve months.'

He slapped his hand back down by his side again, looking not quite smug, not quite despondent. 'So how, my friends, should we ratify the desertion of a Praefector? A man senior enough to lead the XII when our glorious legate and high tribune are elsewhere?' He clapped his hands together, as if he'd made the only point worth making.

'Even with your *fustuarium* as an absolute minimum, how do we begin to quantify the punishment fit to place on your shoulders?' He lapsed into intent silence, watching Orbus keenly. None of the others seemed willing to break it. They had their own opinions, no doubt, but they wanted to see how he'd take this first challenge.

If he folded now, then it was over.

'How is your shoulder, Centurion?' Orbus suddenly asked. Alvanus seemed taken aback for a moment, but couldn't help his gaze dropping to his left arm. Covered by uniform, he looked the picture of health. Beneath the robes and leather, however, there lay a different story, a twisted snarl of scarred tissue from the Gallic arrow that so nearly killed him. 'I may have committed a capital offence that night,' Orbus continued, 'but I also saved your life, Alvanus. I'm no expert in military law, but how does the valour of saving a decorated officer stack up against the shame of fleeing?'

'You crossed my path at an opportune moment,' Alvanus growled, but his heart was no longer in the accusation. 'And it wasn't just you, Orbus. Nicanor was there too. As were others. And they were noble enough to stand their ground, and die with honour.'

'Not the attitude I would expect from you, Praefector,' Urbanus warily added, 'given where you've found yourself. In fact, I had imagined a man with your familial history would be a little... *humbler.*'

Another uneasy silence fell upon the hall, and this time, it was the Legate that no-one dared interrupt. Orbus, unlike more than one of the officers sat in judgement of him, hadn't come from an especially affluent or blueblood family. But no. That was not what Urbanus was referring to. And they all knew it.

For a moment, the Praefector closed his eyes. And suddenly he was back.

Gouts of flame, prickling the hairs on his neck. Blood on his teeth, somehow pleasant in its disgust. Curses screamed in Gallic, and the dying cries of men he'd known as boys.

He breathed out, unclenching his fists.

'Leaving Alvanus' enthusiasm aside,' Marcus Scipio took up the verbal baton, 'we did talk over a number of possible punishments, even momentarily putting *fustuarium* to the wind. This isn't just about you, Orbus. This is about the XII, and its unimpeachable reputation. How you have acted will determine our judgement, but how *we* act will determine how others judge us. There was talk of ostracism, or banishment to the rank and file, but all agreed that losing your position is not enough.'

'You could always kill yourself,' Thracian put in, and there was a gleam in his eyes that Orbus didn't like the look of. 'Honourable suicide. By hemlock perhaps, or falling on your own sword. It would grant the end of your career a dash of Stoicism.'

Thracian, as usual, was mocking while his words were not. The heir ascendant of the Legion, as his many grumbling detractors claimed. A formidable warrior in the shield-line, a masterful tactician from afar and a man of unassailable pedigree, on parchment he was an epitome of the soldier's ideal.

Orbus met his gaze. Was he imagining the smirk on his face? After all, there was more to a man than his qualities on parchment.

'Are those your own words, Thracian,' he asked pointedly, 'or the words of the legionaries whose favour you hope to curry, *First Spear?*'

Thracian made a show of looking outraged, his tanned features contorting with apparent gravitas. 'That is a serious accusation, Praefector. Are you really in a position to be making those, instead of answering them?'

'Enough.' This from Horatian Ardius, lounging across his own bench at Urbanus' other side. On the surface, he appeared the least perturbed of the gathered jury. But appearances could be deceiving. 'This is getting us nowhere.'

'Thank you, Centurion,' Orbus replied. And he meant it.

'Not you,' Ardius replied. 'All I meant was that Alvanus is wrong. There *is* more at stake here than what happens to your sorry neck, Praefector. Other eyes take note of what we decide, within the Legion and without. When I tell my men what has transpired here, I need that example to show them that no-one is above the chain of command. Not even a camp prefect.'

And there was none of Thracian's mockery in *that* claim. Ardius led the Cohort's sole *hastati* century, populated with the newly-inducted and least experienced legionaries. They wore lighter armour than their *principes* fellows led by Thracian and Cascana, and it was their thankless lot to make up the Legion's frontmost ranks, protecting their more battle-hardened kinsmen.

That responsibility – shaping and training up the Cohort's fresh meat – was something the Centurion took pretty damn seriously.

'And how,' Orbus dared raising an eyebrow, 'do you propose to solve this problem?'

Ardius fixed him with a coldly professional stare. 'Delicately. But decisively.'

'Do not imagine,' Urbanus weighed in behind his centurion, 'that this is mercy, Orbus. There is a great gulf between what these men here would *like* to do to you, and what the law allows us to do. Emotion will not rule our judgement.' He didn't feel the need to say anything more, but all Orbus had to do was look to one side. Thracian's twisted smile was enough to make him feel positively damned.

Once again, he was struck by the feeling that all was decided. That Urbanus – with Thracian's snide poison doubtless ringing in his ears – had already made his decision, and simply wanted to watch Orbus flail around in his own guilt before doling out a greater punishment.

'It could be said,' the Praefector slowly began, 'that subjecting me to a public flagellation was rather... emotional.'

A brief, uncomfortable silence fell upon the chamber. Once the slave had transcribed that pithy little remark on the tablet, the Legate turned his icicle-gaze upon the Praefector. He could have shouted, as he often did when his temper was ascendant. Not that he needed to. Urbanus was consummately skilled at conveying a wealth of disapproval with the barest effort.

'Fitting, don't you think?' the Legate replied. 'It could also be argued that betraying the men you lead, and abandoning them to their fate, was a rather emotional decision too.'

Orbus had no retort to that. His silence did the talking for them.

'Perhaps there is a middle ground we can climb to.' Cascana had wisely waited before giving his own verdict. 'A compromise we can all reach, that respects the seriousness of the crime while displaying our wisdom, and our *clementia*.'

Ever the politician, Orbus ruefully reflected with an inward smile. His bond with Iulus was known by every man in this chamber. If Cascana had tried a more emotional appeal, the others would have seen through it at once. But here he was, advocating a merciful approach under the guise of reason.

'A simple demotion to the ranks would send the right message,' the young centurion continued. 'Or at least, demotion from the officers' echelon. Ritual branding, as well, perhaps? There would be no feasible need for us to dirty our hands and consciences any further, gentlemen.'

'No,' Thracian harshly scolded him. 'This man is a deserter, however closely you know him. His punishment must fit the crime. If Orbus is capable of fleeing from battle, and abandoning his men, who knows what other crimes and failures he may have committed in his post? Or, worse, *allowed to happen* on his watch? If *fustuarium* is out of the question, then his presence will only taint the XII further.'

The Praefector scowled appropriately at the First Spear's attempt to fan the flames. *Clever, clever.* Thracian's plan became clear in that moment, and Orbus fancied he wasn't the only one who saw it. He wanted to take Orbus' place as camp prefect, something that, as the Cohort's eminent century commander, was entirely within the realms of possibility.

If any more of the Legion was back in Rome right now, then there might have been some debate. But with the other cohorts all on deployment, the point was moot. The rank was practically Thracian's already.

And it was a cunning plan, all things considered. The other four centurions all had incentive to back it, because if Thracian ascended to the Legion's top brass, one of them would take his place as First Spear.

Through all this, the scribe's stylus *scratched* onward, immortalising every spoken word of Orbus' shame in the Legion records.

'Having heard the arguments,' Urbanus decided, 'I do not believe that termination of your command is quite sufficient punishment, Sertor. Centurions Thracian and Ardius are correct. If your influence is to be truly cleansed from our ranks... then you can no longer have a place in the XII.'

Orbus took a moment to digest that. Losing his prefect's crest was something he'd expected, right from the start. But expulsion from the Fulminata, too?

'This legion is my life,' he began, speaking to all his accusers at once. He hoped he was the only one that heard his voice quiver. '*Soldiering* is my life. How am I meant to carry on? The *auxilia*? That is hardly service fit for a Roman, not least a legion veteran.'

In truth, Orbus was being a little harsh. Plenty of youths from Rome, not lucky enough to win entry into the legions as new recruits, cut their teeth in the Empire's auxiliary Cohorts, alongside foreigners and noncitizens of every colour and creed. But still, Orbus had held his position of authority within the XII for a long time. And he'd earnt it the hard way, through grit and merit.

'There are other legions…' Cascana chose that moment to intervene. Under the Legate's watchful gaze, he tried not to sound too hopeful. 'There are bound to be openings, for a cohort or century commander, fit for an officer of your experience.'

'Then again,' Thracian cut in with venomous glee, 'perhaps not. Maybe no legion's officer class would dare touch you,' he mused. 'I'm sure there would be plenty of demand for a *decanus*. Or simply a rank-and-file legionary.'

A few of the other centurions began to snigger. Orbus had to grit his teeth and bear it, for Thracian was completely right. Even if he managed to wangle his way into another legion – after practically prostrating himself before another legate, no doubt – there was no guarantee his career would continue with any dignity.

Urbanus closed his eyes for a moment, slowly and stately. 'No.'

Thracian frowned. 'Sir?'

'No,' the *Legatus* repeated. 'I will strip you of your place in this legion, Orbus. However you choose to spend your sorry existence is none of my concern. But it will not be under my command.'

Thracian didn't even try to hide his smile, and this time Alvanus and Ardius joined in.

'But,' Urbanus continued, 'that alone is not enough recompense for your sins. A far greater example must be made of you.' He didn't elaborate, but Orbus fancied he could sense where this was going. Suddenly that *fustuarium* didn't quite seem so unlikely.

'Unless, of course,' Thracian added with false indulgence, 'you have anything more you wish to say in your defence?'

The Praefector – and he was still a Praefector, for now at least – looked away. His gaze flickered over to the great bay window, with its unspoilt panoramic view over Rome's northeast. How beautiful it all seemed, when you took the time to look properly. It was sometimes harder to appreciate that from the ground.

Possibilities played out behind his eyes. Claims he could make, defences he could give, excuses for his unforgivable choices. And, each time, a verbal counter-charge appeared in his thoughts. A way they could swat it aside, or twist his words into mockery. It hardly mattered, anyway. Each attempt sounded more craven in his mind than the last.

No. To the gods with this little dance. He'd had enough.

'If you were hoping I would try to justify my actions,' Orbus took a moment to meet Thracian's snide gaze, 'then I'm going to have to disappoint you, officers.'

He rose to his feet, ignoring the centurions' muted surprise. Even the slave at the chamber's edge looked up from his wax tablet.

'Make your decision, *Legatus*.' He smoothed the folds on his crimson tunic. 'I will await your word, for I have nothing more to say.'

And with that, Orbus walked away from the council that held his life in their hands.

'Well.' Alvanus was the one to break the silence, doing so with his customary lack of decorum. 'Good riddance to the chaff, I'll say. The XII will be stronger without him.'

Nobody argued.

'Better prepare the Tarpeian Rock, I suppose,' he added with grimy anticipation.

Cascana cocked his head, eyes full of persuasive life.

'That is one option, my friend. But I dare say I might have an idea.'

Urbanus turned his hawkish gaze upon the young officer.

'I am listening.'

IT WAS NOT a long wait. That couldn't be a good sign.

Orbus had found an impromptu seat hidden from easy view, at the foot of the stairwell leading up to the tower chamber. Hunched down, back against the wall and ignoring the throbbing pain in his scars, all he could do was await the final summons with some semblance of dignity, a praefector in name only.

A surreptitious cough caught his attention, the new arrival pretending to clear his throat. It was the scribe from earlier. The slave whose job it was to record proceedings.

'They are ready for you, sir.' The wretch didn't even make eye contact before scurrying back up the steps.

With a sigh no young man could never emulate, Orbus rose from his place to follow him.

'YOU HAVE SET us quite the challenge.'

Urbanus appeared fairly unmoved since his quarry's abrupt departure, something that surprised no-one. The other six men seemed only a little perturbed by Orbus' sudden exit and reappearance. Alvanus appeared a little more attentive, to the Praefector's eye, and Ardius and Scipio seemed to have lost some of the murderous ice from their gazes.

Most intriguingly, Thracian appeared a touch more neutral than he'd seemed earlier. Not vindictive. But still triumphant.

'On the one hand,' the Legate declared, 'good men – better men than you, have no doubt – seem determined to fight your corner, and vouch for your strength of character.'

Orbus' gaze drifted over to Cascana, who pursed his lips with grim resolve.

'And yet,' Urbanus continued, 'you only seem contemptuous of this entire process, and our attempts to enlighten you. Quite a combination, it must be said. But together, these factors guide me to my decision without doubt.' He cleared his throat, fixing Orbus with a look that could stop a man's heart.

'You are stripped of your rank with immediate effect.'

The scribe *scratched* the words into the wax.

'You no longer belong to the XII.'

The nib went on *scratching*.

'You are no longer entitled to your *veteranus* pension, as such a discharge would normally entail.'

Scratch, scratch, scratch.

'But at the suggestion of one of my officers…' He looked at Cascana. 'Even if your life is no longer our concern, there may yet be a way to put it to use.'

The sixth juryman leant forward in his seat, preparing to add his voice to the Legate's at last.

His presence here today had taken Orbus off guard, for the man wasn't even legion. He was bearded and moustached in contrast to the centurions' shorn and oiled faces, with skin of a darker, more oaky hue than the tanned and seasoned men around him. He was from another world entire, beyond the borders of Italy and far across the Adriatic Sea.

His name was Behemon, son of Dannikos, and his Greek heritage was evident in every aspect of his appearance. A native of the province of Achaea, he captained a phalanx of armoured hoplite warriors who he led in service to the Emperor – a tribute paid to Rome by his Hellenic kinsmen after a long-ago defeat in battle. He'd led his countrymen alongside the XII for the better part of a decade now, and while Romans and Greeks weren't the most natural of barrack-mates, Behemon's men had earned the wary respect of many legionaries they fought beside.

But still… what was he doing here, involved in issues kept within the Legion?

'I was awarded Roman citizenship,' he answered Orbus' unspoken question in thickly-accented Latin, 'as reward for my actions in Gaul. I am retiring from military service, as of today, and returning home to Hellas,' he added, using the Greeks' own name for Achaea. 'In my absence, my cohort of hoplites needs a captain. Legate Urbanus would have you take my place.'

Orbus' hands curled over the braces of his seat. *Auxilia.* A foreign unit of *auxilia.* Quite the demotion indeed. He wondered if Thracian had anything to do with this, or if it really was all down to Cascana. Not that it mattered. Either way, his humiliation was complete.

'Yes, you see.' Urbanus' smile was an implacable thing. 'The *auxilia,* that you turned your nose up at? Perhaps living among their ranks will teach you a little humility before the end.'

'Which may come at any time,' Thracian put in. 'Those Achaeans may fight for our Empire, but they are not funded by it. Behemon's countrymen across the sea saw to that, but as their new officer, it is your pocket those bruisers will live off now. Here's hoping you've been hoarding that prefect's pay,' he added, slyly. 'Because now you're without a salary... and I dare say you are going to need it.'

'How am I supposed to feed these men?' Orbus retorted. 'Or mend their armour? Or supply reinforcements? Or lodge them?'

Alvanus could scarcely hold in his laughter. 'The *Forum* is still bustling, my friend. You had better grab your begging bowl.'

Orbus closed his eyes, his bile rising to boiling point. *You are alive. Focus on that. There will be no* fustuarium *today, even if this is hardly better. The gods must have a plan for you yet.*

'It is settled, then.' Urbanus steepled his fingers together, like a feudal king in his stately element. 'In your absence, Thracian will take the mantle of camp prefect. The rank of First Spear...' he paused, gathering his thoughts, 'will go to Centurion Cascana.'

A surprise, to be sure, but a welcome one. Young Iulus was one of the most popular officers in the Fulminata, and had a service record worthy of a hero. The other centurions nodded at this sudden accession, stoically but not unwillingly.

'Furthermore,' Urbanus regally concluded, 'at a time of my choosing, I will have one final condition for you to honour, as part of your sentence. You will swear to me that when that time comes, you will hold yourself to it. Only then will our judgement be complete.'

Orbus drew a hand back through his thinning hair. What in Pluto did it even matter, anyway? His life, as he knew it, was over. 'It will be so. I swear it,' he replied.

'Good.' Urbanus motioned to the scribe behind him, and the slave abruptly stopped writing. This court martial was at an end, and his work here was clearly done. 'In that case, I pronounce this matter closed.'

And that was all the cue he needed. Orbus rose from his seat once again, barely sparing the others a glance as he turned to leave. And why would he? He was no longer one of them.

'Well, look at that.' Thracian's voice accosted him from behind. 'Still a prefect, Orbus, even if you're not legion anymore. How ironic the title of *Praefector* must sound now.' He could hear the smirk, clear enough. 'Treachery has never been so rewarding.'

Orbus slowly turned, facing jurors still intent on judging him. He met his former legion brothers' eyes one by one – excusing himself from Cascana's pitying glance – before finally matching Thracian's artful smile.

'It is as you say…' he replied, 'Praefector.'

He turned to walk toward the door, into the uncertainty of his new life.

'You were not strong enough to live with honour,' the Legate told him as he left. 'I hope for your sake, that you have mettle enough to die with it.'

II
EXCISION

THERE ARE SOME things that simply cannot be borne. Some lies cannot be allowed to stand.

In this case, *he* was the lie. That was how it felt. Or, perhaps more accurately, the lie had been part of him for so long – twenty-seven years, to pin a number on it, ever since he'd first sworn the *sacramentum* – that he'd come to define himself by it. It had become synonymous with who he was.

Still, times change.

Orbus had known what discharge from the XII would entail, and he'd known the minute he'd left the *Castra Praetoria* what he'd have to do. That didn't make it any easier, though, and the part of his mind not mired in melancholy – the part that knew he had to go through with this – was resolved to rip the bandage off. Delaying would only make it harder.

Cascana had even offered to come, and in the end Orbus had to put his foot down. This was going to be enough of a violation as it was.

'You've seen enough of my shame already,' he'd insisted. 'But what I face now, I must do so alone.' And Cascana had acquiesced without another word of protest. So calm, so collected.

So understanding... There was a voice in Orbus' head, faint and petulant as it was, that resented the Centurion's magnanimity. And it was, all things considered, a rather ungrateful voice too. Orbus wasn't stupid, whatever his faults. Cascana's words had probably saved his life tonight, and they both knew it.

And so it was that Gaius Sertor Orbus, no longer of the XII Legion, found himself wondering, alone, under the majesty of the Flaminian Gate, away from the distant lights of Rome and out into the winter night. He carried no weapon on his back or sheathed at his side, only a small burning torch of oiled russet wood. He wore no armour or battle gear, just a simple, dark robe that shrouded his form and hooded his head. The fewer people who saw him, the better. The men of the Fulminata were off duty, and no doubt many would be roaming the city streets this very hour. Being recognised now would be more than dishonour. It could be a matter of life and death.

Orbus carried on regardless, relishing the cool night air on his face. The Field of Mars was a fine sight tonight – or would have been, if Orbus' eyes could pierce the dark any better. The torch outstretched before him only lit so much. He only had his bearings from the slightly paler line where the sky met the shadows, and the occasional pinpricks of amber that came from distant fires.

Funeral pyres, most likely, for people too poor or unimportant to warrant a proper burial. Or maybe some enterprising souls just trying to discretely burn their rubbish.

It didn't take him long to find his destination. How could he forget?

Orbus was no stranger to the Field of Mars, but it had been a long while since he'd been back *here*. He'd only ever been a handful of times before, and each instance had been a moment that marked him. Stepping-stones on the path of his life, moments he'd found himself referring back to, measuring how far he'd come.

Orbus lowered the torch as he approached the building, letting it snuff itself out. The marble walls were pale enough to shine through the night. He immediately felt the loss of warmth, but he knew better than to bring a light into this place.

The first thing that hit him was the smell. Incense, invasive but not cloying. It was the smell of priests, and as Orbus entered the Altar of Mars on that silent winter night, a priest was precisely what he found.

He had his back to the door when the Praefector entered, tending the candles and lanterns around the ceremonial altar. Orbus couldn't help but notice the way they were placed – each one standing alone, enough to see by but not enough to actually light up the chamber.

'*Pontifex*,' he greeted the kneeling holy man. The priest didn't answer immediately, straightening up on old, arthritic limbs and turning around. He'd been a soldier too, once, if the tell-tale outline of taut, aged muscle beneath his chiton was anything to go by. Each god had their rules of worship, and the cult of the War God demanded no less.

'*Miles*,' he eventually replied, in a voice too dry and hoarse to have ever been young. 'Show me your spear, legionary.'

Always, this pantomime to begin. The ancient codewords of the Martian rites, all of them aping the war-cant commonly used by soldiers in the field.

'My spear,' Orbus breathed the confession, 'lies broken upon the earth.'

Which meant that he'd come here out of shame, not righteousness. That he was not here to commemorate glory, but to mark censure.

'Show me,' the priest growled.

Orbus pulled at the cord that bound his robe, stretching his arms apart. The top half fell off his shoulders, exposing the bareness of his torso to the priest's squinted gaze. The old man moved slowly closer, gently circling Orbus as he reached for his body with one gnarled hand. He traced a finger over three decades' worth of scars and battlefield injuries.

And tattoos. He ignored the four black letters – *SPQR* – emblazoned over his left shoulder-blade, as well as the mass of crimson scarification that covered most of Orbus' back. The campaign names and honour markings he took a little more care over, sparing a faint smile at those he'd been the one to ink. His jaundiced lips moved, tracing the words he saw, as he carefully noted the ones that had appeared since.

Orbus couldn't help but smile as he endured this silent inquisition. How many years had this priest been plying his trade, how many soldiers had he taken the ink to, and yet he could still remember etching these words into Orbus' own flesh, dozens of years since they'd last met?

The priest slowed to a halt as he came back round. Orbus could pick out the liver spots that pitted his brow and face, and smell his ashen breath as it caressed him. The only movement in the chamber came from the flickering lights around them. The only sound, the distant call of the wind.

'Your silence speaks for you,' the priest rasped. One of his eyes had clouded over in recent years, playing host to a growing cataract. 'What shame could force you to my door, that you cannot bring yourself to name?'

But he knew the answer, and Orbus knew he knew. Their eyes drifted down to a patch on Orbus' left pec. To the one tattoo he'd yet to look at.

LEGIO XII

'Black it off,' Orbus ordered him. 'The whole thing.'

THEY ARE YOUTHS, *playing at being men. They believe, in their childish naivety, that they have reached the top of their mountain. But they are barely children, and by the standards of what will follow, their climb is only just beginning.*

The line of boys shuffles and bustles, from one end of the Field of Mars to another. They are in high spirits, and even with their decani *on hand to keep them in line, their rowdiness will not be curbed tonight. They have been working towards this day for the last five months, and every single moment has been a battle.*

Near the line's head, two boys are preparing to step up to the plate. One of them is a pampered princeling of Rome's aristocracy, who sees this queue as his path to the consulship. The other is an uncouth ruffian with barely a denarius *to his name. He waits in line because his father did the same, and has given little more thought on how to spend his life than that.*

War will change them both, in time, but all of that is yet to come. For now, though, they are unhunched by age, unmarked by scars, and too young to even grow a beard.

When their cohort began the training, neither boy could stand the other's voice. Over the gruelling weeks and months that followed, as they watched friends and bullies fall at the wayside or even die beneath the strain, each now cannot imagine a life without the other.

Publius Cascana throws his head back, laughing.

'Very funny,' he grins. 'I think we both know it's me who will make principes *first, not you.' He grabs his comrade's shoulder, looking him in the eye with theatrical compassion. 'I'm sure, if you ask the Centurion very nicely, he'll let you serve on the baggage train instead. It'll be fitting, don't you think? Doing your service with the donkeys.'*

Sertor Orbus mimes jabbing an elbow into his friend's ribs. 'More fool you,' he chides him. 'Just me and all those air-headed runner girls? I suppose, if that's what you're after, then yes. You're probably better off in the principes.'

He calls out loud enough that the lads behind him hear the whole story, and soon they are all joining in the fun, jeering at Cascana and casting aspersions upon his sexuality.

'They'll pass you around like a prize whore!' one boy-soldier crows.

Cascana tries his best to ignore the rising tide of mockery, hoping it is in good humour. In the years to come he will learn to laugh at himself, but now, like all men his age, he takes himself far too seriously. Life hasn't quite managed to thicken his skin yet.

But his mood darkens, and Orbus knows what nerve he has just touched.

'Have you spoken to your father yet?' he asks him. Cascana does not answer.

'Publius, how will he know if you don't –'

'Tell him?' Cascana snarls back at him. 'Gates of Fire, Sertor – do you think he doesn't know how I feel? Do you think that would even stop him?' He is acutely aware of the heads turning around him, so he lowers his voice once more. 'Do you think I had a choice? The matter was sealed and done before father even told me about it.' He snorts with bitter derision. 'I never even met the girl. My father proposed it. Her father accepted.'

At the top of the line, they can hear officers shouting. The queue begins to shift forward once again, and it will be their turn soon.

'Did they kiss?' Orbus asks him, for want of anything better to say.

Cascana shoots him a look that is pure cynicism, distilled through his eyes. Orbus apologises.

'She isn't a bad girl, from what I hear,' Cascana continues, softening. 'Her name's Falvia. From the Rutuli.'

Orbus whistles low. He has heard of that family, even before he began the training. 'That is a sizeable dowry coming your way,' he points out. 'As will her entire fortune, in time. This will pave the ground for the career you long to begin.'

Cascana has no answer to that. He knows his friend is right, but that doesn't make it any easier to stomach.

'She may be pretty,' Orbus adds.

Cascana is still scowling, but cannot help but crack a smile. 'She is beautiful, Sertor. Her hair is the colour of sunset, on an ocean tide.' The wistfulness gradually fades from his eyes. 'Or so my father tells me. She has had her share of suitors already. I suppose I am lucky.'

'Luckier still,' Orbus counsels him, 'if she chose you.'

That finally breaks the spell. 'Her family chose mine to ally with. That is all.' And now, the entitled resentment returns. 'You are the lucky one, Orbus. Lucky to be born to your family. You can marry wherever you damn well please.'

Orbus takes a moment to think on that, recalling the distant smoke-crowned slum complex his father could barely afford on a soldier's wage, and cannot quite agree.

And then they are at the queue's head. The men behind continue to stir with excitement. The Altar of Mars stands before them, cold and regal.

'You there!' Paulinus storms towards them, a wall of muscle and impatience. He grabs Orbus by the scuff of his neck, propelling him towards the steps. 'Move yourself, boy. And pay the priest his due respect, if you want to spare yourself a whipping.'

Paulinus has the foulest breath of any man alive. Strangely, it is this that Orbus and Cascana will remember their old decanus *for most, rather than all the lessons in swordplay, fieldcraft and hand-to-hand combat, or the incessant marching drills they will pass on to the next generation of infantrymen.*

Orbus finds himself inside the Altar, his heart in his mouth. He has been dreaming of this moment since he began the training.

The priest is waiting for him when he arrives, haloed by small candles and lanterns that hang from the ceiling. Orbus must be the thousandth visitor to the Altar tonight, at least, and yet the priest seems in no particular hurry.

*'*Pontifex*,' he greets him using the formal title.*

*The priest smiles without warmth. '*Tiro*,' he responds in kind. 'Show me your spear, young one.'*

Orbus has prepared for this. He replies, using the phrase he was told to rehearse.

'My spear...' he stumbles over the words. 'My spear lies unbroken in my enemy's heart.'

That seems to satisfy him, as he draws closer. The priest is no feeble old man. He is young, muscular, and were it not for the paint and henna adorning his face, Orbus would have taken him for a soldier too.

'Bare yourself to me,' he demands, and Orbus complies, pulling the thin red tunic off his torso and letting it fall. He should have felt exposed, baring his unspoilt physique before a total stranger, but something about this soldiers' temple puts him at ease.

The priest approaches, blade in hand. The blade is stained with holy ash, mixed with dark ink. Orbus knows what it is for, and how much this will hurt.

He clenches his teeth, closing his eyes...

... and leaves the Altar, the Rite over. The mark on his torso will take some time to heal, but once the ink has set and the swelling has faded, he knows what he will see.

LEGIO XII

He will wear it every day, for the rest of his life, even if he leaves the army. He will be proud to do so.

It will become part of him, synonymous with who he is, just as he imagines it will be for Cascana and all the others waiting in line.

It will be his truth.

The tattoo shows that they have completed their training, and are no longer tirones *to be corralled and jeered at. They are* milites *now, legionaries in truth, and they now belong to a legion.*

All they need now is a war. They are lucky in this regard, because Rome has no shortage of those.

ORBUS WONDERED, AS that very same priest went about his excruciating work all these years later, if he would ever feel that sense of pride again.

He missed those days. He missed Publius Cascana the young aristocratic braggart, even as he'd grown to love Publius Cascana the wise old man. He would have laughed in that moment, if he'd not been in quite so much pain. He'd barely thought about Publius in months. Perhaps it was time to visit him again, whenever Iulus was next off duty.

He felt a fresh splash of pain as the priest concluded. This work was less precise, as the priest hadn't been looking to inscribe letters upon his skin.

He had obliterated them outright, under a crude covering of black ink. As if his service had never happened.

Which meant that now, the XII Legion's shame was gone. Anyone who saw the dark patina over his torso would know what it signified. That whichever Legion he'd once fought in, he'd been shamefully cast out of that brotherhood.

The priest was slowly straightening up now, as fast as his aged back would let him. Orbus halted his rise with a hand on his shoulder.

'No.'

That got him an earthy growl of displeasure. You did not say no to a *pontifex* lightly, whichever god you worshipped or sought favour from. '*No?*' he rasped back as he straightened.

Orbus waved a hand over his torso, taking in the other tattoos. 'Black them off.'

The priest took a moment to process that command. This was not proper. '*Miles…*' he began.

Orbus wouldn't be denied. Not now. Not today.

'Take your blade,' he hissed, 'and *black it all off.*'

YEARS HAVE PASSED, and youths have become men. This is less to do with age, and more about how they see the world.

The line of tirones *troops unceremoniously forward, filing across the Field of Mars to their holy destination. Two centurions observe them from a little way off, taking stock of the men who are joining their legion.*

'You would think,' Publius Cascana muses out loud, 'that all that marching practice would have made a difference by now.' There is no real annoyance there, though, and he seems content to let the matter lie. There are harsher men in the XII to crack down on such things, and he feels no need to do it himself. For now. Once they are part of the Legion, and have been given centuries to join, it will be a different story.

'They'll get their fill of marching,' Sertor Orbus assures him. 'I was speaking with the High Tribune

last night. Apparently it's Germania we're headed to next. We'll be deploying with the Ubii, or some offshoot tribe of theirs. Some chieftain called Arminius.'

Now that raises Cascana's eyebrow. 'Germans, eh? That'll make for a fun scrap. It might cancel out the drag factor of marching through those gods-forsaken swamps and mires.' In actuality, the Legion will not be committed to that campaign, for reasons neither man is currently senior enough to know. History knows this is just as well, for if the XII had been dispatched to Germania it would have never come back.

'Afraid to get your boots dirty?' Orbus gently teases him.

'Oh, you're planning to wear boots?' Cascana ripostes. 'Amateur.'

In recent years Cascana's jowls and chest have started to fill out. Woe betide any man to mistake that for indolence, though, on the battlefield or the parade ground. Cascana remains a prince among men, no matter how age and command have changed him.

Orbus, if anything, has become a little leaner than his younger self. His new muscles cling to his bones more sparely. His hair is a touch thinner, with a slight loss of lustre, and his cheeks and jawline are now framed by a closely cropped beard. It makes him look older, and less approachable, which had been his aim all along. He doesn't like the beard, in all honesty, but he is too particular to admit that to anyone.

He will shave it soon, and in the long run it won't matter. Time and battle will work their course, and before long looking old will not require much effort.

*A wave of jeers downfield draws the centurions'
attention. One of the* tirones *has taken a tumble, and
three of the youths ahead of him have gone down too.
The ground has been churned into slurry by the
hundreds of boys who came before them, and the four
of them are now a muddy shambles.*

*Cascana actually laughs at that. Orbus does not,
for he has something else on his mind.*

*'You know they're going to make you First Spear,'
he says. It isn't a question.*

*Cascana does a fair job of feigning surprise. 'It
isn't official,' he tries to explain it away. 'And nothing
is set in stone. It could be any one of the others.
Evander won't just hand it out on a whim, he'll want
to –'*

*Orbus stares at him for a few moments, daring
him to keep going, until Cascana can't hold the
chuckles back.*

*'Alright,' he concedes. 'I had heard, unofficially. I
don't think it'll be public for another week at least.
How did* you *know?' he asks, suddenly guarded.*

*Now it is Orbus' turn to laugh. 'Arcites is dead,
and Urbanus is staying in Rome for the quaestors'
elections. Who, realistically, did you think was going
to replace him?' He snorts, a little less amicable now.
In theory, First Spear is a role that goes to the finest
centurion in the cohort. Of course, in practice, 'finest'
usually means whichever centurion has the bluest
blood or the most family wealth to call upon. All the
better for them to lead a political life with a deep
understanding – and more importantly, the loyalty –
of a swathe of the Roman army, or return as a* legatus
and command one, or even multiple legions.

'I suppose it is obvious, when you frame it that way.' Cascana suddenly seems a little crestfallen. *'I've been having some doubts lately,'* he confessed. *'I'm not entirely sure I want to keep to my old plan. Maybe I want to stay with the XII.'*

Orbus needs a moment to process that. Hearing his closest friend is willing to shelve his entire life's ambition is enough to rob him for words. Cascana joined the military for this very reason, and has never shied away from hiding it.

His years of service, as distinguished and noble as they are, are merely a rung on the ladder of his ambition – the cursus honorum beckons, and Cascana's family money will grease his entry into the Senate. And from there, with the right choices and alliances made, the possibilities are endless. A praetorship, certainly. Maybe even a move for consul, provided he can stay in the Emperor's favour.

This has been a part of Cascana's life from the day they met. Orbus can scarcely separate the man from his ambition.

Or perhaps, he notes melancholically, his family's ambition for him. Who would Cascana be without it?

'I suppose it is hard for you to understand.' Cascana takes his silence as judgement. *'There is no other path for you. The Legion is your whole life.'*

And that is a rather tactless way of putting it, but Orbus decides against telling him that. He doesn't want to interrupt this moment of introspection.

'I could stay as I am,' Cascana continues. *'Running around with the* principes, *First Spear, maybe even command the* triarii *if I'm lucky. And then I wait around, on the off-chance I take the Prefect's crest. Or I enter public life, as my family expects,*

swan around as a senator for Jupiter knows how long, and what then? Wait for a rise to glory that might never come, growing fatter and more gluttonous all the while? Or return as a high tribune, or legate, to command a legion that no longer knows me? Perhaps not even this one.'

Orbus gives this a moment of thought. 'So in essence,' he surmises, 'you need to choose between what you've wanted your entire life, or at least, what you've told yourself you wanted...' He gives his friend a telling look. 'Or the thing you think you want right now, which may not even exist?'

Cascana cocks his head wryly. 'My own fault for asking, I suppose.'

'I didn't mean it like that. But you're right, Publius. It is hard for me to see it, from my perspective.'

He doesn't need to elaborate. Orbus may have soldiering in his blood, but little else. No noble lineage, and certainly no family fortune. He cannot even enter the Senate as a novus homo *– a sneeringly-titled 'new man' – for he has little money of his own, and hasn't been lucky enough to marry a woman of means. Tribune, legate, any higher rungs above that... a patrician or even a knight could rise to such stations, with luck and gold and favour. But as a plebeian, those paths are firmly closed to him.*

The Legion really is his life. Praefector, that role that Cascana may turn his nose up at, is the highest peak he can ever climb to. A man can't even hold it until he has served his first full tour of service. Twenty-five years, provided he lives that long, and doesn't wish to retire at the end of it. It will be another seven years before Orbus even qualifies.

And does he even want it, anyway? Does he really want to spend his days corralling officers with better manners and more august surnames? Men and boys who will inevitably outgrow him, and ride their pedigree toward grander, loftier heights?

'Look on the bright side, though.' *Cascana seems to sense his thoughts.* 'At least you don't have to agonise over any choices. For you, the only way is up.'

Ah, the tortured hero. Even now, after the horrors of war and burdens of duty have knocked the snobbishness out of him, Publius Cascana still has a way of making his own problems ring louder than anyone else's.

'Still,' *he muses.* '"Praefector Orbus"? I can't really picture you as a camp prefect.'

'No?' *Orbus quips.* 'You think I couldn't bash the centurions' heads together?'

That makes Cascana laugh. 'I think you'd be too good at it. That's the problem.'

Only Orbus has stopped listening. 'Look sharp, Publius.' *He points to the slowly-trailing column of* tirones. 'What have we here?'

Cascana follows Orbus' finger, but already knows what he will see. It is the only reason the two of them volunteered for this duty today.

There, shuffling along in the moving line. A sixteen-year-old mass of gangly limbs and thick hair. Little Iulus Cascana, in his ill-fitting soldier's uniform. Well. Not so little anymore. Every time Orbus stops to consider Iulus' coming of age, it makes him feel positively venerable.

But he has to admit, it is pleasantly disconcerting to see the boy he once held as a baby, and used to help teach and train as a child, about to follow them across this same glorious threshold.

'Shall we?' Orbus asks.

'Why not?' Publius has a knowing glint in his eye.

The two centurions march their way down to the line of youths. This has the exact effect they'd hoped for, as the group of boys with Iulus among them suddenly freezes in panic. And why wouldn't they? Today is the apex of their training, and here are two seasoned officers bearing down upon them.

'Tirones!' Cascana shouts. 'Attend my words!'

That does the trick, as the four or five youths around Iulus suddenly stand to attention. Iulus must have recognised them, but he says nothing and nor do his compatriots. He must not have told them who his father is, and that is wise. The training grounds are no place for nepotism, and the open knowledge that he is a centurion's boy would have only made the last few months harder.

'You there!' Cascana singles out his own son, indignation and spittle flying from his mouth. Orbus says nothing, letting him have his fun. 'Look at those caligae! Soaked in Martian dirt right up to the bootstraps! Explain this at once, or you'll feel the vine!' He doesn't need to brandish his vine stick menacingly. The favoured symbol of office for centurions off the battlefield, every single tiro feels the crack of a vine stick over his back at least a dozen times during training.

'I... I...' Iulus' disarray is entirely genuine. His caligae aren't bad looking, in truth, and his friends' are far dirtier. 'I don't un-'

Cascana shoves his son forward, sending him reeling. Iulus crashes face-first into the mud. The *others scatter out of his way. This time no-one laughs, because no-one dares court the wrath of a bad-tempered centurion.*

'You dare talk back to an officer?' Cascana thunders. 'You forget yourself, tiro!' He grabs him by the tunic and hauls him bodily upright. Iulus is a picture of muddy confusion, and Cascana grabs him by the cheeks, his gaze boring into his eyes.

His face is a mask of intense anger, but Iulus sees the smile in his eyes. And hears the pride in what he whispers next, so faint Orbus almost misses it.

'I am so proud of you, boy. Here, today, I am the happiest father alive.'

'PRAEFECTOR?' A REEDY voice called from outside. 'Do you have a moment?'

Thracian lowered the scroll he'd been reading from, smiling a knowing smile. *Praefector.* He was still getting used to that.

'Enter.'

The legionary who shuffled into his quarters was a fairly weak and diminutive specimen. One of Ardius' little whelps, from his uniform markings. He seemed more comfortable looking at the floor, and Thracian felt no urge to set him at ease.

'Is there something I can help you with, *miles*?'

The *hastatus* composed himself, meeting Thracian's steely gaze. 'Your orders to our unit, sir. To stand watch over the Flaminian Gate. You instructed us to come as soon as we had something to report.'

Thracian's eyes momentarily flickered with emotion. *Already?*

'Go on.'

'The deserter was spotted, making his way to the Field of Mars.'

'When?'

'Approximately twenty minutes ago, Praefector.'

This was quicker than Thracian had anticipated. He steepled his fingers together. What a pleasant surprise.

'Return to your post, *miles*. Let it be known throughout your formation that "the deserter", as you so eloquently put it, will be returning to Rome through the Flaminian Gate before daybreak.' He gave the man a gentle smile. 'And don't feel the need to be discrete, either. This is not a matter of particular importance, or secrecy.'

The *hastatus* needed a moment to digest that in silence. They both knew what Thracian was really suggesting, that tacit truth he'd left to hang in the air. Still, orders were orders, and unless Legate Urbanus appeared from thin air to countermand it, a Praefector's word was law.

'Would that be all, sir? Is there any message I should convey to them, at the same time?'

Thracian smiled viperously in the dim candlelight. One last attempt to get his intentions out in the open. You couldn't blame a man for trying.

The new Praefector waved a hand through the air, feigning nonchalance.

'Just tell the men to follow their consciences.'

THE MEMORY OF that day, of Iulus' happy acclamation, almost made him forget the pain.

Almost, but not quite. Taking the ink was never a pleasant experience, and Orbus had never before been carrying a host of wounds from flagellation either.

And, tellingly, each tattoo in the past had come with a measure of martial pride. He had none of that particular salve tonight.

Still, it was done. Orbus' marks of allegiance to the XII Legion, as well as all the other campaigns and battle honours he'd accrued since, were gone. The words had been smothered by the priest's crude handiwork, uneven patches of black liberally covering his torso. And that was before you even considered the swelling, tell-tale patches of faint red visible beneath that spoke of muscular inflammation. It would settle, in time, but they didn't exactly make the healing wounds hurt any less.

What a wreck. He idly wondered what Merope would make of it, next time the two of them were undressing each other.

Orbus was lucky enough not to have company as he hobbled back beneath the Flaminian Gate. Robed, there was little chance of a stranger recognising him for what he was. Even for anyone who knew him, without his armour and uniform it was unlikely that they'd pick him out from –

'Halt.'

Orbus froze. This couldn't be good. The only souls still awake around the Gates of Rome would be armed guards, and why would they want to know his business?

He turned, smiling a cynical smile. *Because they knew to look out for him.*

The city guards were locking onto him, weapons in their hands. Other figures melted out of the darkness behind them, around them, behind *him*.

Armoured figures. Figures wearing legionary red, bearing the iconography of the Fulminata.

'Praefector,' one of them called with his best attempt at gravitas. 'I think it best that you come with us, now.'

'*Milites*,' Orbus growled. 'Whatever it is you want from me, I –'

THE GROUND TASTED awful. That was his first thought.

The pounding, splitting ache from the back of his skull was the second. What had they used to hit him with? A brick?

They were dragging gravel over his face. No, that wasn't quite right. Hold on.

No, they were dragging him over the gravelly road, ankle first. As Orbus' eyes drifted open, blood running down his temple, the crashing crackle of bootsteps all around told him all he needed to know.

It must have been at least twenty men around him. He swallowed. That had implications.

He didn't need to crane his head to know where they'd be taking him. Back down towards the Flaminian Gate, the quickest way out of the city once more.

Where nobody could see them, and nothing prohibited them from bearing weapons.

THERE WERE MORE men waiting for them on the Field of Mars. Orbus heard more than saw them, his head still swimming from the blow, his eyes leaking tears of molten agony from all the grit and mess they'd dragged him through.

Jeering, all around him, mixed with honest anger and bitter taunts. It washed over him, enough to make him lose his balance. Only there was nowhere to fall.

Strong hands hauled him up by each shoulder, and they were not gentle.

They were leashing him, Orbus sluggishly realised. Bound to a post, once again, for punishment. Fortuna had a twisted sense of humour.

The world around him slowly swam back into focus, even as the shouting grew more distinct. Soldiers, all of them, and all from the XII. Infantrymen, rank and file for the most part, although Orbus recognised a couple of *decani* among the throng of indignant faces.

A chill wound its way down his bruised spine. There were legionaries here from across all five centuries, even Cascana's. Iulus hadn't been lying about how unpopular he'd become.

Their officers had decided Orbus' fate, and had ordered them to endorse it too. They would, in time. But first, they needed to make it right with them.

The only question that remained was how far they planned to take it.

A giant of a legionary bore down upon him. The baying of the soldiers reached a climax as he abruptly grabbed at Orbus' robe, tearing it open to expose his bruised and battered physique.

'Got some new war paint, have we?' he boomed, more to the crowd than his target. 'Don't think that's going to get you out of this.'

'Spare me...' was all Orbus could manage. His head lolled to one side as he fought to remain conscious.

'*What?*' the brute hissed back at him, still loud enough for everyone to hear. He grabbed Orbus under his chin, forcing him to meet his gaze. '*What* did you just say?'

'Spare me…' Orbus forced the words through his drooling mouth, 'this bloody… lecture.'

The legionary's face froze, curled in a rictus of growing anger. 'Where's that cudgel?' he snarled. Someone from the crowd tossed a brutal-looking club in the big man's direction, and he grabbed it right out of the air.

'Place your bets, boys!' he roared. The crowd's jeering rose to a fever pitch. They smelt blood, and they wanted it.

'How many blows before the deserter falls?'

III
THE PRODIGAL SON

'I SUGGEST,' CASCANA began, fighting so unbelievably hard to keep his façade of calm, 'that one of you start talking.'

Nobody spoke.

Few were the times in Cascana's life he'd considered striking a fellow officer – outside of a formal duel of honour, anyway – but now, as he glared at the centurions he supposedly led, he would have happily fallen upon them like a slavering jackal.

'If it helps, you can consider that a direct order.' Inwardly, Cascana winced. Barely a week since he'd made First Spear, and here he was pulling rank on his former peers.

'We weren't the ones to put it in motion,' Scipio began. 'I don't know how word got out. Somehow, the men posted on the *pomerium* learned that Orbus was heading for the Altar of Mars. They must have known why he was going, and took that chance to ambush him.'

Cascana leapt on the Centurion's words. 'And why, exactly, were any of our men even stationed at the Gates? Much less, the one Gate that led right onto the Field, where any man with half a head could figure Orbus was bound to go?'

Scipio had no answer, lapsing back into awkward silence. He tried to affect an air of indignation, sitting there all prim and proper. It was common practice sometimes, after a particularly gruelling campaign or battle, to put returning *milites* on wall-duty upon return to Rome, as a means of making the jump to peacetime a little gentler. Or, more often than not, keeping potentially unstable men on a disciplined leash. But Scipio was fooling nobody today.

'Some of my men were among the mob,' he eventually admitted. 'But they weren't the ones to start it, or who leaked the news to begin with. The legionaries on wall duty were all *hastati*.'

And with that, Scipio doubtless believed himself blameless. Cascana, Alvanus and Pylades all turned to stare in the same direction.

'Alright,' Ardius conceded. 'I had some of my century on the wall. But I didn't set them on watch for the deserter, let alone anything else.'

'"The deserter",' Cascana aped back at him, 'is what they called him. Precisely.'

'Which proves what is plain as day,' Ardius tried to recover his footing. 'Someone else in this room must have ordered them to accost the d- accost *Orbus*. Or, at least, someone knew what was happening and didn't stop them, but had me kept out of the loop. That order did not come from me.'

That did it. The other four centurions erupted in a burst of sound – half-indignation, half-laughter. Even Cascana couldn't help joining in. Horatian Ardius, the most terrifying and unforgiving commander the *hastati* had ever had, outplayed by his own *milites* so easily?

'I don't believe that for one second,' Cascana assured him when the furore died down. 'And I don't think you do either, Centurion.'

'Look, sir,' Alvanus began, 'I had a hunch the men were *planning* something—' He stalled Cascana's next protest with a raised palm. '—not *what* they were planning. I don't see what you're that put out about, frankly. The *milites* needed to get their frustration out at some point. The longer they were denied that release of pressure, and the more we tried to clamp down on it, the worst it would have got. It's not like they killed him, or anything.'

Now *that* set Cascana's teeth on edge. That utter apathy, masquerading as pragmatism. Was this what being First Spear would entail, for the rest of his days? His father had always made the role sound so… dignified.

'They didn't kill him,' he sighed, 'because one of those loose-lipped conspirators ran his mouth off within earshot of my *optio*, who reported it to me at once. The only reason Orbus is alive today is because I came rushing out there with half my bloody century, and broke the party up before it could go on longer than a few minutes.' He straightened up, folding his arms. 'My thanks, by the way, for your utter lack of assistance. If I didn't know better, I would believe you wanted this to happen.'

Scipio cleared his throat, all eyes on him now. 'Come down from your high horse, First Spear. There were men from all five centuries on the Field last night. Even yours.'

Cascana's inner monologue swore repeatedly. Scipio was right, and he knew it. But that didn't detract from anything Cascana was saying, and he needed them to see that.

'Every man from my century who was involved will face their dues,' he told his fellow centurion. 'You have my word on that. And anyway,' he took on a harder tone now, 'some men on the Field may have been mine. But *every* man who arrived to break it up was mine. So no, Marcus. I don't quite feel I'm in the same trireme as you today.'

He took in the passive gazes of the four officers around him, wondering what exactly would get through to them.

'So do you mean to tell me,' he began, 'that all of you had "some inkling" that this was going to happen, and yet not *one* of you had the initiative or perception to find out exactly what, where or when?'

None of them seemed inclined to take the bait. Oh well, thought Cascana. Time to ram the point home.

'Or maybe you did, and simply didn't want to stop it?' He glowered at the lot of them. 'Thracian may have been happy to let you play your little games, just so long as he came out smelling of roses. But I am First Spear now.' He fixed Alvanus with a particularly pointed look. 'And I will have truth from my officers.'

For a moment, he felt like he'd convinced them. Like he finally had the moral high ground he'd hoped for. But that all came crashing down a moment later, as the cohort's newest centurion said his piece.

'Why do you care?' Where the others tried to fake nonchalance, Manius Pylades almost seemed louche. 'Why strive so hard to protect him? He is no longer part of the Legion. He is no longer our problem.'

This again. Cascana wondered how many times he'd have to go through this with them, before Orbus was safely out of the way on some other gods-forsaken battlefield or province.

'Because this whole affair isn't just about Orbus. The entire cohort's reputation lies on how we handle this.' He grimaced. 'The entire Legion, damn it. *Yes.* Our image took a battering in Gaul, which was compounded when Orbus did what he did. And yes. The fate we exiled him to? That was a cold, calculated attempt to mend that image. How *we* came out of it was more important than how *he* did, no matter how much anger at him remained in our ranks. And now—' He rubbed the stress out of his eyes. '—you've let your own troops completely undermine the whole point of it. It was a choice between looking weak or looking out of control. And now, thanks to the four of you, we appear to be both.'

Pylades thought on this for a moment. As it stood, Cascana didn't know the man well enough to tell if he was deliberately trying to insubordinate him, or if asking such painfully obvious questions was merely how his mind worked.

That doubt was banished a moment later, however.

'It could be argued,' Pylades mused, with craven impartiality, 'that your intervention, First Spear, was what made the cohort look weak. Before, it could be simply written down to a few legionaries' undignified exuberance. But riding out there to put a stop to it?' He raised a scarred eyebrow. 'That announced to all of Rome just how serious the problem is.'

'Undignified... *what?*' Cascana almost did a double take. He was not an irate man by nature, but here he was being pushed to it, nonetheless. 'A man was almost *killed.*'

'A man who is no longer of our ranks,' Pylades retorted with murderous calm. 'A man who is no longer our concern or responsibility, and who arguably deserves to die anyway.'

Cascana treated the Centurion to a glare. 'You're new to your rank, Manius, and I appreciate that.' He smiled with a warmth he did not feel, and a malevolence he certainly wasn't used to. 'The step up from legionary to *decanus*—' He waved a hand in the air to simulate that step. '—takes a certain man, no doubt. And a certain broadness of thought.' He then waved his hand in the air again, considerably higher this time. 'But the leap to centurion, on the other hand, is something altogether broader. And *more daunting.*'

The other three men shifted uncomfortably where they were sitting. This was a Cascana they hadn't seen before, and the change was not a particularly welcome one. The leap to First Spear must clearly also be quite something, and seeing the man flex his newfound power was something they weren't keen to challenge.

'So let me tell you, *Centurion* Pylades. You may have been able to keep your head down as a *decanus*, basking in your influence and lording it over your tentmates. I'm sure Thracian had no issue with that. But you are an *officer* now,' he growled. 'You are not a unit leader with a fancy title. You have *responsibilities*, as heavy as your rank itself.' Pylades seemed a little less certain of himself now, and that was good. That was a start.

'And let me tell you, *Centurion*, from the perspective of your First Spear, it really doesn't do well to begin your role by failing to control your men so utterly. *Much less* by trying to worm your way out of responsibility afterwards.'

Pylades still didn't say anything. To open his mouth would betray the truth – that Cascana had read his thoughts so adroitly he might as well have shouted them to the sky.

'It is a large pair of *caligae* you are stepping into, Manius.' Cascana had softened a little by now, just as he'd intended to. He'd shown him the stick. Now for the carrot. 'There are men, I'm sure, who see you as nothing more than a proxy for our new praefector. Who believe that your century, from this point on, will be nothing more than an extension of his will.' He laid a hand on Pylades' shoulder, somehow brotherly and disconcerting all at once. 'I'm sure you're keen to prove them wrong.'

Cascana walked away from Pylades, turning to regard the four of them as a whole. 'At present, I'm not planning to escalate this any higher. More scrutiny will only hurt the Fulminata's reputation further. But since you all seem keen to chalk this down to legionaries acting alone, let me be clear. From now on, regarding any attempts on the life of Sertor Orbus made by any man in this cohort, I will hold the commanding officers of the men in question personally responsible.' His eyes met Pylades' once again as he added, 'And you can be damn sure that I won't be taking my concerns to Thracian. I will go straight to the legate and tell him everything.'

And so began Iulus Cascana's tenure as First Spear.

'Dismissed, all of you.'

THE MOOD WAS not exactly buoyant as the four centurions departed. Ardius and Alvanus had no desire to tarry, their short-sightedness exposed for all to see. While each of them hurried back to their respective barracks, Pylades was a little slower out the door.

'Wait, Manius,' Scipio called out from behind him, as soon as they were out of Cascana's earshot. 'A moment.'

Pylades turned on his heel as the *triarii* commander approached him. Outwardly Scipio seemed as stoic and composed as ever, but looks could deceive, and Pylades doubted his fellow centurion wanted to exchange pleasantries.

'You think us blind to your little ploys?' Scipio hissed at him. 'I know you're acting in lockstep with Thracian. Do you really think young Cascana won't have worked that out? Or the others?'

'*Praefector* Thracian,' Pylades gently corrected him. 'And that is quite the accusation, Marcus. Especially without the proof to back it up.'

Scipio glowered at him as Pylades reached into his tunic pocket. 'The Praefector sent one of these to you last night, as well as me. As I'm sure he did to Alvanus.' He brandished the folded despatch with its wax seal broken, glancing across the courtyard to make sure they were unobserved. 'Did you think you were the only one to receive it? Perhaps *someone* put it about the barracks last night that Orbus was planning a trip to the Altar of Mars. But the fact is, you knew this was on the cards. And there are couriered papers, with the Praefector's personal seal on them, that corroborate that fact. So I suggest you take a moment to think on how you'd like to play this.'

Scipio grabbed the other man by the tunic, ramming him up against the barrack walls.

'You treacherous bastard,' he spat, but relented. Pylades was exactly right. Scipio had known the truth as soon as he'd received Thracian's message. The assault had been happening, whether he liked it or not, and by couriering the news to the other centurions, Thracian had essentially painted them as complicit. It was all there, inked upon parchment.

And why? Scipio didn't even need to guess.

'All this to keep us from looking into the truth,' he murmured, calming down. He released Pylades from his grip, letting him slide back down the wall. 'That it was Thracian behind all of this. He set the legionaries up on lookout, and stirred the others into a killing frenzy.' A part of him almost wanted to laugh. Thracian had always been a worm. An infuriatingly competent worm, but a worm nonetheless. But this? This was nothing short of conspiracy to murder.

Pylades was dusting himself off, seemingly recovering his poise. 'I cannot speak for the Praefector's private feelings, but take this as a warning, Marcus. One centurion to another. To look any further into this incident, or interfere any further on the deserter's behalf, will surely invoke the wrath of our masters.'

Scipio shook his head, defeated but still derisive. 'By *interfere in*, you mean *defend*. And by *our masters*, you mean *Thracian*.'

Pylades was already drawing away. He'd made his point. 'I couldn't possibly comment.'

And just like that, he left. By Scipio's reckoning, you would think they'd been discussing the winter training regimen, or placing bets on when the *Principia*'s next ale shipment would arrive.

For a few languid moments, he did just as Pylades had asked. He wondered how exactly he was going to respond.

Scipio had his faults, various and great in number. But he was no simpering fool like Pylades, to hide behind the words of others. He wasn't a scheming little rat like Thracian, either. He was a soldier of Rome, and he led a century whose standards were as high as his own. He wasn't the kind of man who walked away. Not when a gauntlet was thrown down.

Decision made, then.

THRACIAN DIDN'T TURN out to be in his new praefector's quarters, and the spotty little tribune transcribing papers at his desk wasn't sure where he'd gone either.

Now that had made Scipio smile. It was too late in the day for the Praefector to stray particularly far from the *Principia*; his private villa wasn't close enough, and he'd still have duties in the evening. But it was too early for the brothels and pleasure houses to be rolling out their star attractions, and that ruled out the other most likely option.

The Quirinal, perhaps, where his family estate lay? Doubtful.

Which left only one other place.

Scipio was almost tempted to strip off his centurion's garb, but it probably wouldn't hurt to look like he was on official business. He was vindicated a little later, as he wound his way through the bustling, shouting crowds of the Roman *Forum*. This was peak time, and passing through the Empire's beating heart – the throngs of merchants and traders flogging their wares, ranting quacks preaching from makeshift rostra and even the occasional priest or travelling hierophant – was never easy even on quieter evenings.

Today's trip was mercifully smooth, the prevailing foot traffic not wanting to impede a legion officer going about his duties. Most of it was moving the other way, toward the Temple of Peace, instead of the Tiber's banks where he was headed.

Passing under the *Palatium*'s expansive shadow, it didn't take him long to reach his destination. The streets of Rome were broad and direct, and his target, nestled between the Aventine and Palatine Hills, was accessible by roads from practically all points of the compass.

A long, circular edifice stretched across the entire length of the *Palatium*'s south border. Walls almost as high as the Imperial Palace itself hugged a cavernously empty interior, nestling multiple tiers of seating that overlooked a vast floor of sand.

Chariots raced over that sand. Gladiators fought death bouts over it, and their blood ran into the dirt at each battle's end. Unluckier souls were pitted against beasts and animals in matches that were decidedly more one-sided. In those cases, the blood that ran into the earthen floor was more often from prey than predator.

The *Circus Maximus* had, in better days, been a beacon of all that was noble and patriotic about Rome. Fire damage and exotic foreign reliquaries had rather maligned that aspect of it; Scipio couldn't quite appreciate the aesthetic pairing of an obelisk of darkened quartz, once part of sun-worshipping rites in far-off Egypt, with hastily-repaired tiers of seating that looked sourced from the most readily available wood to hand.

Still, if you liked the taste of blood in the air, and were happy to see fortunes made and lost, then there were few better places to be. Of all Sallus Thracian's favoured haunts in Rome, Scipio was certain he'd find him here.

And he wasn't disappointed. Thracian had, naturally, taken one of the most prestigious seats in the house – a middling position on the front straight, but behind the row reserved for members of the Senate – which he held via his birth-right as a patrician. And there he sat, lounging back like a king at rest, watching the chariots thunder on their way with idle detachment. He was the only spectator present in this prestigious row of seating; hardly surprising, as given the time of day, any other man of such a rank would be occupied with duty and work, not leisure. Another figure in legionary garb, presumably his *optio*, stood by his side, apparently here just to pour out Falernian red and cut it with the right amount of water.

Part of a prefect's responsibility was reviewing and maintaining all equipment and resources in the cohort or legion they served in. And here was Thracian, using his designated First Legionary to wait on him hand and foot.

'Praefector,' Scipio called out. He tried to inject some respect into his voice, a slight measure of deference. Tried, and failed completely. 'Praefector, do you have a moment?'

The man who had until days ago been Scipio's peer turned his head. 'Centurion,' he called out, pointedly making no effort to get up and greet him properly. 'What brings you to the *Circus* on this fine evening? I didn't have you pegged as a man for blood sports.'

'I'm not, usually,' Scipio confessed. 'Nor are most of my fellow officers. Our duties demand much of us, and we rarely find the time for such pursuits.'

That was suggestive enough to prick the man's attention. Thracian shifted upright in his seat, waving the *optio* away. If anything, he looked more bothered that Scipio had disturbed his afternoon of sun and racing than he did at the Centurion's insinuation that he was neglecting his new obligations.

'What can I do for you, Marcus?' he asked him, his choice of words amenable where his tone was not.

'I just had a rather interesting conversation,' Scipio continued. 'With your man Pylades, and our new First Spear.'

'My man?' Thracian repeated. 'Manius may once have served in my ranks, but I assure you he is nobody's *man*. He is no more or less under my command than you are.' He smiled, enjoying rubbing salt in that particular wound.

Scipio gritted his teeth. 'We know it was you behind what happened to Orbus last night. And Cascana isn't stupid. He knows we can't affirm that, because of those accursed messages you had sent to us before it happened. I've got to hand it to you, really. We couldn't look anymore guilty if we'd tried.'

Thracian's smile was almost beatific. 'A masterful move, no? Don't take it personally, Centurion. Think of it as a gentle lesson of who is who in the hierarchy.

A way to mark my new tenure, just as Cascana marked his by riding out onto the Field of Mars last night.'

The racing chariots took that moment to storm past, making for the turning post at the arena's other end in a cloud of stampeded dust.

'What do you have against him?' Scipio could only ask. 'Why go to so much trouble to ruin him?'

'That is none of your concern.' Thracian had already turned his attention back to the race. 'All you need do is leave it alone.'

'*No.*' Scipio's avowal was ironclad. This would not be how he lived his life. 'No. This is not how the XII operates. I'm going to the Legate about this. And about last night.'

Thracian's gaze slid back to him, slowly, malevolently, like an apex predator tracking the movement of prey. 'Is that so?'

'The ramifications be damned.' Scipio wouldn't be swayed – he was set on this course now, for good or ill. 'I don't care how Urbanus reacts. Even if it means I lose my damn century. I will not be a pawn in these games of yours, *Praefector.*'

Thracian was standing up now, slowly rising from his seat to Scipio's own level.

'I was conducting an inventory over our cohort's paperwork,' he began to explain, 'as part of my new responsibilities. Little that would interest you, Centurion, unless you want me to inundate you with the minutiae of legionary battle-gear and camp logistics. But Orbus' collected files on the officers had a few surprises, I can assure you.' He let that scandalous suggestion hang for a moment. 'How is the lady Murina, by the way?'

The question died in Scipio's throat. He knew, right then, where this was going.

'You and lady Murina were once engaged, were you not? It must have been... what, seven, eight years ago now? Oh, what a coup that would have been, Marcus. The Helveticae are a powerful family.'

'Indeed,' the Centurion replied through gritted teeth.

'Only it was not to be. Alas, love is a fickle thing. The two of you parted ways. For you, a beleaguered return to the Fulminata. Her, to the Hearths of Vesta.'

Scipio's jaw was set like rock. He had little issue with his romantic past being paraded like this, even if that old wound still stung. Murina had taken the virgin's robe for her own reasons. He'd married another woman and returned to military service for much the same. But no. These facts, alone, did not concern him – that honour fell to the sordid direction Thracian was going with this.

'Your wife resides in her family estates in Arpinum, and rarely even comes upcountry, let alone lodges here with you in Rome.' The Praefector smiled ruefully. 'A man can get lonely. But if you're going to debauch a Maid of Vesta...' He trailed off, relishing every moment. 'At least entrust your love letters to a slave who can't be bribed.'

Scipio had no answer. What could he have even said? Thracian had him dead to rights, and they both knew it. The racing chariots pounded past them yet again, to a renewed set of applause, but he barely heard it.

And if one of those letters had been on file... had Orbus known, all these years, and not said anything? Had he even told anyone?

'You…' Scipio could barely even frame a riposte. 'You *bastard.'* For the second time today, the capriciousness of legion politics had blindsided him.

The cursing renewed Thracian's saccharine smile. 'I may well be, Scipio. But I'm a pragmatist, first and foremost. You're a good soldier, and a good officer as well. If I'm going to serve my legion as well as can be, I need men like you. A dead or disgraced centurion is useless to me.' His gaze took on a new, rather more predatory light. 'But so is a disobedient one. I have asked you to leave our cohort's disciplinary… *lapse* behind us. Since you have so little respect for the chain of command, now you know the consequences of disobeying me.'

And Scipio did. Sleeping with a Vestal Virgin was beyond a transgression. It broke all holy writ. If exposed, then the punishment for Murina would be a long and painful death, and his own would be little better.

You fool. You proud, blind fool.

'Return to the *Principia*, Centurion.' Thracian was already sinking back into his seat, beckoning his *optio* back to him. 'I have no wish to keep you from your duties. Move on from the past day's events, and go back to your men. I have little doubt we'll be marching back into war before long, and I need you at your best.'

HE SPLASHED WATER over his face, idly exploring the bumps and marks with his fingers. Truth be told, the retribution hadn't been that bad. The blow that knocked him out had been the worst, and Cascana had arrived to deliver him soon after the beating had started – before the men could really get down to it.

The ink still ached. The swelling had started to fade – although, with the scars and kaleidoscopic bruises over his torso, you would never know it. With time and proper care, the sores and redness would diminish further.

Still. Looking at it wasn't getting any easier.

'Uncle?' Cascana's voice called from the outside portico.

'I'm here,' Orbus replied. He dabbed a saffron cloth over his lips and face, and for the first time since last night, it didn't come away with any blood.

Cascana ducked into the small chamber, briefly taking in the view from the window. This was far from the only property his family owned across the city, and though the Cascanae laid claim to far grander villas and townhouses, this small tenement overlooking the *Forum Caesaris* had been judged empty and nondescript enough to hide Orbus from the malice of his former *milites*. The faint yammering of wild dogs carried over the evening air.

'You are looking well,' the First Spear ventured.

'Is that so?' Orbus replied. 'I rather thought I looked like shit.'

'You could have looked shitter.'

The Praefector nodded, putting his sarcasm momentarily aside. He'd already thanked Cascana last night, as profusely as his pride and the concussion would let him. And, of course, the younger man had deftly sidestepped every word, telling him to think no more of it. 'So, you mean to go through with your plans?'

'I do.' Orbus cocked his head towards the small bedspread, where his legionary belt lay on his praefector's uniform. Puli had had the tunic steamed and pressed. And, quite tellingly, he'd had the sigil of the XII removed from the right epaulette. May the gods bless him. He'd saved Orbus having to order it done. Or do it himself.

'They're not a bad formation, those Achaean fellows,' Cascana mused. 'What I wouldn't give sometimes for a phalanx of armoured hoplites to back up my shield wall.'

'Indeed.' Orbus's gaze searched the First Spear for a moment. Cascana was trying to make the future sound promising, just as any true friend would. But all he was doing was telegraphing his own thoughts. The hoplites were not a numerous troupe, and Orbus barely had the funds to even keep their equipment serviceable, let alone pay any more for reinforcements.

And if he could? He had no legion to seek support from. He could volunteer their service to another *legatus*, assuming they deigned for whatever reason to show him any favour. That, or march his new *auxilia* out alongside another Roman army on deployment, trying to scavenge any insight he could from their war councils, and hope to make a difference in whichever battle they found themselves in.

And they were just one force, after all. They'd lose men, battle by battle, and Orbus would have no real way to replace them. Or maybe they would be broken in one fight, and massacred by a victorious foe. At least Urbanus' hope for him to bloodily redeem himself would be more quickly achieved.

So, no. The Praefector didn't quite share the First Spear's optimism.

'Well, no time like the present.' Cascana's thoughts were already moving on. 'When will you meet with Behemon's men?'

'I'm not, just yet.' Orbus reached for his legion robes, pulling the tunic over his battered chest. 'Not for a few days. They're still billeted here in Rome; they won't exactly be going anywhere soon. No.' He pulled the belt around his hips, locking the silver buckle in place. 'I have business to attend to first.'

Cascana sensed at once what he was getting at. 'You're going back to Baiae, aren't you?'

'I am.' Orbus was already pulling on his *caligae*, refastening their leather straps. 'I thought a little homecoming was due, after all this time. Anyway, I need to set a few affairs in order, before I take command of the phalanx.'

'I'll wager Sextus would relish the chance to see you,' was all Cascana could say. 'But are you sure the timing is quite right, uncle?'

Orbus took a moment to regard his soldierly reflection in the basin mirror, before reaching for the long dark over-cloak that hung over the bedspread. 'You always call me *uncle* when you're trying to make me do something,' he drily observed.

Cascana chuckled nervously, forgetting himself. 'A habit I must break, Praefector.'

'You're already persuasive enough as is,' Orbus jokingly assured him. 'I'm still alive, aren't I?'

The First Spear smiled, genuine enough to warm the soul. 'I think that's the first joke I've heard you make since Gaul. Well, before you make any grand exits,' Cascana added, 'I have a couple of things for you.' He got up and moved towards the door, calling out for someone in the portico – one of his household, presumably.

'Oh?' Orbus' brow furrowed. He got his answer a moment later, as Cascana reappeared with another man of similar age. He was tall and lanky, and his faded red hair had been given a military cropping. He held himself too rigidly for a civilian, and the slight indent marks on his scalp and temples spoke of a life lived under a battle helm.

The legionary extended a bony hand. Whatever he thought of Orbus' battered physique, he made no comment on it. 'I am Titus Argias, Praefector.'

Orbus clasped the hand firmly. 'Greetings, Argias.' For want of anything better to say, he turned to Cascana. 'You're one of his, presumably.'

'That, I am.' Argias seemed a little thrown, as if he he'd expected some other response. His officer stepped in helpfully.

'Argias serves in my century as a *duplicarius*,' Cascana explained. 'His *decanus* speaks well of him, although until I bury some more poor sods in the earth there's little scope for promotion. But,' he said, smiling wryly, 'I suspected there are other units he could join. And you could probably use a good *optio*.'

Once again, Orbus felt an avuncular pride warm his heart. Traditionally, every centurion relied upon an *optio*, a 'second in the century', to dispense their bidding. But it wasn't uncommon for higher ranking officers – praefectors, high tribunes and the like – to carry on the practise too, using such men as adjutants and seconds. Since Salius had died in Gaul, Orbus hadn't even begun to think about replacing him. Till now.

'Thank you, Iulus. That is a fine gesture.'

And he meant it. Looking at young Argias here, Orbus had little doubt that this up-and-coming legionary would be a valuable investment for his new command.

Still, no need to tell him that. Hierarchy was hierarchy, and the legions had standards for a reason.

'So,' Orbus fell back into his prefectorial role, looking Argias up and down. 'A double-wager, eh? That's quite an endorsement, from the First Spear here. But you want to be my *optio*? My First Legionary?'

'Yes sir!' Argias saluted, crisp and snapped, with an enthusiasm Orbus no longer recognised in himself.

'I hope you realise what you're getting into. This is an all-Greek phalanx, who know what they're doing, and have been doing it their own way. You're not going to earn their respect that easily. You'll also be the only clerical pair of hands. I don't exactly have tribunes falling out of my arse, so all that shit will fall on your shovel.' How naturally it came back to him, the ordering, the delegating, the weighing up and down. 'You can read and write, can't you?'

'Yes sir!' Argias repeated, beat for beat.

'Enough of that.' Orbus cantankerously waved the formality aside. 'You're not a *tiro* anymore, and we're not on the parade ground. Return to the barracks, and make yourself known to the Achaeans. They're still billeted at the Legion *Principia*, in the auxiliary quarters. As far as I know, anyway.'

'Sir.' Argias nodded, less formally. 'Should I pass on any orders to them?'

'Just take a message to whoever Behemon's left in charge. Tell him I'm taking a trip down-country,' was

Orbus' cryptic reply. 'Personal business. I will return to Rome in three days.'

His thoughts began to flow. 'In fact, that can be your first job. Take an inventory of all the men, whoever Behemon has left. I want their service histories, combat status, and an account of all their weapons and armour.' The *auxilia* didn't have access to legion armouries, and hoplites usually saw to their own battle gear. 'Find out what's damaged, what needs replacing. What will take another trip to the smithies, and what just needs a bit of whetstone.'

'Done.' Argias nodded, shifting from eager young pup to level-headed administrator. 'I can get an estimate of cost, too. There's a forge I know in the *Subura*. They do good metal, and they'll give us a fair price. The owner's son is a legionary in the IV. We were *tirones* together.'

Orbus stopped himself from smiling, but he fancied Argias saw the flicker of pleasure in his eyes. 'Very good,' he told him. 'Well? Don't let us hold you up, *optio*.'

Argias snapped around on his heels, briskly marching off before they could see his smile.

'Someone's keen,' snorted Orbus after he'd left. 'He's your sort of man, and no mistake.'

'We were all like that once,' Cascana gently chided him.

'Some of us were.' Orbus' eyes were glinting again, with that roguish energy Cascana hadn't seen since the court martial. 'Thank you once again, Iulus. If there wasn't anything else...' He started to fasten the togs on his over-cloak.

'Actually,' Cascana began, resting a hand on his sheathed sword pommel, 'I think you'll want to see this.'

It was only then that Orbus paid the sword at Cascana's side any heed. Hidden as it was in its leather scabbard, it looked too long and tapered to be the *gladius* he normally favoured. This looked more akin to a longsword or *spatha* – although, as Cascana drew it in one smooth motion, that was far from the first thought in his mind.

'No...' The Praefector was lost for words. '...How?'

Cascana still hadn't lowered the sword. 'Some men from Alvanus' century recovered it, when we regrouped in the ruins. I think they were hoping to flog it as spoils, but I gently persuaded them to part with it.'

The sword was not made of iron, bronze or even steel. It was forged from alloyed silver – the purest, strongest silver there was, quarried in the mines at Laurium in faraway Athens. When Orbus had first learnt that, he could never see it without imagining the many slaves who'd toiled their lives away in those mines, those hellish caverns that swallowed men and spat out ore.

It was *his* sword, and his father's before him, and it gleamed like sunlight on the tides. In the tongue of the Greeks, the sword was called *Ananke*.

'Necessity,' Aruxeia had once translated it, doubtless weary of Orbus' ceaseless questions as she tried to scrub his father's floors clean. 'Necessity, in both of its guises – the righteousness of heroes, and the excuses of cowards.'

And now it was here. Not lost in the ashen remains of the cohort's ransacked *castra*, or carried off in the grasping hands of thieving Gauls. Here, back in his grasp, and it felt like a part of him had returned home.

Orbus took a second to savour the moment. The feel of the cold hilt in his sword-hand, the glinting of the evening light across the flat, the gently upward-tapered halves of the crossguard…

'Uncle?' Cascana cut in, wryly. 'Do the two of you need a moment alone?'

Orbus lowered the sword, reluctantly. 'Very droll of you, Centurion. But I'm afraid I really do have somewhere to be now.' He took the scabbard from Cascana, sheathed the silver blade in place, and fastened it over one hip.

'Baiae already?' the First Spear replied. 'It's a little late in the day to charter a wagon.'

'I'm not going to Baiae just yet,' Orbus replied. He was already heading for the door. 'I am going to see Merope.'

He was already gone before Cascana could reply, striding across the colonnade as briskly as his many wounds would let him.

'Lucky her,' Cascana mused to the open air.

IV

BAIAE

IT MUST HAVE been three hours since sundown. That much was obvious from the sky, and more subtly intimated by the fading night's warmth. But beyond that? He'd rather lost track of time.

Orbus reclined in the bed, the sheets up to his hips. The breeze on his midriff was just the tonic to his sweaty skin. Another languid burst of wind poured through the open shutters, and he felt that relief in his bones.

He turned over in the sheets, running a glance down his companion's naked back. She never saw his smile in the half-light.

He'd always taken a dim view to legionaries keeping whores around the barracks or on deployment, and no doubt any *miles* that caught the two of them here would cry hypocrite. But then he had no legionaries anymore, not really, and this woman belonged to him and him alone.

And he supposed, in a small way, that it worked both ways.

She was sitting up now, pulling her unruly dark hair back into some semblance of tidiness. Her skin was a similar shade to Behemon's – as was the way of so many born in Etruria.

She turned to look at him again, gently reaching for his torso. Her fingers tenderly ran over the crude splodges of ink eclipsing the Legion mark and all his former honour-scrawls. He winced a couple of times as her fingers found his bruises, but that didn't stop the question on her lips.

'Why would you do this to yourself?' she asked him. It was the first words she'd spoken since they'd gone to bed.

Orbus saw no reason to lie. 'To break from the past, Merope. The Legion could not suffer the shame of my cowardice. It could not wear the stain on its honour. The only way to remove that stain was to remove me, and remove my piece in its history.' Now he ran his own finger down the new ink. 'Now that stain is gone. It is as if I was never a part of the XII.'

'The Legion's shame,' Merope echoed. 'But what about yours?'

Orbus' gaze shifted. He hadn't expected this. 'My shame? Mine is mine to bear. There is no salve for me, no balm to ease that wound. All I can do is let it fester.'

'Why?' Merope retorted. She was dressing herself as she spoke, pulling her dress back over her body. 'Why does your legion's honour matter so much more than your own, if both were sullied?'

'Because…' Orbus groped for a reply that would appease her. *Gates of Fire, woman.* 'Because I chose to do what I did. The Legion did not. I chose to run from a war, after I had sworn an oath to take no backward step.'

'Because you were afraid?' Merope asked him. There was no judgement there, and there never would be. That was just one thing that had drawn him to her.

'Because I was a coward,' Orbus corrected her.

'Because you were human,' she tenderly retorted.

From any legionary, any fellow officer or indeed any other living soul, Orbus would have snorted his derision and shaken his head. He might be mercurial, but he wasn't profound. He had little regard, or patience, for this kind of discussion.

But here, in a lover's bed, with the courtesan he shared so many of his secrets with, he briefly allowed himself the luxury of an open mind.

'We are soldiers,' he confessed to her. 'We are trained to a standard, and we hold ourselves to a code. We can't just *be human*. We can't allow ourselves that luxury. We have to be...'

'Better?' Merope raised an eyebrow.

'I wasn't going to say that,' Orbus drily replied. He made no effort to rise as Merope put her clothes back on, seemingly content to stay in bed. 'And if it's all the same, I'd like to change the subject. This is literally all I've thought about since Gaul. I don't ask you about your ink.'

Merope pulled the neck of her dress, letting her collarbone show. The thin black cursive etched into her skin, that she'd had from the day she'd been born a slave, was visible even in the candlelight. 'That is because you don't need to. You learnt what you needed when you purchased me, *master.*'

Scarcely had the word *master* sounded less masterly. Orbus let it go. She wasn't exactly wrong, and she knew he valued her for her candour as much as anything else.

Alright, so maybe that was wrong. She was a beautiful woman – young, but with the gentle grace of someone much older – and they both knew it. Orbus told himself that that was the case; that he cared about her simply because he burned for her, and that he kept her just for that reason, and not because no-one else in Rome probed him so deeply with their questions, or guessed the way his thoughts were flowing quite so adroitly.

'No gold or jewellery for me, this time,' Merope scolded him. She tried her best to make it sound like a joke. 'You've never come back to me empty-handed before.'

'And I have never been cast out of my legion before,' was his rather scathing retort. That was more venomous than he'd intended, and he regretted it immediately afterwards. 'So much has happened, even since I returned to Rome,' he added, softening his tone. 'I've barely been able to get my thoughts in line.'

'In line enough to make your way here, though?' Merope smirked, but Orbus wasn't really listening.

'I'm going to Baiae,' he announced, apropos of nothing.

'For good?' she asked him.

Orbus shook his head, still not really looking at her. 'Just for a visit. I need to see my brother again... and I should visit my wife.'

Ah. So that was why he was being so cagey. Merope didn't really know how to respond to that – or, for that matter, how Orbus expected her to take the news.

'If you're saying you intend to bring me with you,' she began, 'then I would request, in the strongest possible terms, for you not to.'

'I wasn't going to make you,' Orbus assured her.

'Then why bring it up at all?' she snapped at him, most unladylike. Orbus didn't choose his slaves for their backtalk, but he'd always given Merope a longer leash.

'I understand it is… hard for you,' he began. 'Hearing me talk about her like that.'

'How very self-flattering of you,' Merope started to reply, but they both could hear how defeated she sounded. She came back round to the bedspread, sitting on it next to Orbus. 'You're not looking forward to it. I appreciate that. So why share that confession with me?'

Orbus didn't respond, but Merope wasn't an idiot. She ran a finger through his thinning hair. 'I don't know what went on with you in Gaul. And I don't know what's going on in there,' she stroked his temple with her knuckle. 'But I'm your slave, not your conscience. Please don't place that burden on me, master. Please don't make me your confessor.'

'You are my slave,' he coldly replied. 'You'll be whatever I need you to be.'

Suffice to say, that rather broke the spell of the moment. Merope pulled her hand away, getting up off the silken sheets.

'If that is what you wish.' There was no tenderness at all there, not anymore. He'd had his chance for that. 'Then seeing as I have performed my service, *master*, may I take my leave of you now?'

Merope didn't even wait for a response, pulling another sheet off the bed and retreating to the other room, and the divan she usually slept on when her master didn't come knocking.

Orbus stayed where he was, propped up against the headboard, with only his thoughts for company.

DAWN FOUND HIM much the same way, still contemplating, still alone. He hadn't slept. He'd barely even moved, still semi-upright in a bed that felt understandably lonelier than usual.

Merope only half-heard him leave; she fancied she still must have been asleep. She herself didn't stir from the divan until a polite knocking truly woke her a couple of hours later. It was late morning now, with sunlight and warmth streaming through the shutters.

It wasn't Orbus knocking at the door, she knew that much. His knock was less dignified, and more insistent if he was particularly craving some female company. She had a fleeting idea of who *had* come calling, and was pleased to see her guess was right when she opened the door.

'Centurion Cascana.' She stepped out of his way. 'Do come in.'

'My thanks, lady.' The First Spear ducked his head as he made his way inside. Cascana always called her *lady*, and privately she found that endearing, if a little cringeworthy. Women weren't really his area, and it showed in his awkward and earnest smiles.

'Can I offer you refreshment?' she asked, mainly to fill the silence. 'Water, perhaps? The day is hot.'

'No, thank you.' Cascana shook his head, nonplussed at her deference. She wasn't his slave, but she was *a* slave, and he was a free man. 'I was hoping to catch your master. He told me he was coming here, but I confess I don't know if he planned to spend the night.'

'He did.' Merope and Cascana knew each other well, if not closely, and Cascana knew what her duties to Orbus entailed. Still, she felt a little sheepish talking about it openly. 'You just missed him, actually. He left a couple of hours ago.'

'Quite early.' It wasn't a question.

'Indeed,' Merope replied. 'He was going back to Baiae. I think he wanted to make good time.'

Cascana nodded. 'Yes, he mentioned he'd be going home for a few days.' He walked through the vestibule, sitting himself down on an oaken chair that overlooked the small balcony. The view wasn't exactly idyllic – unless you counted an identical empty tenement block, practically spitting distance away, as idyllic – but as an anonymous apartment to stash one's courtesan in, Cascana couldn't fault it.

'How did he seem to you, last night?' he suddenly asked.

'He...' Merope didn't answer straight away, as she'd honestly being mulling this over herself. 'He wasn't himself. Sometimes he's different, or a little out of sorts, if it's a hard campaign he's coming from. But this time...' She thought back to last night, when Orbus had coldly reminded her of her lowly station. 'He wasn't himself at all.'

Cascana nodded, sagely. 'That is the conclusion I've drawn since we returned to Rome.' He went on to gently describe the ambush to her, and Orbus' shameful part in it. Merope seemed markedly less open as his story went onto the court martial, and by the time he was done narrating the attack on the Field of Mars, she wasn't stopping to ask questions at all.

'Blood of Teucer...' she breathed.

'Did he not tell you?' Cascana asked her.

She shook her head. 'He did. It just didn't sound quite so... serious, coming from him.' She dragged a tangled strand of hair out of her face. 'He just said that he got jumped by some rowdy *milites* off-duty.'

That made the Centurion smile apologetically. 'I doubt he meant to mislead you. He probably just didn't want you worrying.'

Merope almost laughed. 'I doubt that. He wasn't at his most... receptive, yesterday.' Her face must have darkened, as Cascana cringed.

'He feels he is alone,' the First Spear tried to explain, pointing at his temple. 'Up there. He has me. And you,' he added gallantly, 'but what he's going through, he's going through alone. So, with that in mind...' He paused, finding the right words. 'Maybe cut him some slack for a while.'

Merope's own words came back to her, echoing through the night. *Please don't make me your confessor.*

'I don't know what happens to him without a legion,' Cascana confessed. 'And I don't think he knows who he is without one.'

She didn't think much to that, by Cascana's reckoning. Whatever Orbus had said to her last night must have really stung.

'It will get better,' he tried. 'Just give him time. I know how much he cares about you.'

'I care about him too,' Merope replied, and that wasn't a lie. 'Sometimes it is just... hard.'

Cascana knew at once what she meant. 'I know. It isn't a simple thing. He longs for you, in his own way... but not like Caesula. We both know he'll never move on from that.'

BAIAE BECKONED, AND in truth Orbus felt shamefully glad to be leaving Rome again.

The weather was blessedly dry for winter, which meant firmer ground, which meant faster travelling. For a while, Orbus was transported back to the winding mountain pathways of Gaul. The roads there were scarcely worthy of the name, crossing plains of uneven land which couldn't quite be considered hills, and rarely ran straight at the best of times. Or more often they simply stopped, ebbing away beneath the grasslands or rubble of times gone by.

Here, in the heartland of Rome's Empire, he didn't have quite so much to worry about. The *cursus publicus* connected every town and city on the Italian peninsula, and when every road led to Rome, then every road could, in theory, lead anywhere else too. The white marble markers by the roadside denoted the passing of miles, and although there would be more than one waystation to stop at for the night, Orbus had every reason to hope for an unbroken journey.

Evening became night as they crossed Campania's fertile plains. Orbus' chosen route hugged the coast, mainly for ease of navigation but also to take in the coastal lights. The settled areas across the Tyrrhenian Coast were visible from a long way off, the pinpricks of light from faraway torches and beacons casting a fractal amber aura over the distant moonlit tides.

'Now that,' Orbus murmured from the carriage, 'is always worth seeing.'

'Praefector?' Argias chipped in from opposite, where he'd been sat for the journey thus far. 'Did you say something?'

Orbus cursed inwardly. Puli usually knew better than to disturb his introspection, but he'd assumed Argias had fallen asleep.

'Just... at ease, *optio*.'

NOT LONG AFTER, they reached the outskirts of Baiae.

If Rome was the crown of the Mediterranean world, then Baiae was a particularly prized jewel in that crown. It had no strategic importance, a populace too small to canvass or tithe from, and yielded little agriculture to the Empire's capital.

But then, its main export was pleasure.

Untamed beaches led into the Gulf's viridian waters. Geothermic pleasure pools warmed the soul as much as the body. Idyllic mountain retreats overlooked the rustic landscape. Small wonder the imperial household had bought up so much of the ancient town already. Even emperors needed a holiday.

Julius Caesar himself had once owned a villa here, and that very building still served its purpose as a holiday home. Its purchase history only added to the villa's renown and high demand.

A good way off from Baiae's outskirts, Orbus' wagon turned a little further inland, taking a narrower and poorer-kept road down the verdant peninsula. Each time he peered outside the wagon's cramped *carruca*, Baiae grew a little more in his field of vision. Their true destination was close to the town but less populated, and in Orbus' opinion that made it lovelier still.

Before long they passed the first sign, inked upon some gilded driftwood hanging at the roadside.

ELYSIA

The evening air was quiet and still; not especially cold, for few places in Italy were ever truly cold. Gone were the sounds of merry travellers on the air, and horse-drawn traffic from the country roads and streets. Out of season, Baiae was a quieter, queerer place.

The town's soul had been taken by the privileged merrymakers who loved it so. Perversely, this only seemed to make Orbus feel more at home.

'We're here,' Puli told them. By that point, the slave must have been wearied unto death, but then they all were. They'd been on the move for almost eighteen unbroken hours, and somehow even passengers found long days on the roads particularly draining. But professionalism was Puli's watchword, and his master expected no less.

'What is this place?' Argias wondered, eying the gates that stood before them. 'A leisure resort?'

'Of sorts, yes.' Orbus was pulling a cloak on. 'Although I doubt it's in service, this time of year.'

'And this is your home?' the *optio* pressed him.

Orbus smiled, buckling on *Ananke* with his belt. 'My father bought this estate when he... retired. These days I own half of it.'

The mules were quietly braying, in need of rest and sustenance. Puli was already half done unloading the baggage.

'So who owns the other half?' Argias asked.

'I'M NOT A man who likes jokes, brother. And you're not much good at making them.'

Sextus Sertor Orbus was a rugged, ruddy bear of a man. His hair was thick and bouffant as opposed to sparse and cropped, and his face was puffy and vital where his brother's was lined with care and concern. Where Gaius was slight but powerful, Sextus was imposing *and* powerful – at least, he would be, if he'd ever tried to shape his body with a soldier's discipline.

And tonight, as the two of them sat in his study with drinks in their hands, and the soldier confessed everything he'd done, it was all the businessman could do not to scoff in his face.

'So, you ran and left your men to die, weaselled out of the death penalty you ardently deserved, and had Cascana bail you out when your men tried to punish you the hard way.'

'That,' Orbus gently pointed out, 'is an interesting interpretation.'

'That's *my* interpretation. And that doesn't make it wrong.' The older man snorted. 'How is the little prince, anyway?'

'Well,' Orbus replied. 'He's just made First Spear, actually. I dare say his star is on the rise.'

Sextus grunted noncommittally. 'Fascinating.'

Even Sextus' accent was different to Gaius'. It held the same root of lower-class Latin, a legacy of the slum-childhood they'd shared in the *Subura*. But now it seemingly owed more to the country types found across the Bay of Naples and wider Campania.

When he'd first taken over Elysia, that had been a deliberate affectation to charm his clientele. These days Orbus suspected it was entirely unfeigned, having gradually become part of who Sextus was. He distantly wondered what he sounded like, in his brother's ears; doubtless an urbane melange of regional, soldierly drawl.

'Let's have a look, then.'

Orbus pulled the lapels of his tunic apart. Under the metal *phalerae* that denoted his officer status, the wounds he'd taken in Gaul and on the Field of Mars were still slowly healing. But it was the tattoos that drew Sextus' eyes most, more specifically the one that covered the Legion numeral.

Sextus swore out loud, multiple times. He wasn't a particularly reverent soul, but he was a superstitious one, and Orbus' blacked markings didn't sit lightly with him. There were no such tattoos on *his* body, because Sextus had never served in the legions, but he knew well enough the import of his brother's ink.

'If father could see you now...'

Sextus caught himself glancing out the southwest window, as if old Ascanius Orbus, interred out in the central villa's adjoining field, was actually about to spring from death and admonish his son's desertion.

'Oh, don't start all that.' Orbus' tone was uncharacteristically snide. 'Allow me to cut the *favoured son* tirade short. I didn't come here for a lecture on how I'm failing our father's legacy.'

'Failing it?' Sextus scoffed. 'I'd wager you're more our father's son than ever, Gaius.' His smile took on a venomous edge. 'A penniless soldier, who claims to have a cause, even if the words don't ring true. Who when faced with the end, chooses a life of cowardice instead of a death with honour.' Orbus didn't like the glint in his brother's eye.

'And look, you even have the same damned sword!' Sextus shot an envious glance at *Ananke*, hanging behind them with his brother's cloak.

'Our father had to do what he did,' Orbus warily replied. 'And so did I.'

'Ah, so you had no choice?' Sextus wouldn't let it lie. 'But no-one ever does, do they? When a man believes he has no choice, that is the moment you see who he truly is.'

A rather caustic silence fell upon the room. The only real sounds were the lowing of the donkeys outside, as Sextus' slaves fed and watered them. Orbus had worked them hard, and they'd need some tender care indeed before the journey back.

'I am not him.' Orbus took a sip of his drink – not ale, not even the wine he pretended to like, but a good draught of old British mead. Ascanius had brought shipments of it home from his first tour of service, as a freshly-minted *hastatus* in faraway Britannia, and this particular vintage – brewed by the old Iceni, rumour had it – had become a firm favourite of his sons. Orbus had a fair amount stashed back in Rome, but he didn't break it out regularly. It wasn't easy to acquire these days, and some things were for savouring instead of squandering.

'I am not my father,' the Praefector gently murmured.

'Maybe not,' Sextus mused, taking a swig from his own goblet. 'At least he stood and fought. Surrendering isn't quite the same as running away, I suppose. And at least he *earnt* his reprieve.'

Orbus said nothing, as more memories unwound themselves in his mind's eye. Their father, and the stories he'd told them about Actium… the seas catching fire, the fleets crashing together, and how it felt to be on the losing side of a world at war.

Sextus seemed to sense his thoughts, or else had long learnt how to guess them.

'You may not be granted the *clementia* he was, brother,' he told him. 'But I know you still believe.'

Orbus wasn't sure if that was a compliment or not. 'You were always more of a believer in the cause than I was, Sextus. Maybe even more than father.'

'You bet?' Sextus' brow furrowed with grim resolve. 'I can tell you *I* wouldn't have surrendered to my enemy's mercy. Better a blade at my throat than *clementia* on my knees. Maybe you're more our father's son than me after all.'

'Oh...' Now *that* prickled Orbus' temper. 'You think you know anything about dying for a cause? You've never even picked up a gods-damned sword, let alone fought. Do you know what it is to risk your life, Sextus? To *actually* draw a blade in the knowledge that it might be you that falls? You can *talk*—' He gesticulated with his non-drink hand. '—talk and talk and talk, about the cause, about your beliefs, to your cursed heart's content. But do you know what it is to *fight* for them? Even a creedless, unprincipled sell-sword has more conviction than you, if he's man enough to draw iron!'

'And of course *you'd* know!' Sextus shouted back. 'All you *do* is fight! Following orders because that's all you know. Never stopping, never questioning. Bleeding for the lies your legates tell you, dying for causes you don't understand!'

'That's what being a soldier is!' the Praefector bellowed.

'*Well it wasn't this time!*' Sextus roared. '*Because this time you ran away!*'

They lapsed into another, more static, silence. The scuffing of footsteps in the vestibule outside betrayed the uneasiness of Sextus' slaves; he had several who worked in the household, as well as across the other villas and dwellings that made up Elysia.

They weren't accustomed to their master's temper.

Sextus moved to pour himself some more mead. He'd knocked his goblet over in the heat of the moment, and he hoped the drink would douse his anger instead of fuelling it. Across the table from him, Orbus was similarly brooding.

This was hardly the brothers' first dance, anyway. How many times had they had this argument in the years since Ascanius had died? How many times had Sextus called him a sell-out, an unprincipled thug in legion red, an institutionalised bully who would never step outside his regimented life and speak the truth?

And how many times had Orbus hit back, deriding him as an armchair philosopher, a self-righteous messiah who hid miles away from Imperial Rome, and had never fought against his fellow men?

And, of course, each coin had two sides. How many times had Orbus considered if his brother was right, and wondered if he'd truly lost his family's ideals, or simply tempered them with realism? And how many times had Sextus put himself in his brother's shoes, questioning if his ends would always justify his means if *his* life lay on the line?

Some questions have no answers. Truth can be simple, or it can be labyrinthine, but it is always subjective, and the brothers Orbus were no exception to this.

As ever, Sextus was the one to cut to the quick of it.

'We're Republicans, Gaius. We always will be.' He took a long swill of his mead, relishing the faintly pleasant burn in his throat.

'And we live in a republic,' Orbus stressed. 'Only one that is changing. We–'

His brother cut him off, not unkindly. 'Not changing. *Changed*. We are led by one man.'

'A first citizen,' Orbus replied, although he sensed where this was going.

'An emperor,' Sextus pressed. 'We live in a *principate*, brother. But enough quibbling with terminology. Is a republic a republic if one man has a boot on its throat?'

Orbus didn't answer immediately. There was a part of him – a small, rebellious part he'd ever admit to – that perversely warmed to this kind of debate. In Rome you simply couldn't talk like this. Challenges to the throne's power were not allowed to stand, no matter how flippant or philosophical.

'We threw out the last king of Rome centuries ago.' This was Sextus' popular refrain, and he took his brother's silence as accepting of his righteousness. 'Are we really going to let another one take his place? And what happens when this emperor dies? Do we go back to the way things were? To the Republic of yore?' His passion become more brittle. 'Or is a new man picked to replace him? A man picked by the Senate? Or worse, by *him*?'

'The people will choose,' Orbus allowed. 'Such a choice couldn't be made lightly, or without their will.'

'The people,' Sextus spat, 'will choose whoever is put before them. There may not be a king, but there will be a kingmaker. *One man. That* is the basis of a tyranny. He folded his arms smugly, as if that had made the whole case for him. 'Mark my words, brother. When Augustus dies, then I'll be proved right. That is the moment on which all will turn. That's when we'll know we've fashioned ourselves a king, at the head of his own foul dynasty.'

'Augustus is not a king,' Orbus wearily replied. 'And he does not have an heir.'

'He sits upon a throne.'

'He leads the Senate.'

'He *is* the Senate.'

'How would you know?' Orbus tried to steer the debate from its accustomed path. 'What news do you even hear out here, in the Bay? I thought that was the point of this place. A secluded haven, where the wearies of the outside world cannot reach you.'

Sextus grimaced as his own words were repeated back at him. 'Everyone knows,' he vaguely replied. 'And I hear things. I… have contacts.' He stopped abruptly, and an odd look flashed across his face. As if he'd been caught out. Let slip something he shouldn't have.

Orbus' eyes narrowed. 'What?'

'Nothing.' His brother seemed keen to move on. 'So this emperor of yours… this is a man you love, and swore to fight for in your *sacramentum*, despite the fact that he took everything from our father, and has brought us to this point?' He gestured out the window with his arm, and Orbus knew the point he was making at once.

Ascanius Orbus, like so many who'd been caught on the wrong side at Actium, had begged for *clementia* from the new emperor and been granted it – at a price, of course. That price had been the forfeiture of his military standing, and the bulk of his amassed savings.

Ascanius had retired from the legions under this dishonourable cloud, and the last of his money had been spent here, on Elysia. A fading pleasure ranch, far from Rome's eyes, that his oldest son now battled to keep afloat. Meanwhile, his other son followed in his military footsteps, fighting for a cause and man his father once waged war to defeat, holding a rank he couldn't move past, and hoping his peers would see him as anything more than his father's mistakes.

Orbus took a moment to consider his own choices, and the loss of brotherhood he'd suffered. Truly, sons were their fathers.

'You know, half of Baiae is owned by the Emperor's household,' he cautioned Sextus. 'Your holidaymakers aren't exactly going to give you a sympathetic ear, brother. One day, you'll say the wrong thing to the wrong person and then...' He didn't need to finish the thought. It was that obvious.

'I have never seen you like this before.' Sextus' introspection usually ended at the boundaries of his own self, but from him, those words struck Orbus as unconscionably melancholy. 'You usually hit back at my words, Gaius. You don't actually listen to what I have to say.'

'I usually have a place in the world, brother,' was Orbus' equally despondent reply. 'I've lost everything. My rank, my legion.' He sucked in a breath. 'My life.'

'So is that why you're here?' Sextus raised an eyebrow. 'Because you think I'm right? That I can somehow absolve you?'

Orbus' eyes darkened, his gaze flashing with the fortitude of the truly nihilistic. 'I'm not here for absolution, brother. I am here to atone.'

Sextus' silence was invitation to continue.

'I want to sell you my shareholding,' Orbus announced. 'Well, most of it. Thirty percent. Which will put mine to twenty, and yours at eighty.'

'I have been working here a while,' his brother drily replied. 'I can count, Gaius.'

'And my land as well,' Orbus continued, heedless. 'Everything except Numa's Cairn, and the adjoining field.' That was the villa in Orbus' half he called home during his visits. 'Buy all the rest from me. I know you've always wanted it.'

Sextus didn't need to think. The brothers Orbus rarely agreed with one another, and frankly sometimes didn't even like each other. But they always trusted each other.

'Done. I'll have Aruxeia draw up paperwork in the morning.' He sniffed, rubbing his bulbous lips together. 'I can't give you the market price, though. You'll have to settle for less.'

'Business that bad?' Orbus remarked, although he was sure he knew the answer. It was pitifully evident, from the shambolically picturesque chaos of this study to the peeling paintwork on the neighbouring villas.

'I'll get through it,' Sextus replied. 'And I'll build it back up. You mark my words, Gaius – everything Father put into this place, I'll restore.'

Orbus had no answer to his brother's ardent conviction. Sextus had had many ardent convictions in his life. He wondered if this one would be any different.

'Well then, consider this your first step on that path,' he said, as diplomatically as he could. 'Make sure we can start the ball rolling quickly, though. Tomorrow I leave, the earlier the better.'

'Your mules may need longer,' Sextus conceded. 'As will Puli. You put him through a lot, to get here so quickly. Driving a wagon isn't easy, Gaius. He went out like a light, the moment his head hit the pillow. My footmen told me.'

'Puli will be fine by morning.' Orbus drained the last of his mead, slapping the goblet down. 'He has worked to tighter margins before.'

Sextus' smile was a thing of lopsided honesty. 'Was he really fine?' he countered. 'Or did he simply not complain?'

Orbus let it go, as his brother was probably right. That was the problem with legionary training, and holding yourself to military standards. It was easy to forget that not everyone else did.

'Speaking of slaves,' Sextus added. 'How's that little Etrurian beauty of yours?'

Orbus rolled his eyes at his brother's crudeness. 'I think I'll go for a walk, before bed. Goodnight, brother.'

'Rest easy.' Sextus was already going back to the papers at his desk – details of rents, no doubt, from the villas, beach and geothermic pool that made up Elysia. 'Aruxeia is probably still awake. Do give her your regards, if you see her.'

Orbus snorted. A Greek slave Ascanius had acquired with the resort, Aruxeia had moulded them into boys and then young men with harsh, scolding fairness. But her talents were far wider, and an older Sextus had freed her, employing her as a business manager. These days she helped him run Elysia, commanding the small army of slaves and scribes it took to keep the estate ticking over.

'I'll keep an eye out.' Orbus rubbed fatigue from his eyes as he rose from his seat. It had been a long day, and mead always had this effect on him.

He was almost at the door when Sextus spoke again.

'If you're here,' he ventured, 'are you going to see Caesula?'

The two brothers met each other's eyes for a moment. Some things cannot quite be said with words.

'I thought I would, when I came out here,' Orbus told him. 'But on reflection, no.'

THE NIGHT WAS finally losing its warmth. Or maybe that was the mead wearing off.

Orbus found himself walking through the arid pasture, pushing his way through grass that grew up to his knees. It didn't take long to reach his destination. He knew the way. He'd been enough times.

It wasn't a particularly flamboyant funerary marker, but then neither was the man whose ashes were buried in it. One simple stone monument, with a grille for pouring libations. The ground around it was perfectly earthen, but it had been a long time since any man had planted flowers here.

ASCANIUS SERTOR ORBUS

Father and soldier both

Orbus wiped away the dust of ages, making the faded inscription a little more legible. His eyes moved past the record of his old legion, the title of his century, and the many stories and battle honours accrued over a life in the Red. Only one part of the inscription truly mattered, and it was the part he always read. He'd come here so many times before, and each time he pondered his father's melancholy choice of epitaph.

'The true hell of life is that every man has his reasons.'

This time, as he looked up at the stars above him, the words didn't quite feel so aloof.

PART II
LIBERALIA

V

IN PAINTED CHAINS

BYDRETH'S EYES SNAPPED open. Pain, as usual, heralded the coming of dawn.

Sweaty, calloused hands roused him awake, and they weren't particularly gentle about it. He was dragged to his feet, still half-asleep, and almost smiled when the familiar slap to wake him up came.

He felt himself actually smiling. Somehow, this never seemed to ever dampen his spirits – not today, not yesterday, or any day in the years of captivity leading up to this moment.

'Hello, Barcus,' he greeted his tormentor. 'How are you, this fine morning?' There was no mockery there, no baiting edge. This was his life. It wasn't an easy or happy one, but what else could slaves expect?

'Shut up.' Barcus was already shoving him out of the wooden caravan, into the cold Januarius air. That didn't affect his mood much, either. He'd always relished the outdoors, even at its coldest and greyest. It reminded him of home – at least, of what home should have been like.

Today the sky was a little hotter and brighter than expected. The countryside extended in each direction, with the great road scarcely visible at the horizon's edge. Baiae and the Bay of Naples lay one way. Cumae, and the route further inland, another.

No matter how he much he longed for his ancestral, half-remembered homeland, Campania never failed to take his breath away. This warm, verdant land of wine and swords – what place in the world was like it?

Barcus and the other heavy-hands were putting them all to work, forcing Bydreth's companions awake with barked commands and the occasional slap. Like Bydreth, most of them didn't feel like fighting back, mainly because their thoughts were too tired and sluggish to move properly, and more likely because like Bydreth, this was the only life they'd ever known.

A part of him felt a twinge of irony. Back home, men of the Ulthaini fought each other over women, over spoils and their own honour. But then, these men weren't Ulthaini anymore. They were descendants of that great tribe in blood, if not in heart. They could speak the tongues of the Picts, and they wore the blues and reds of their bloodline on their skin and faces, but few of them could truly explain what either meant anymore. That part of them had been stripped away.

Maudlin thoughts weren't in Bydreth's nature, but even *his* morning bonhomie faded at the thought.

A few wooden pails of valley water were waiting for them outside, and Bydreth found himself joining the queue of his fellow men to dunk their heads in it. The water was ice cold, though not especially clean, and that freezing immersion – and the shock that followed – was all the slaves were allowed each morning to freshen up. Bydreth was quietly glad he'd joined the queue early. After too many visitors, the water would be thick with mites and muff.

He pulled his face out of the water, rubbing hands through his waterlogged burgundy locks. He caught a glance of his fractured reflection in the churned liquid: a broad, roguishly handsome face striated with fading war paint. Smiling at it rather ruined that illusion, displaying a set of rotting, yellowed teeth that no physician would ever be able to save.

'Come on now,' grunted Barcus, somewhere behind him. 'Quit admiring yourself. There's others waiting.'

Soon, others began grumbling with lethargic impatience. 'Sorry, Barcus,' Bydreth called out as he left. 'With a view like this, can you blame me?'

He grinned, displaying that foetid mouth for all to see.

HE FOUND BRAUDA a little later, as the troupe was warming up. The other man was crouched on one knee, morosely scratching at his scalp, seemingly displeased with what his fingers felt.

'That's the name of the game, cousin,' Bydreth quipped as he drew near. 'Later you are in the queue, the more lice you're getting in your brow.'

'I barely have any damned hair, anyway,' Brauda growled. 'How can it hurt this much?'

Bydreth stood there for a moment in the morning air, marvelling at his cousin's banal concerns, before walking over behind him.

'Alright,' he decided. 'Let me take a look.'

Brauda grunted a second time, which Bydreth took as acquiescence to his offer of help. He reached out with gnarled hands, gently running them through the tatted strings of Brauda's thinning hair.

He hadn't been exaggerating about the mites.

The other once-Ulthaini slaves around them paid him little heed, most of them in the midst of stretching their muscles, warming up their fatigued and abused physiques, or simply snatching what little rest they could before tonight's preparations would begin proper.

'So,' Bydreth began, still gently attending to his kinsman's scalp, 'are you going to tell me what's really eating at you?'

He couldn't see Brauda's face, but fancied he could feel it contort in boyish annoyance. Brauda was a man of varied and surprising talents, but concealing his emotions was rarely one of them. He was a decent man, a straight man up and down. Although that could be less charitably called narrow-mindedness.

'Take a running guess, Byd,' was Brauda's only reply. Bydreth wasn't an idiot, and he knew Brauda meant the red-ribbon scars down his back. Scars that hadn't been there the day before.

'What did our master take exception to this time?' Bydreth asked him archly.

'He is *not* my master,' Brauda hissed under his breath, fervour trumped by a desire to not be heard.

Bydreth let that claim go unchallenged, raking more lice from Brauda's mane. 'So what did you do, then?'

Brauda spat into the earth, standing up and turning to face his older cousin. Grooming time, clearly, was over.

'You don't have to play their games, Brau.' Bydreth gave him a gentle slap on the shoulder, playful yet still comradely. 'You don't have to rise to every slight.'

That didn't quite lighten his cousin's mood as hoped. 'Well,' Brauda retorted, 'you certainly seem quite good at it.'

For a man as perceptive as Bydreth prided himself on being, he didn't clock the undercurrent of bitterness in Brauda's voice. Bydreth was a magnanimous soul; Brauda was not. Bydreth loved Brauda for it, while Brauda resented Bydreth for much the same. Brauda had a thinner skin, and like all such men, no-one else was more aware of it – and frustrated by it – than he was.

'Come on, then. We should go and join the others.' Bydreth motioned towards a group of their troupe-mates, who were practising their juggling of oiled wooden clubs. Those would be set alight come the actual performance, with little thought given to the jugglers' safety. Another man, nearby, was working on his handless headstands, and Brauda idly wondered how long it would be before he pulled his back again.

'Tuggi, Klaujan,' Bydreth called. 'Mind if we join you?'

The once-tribesmen grunted, and Bydreth picked up a wooden play-spear from the ground. 'Run through the routine with me?' He gave the dummy weapon an experimental spin.

A sudden commotion turned all their heads.

'Behold,' Brauda murmured sarcastically. 'Our lord and master cometh.'

AGAMEMNON II CLAPPED a hand to each cheek, yawning the night's fatigue away. My, oh my, this was going to be a good day.

It was pushing noon. He'd been awake all of twenty minutes, but the troupe would have risen hours ago, put to work by Barcus for morning practice. Baiae wasn't a widely populous town, but there'd be enough paying spectators to form a crowd, and spread the word.

Enough *rich* spectators. He allowed himself a predatory smile. *Rich, young, female spectators...*

He couldn't hear much from outside. Just the wind, the thump of wooden weapons clashing, and the calls of livestock rehearsing their acts. No-one was crying out from a whipping or clubbing, which meant that no-one had tried their luck with a nocturnal escape attempt.

Fifty men, mottled in Ulthaini blue and scarlet, glistened with sweat and exertion. They practised their aerial acrobatics, flipping and vaulting over their earth-bound comrades. Others sparred with blunted weaponry, engaging in all manner of flowery, impractical swordplay that would probably amuse an actual soldier. The remainder were lighting up their oaken juggling torches.

They were all the more diligent for Barcus and his muscle's constant malevolent scrutiny. Hands never strayed far from cudgels, as if the slaves needed that reminder. This was their life, and life didn't change.

'Look sharp, all of you!' Agamemnon II called out. 'We're taking the show north. Back to Baiae. The spoils will be rich for the picking.' He licked his dry lips assuredly.

'Baiae?' Bydreth called out. Wasn't it always Bydreth? 'Baiae will be out of season. Surely we'd do better back at Cumae?' Bydreth looked up, noting the sun's position in the sky. 'If we set off now, we could make it there in time for evening… if you think that best, master.'

For a moment, the slaver was lost for words. *We? We* would do better? The idea of this performing monkey on a par with *him*, Agamemnon II?

His liver-spotted hand tightened around his cane's jewelled head. Time for a little lesson in manners. He was a showman, and all life was showmanship. The troupe would serve as audience, and the performance would be the punishment of an insolent slave.

'Come here, young man,' Agamemnon II beckoned him closer with a spindly, gnarled finger. 'I can't say I heard that.'

Brauda grasped Bydreth's wrist, only to be shrugged off. Bydreth begun to walk closer, his kinsmen's eyes all on his back.

'Now…' huffed Agamemnon II, masking some very real anger with some very theatrical innocence. 'I must have misheard, because I thought for a moment you were questioning my decisions. But you wouldn't do that to me, boy… *would you?*'

Bydreth halted. He enjoyed believing himself brave – as would any of his fellow Ulthaini, he wagered – but his master's unchecked mania was always enough to disturb him. He didn't just look raving mad. He looked… ill. Like he was coming apart from within.

'Don't you…' began Agamemnon II, his words practically falling over themselves. Somewhere in the sky a bird called out. 'Don't you… just… *contradict me!*' His free hand bunched into a fist.

Bydreth mirrored the gesture, as Barcus's goons ghoulishly appeared at Agamemnon's back. He thought of his life, all the years he'd grown to manhood under the sinister aegis of this monster. He thought of himself, and every joke he'd ever made to put his friends at ease, every battle of words he'd chosen to avoid, all for the sake of living another day.

Bydreth met Agamemnon II's eyes for a moment, and told him, gently and politely, to go to hell.

The slaver never got to reply to that, as one of Barcus' servile thugs chose that moment to run to his master's side.

'Lord Agamemnon,' Truja spluttered, coughing. He'd been running hard. 'We're being approached. A wagon's come off-road, a mile or so south. It's headed straight for us.'

Agamemnon II narrowed his beady eyes. *Off-road?* Then whoever was inbound wasn't simply passing. They were specifically looking for the caravan site.

For him.

He forgot his righteous indignation, worry plastered across his face. Agamemnon II had his fair share of enemies. These newcomers, whoever they were, must undoubtedly have an axe to grind with him.

'Look!' someone shouted, pointing. 'Are those soldiers?'

Everyone – Agamemnon, Barcus, Bydreth, Brauda, and every slave-performer, heavy-hand and ass-driver – turned to the south.

Where a pair of red figures were approaching over the crest of the ridge.

'Who are they?' Bydreth muttered. With the sudden shift in focus, he'd stealthily returned to Brauda's side.

'Haven't a clue,' his cousin replied. 'What are legionaries doing this far from Rome, anyway?'

And legionaries they were. Bydreth made them out better as they came closer; the first was a gangly young man in army red, wearing the traditional segmented body armour he associated with soldiers.

The second one was shorter but more solidly built, and Bydreth could tell at once that he was the more grizzled of the pair. He was also clearly older, as neither man had donned a helmet. His hair was dark and thinning, slicked back from his gently balding head. The younger one's was thicker yet more studiously cropped, of a similar shade to Bydreth's.

The heavy-hands had grouped around Agamemnon and Barcus, on edge for obvious reasons. But the slaves seemed to be on guard, too. A Roman soldier butting into Agamemnon's livelihood, and seeing all the illegality of his dealings, would likely end one of two ways – with all his slaves freed, or executed.

The new arrivals halted at the cusp of the Ulthaini ring. The members of the troupe recoiled, clustering around each other in a loose semi-circle crowned by Agamemnon and his thugs. Behind them, the caravan's wagons and carriages were moored in various states of disarray, the asses and beasts of burden grazing and paying their masters little heed.

'Which one of you is Licias Verdas?' called out the older legionary. He panned his gaze across the whole gathering, his eyes briefly passing over Bydreth and Brauda. Hearing no answer to his question, the man rephrased it with a frown. 'Which one of you was born Licias Verdas, who now addresses himself as *Agamemnon the Second?*'

Whispered laughter began to weave its way through the slaves. Bydreth and Brauda found themselves joining in. *Licias Verdas?* Few of them had ever believed their master's real name was Agamemnon, but *Licias Verdas?* What a burden to bear that must have been.

Agamemnon II drew himself up to his unimpressive height, striding out from his henchmen towards the newcomers. The gods alone knew how much brutally-forged authority he'd just lost among the troupe.

'I am he.' The slaver came forth, as fast as the cane would let him. He extended a spindly hand in greeting, hoping no-one noticed how it shook. 'And who do I have the honour of addressing?'

The legionary looked down at his hand without touching it. 'I left Baiae this morning,' he begun emotionlessly, 'having heard some rather troubling reports about your good self. In particular, concerning the legality of your purchasing of slaves.'

Agamemnon balked, believing he did so subtly. 'And why,' he stuttered, 'would my livestock be the concern of the people of Baiae?'

Bydreth saw something in the legionary's face darken. Clearly, this answer hadn't pleased him. How interesting it must be for Agamemnon, to be on the receiving end of fear. How educational.

'Because,' the legionary replied, 'the people of Baiae have taken exception to you in the past. To you bringing your performing circus to their borders. In particular, the lewdness of the acts you force your slaves to perform. Their *services*.'

Agamemnon II smiled a grimy smile. 'Roman women like barbarian men. And who can blame them? Closeted up in Rome, under their fathers' locks and keys. They all come to Baiae to be free, to let off steam.' The smile broadened. 'All I do is help them scratch an itch.'

The old soldier's accusations were implacable. 'You seek out rich men's wives and daughters as they holiday miles from home, and prostitute your slaves to them for gold.'

Something turned sour in the pit of Bydreth's stomach, for he knew this to be entirely true. Brauda let out a low growl from beside him, similarly shamed. None of the others seemed keen to dwell on that, either.

'These men are my property.' Agamemnon II swept a stiffened arm across the whole site. 'And I can dispense with my property as I see fit.' His smile became a little less saccharine now, indulgence replaced by malice. 'No law has been broken here, whatever you think of my business practices.'

'Perhaps not,' the younger legionary chimed in. 'But you do, I presume, possess the correct paperwork and doctrines of sale for every man you own? At least, for every man you force into such services?' He folded his arms, with a smug light in his eyes. 'It would be easy for us to check. The Curule Aediles' edict is particularly clear on the subject of illegally and improperly obtained slaves.'

'And as a praefector in the Emperor's legions,' the older man continued, 'and a servant of Rome, I feel obliged by my public duty to check.' Bydreth could hear the smile in his voice. 'And if you're not willing to show me, then I would feel equally obliged to alert the relevant authorities on our return home.'

The lanky soldier smirked. 'All down to our public-spirited nature.'

Agamemnon looked between these two legionaries, as they calmly and courteously laid out their intentions of ruining him. He doubted whether any public body in Rome would feel the zeal to delve into Campania and prosecute him, but his trade relied on word of mouth. Once the truth got out… it would all be over. Assuming the livestock didn't try to take matters into their own hands, now the charade was blown.

'You cannot do this.' He clutched the cane's head tight enough to whiten his knuckles. 'I will not… be intimidated like this!'

The soldiers didn't need to answer. Agamemnon's slaves had that honour, as each and every last one of them begun to laugh. Bydreth and Brauda found themselves joining in, swept up in the moment. Barcus' goons weathered this storm of hysterics in uncomfortable silence, but quite tellingly, made no effort to stop it.

To Bydreth's eye, that was probably the moment that Agamemnon – *Licias* – realised the die had been cast. His ego had been punctured, his illegality brought to light… even if the ground opened up and swallowed these two legionaries, even if no-one in Rome was ever the wiser, the damage had been done. His tenuous authority, built upon years of fear and subjugation, had been cracked asunder. Even the muscle couldn't help him now, assuming they would even try. A tide had been turned, and there would be no turning it back.

'No,' Agamemnon II cried, half-sob, half-roar. '*No!*'

He lashed out with that cane of his, faster than any man present could believe him move. The jewelled head collided with the older soldier – the Praefector, he'd called himself – smacking him right in the temple.

Only it didn't. Somehow, the Praefector had caught it in mid-air. A blow that should have concussed or fractured bone – and Bydreth had seen that happen before – was halted, scarcely inches from the veteran's face.

'Enough of that,' the Praefector growled. He wrenched the cane from Agamemnon's rheumatic fingers. And smashed him to the ground with one swinging blow.

Bydreth found himself looking away. If Agamemnon II ever survived to have children, he fancied that *their* offspring must have felt that. He couldn't stop himself from grinning, and he wasn't the only one.

'He'll be shitting teeth after that,' Brauda noted.

Agamemnon frolicked on the ground, frantically scrabbling out of the soldiers' way on his haunches. He spat a string of blood and mucous from his mouth, revealing that Brauda's guess had been right. A series of shattered stumps remained where his front teeth had once been.

For a moment no-one moved. And then Barcus was charging, followed by four or five of the heavy-hands. Cudgels raised, they hurtled at the new arrivals, even as Agamemnon shrieked his helpless rage.

'Argias,' the Praefector addressed his companion, 'these are yours.'

The younger soldier – Argias – drew his *gladius* in one smooth motion, holding the blade in reverse grip. He didn't charge, or scream a battle cry. He didn't even seem tense.

A flash of steel. Then Barcus was down, screaming, his hands not stopping the blood gushing from his head. That same blood stickily coated the *gladius* pommel, but Argias wasn't finished.

'*Shynnach,*' Brauda swore. 'The lanky child can fight.' Bydreth didn't disagree.

But the rest of them were on him then. A burly, thuggish man went for his torso, trying to tackle him to the ground. The young legionary rolled with the takedown, stabbing a booted heel into his attacker's face with a *crack* of pulped cartilage. And then Argias was moving, bolting out of the dust, ignoring the mewling, bloody man at his feet. His weapon pommel struck another thug's navel, winding and flooring him, even as he threw a fist at the next man's jugular.

He didn't stop. He didn't slow. He was a blur of crimson motion, weaving, attacking, and somehow never even slowing to take a blow. And he hadn't even used the blade.

Argias abruptly dropped his *gladius*. That wrongfooted his opponent, just as planned. He grabbed the ruffian's head with both hands. And kneed him, hard enough to shatter his nose.

In the aftermath, Argias sheathed his sword and started wiping the bloodied dirt off his tunic and breastplate. He was coated head to toe in grit, with the odd spatter of blood garlanding him like badges of honour, and frankly seemed all the more at home in it.

'Does anyone else,' the Praefector called out in a haggard, booming voice, 'have any objections?'

Pained, muffled groans were the only response from the victims of Argias' self-defence. A couple of the less injured tried to crawl away, not daring to risk the slaves' mercy. The rest were too stunned and flustered to even move.

'You've got to hand it to them,' Brauda grudgingly acknowledged, and Bydreth knew what his cousin meant. This Argias could have simply ploughed into them with his *gladius*, slaughtering the lot of them. But there would be ramifications to that, a judiciary trail with evidence to follow. And it would have probably turned this whole encounter into a riot, with slaves running in every direction as they took the chance to free themselves.

'Good.' The Praefector wiped a hand on his chainmail vest as Argias rubbed his gory pommel on his tunic. He grabbed the mewling, whimpering form of Agamemnon and hoisted him upright.

'Now,' the old soldier told him, loud enough for all to hear. 'I can have your thuggish little retinue slain, right here, to a man. And I doubt your slaves will see you in quite the same way with all your muscle gone.'

Agamemnon's ruined face made a poor show of remorse. The Praefector ignored him anyway.

'Or,' he continued, 'you can take a nominal sum of *denarii* from my coffers, leave with your brutes *and* your life, and formally waive any claim you have over these men, in favour of my own.' The legionary cocked his head, as if in thought. 'Of course, if anyone looked at *my* papers, it would seem you *had* legally owned them in the first place.' He half-smiled as he threw Agamemnon back down in the dirt. 'I know which offer I'd choose.'

That made Bydreth smile. It was a calculated offer, and a shrewd one – putting the bruisers' lives in Agamemnon's hands. If he declined, then they would surely kill him in retaliation. If he accepted, there was nothing to stop the Ulthaini from doing the same.

Bydreth had no idea who this praefector was, or why he was so interested in acquiring a mob of Celtic slaves, but you didn't need to know someone to like them. Or to appreciate a kindred spirit.

'Alright. Alright!' The once-slaver hunched up to look at him, but tellingly didn't try to rise again. He clearly wasn't getting the cane back, and if he couldn't return to his feet unaided then the humiliation would probably kill him alone. 'I'll... I'll have to draw up papers.'

'No need.' The Praefector turned back to the horizon, where the soldiers' wagon lay. He waved a hand, and a small figure began scurrying out in their direction. 'Puli has them all ready.'

AGAMEMNON II DEPARTED later that evening, with nothing but a pitiful handful of cash and followers. They travelled on foot, with nothing that belonged to them from the caravan site, not even to protect them from the weather. Still nursing their injuries and their pride, they took their leave, and that was that.

Their new masters hadn't said or done a great deal afterwards. Their manservant, Puli, had had their one wagon brought right up to the site, and the Ulthaini had been pleased to discover that the Praefector and Argias had filled it with disposable food, in anticipation of their run-in. It wasn't much, mainly stoned bread, cured pork and fish, but it was better than anything the slaves had enjoyed for years. The young soldier Argias had directed a few of the burliest tribesmen, tearing down Agamemnon's opulent wagon and all the moronic paraphernalia inside, and after torching it, the troupe had enjoyed an impromptu firelit feast as night drew in.

No-one seemed worried about the beacon they'd created. Down-country, in the land between cities, there weren't bound to be many winter travellers. And Bydreth's kinsmen looked a rough and ready lot. He doubted any onlookers, seeing a distant fire, would want to meddle with a horde of painted barbarians anyway.

'This is good meat.' Brauda put down the bone he'd been gnawing, picking stringy sinews from his teeth. 'Don't get this often.'

Bydreth wiped perspiration from his forehead, as he bit into the last of his own helping. It tasted of oil and cooking fat, but filled a hole nonetheless. 'I wonder what'll happen to Agamemnon?' he asked.

Brauda snorted. 'To *Licias*, you mean. I knew he was screwed up in there—' He pointed to his own temple. '—but talk about delusions of grandeur.'

Bydreth bared his rotted teeth and gums in a singularly unpleasant smile.

'Let's go and meet our saviour, eh?'

'THEIR SAVIOUR' WAS sitting a little way off from the fire, thronged by a loose ring of Ulthaini. They were sharing the last of the feast's dues, lightly joshing and gossiping with each other as they ate, and Bydreth could tell from a glance that the Praefector lay on the conversation's periphery. Another subtle touch, Bydreth noted. Their new master was letting them be themselves, stretching their newfound freedom, before asserting his authority. Clever.

He didn't strike Bydreth as a charismatic or gregarious man, but hardly a taciturn or brooding one either. Bydreth found himself trusting him instinctively, a fact he had no intention of sharing with him.

The ring of men parted as Bydreth and Brauda drew near. Bydreth smirked at a few of them, while Brauda gruffly nodded in greeting.

'Here's the one I was telling you about,' Tuggi said through a mouthful of meat.

'So I see,' the Praefector rose, stretching out a hand. 'You must be Bydreth.'

'Aye, guilty as charged.' He gave another of his roguish smiles as they clasped wrists, his degraded teeth on display once again. 'This here's my cousin, Brauda.'

'Bydreth. Brauda. Good to meet you both.' The soldier took his hand back. 'I am Gaius Sertor Orbus, Praefector of –' he broke off, apropos of nothing. 'Praefector of the Roman army,' he finally managed. He gave Bydreth a discerning look. 'I'm told you're the man in charge around here, Bydreth.'

Tuggi and a few of the others gave that claim a good-natured jeer, slapping his arm with feigned severity. Brauda, quite tellingly, didn't join in, and it was probably a good thing no-one saw the look in his eyes.

'You could say that,' Bydreth answered, to more mock-mockery. 'Mind if I bend your ear, *Praefector*?'

Orbus seemed taken aback, but eventually nodded. 'Excuse us, lads,' he addressed the other Ulthaini.

'Save me some meat.' The others grunted as they returned to their food, not really listening.

'Let's take a walk,' Bydreth suggested. 'Come on, Brauda.'

Brauda had been going to join them anyway, but now did so somewhat bristling.

'So let's say I am in charge,' Bydreth began as they drew away from the fire. 'If you're the one who owns us now, Praefector, then I've got questions.'

'Fire away,' Orbus replied as they walked. 'I'll answer what I can.'

'Well for a start,' Brauda cut in, 'what are you planning to do with all of us?' He swept a hand over the gathering. 'Because they might be happy to live in the moment, now that bastard Agamemnon is gone. But I'm not fooled. That dubious legal shit you pulled on him doesn't have pillars to stand on. If he didn't own us legally, then now neither do you.' He ignored Bydreth's scowl at this hostile line of questioning. 'And once the euphoria's worn off, they're going to realise that too.'

'Much as we appreciate the gesture, Praefector,' Bydreth amended, 'you still haven't told us why you ousted Agamemnon. Or what you plan to do with us now. How did you even find us, anyway?'

'My brother lives on the outskirts of Baiae,' Orbus explained. 'He'd heard word that your troupe had been making trouble in Cumae, and rumours that you were headed this way.'

Bydreth snorted. 'That's true enough. Although the trouble was all Agamemnon's. He was all for attracting punters to the circus, that's for sure. He just never really knew when to stop.'

'What he said about the women,' Orbus replied, looking over to him. 'Was that true?'

The three of them had come to a halt now, far enough from the fire to not be overhead.

'You may have taken us out of the cooking pot,' Bydreth told him, 'but I'm not about to let some stranger put us right into the furnace instead. So tell me, Praefector. What do you plan to do with us?'

'Wouldn't anything be better than this?' Orbus asked.

Brauda's guttural sniggering stalled whatever reply Bydreth had in mind. 'We're slaves, Praefector. That claim's never true.'

'We may be barbarians, Orbus,' Bydreth added. 'But we're not fools. That wretch Agamemnon owned us. He abused me and my kinsmen all our lives.' His fist curled, a needlessly theatrical touch. 'I'm not going to let that happen again.'

Orbus paused, noting the man's sincerity. 'No,' he replied. 'I see that.'

Brauda frowned fractionally, feeling once again like the third party in this moment of intensity. 'So what do you want with us then, Praefector?'

Orbus didn't answer immediately, losing himself in the swirling crimson and cobalt of Bydreth's tattoos. 'You and your comrades... you are Picts?'

That made both the cousins chuckle.

'*Pict. Celt. Briton. Gaul.* You Romans can drape whatever name over us you please.' Bydreth enjoyed this chance to be the one giving the answers. 'I can't speak for all the tribes of our land, but us here? We're Ulthaini.'

'*Ulthaini*,' Orbus repeated, mangling the pronunciation. 'And whereabouts in *Terra Picta* were you originally from?'

Brauda smirked again, at that phrase no-one beyond the Tiber's banks had ever used, before Bydreth offered enlightenment.

'Our home was about thirty leagues south of Fortriu,' he told him. Not that it mattered, as Orbus was clearly none the wiser.

'And you said your *kinsmen*...' The Praefector trailed off.

'That's right,' Bydreth replied. 'We all came from the same settlement, the lot of us. For Brauda and I, the same family.' He nodded at his cousin.

'So when you were captured...'

'Yes. You think Agamemnon built this troupe from the ground up? He bought the lot of us, at auction.' Bydreth lapsed into silence, and Orbus sensed he wasn't as comfortable talking about this as he pretended to be.

'We were taken, in a raid.' Brauda took up the baton. 'We were children. Following our fathers, venturing onto enemy soil. Our first taste of battle, although most of us were barely old enough to carry our fathers' spears. Didn't end particularly well. It was an ambush. The men were killed, and our oldest and surliest put to flight or slaughtered. They knew the children could be taken alive, and sold as slaves.'

'And that's how you came to Licias,' Orbus inferred.

'Aye, Praefector.' Bydreth had resurfaced from his reverie. 'He saw our ink, and heard our accents. He wanted something exotic, people he could make into circus attractions.' He sounded every bit as bitter as Brauda in that moment, for all his pragmatism. 'And he knew people wanted that. Something they don't see in Rome. Something for them to laugh at, and remind them that they rule the world.'

For a moment Orbus was speechless. He couldn't tear his eyes from this man, and the caustic dignity that coloured his words.

'I am no slaver,' the Praefector told him. 'And I'm no ringmaster, either. I won't lie to you, Bydreth of the Ulthaini. By this paperwork, you are all now mine, and the truth is that for now at least, it suits me to keep it that way.' He turned to look at Brauda as well. 'But I am taking you with me to Rome, and when that happens, you have my word as a legionary that I will grant you the freedom you deserve.'

Now that got their attention, and Orbus knew it well. Manumission was not a word that got thrown around lightly. Most slaves worked their lives away in servitude before their masters granted them freedom. The ones who bought it usually had to sacrifice half a lifetime saving up the funds, assuming manumission was even on the table to begin with.

If Orbus was dangling that prize now, within *hours* of taking their collars, then it hinged on something. Something of colossal importance.

'You buy us, just to free us days later?' Brauda spoke his cousin's thoughts with less tact. 'Why go to all the trouble to begin with?'

Bydreth made the instinctive leap first. 'You don't want our freedom,' he told the Praefector. 'You want our service.'

Orbus' smile was barely visible through the firelit night. 'Indeed. Licias sought slaves, Bydreth. I seek soldiers.'

'You want us to fight beside your men, is that it?' Brauda didn't seem rapt with the idea. 'Meat shields, to take the blades and arrows meant for Roman throats?' He snorted. He seemed to do that a lot. 'You'd be better off going to the fleshmarket. There are slavers who ply that particular trade, anyway. Hell, at least Agamemnon kept us breathing.'

Bydreth shot the younger man a warning look, but Orbus replied regardless.

'No, Brauda. I don't want you to die for my men. I want you to *be* my men.'

Brauda scoffed at that, but Orbus carried on anyway. 'I have left my legion behind, and my next command is to be a cohort of *auxilia*. A cohort I am building, from the ground up. I want you and your kinsmen to be a part of it.'

He gave Brauda a scathing look. 'And say what you will about our tactics, Brauda of the Ulthaini. A legate may command from afar, but a praefector's place is with his men. So if they send you into battle's maw, to bleed and die in place of your betters...' He laid a hand on Brauda's shoulder. 'Then I will be bleeding with you.'

Brauda shrugged the grip off, but both Orbus and Bydreth could see him starting to soften.

'We were tribesmen,' Bydreth gently pointed out. 'We're born of warriors' stock, and are used to punishing labour... but we're not soldiers. We can't fight like legionaries. We couldn't even *think* like legionaries. We weren't born to march in shield walls. That was never the way of our people.'

'You will be trained,' Orbus assured him. 'I will deal with that.'

'We don't have weapons,' Brauda added, more aggressively. 'Or armour. We don't own anything.'

'I will deal with that, too.' Orbus was hardly looking at them now. His focus was on the distant fire, and the painted men revelling in its warmth. 'Argias will have more wagons from Baiae before long. Put the word out, Bydreth. We leave at first light, tomorrow. Anything that can be left, throw it to the flames. The less evidence we leave, the better.'

'We're going to Rome?' Bydreth asked him.

'Indeed we are.' Orbus was already walking away, back towards the others. This private conclave was seemingly at an end.

'So what do we call you then?' Brauda called after him, half-sarcastically. '*Master?*'

'Praefector is fine.' Orbus didn't stop, or even turn. 'Although a little more respect would be nice. You're talking to your master, after all.'

VI

POWER GAMES

THRACIAN NARROWED HIS eyes, far from pleased at what he'd witnessed.

'Spears down, all of you.'

The atmosphere on the Field of Mars was uncharacteristically tense, as the Legion's new praefector wound up the morning training regimen. The Fulminata were used to being put through their paces – indeed, every legionary in the Roman Empire was – but few among them had anticipated the level of zeal forced on them today.

Today had been Thracian's first official operation as camp prefect. The easiest way for a new officer to establish authority was to make his mark early on, and the easiest way to do *that* was to push the troops harder and more brutally than the post's last incumbent had ever deemed necessary. It wasn't sustainable, and probably wasn't even sincere – the *milites'* training schedule would surely slide back to normal over the coming months – but for now, the rank and file resigned themselves to aching bodies, scarred hands and a lack of sleep for the foreseeable future. They were still getting the measure of their new praefector, and he was still learning to fit the role.

'I've seen you all move sharper than that,' Thracian called out, but there was no heart in it. 'Parade rest.'

The legionaries obeyed, slackening. Not quite *at ease*, not quite *spear-ready*, *parade rest* was the middle ground that kept them calm, yet alert.

Thracian had three of the cohort's five centuries drawn up here, a little under five hundred men. He'd taken a century from each class of legionary to begin his work; the entirety of Ardius' *hastati* were here, the newest recruits to the XII who had barely outgrown the *tirones*. Next to them, the *principes* of Pylades' century, men who formed the mainstay of Rome's legions, the formation that Thracian had commanded as First Spear till now. And finally, on the other flank lay the *triarii* of Marcus Scipio, grizzled armoured veterans, many of whom boasted careers longer than Thracian's life. Every man stood to attention, stoically ignoring the beads of perspiration running down their armour and making their underclothes sodden.

Their centurions were absent, something of Thracian's own doing. He didn't need that kind of interference. Thracian had his own methods for getting the best out of the *milites*, and while they weren't the most tasteful, they were effective. What the other officers didn't know, wouldn't hurt them.

True, their *optios* and *tesserarii* were here, and could report anything back to the centurions they served, but they were small fry. What was an infantryman's word against the third in command of the Legion? Especially one with the means and power to make their lives a sorry hell if they squealed a protest?

Thracian was a man who thrived on direct control. It was how he'd run his century, and how he'd made it into one of the finest in the XII, if not necessarily the happiest. Still, what the hell did it matter? The men beneath him may have resented it, but the men above him were satisfied with it, and they were the ones who mattered. Urbanus had praised him many times for the ironclad grip he'd had on his *principes*, and even Orbus had come to grudgingly respect it. Results talked, and Thracian had made First Spear off the back of those dictatorial efforts.

And so it was today that Sallus Thracian started his tenure as Praefector in the most bullish way possible, taking the reins of command from his centurions' hands. Pylades had agreed, but Thracian would expect no less from his favoured pawn. Ardius and Scipio hadn't been quite so willing, but they were professional enough to acquiesce without a struggle. Orbus may have cared enough for appearances to work in lockstep with them, but Thracian had no such qualms.

Perhaps they would lodge a grievance with Cascana, and the thought of that almost made him smile. The new First Spear couldn't help them now. With Urbanus occupied and the High Tribune elsewhere, Thracian's word in the Legion was law.

'I can't say I'm pleased with what I've seen today.' Thracian marched forward, closer towards the frontmost rank of *milites*. The weak morning rays glinted off the iron of their battle helms. 'Is this the best you can do?'

No-one seemed eager to reply to that, and he couldn't blame them. During training, any *tiro* stupid enough to answer a drill-*decanus*' rhetorical questions got subjected to blistering shouting, a degrading nickname that would haunt him for years, and more often than not a trip to the whipping post. Still, Thracian wanted to hear them roar today, no matter how much coaxing it took.

'I *said*,' he called out more belligerently, his words carrying to the back, '*is this the best you can do?*'

'*No, Praefector!*' The legionaries didn't need any more prompting, but Thracian wasn't finished.

'Are my men falling short, their standards growing sloppier, like the wretched deserter who once commanded them?'

'*No, Praefector!*'

'Is my name Gaius Sertor Orbus?'

'*No, Praefector!*'

'Was Sertor Orbus fit to lead these men?'

'*No, Praefector!*'

'And were you expecting more of the same from me?'

'*No, Praefector!*'

'*Good!*' Spittle was flying from Thracian's mouth now. He fancied the whole Field of Mars had heard that, everyone up and down the Tiber's banks. He loved this, loved shouting in their faces, feeling his choler rise as he stoked the cohort's fires. These men were a forge, building in temperature to the white-hot intensity needed to ply their bloody craft.

The metaphor was apt, as forging weapons of war was exactly what Thracian was doing here.

He strode firmly down the lines of men, legionaries stoically refusing to register his passing.

'Are we the XII Fulminata?'

'*Yes, Praefector!*'

'Are we in the habit of fleeing from battle?'

'*No, Praefector!*'

'Or do we stand our ground, and die with honour?'

'*Yes, Praefector!*'

Thracian didn't stop marching. Each time he reached the end, he about-turned and paced the way he'd come. Every rank he passed, he felt his pride and anger roil and grow.

'Do we suffer the cancer of cowardice in our ranks?'

'*No, Praefector!*'

'Or do we excise it, with blade and fire and fury?'

'*Yes, Praefector!*'

Thracian halted, catching a fervent breath. He paid the man beside him no heed.

'Who is it we fight for, men?'

'*The Emperor, the Senate, the people of Rome!*'

'And whose orders will you follow to Pluto's shores?'

'*The Legate, the Prefect, the lord of my tent!*'

He resumed his marching, living out this moment for as long as he could.

'Who will protect you, when battle is joined?'

'*The man on my left and the man on my right!*'

'And whom will you guard, when sword-hand draws steel?'

'*The man on my right and the man on my left!*'

'Who is it you fear, men?'

'*The gods far above and the gods far below!*'

'And who of the pantheon will you bless as you kill?'

'*Brazen Mars, in his cuirass of bloodstained bronze!*'

'What will you lose when you march into war?'

'*My doubt, my fear, my limits and my shame!*'

'And what will you leave, when battle is done?'

'*Widows and footprints and foes rent in two!*'

Thracian had reached the front now, taking his place before his gathered troops.

'Is this the standard you hold yourselves to, *milites*?'

'*Yes, Praefector!*'

'Is that the standard you seek to earn?'

'*Yes, Praefector!*'

'And do you think these words mean much without actions and deeds?'

'*No, Praefector!*'

He took a moment to consider that, the passion gradually receding from his eyes.

'Very well,' he told them. The sunlight had started to fade as clouds streaked the falling rays. 'Maybe you do still have the fire in your belly after all. I know how the deserter used to run the training regimes, and how your officers followed suit. I know the type of ship he ran, for I was part of it. But I am camp prefect now. I will be taking a more direct and hands-on role in maintaining the fighting vigour of you legionaries. I will not let the prowess of our legion degrade any further. I will not let the deserter's laxity taint this cohort, and have you infantrymen pay the price for it!'

That was a rather tinted view of Orbus' tenure, a tenure that had seen standards met but not abused, and had pushed legionaries to their limits while still respecting their humanity, but such was life.

Another reason why Thracian hadn't wanted the centurions here. Now he'd announced it, nothing short of a direct missive from Legate Urbanus could take it back. The century commanders may well have had something to say about this new approach to Legion training, but they wouldn't dare soil the chain of command by countermanding him.

The ranks of legionaries waited this out in tightly-focused silence, but Thracian fancied he saw the ripple of unease pass over them. No doubt they all believed, with good reason, that this escalation meant the XII was headed into a singularly arduous and demanding warzone. One that would swallow up their lives for untold months and reap the mother of all butcher's bills. And Thracian let that doubt ride in their minds, saying nothing to disabuse them of that notion. Fear of the future would push them to their best, just as much as fear of him.

The Praefector strode forward abruptly, almost within spear range of the closest rank of men.

'So what say you to this challenge, *milites*? Will you fall at the wayside, before your travails even start?'

'*No, Praefector!*'

'Or will you rise to the occasion, and prove the *Legatus* right when he measures our prowess against the IV Scythica, or the XV Apollinaris?'

'*Yes, Praefector!*'

'So *prove it!*' Thracian was face to face with the forwardmost *decanus*, a man of Scipio's he didn't know. '*Ciringe frontem!*'

The man dropped into sword stance, shield up. They all did.

Thracian almost purred with anticipation. Seeing almost five hundred finely-drilled legionaries take position in the same moment was a sight that sent chills down his spine.

He nodded, formally. '*Tecombre.*'

The sea of shields came down. The ranks resumed their parade rest.

He dared another inch closer. '*Contendite vestra sponte!*'

Two hundred spear-points shot into focus, every man on the Field stretching their *pilum* out past their shield-ridge in a killing thrust. The *decanus* out front could almost touch Thracian with his. Another inch and it would have pierced his sternum.

Thracian met the unit leader's flint-grey eyes, drawing breath and shouting the command again.

'*Contendite! Vestra! Sponte!*'

The phalanx of *pila* pulled back, and then, like a set of colossal iron teeth, shot out a second time.

Thracian exhaled his pleasure. Few things in this world could make him feel alive anymore, but the Roman military never failed.

'*Tecombre,*' he ordered them once again, setting the legionaries back into readiness. 'That will be all for today, men. *Decani*, lead your units back to the *Principia*. I want to see each one of you working your tentmates bloody come the morrow. Any *decanus* unable to train his men to such a standard will be held as accountable as the failing legionaries themselves. Think on that, when you consider how to motivate your boys.'

The new praefector gave his men one last brutal, searching look. 'Dismissed, all of you.'

THE RETURN JOURNEY from Baiae had been blissfully uneventful, if you could call managing the logistics of moving almost sixty men upcountry uneventful. Orbus had dispatched Argias back to Baiae to rent more wagons, letting the Ulthaini travel more like people than beasts of burden.

They'd made decent time, with the weather warming up a touch as they neared the Seven Hills. For the final stretch of flatter road, they'd even taken to walking behind the wagons, turning their loose convoy into something of a procession.

Far ahead of them, the Aventine Hill loomed almost benevolently in their gaze, with the Appian Gate that would lead them across the *pomerium* and into the city holding the foreground. No burly guards or legionaries were waiting to ambush Orbus this time, and he wryly wondered if he should take a barbarian escort with him more often.

'So *this* is Rome.' Bydreth was shamelessly lost in awe, utterly taken by the grandeur of his surroundings. The immense stone gate they'd passed under, the towering walls of lovingly polished marble, the gilded ranks of exquisitely-wrought tombstones, statues gazing down on either side from regimented colonnades…

The *Via Appia*, Orbus had called it. The Appian Way. Never mind the rest of Rome, this marble avenue alone seemed to stretch on forever.

This was where gods would come to lay themselves in state.

'Enough with the gaping,' Brauda growled at him. 'You're like a child who's just been taught to wield a sword.'

'Maybe I am,' Bydreth readily conceded. He felt no shame in it. He'd always wanted to see the Eternal City.

'Welcome to Rome, boys.'

IT DIDN'T TAKE long for Thracian's ripples to spread. The men of the XII were filing off the Field of Mars, heading back past the *Villa Publica* in the rough direction of the city. The Praefector picked out a figure standing sentinel as the legionaries trooped past. Cascana, replete in his uniform and badges of office. As if it would be anyone else.

'First Spear,' Thracian greeted him coolly. The line of *milites* continued to march on beside them, oblivious to their exchange. 'I don't recall summoning you to the drills today.'

'I need no summons to go where I please,' was Cascana's equally ambivalent reply. 'I am the foremost centurion in this legion. Whatever new ideas you have for drilling the men, I'll thank you to keep me abreast of them.'

Cascana didn't possess a great well of anger for intimidating people, but he'd learned over the years that weaponised civility did the job just as well. Today, his courteous smile wasn't fooling anyone.

'I can tell what you are thinking, Centurion,' Thracian assured him. 'Standards of performance in this cohort have become inordinately sloppy. In a way, Orbus' desertion may turn out to be a twist of fortune, as it has also exposed his dereliction of duty. I will be instituting a new, more vigorous regimen from now on, and will be taking a more active role in implementing it. It would appear that the deserter had become... lax.'

Cascana narrowed his eyes, unimpressed by that level of spin. 'Or maybe you seek to make him *look* lax, Praefector.'

'The *Legatus* has trusted me to handle affairs in my own way.' Thracian's tone had hardened. 'Just as he would trust any praefector. I will not abuse that trust, as Orbus did.' He smiled at the younger officer ruefully. 'In truth, raising the stakes on the training grounds was child's play. I was genuinely surprised at how much slack there was to be played with.'

Cascana almost swore under his breath. It wasn't slack. It was breathing room, a level long-agreed by generations of instructors and *decani* that pushed legionaries as hard as could be, without physically or mentally destroying too many of them in the process. Morality barely came into it. If Thracian started toying with that balance now, in the coming months there may not be enough *milites* to form into centuries.

'Urbanus will hear of this,' was all the First Spear could manage. 'Putting your own ambitions and record ahead of the Legion's best interests…' He trailed off.

'Urbanus will hear what I want him to hear,' Thracian corrected him. 'And he'll see what I want him to see. In this case—' He inclined his head towards the departing soldiers. '—quick results.'

'Quick,' Cascana conceded, 'but temporary. You will burn the men out. Morale is just as important as aptitude, Praefector. You cannot trade one off against the other.'

Thracian waved the Centurion's concerns away. 'Is this what all your father's money bought you? All that Hellenic education? Just tenement-wall philosophy, from the mouths of sophists?' He turned away and begun to march after the men he'd brutalised. 'Return to your duties, Centurion. We both have much to do.'

Cascana didn't say anything. He'd never liked Thracian one iota, and he fancied the man felt the same way about him. He didn't like him, and had little taste for his methods, but he'd always had a grudging respect for his talents. Thracian was a good officer, on the whole, even if he didn't always go about things the right way.

But this? This was not right. This new culture that Thracian would be undeniably fostering within the cohort's ranks… no good would come of it.

How else would legion life change, now Thracian's dictatorial tendencies had come to the fore?

'PRAEFECTOR,' THE MESSENGER wiped brow-sweat off his vambrace. 'You're wanted, sir. Immediately.'

Orbus cast a weary glance up from his writing desk. Argias did the same from his own seat opposite, his expression similarly haggard.

'Wanted by whom?' Orbus asked, raising an eyebrow. It had been a trying morning, all things considered, and his assorted wit and pep had simmered down to snappiness. 'If I am allowed to know?'

The two of them had set up shop in one of the *Principia's* disused quarters, blissfully out of most of the cohort's way. Between the centuries' casualties taken in Gaul and the departure of most of Behemon's auxiliaries, the Fulminata's urban headquarters felt a little emptier of late. Blissfully, this meant that Orbus only rarely crossed paths with other legionaries, the very same reason he hadn't taken an office in the *praetorium* with the centurions.

The messenger – a tribune, if the purple gilt on his toga and fleshy, pampered face were much to go by – handed Orbus the sealed scroll he'd been carrying. The Praefector broke it open, pulling the vellum apart.

'Legion command,' he murmured, more for Argias' benefit than the Tribune's. 'That's the Legate's seal. Him, or the High Tribune. I didn't realise Verrinus was back in Rome.'

The messenger didn't feel the need to reply. He just stood there, regal and vapid, waiting for Orbus to confirm the obvious. How much family money had been spent to get him this position? How much favour had his patrician father curried?

'Very well, Tribune.' Orbus rolled the message back up, stacking it on his pile of papers. 'Thank you,' he pointedly added a moment later before the boy finally took his cue to leave.

'You know you're getting older,' the Praefector mused afterwards, 'when tribunes start looking younger.'

Argias didn't look up from his writing. He didn't feel familiar enough with Orbus to run with the joke, so he nodded at the delivered scroll instead. 'The Legate wants to meet with you then, sir?'

'Him, or someone of his rank.' Orbus scratched his stubble. 'No, it must be him. I've barely talked to another *legatus* in years. Whoever it is—' He unfurled the message again with one hand. '—I'm to meet them at the Gardens of Sallust in an hour. Urgent business, apparently.'

'That sounds pleasant,' Argias remarked.

Orbus didn't rush to agree. He thought back to Urbanus' words in the *Castra Praetoria*. That promise of another due yet to come. Orbus had an unwelcome feeling that the other *caliga* was finally about to drop.

'As if today hadn't been difficult enough already.' He didn't need to elaborate, for Argias had been with him the whole time. 'How by Pluto did I think taking them to the *Baths* was a good idea?'

Was that a rhetorical question? Argias couldn't be sure. He certainly agreed, though. They'd planned to take the Ulthaini to the Baths of Agrippa, along the Viminal Way. Bydreth had sworn he could keep his kinsmen in line, and it should have been both an uneventful exercise in cleanliness and acclimatisation to a key Roman custom.

The reality had been rather more anarchic, and had seen the *apodyterium* mobbed in a Celtic frenzy to get hot water, a stampede of terrified, sodden patricians running out into the street without their togas, and a lifetime ban for any man who claimed to be an associate of Sertor Orbus.

Right now, while Orbus and Argias worked in one of the *Principia*'s emptier billets, the sorry tribesmen were holed up in a temporarily empty barracks further inland with the remaining Achaean hoplites. Cascana had helped arrange it, as Orbus had no desire to bring his new charges here, and risk them crossing paths with his former men. Behemon's second, Arxander, had been left loosely in charge of the whole group as they feasted and mingled with the Greeks, and Orbus had instructed him to kneecap any one of his new followers who misbehaved or tried to leave.

'I suppose I'd better get over there.' The Praefector rubbed a hand over his face and eyes. Damn him if he didn't feel a little wearier each day. 'Where are we at with our enquiries, *optio*?'

Argias snatched up some of the papers he'd been reading and writing, holding them up for Orbus to glance at. 'I scouted around the drillmasters and unassigned *decani* still based around the city. The ones I know, anyway, and the ones who would talk to me.'

'And?'

'And they all clammed up fairly quickly when they realised what I was after. I suppose you cannot blame them, sir. Sniffing around for stray or unwanted *milites* isn't going to go down well, even *tirones*. Not now we're outside the club looking in... sir. I just heard the same story, time after time. "The legions will look to their own, and the *auxilia* must do the same." With varying levels of politeness, as you would expect.'

'It wouldn't make a difference if they were *tirones* or not,' the Praefector told him. 'We'll still have to commit the others to the training, and we'll barely have the time to do that anyway.'

Orbus screwed up his face. This was exactly what he'd been fearing. The Legions by and large did their own recruiting, either reaching out for malleable young men themselves, or taking their pick of whichever youths flung themselves at the chance to join their ranks. Conscription wasn't something particularly common, or welcomed, and the rate of recruitment was rarely so uniform either. It was usually dictated instead by the legion in question, wherever a front was faltering, to whichever formations found themselves with boots that needed filling.

Argias had a point, even if he'd chosen his words carelessly. They really *were* on the outside, looking in. Without the infrastructure and renown of the XII, the prospect of adding any actual Roman legionaries to this little band Orbus was building had gone from remote to utterly laughable.

Had he been expecting any differently? He was a disgrace, a legion exile. He had no familial ties, and no real means beyond the dwindling lump sum he'd liquidated from Sextus. It didn't exactly scream confidence, even if other legions had been willing to play along.

'So, no legionaries,' Orbus bemoaned. 'What about the rest?'

The look on Argias' face said it all, but the *optio* dutifully shuffled some papers around before handing them to his officer. These were considerably less tidy, just handwritten scribbles based on what he'd been told rather than copies of anything particularly official.

'Well there were certainly plenty of reports to go through, Praefector. The people do like their gladiators.' He idly flicked through a couple more scrawls on his side of the desk. 'It took me a while to sift through the hyperbole and sort the chaff from the genuinely talented, and a good while longer to separate the most entertaining fighters with the ones who have actual skill. Skill fit for harnessing.' He put his parchment down and nodded at the one Orbus was holding. 'They all seem to come back to our friend, here.'

'Vinculex.' Orbus read the name on the parchment. *Chained One.* That could only be an arena name. 'This is… quite a record.'

'I agree. That number of wins, duels and pit-kills speaks for itself. But that isn't all, sir.'

'No?'

'Keep reading.'

Orbus did so. The various reports and accounts Argias had jotted down weren't exactly complimentary, but they didn't surprise him either. They seemed in character, whichever way you sliced it.

'So our friend has a slight... temperament, as well.' His eyes scanned down the rest of the yellowed parchment. 'I can't say I'm s–'

And then he saw it. 'Oh.'

'Indeed, sir.' Argias seemed to have already made up his mind. 'With such an... affliction, how can he be useful to us? How can he be relied upon?'

Orbus cast another glance over the gladiator's tally of victories. 'With results like that? I'm sure he'd have his uses on a battlefield.'

'A unit of legionaries requires discipline to work,' the *optio* pressed. 'Not just fury. It is a cohort you are hoping to build here, or at least a century. Not a mob.'

No-one spoke, and the air between them seemed to harden as Argias realised just how far he'd stepped out of line.

He tried to backpaddle. 'I just meant, Praefector, that–'

'I *know* what you meant, First Legionary.' Orbus clamped down hard on that fumbling apology. 'That the sort of lip you'd give Cascana? Give your *decanus?* No wonder they wanted rid of you.'

Argias hung his head, saying nothing. His shame was burning, unfeigned and entirely warranted. *Optio* or not, speaking to your officer like that in a legion's ranks was practically begging for flagellation.

Orbus sighed, exhaling his anger. But then, he wasn't in a legion's ranks anymore. Neither of them were. Argias was only trying to help, and he had a point anyway.

With hindsight, it seemed a little trifling for an officer as tarnished as him to get riled over something like respect. Especially from the one man who seemed actually willing to work with him.

'Forgive me, Argias. The day has been long.' He stood up from behind his desk, walking over to where his cloak still hung. Orbus was still wearing the leather *subarmalis* over his tunic, and indeed the *optio* hadn't seen him without it since the ambush at the walls. 'Maybe it's time to look somewhere else for our legionaries. I need you to go back to the *praetorium*,' he bid him, pulling the cloak around his shoulders. 'Legion records, relating to discipline and discharge. See how many names you can put together of men like me.'

'Like you, sir?' Argias' eyes flickered with confusion.

'Disgraced men.' Orbus proffered a grim smile. 'Legion exiles. Proven deserters, or those on file for decimation who didn't end up taking the sentence. Get me a list of the damned.' He crossed the room towards the doorway, ready to set off for the Gardens of Sallust.

'Expand the search, if you can. The same crop, from other legions. The IX Hispania is currently on deployment, as is the I Classica and the XXII Primogenia. You'll have no trouble slipping into their fortresses, if you say you're on official business. Use my name if you have to, and that of the XII.' He smirked. 'By the time they've verified the lie, you'll already have what you need.'

'Yes, sir.' Vim was gradually returning to Argias' cheeks. 'Having legionaries in the cohort will truly make a difference then, do you think?'

'We need Romans,' Orbus explained. 'Gods-honest Roman soldiers. It's all very well to go trooping around with whatever gutter trash or foreign swords I can dig up, but we need that legitimacy. We need some of our own in the ranks, else they'll never take us seriously. Who knows,' he mused, 'if we're lucky we might even scrounge ourselves another officer. Someone to open more doors for us. Blood of Teucer, we'll need every open door we can find in the coming months.'

The *optio* nodded. 'If we ever find ourselves fighting beside a legion,' he reasoned, 'they might be more inclined to protect us if they see their kinsmen in our ranks, rather than just a sea of foreign faces.'

'Exactly. And it might help get some of the others in line,' Orbus agreed. 'To make them realise we all want the same thing.'

Argias frowned. 'Sir?'

Orbus cocked an eyebrow. 'To atone.' He made to leave, disappearing out into the corridor. Only he stopped, and turned back.

'And Argias?'

'Sir?'

'My mind hasn't changed. Go to the *Circus*. Bring that Vinculex to me, and anyone with him we can make a *miles* of.'

HE HADN'T BEEN here in years.

The Gardens of Sallust, a beacon of calm and beauty in a city that screamed awe and purpose from every marble rooftop. An oasis of peace and verdancy in the bustling greyness of the Empire's capital.

Gaius Sallust had once governed the province of Africa Nova, and echoes of that regency were displayed all across the Gardens, if you knew where to look – a statue of Maecenas mounted on a bust of black quartz here, an inscription carved on an icon of pink-veined rock there. Looted treasures, all on display like stately spoils of war, taken off the Numidian sands.

The place was quieter than it had any right to be for its proximity to the eternally-congested *Argiletum* and Rome's vibrant northeast. Orbus had never really understood how that could be. He'd asked someone once, one of the Legion's *immunes* who were paid to understand such things. The engineer had explained it to him in detail, but the Praefector had barely grasped it; something to do with the flow of sound down the *Via Salaria*, and the way it reflected off the Pincian and Quirinal Hills.

The great and the good thronged every space and avenue, those who could afford the luxury of a carefree sunlit afternoon without worrying about something so mundane as a hard day's work. So much for being open to the public and penniless of Rome. The only plebeian souls here were the municipal slaves, those city-owned wretches who tended the garden's plants and upkeep. And they were the lowest of the low.

Urbanus was already here, lounging on a bench out the sun's way, overlooking a bed of neatly-pruned Hispanic hydrangeas.

'*Legatus*,' he greeted the older man neutrally as he approached.

Urbanus turned to regard him, the movement slow and almost reptilian. 'Praefector,' he replied. 'I see your wounds are recovering.'

He didn't apologise for those injuries *he'd* inflicted, or concede that he had gone too far. He didn't mention the ambush, or express any regret that he hadn't been able to prevent it. All he did was stick to the facts.

'I heard what happened at the Baths today. Doubtless half the city has, by now.' The Legate tilted his head a fraction at the bench, a bare-bones encouragement for Orbus to take a seat. 'Well, the uppermost wealthier half, at least. I've no doubt you'll be the talk of all the country villas and private clubs for weeks to come. It has been all of ten days since I led the First Cohort back to Rome, and still you seem determined to make a name for yourself.'

Orbus didn't reply to that at once, gauging what to say. How much did Urbanus really know about what he'd been up to?

'A mob of Picts, I hear.' The Legate dashed his momentary hopes. 'Painted barbaric fools, more fit for the *Circus* or the arena than the barracks. You really don't know when to let go of the reins, do you?'

Orbus chose not to let his wryness speak for him. 'I have disappointed you, *Legatus*. Haven't I?'

'What I feel is irrelevant.' Urbanus remained as prim and tight-lipped as ever, at odds with what lay within. He was a man who felt, no matter how hard he tried not to. 'Regret is unprofessional.'

The old general turned to Orbus, finally looking him in the eye. 'They didn't want to make you praefector, you know.' For a moment, their surroundings were forgotten – no opulent Gardens, no meandering visitors, no slaves tending the thickets and flowerbeds. 'Evander didn't think you equal to the rank, and nor did Arcites. They didn't think you were prefect material.' That actually made him smile, only to himself. 'What a thing is fate, Orbus. If not for one little twist, one word in the right ear, you might have lived out your days as a bitter old centurion.'

Orbus considered that for a moment. He might have preferred that life.

'I vouched for you,' Urbanus continued. 'As did Cascana the Elder. We believed that you were the right man for the role.'

'I… did not know that,' Orbus replied. Which was only half true. When the promotion came, he'd always suspected Publius had something to do with it – the man could be subtle, but far too self-regarding not to hint it when the wine was flowing – but that Urbanus had spoken in his favour too? That, he hadn't expected.

Evander had never had much time for him, but that was more from reliable patrician snobbery than anything else. Arcites was a more surprising case. The man had been praefector himself for much of Orbus' and Publius' early careers in the XII. The younger Orbus had always considered him a brother in arms, an easy man to call comrade, no matter what your rank was or how much money your father had.

'I'm sorry,' Orbus said eventually. 'I had no idea you did that for me, *Legatus*. I'm sorry I couldn't repay your trust.'

Insofar as Urbanus could look sheepish about anything, he did so now. In reality, the expression wasn't far off his default squint, which rarely seemed to change.

'You did repay my trust,' he replied. 'Every day you did your damned job.' He sighed. 'You ran my legion well, Orbus. That is why I valued you.'

The sun chose that moment to re-emerge from its caul of clouds. 'But you failed,' the Legate continued. 'That was your sin. A man of your rank cannot be allowed to fail.'

That was a slightly rosy view of the situation, Orbus decided, considering everything that had followed. But he chose not to say that out loud.

'I have accepted the punishment you deemed for me,' the Praefector admitted. 'And I will continue to accept it, as it was rightfully earnt. But if there was something I could do to regain your trust...' He let the words trail off. It was a hint he'd considered dropping since setting out from the *Principia*. If building a unit of *auxilia* from scratch was proving difficult, then perhaps it wouldn't hurt to have a legion legate on side. Or, at least, one not actively disposed against him.

Only that made Urbanus' face harden, and Orbus knew at once had he'd phrased it the wrong way. He'd hoped to sound sincere in his wish. Instead, he'd merely come across as craven.

'As it happens,' the older man replied, 'that is why you are here. In a way.'

Orbus shuffled uncomfortably in his seat. He didn't like the note of anticipation in Urbanus' voice. The memory of the court martial came back to him, the dangling of an obligation yet to come. It was like he'd told Argias – the other *caliga* really was about to drop.

'Have you ever heard of the brothers Lemnon?' Urbanus asked him suddenly. He framed the question casually, but Orbus knew his legate, and he knew this was leading somewhere.

'I've heard the name. Well, names.' And more. The brothers Lemnon were plutocratic stone and timber merchants, Achaeans by birth, who had branched out across the provinces before amassing enough to settle in Rome.

Under the newly-crowned Augustus they'd truly made their fortune, helping rebuild Rome in marble to mark the Principate's birth. Now they plied their trade for anyone who had the right money.

'Then you know what they're about,' Urbanus decided. 'What you may not have known is something that happened a few years back, while we were on campaign in Judaea. Do you know Lady Aemilia, of the Volscani?'

Orbus frowned. 'Not personally. The family, I've heard of.' And who hadn't? A wealthy yet unremarkable offshoot of the old Sergian bloodline, the family's matriarch had tragically died giving birth to their second son, a heartbreak that had killed the elderly father too. The older son had persisted a little longer, before dying in some backwater campaign no-one remembered. That had left the middle child. A daughter, on the cusp of maidenhood, and now heir to a venerable patrician fortune.

The good Lady Aemilia, presumably.

'The brothers adopted her. Formally,' Urbanus continued the story.

'I suppose that makes them the *uncles* Lemnon, now,' Orbus quipped. The Legate shot him a withering glance before carrying on.

'They took her as their ward. Why would that be? What is it, with all these Greeks and provincials, that makes them so determined to appear Roman? *Pedigree*, Praefector. One thing all that new money can't buy you. These up-and-coming foreign types can study our philosophy, learn our languages, ape our manners... and frankly, that is to be encouraged. That is how we grow as a people, by reaching out to others and letting them put back into us. But *legitimacy*. That is something these hoi polloi cannot buy, or barter over.'

Orbus didn't say anything, bile rising at the Legate's heavily-implied snub to his background.

'Is that why you think they adopted her?' he asked.

'It stands to reason,' Urbanus answered. 'An act of charity like that. How better to appear as an upstanding pillar of Imperial society?'

Orbus wrinkled his brow.

'I suppose her being a young and orphaned heiress may have had something to do with it,' was his knowing reply.

'You needn't sound so arch, Praefector. I was simply making a point.' In reality, they both knew it. People like the brothers might aspire to be socialites, but they were businessmen first and foremost. They knew an opportunity when they smelt one.

'What does this have to do with me?' Orbus asked.

'Everything,' was Urbanus' reply. The man had a talent for inscrutability. 'Making a ward of a girl like that? That speaks of a need. A need to step up a rung on the ladder of legitimacy. One of them could have married her outright, I suppose, only that would be too flagrant. Too *tasteless*. It would have shown just how mercenary their intentions were.'

'Indeed it would,' Orbus replied. *And it would doubtless have driven a wedge between them. How would they pick the groom?* 'But again, what does this have to do with me?'

Urbanus smiled, slowly and thinly. 'Because they wish to climb another rung on that particular ladder. Times change, and now the brothers wish to align with another pillar of Rome.' He looked Orbus up and down, taking stock of what he saw. 'The legions.'

Orbus narrowed his eyes, more from intrigue than suspicion. Some punishment. Urbanus was a man of pragmatism, and Orbus' penance could simply be fulfilling a need. This could mean opportunity. Opportunity that he desperately needed.

'And I'm the man to help them, is that it?' He searched the Legate's face for clues.

'Indeed you are. And young Aemilia is the key.'

Ah. So *that* was it.

'Well.' Orbus nodded sagely, glad that they'd finally cut to the truth of it. 'Then I'm to join the brothers, as a ward to this young lady. You're right, I suppose. Having a Roman on their level, with the same responsibilities, will only make them seem more legitimate and high-intentioned.'

And there it was. How quaint, to finally hear Urbanus' will for him spoken out loud. It could have been worse. Being saddled with some spoilt eighteen-year-old rich girl wouldn't, feasibly, make too much difference to his life. She'd have expensive tastes, no doubt, but at least it'd be her own dead family she'd be eating out of pocket, or the brothers Lemnon. Not him.

And her money… he'd be entitled to a little of it, as one of her official guardians. Suddenly, the dwindling amount he'd chiselled away from Elysia didn't seem as much of a worry. More scraps of soldiers and ex-slaves, and better armour and weapons to clad them in. With a little luck, might even be able to entice some actual legionaries.

The ghost of a smirk drifted across Orbus' face. Maybe she could go to live in Baiae, in *his* ancestral home. The thought of this Aemilia learning to get along with Sextus and Aruxeia was almost enough to cheer him up, on this day of days.

And then he took another look at Urbanus, and realised something wasn't right.

'I think you misunderstand, Praefector. That is not what we intend for you. You will form part of an alliance with the brothers. It will simply be a little more… permanent.'

Orbus didn't say anything for a moment, because he didn't know what to say. He couldn't quite grasp what Urbanus meant.

And then it hit him.

Slowly, inexorably, the *aureus* finally dropped.

Once again, there were no visitors around them. No slaves. No Gardens of Sallust. Just the two of them on their bench. Orbus' head was still ringing from the dropped revelation.

'No,' he finally managed. 'You cannot be serious.'

'I'm as serious as the grave,' was the Legate's retort.

'But…' Orbus could barely string a sentence together. Such was the turmoil. '*No.*'

'Yes.' Urbanus was implacable. 'The brothers Lemnon have agreed that marrying Aemilia into the Roman army would be a desirable endgame, for both parties.' He tilted his head a fraction, regarding the Praefector like a hawk. 'You will marry her.'

Orbus' mouth had turned to desert. 'I c–'

'Can't?' Urbanus suddenly thundered. He never usually thundered. 'You *can't* marry the Volscani girl? You swore to me at your sentencing that you would follow my will in this! In whatever path I laid for you! Are you a liar, and an oathbreaker, as well as a coward?'

That outburst was loud enough to turn a few heads. The slaves continued to go about their work – it was quite literally more than their job's worth to worry about such things – but some of the Gardens' other patrons didn't appreciate their daydreams being disturbed. Most undignified.

Orbus felt himself on the verge of crying, something he hadn't done since... well, he couldn't remember. He never shed tears. He hadn't in Gaul, not when the Legate had scourged him, not even in all the empty nights that had followed.

Urbanus' face didn't change, but the Praefector could sense the torrent of disgust roiling behind his eyes. Urbanus had a talent for that, for showing his feelings without *showing* them. *You never see his fires*, Alvanus had once drunkenly put it. *You simply feel the ground you stand on burn to ash.*

'I know you have been married before,' the *Legatus* told him. 'And that you had no desire to be so again. But give me one good reason why you cannot wed Aemilia.' Urbanus sat there, taut as a bowstring, awaiting a fitting reply.

Orbus found himself leaning forwards on his seat. It was all he could do to not bury his head in his hands.

Caesula...

'Excuse my ire,' Urbanus attempted to sound conciliatory. 'In honesty, I thought you would be pleased. This will be a good match for both of you.'

'You mean for you,' Orbus acidly replied, 'and the brothers.'

'No, Praefector. I meant for you and Aemilia. From her perspective, it's an easy win. You are an older man, with all the responsibility and self-assuredness that brings. As it stands, you have no money, pedigree or family connections, all of which means you couldn't feasibly stray beyond the marriage bed even if you wanted to. And anyway, half of Rome knows you're a man scrabbling to recover his honour. It is undoubtedly in your best interest to play the faithful husband.'

'So I see.' Through his chagrin, Orbus had to hand it to the man. He'd planned this to perfection. 'And what about my end?'

Urbanus smiled that thin-lipped smile again. 'The girl is young, and beautiful. And more importantly, she comes from money. *Old* money, and an ancient family name to go with it. A good amount of which will surely come to you through her dowry, and even putting that aside for a moment... the Volscani family will have, in you, a new patriarch. Her family fortune will eventually be yours. So yes, Praefector. I think I'm right in believing that an heiress hanging off your arm will only enrich your life. After all, this new unit of *auxilia* you're hoping to build – maintaining soldiers isn't exactly cheap, is it?'

It was then, and only then, that Orbus saw the whole matter in more clinical terms. Urbanus had known what he'd been up to, ever since he'd set off to Baiae. Perhaps even before that. And he'd factored it into his accursed plans.

With this ultimatum, he'd blended together his political machinations, his desire to punish Orbus, and the Praefector's own plans for the future, concocting them all into this foul little arrangement.

'Is this what you truly want?' Orbus asked. He could hear the defeated impotence in his own voice. 'You would do all this just to spite me?'

'I am not spiting you, Sertor.' Urbanus wouldn't be deviated from his goal. 'I am making an example of you. You've served under me for long enough. You know I am not a cruel man. I'm a pragmatic one. And as it stands, this marriage of convenience will advance my agenda, as well as the brothers'.

'And what agenda would that be?' asked Orbus. Whatever the answer, he doubted he could bring himself to care.

'Because the brothers Lemnon are expanding into a new field,' Urbanus explained. 'It never ceases, does it? The quest to stay relevant. And that quest has led them into weapons design. They have started designing their own *ballistae*, and other such siege-engines. They believe they can improve, and revolutionise, the way we Romans wage war.' He allowed himself a smile. 'I have seen some of the results, and it must be said their beliefs aren't without grounds.'

Orbus had nothing to say. The Legate wanted to prostitute him to these two Achaean moneymen, all to court their services and have the Fulminata's ranks supplemented by top-of-the-range artillery. How could you even improve a *ballista*, anyway? It did what it did. It hurled rocks at city walls.

'Why me?' Orbus heard himself asking. 'If you needed an eligible bachelor, what about one of the others? Why not Cascana?' he almost spat. 'He's young, handsome, from her sort of family. And unlike me, he's actually on the rise. Or Thracian? He'd jump at the opportunity, to cast aside his *familia* for a loftier match.' In that moment, the Praefector sounded as bitter as Brauda.

'Because I chose you,' Urbanus insisted. 'And because Cascana is a young and earnest man. I care for him, as I did his father. As I once did for you. Truthfully, I fear the First Spear will make the same mistake you once did, and marry for his heart and not his head.'

That actually made Orbus laugh, softly and derisively.

'*That* is your reasoning for passing on him? You actually care that much about his happiness?' His surprise wasn't unfounded. Marriage for a man in the Red wasn't a simple business; for an officer, scarcely less so. Weddings in wartime were strictly forbidden, and even to take a bride in times of peace required weighty authorisation from a *legatus* or high tribune, not to mention the priests who would perform the rites. Yet another aspect of army life that had changed with the coming of the Emperor.

'Cascana is an excellent officer,' Urbanus maintained, 'and one of the finest soldiers I have ever known. So yes. In matters of the heart, he has earned the right to make his own mistakes.'

For a moment, Orbus was taken back to that distant morning on the Field of Mars, when Publius had been the one in this position. Being forced to take a bride of status, by a man he had sworn to honour.

'I knew you would see the truth of it.' Urbanus took the other man's silence as a sign of vindication. 'She isn't a bad girl, from what I hear,' he added, unknowingly echoing Publius' own words on the subject all those years before.

'Well,' Orbus rose to his feet, not even giving his former legate so much as a glance. 'Given I don't appear to have any choice in this matter, I guess we have nothing more to say.' He cocked his head at the sun, gauging the time of day. 'You could have just had a message couriered over to me. My time is busy these days, as I'm sure is yours.'

He begun to walk away, back down the path he'd come. The beauty of the Gardens didn't move him, because he barely noticed it.

'Why are you doing this, Orbus?'

That halted him, making him turn. Urbanus hadn't moved from his seat, still passively enjoying his surroundings. Or so it seemed.

'You will have to be a little more specific, my *legatus*.'

'I am no longer your *legatus*,' Urbanus told him. He still didn't make any move. In truth he'd barely raised his voice, but it carried across the boulevard well enough. 'And you know well of what I speak.'

Orbus found himself walking back to him, but this time he didn't sit down.

'Your future in the army was over. You were given a handful of *auxilia*, and you just had to lead them until your death. Such was your sentence.'

'Do you think so little of me?' the Praefector archly replied.

'It doesn't matter what I think.' Urbanus confessed. 'You ran away from your old life, and thus forfeited your right to it. Such was the sentence. But now? Now, instead of embracing that rightful deliverance, you cashed in your meagre inheritance to buy a mob of Gallic savages.'

'Ulthaini,' Orbus gently corrected him.

'Shut up,' Urbanus replied. 'And now I hear your *optio* is off to the *Circus Flaminius*, to shop for gladiators and other worthless killers.'

Orbus swallowed. *Gates of Fire...* how did the Legate even know that? It had literally been Orbus' last command to Argias before he'd left for this meeting. Urbanus had always had a politician's cunning, a legacy of his many years in the Senate. He was a statesman, as much as a soldier.

'You scrape the dregs of the Roman barrel.' And now he wasn't finished. 'You hunt around for scum and gutter trash, bankrupting yourself to do it. You would clad these wretches in legionary arms, marching them out in a century? Do you simply seek to put more bodies between you and your enemy's spears? Is this you trying to evade your rightful fate, yet again?'

Orbus shook his head. 'I'm not evading anything, Urbanus. My sentence was, indeed, to die leading the *auxilia*, with no legion's *aquila* to look up to. I don't see why I couldn't take that *auxilia* and forge it anew, before that happens.'

Urbanus thought about that for a moment. 'Is that what this is truly about, then?' he asked. 'Atonement?'

'If you can call it that, yes.' But of course it was. What other word fit?

'And you intend to keep at it?' Urbanus continued. 'Building this cohort of hollow, worthless men?'

Orbus nodded. 'I do.'

'I see.' The Legate slowly folded his arms, his focus again on his paradisiacal surroundings. 'Then you will almost certainly run out of money before that happens. Of course, being married to a woman of wealth could go some way to mitigating that...' He sniffed the air abruptly. 'And being a man of private means yourself, which you will be once the marriage is sealed, the *Aerarium* could well grant you a line of credit. You might actually be able to pay those men.'

Orbus weighed that up for a moment, before nodding once again. 'You know I can't say no to this,' he assured him. 'I swore to you not to. You don't have to sweeten the draught for me.'

He turned away, for good this time, ready to leave the Gardens.

'I'll do as you wish,' he called out as he departed. 'Inform the bride of her engagement.'

VII
THE GUTTER PRINCE

THE DAY DARKENED, and Rome still lived.

In the heavens of the *Palatium*'s topmost chamber and ramparts, an Emperor of Rome watched the flow of life pass by on the streets countless feet below, drawing his plans against what reaches of the world were yet to fall beneath his laws.

In a lonely corner of the XII's *Principia*, Sertor Orbus poured more Iceni mead down his throat, eyes glazing over as he contemplated his imminent marriage.

Somewhere out across the great city, another praefector was also drowning his blood in alcohol, although the context was profoundly different. In a rather tasteful boudoir in a less tasteful *Subura* brothel, Sallus Thracian enjoyed a gaudy evening of passion, courtesy of the trio of pretty young things he'd freed from slavery just for the purpose.

Iulus Cascana had spent the evening not far away. At an exclusive bathhouse off the Viminal Way, one solely open to gentlemen of the *equites* class and above, he'd enjoyed a thorough cleanse of the afternoon's sweat and dust from his supple skin. Attendants oiled him down with warm unguent, scraping the watery muck from his torso with strigils as the First Spear spared a few thoughts on both the prefects in his life.

His mind even strayed for a moment out of Rome, to the small country estate half a league from Capena Gate. Old Publius Cascana still eked out a living there, counting the many laurels and valour crests he'd earnt in his career, as well as the number of crops each morning that had gone unravaged by vermin.

Not too far from that secluded little villa, the Field of Mars dominated the north-western quadrant of the city landscape. As had become depressingly necessary in recent years, rank upon rank of legionaries could be witnessed training their battlecraft there on more days of the year than ever before. This was an evening like any other, and of the thousands of marching, drilling, sparring soldiers, a handful of them were from the Fulminata.

Marcus Scipio was just one officer who'd taken the Field this evening, and as the sun drew into the west and his men waged mock-war into nightfall, he took a moment to consider the mistakes that had led him to this point.

He looked out across the Tiber, running like a great artery to Ostia and the open sea. Of course, the truer arteries were probably the streets and walkways of Rome herself, the lattice of paths and roads that connected each district of the city. The *Argiletum* ran through the innermost core of Rome in all its messy glory, linking the *Forum* – that great microcosm of the Empire entire – with the many districts of the *Subura*, and its motley assortment of slums, shantytowns and seediness.

In an apartment within one of the quieter tenement blocks, Merope pulled her shutters closed, wondering when she'd see her master next.

He could be anywhere, for all she knew. Anywhere out across the twilit city, perhaps even passing through one of the immense gates, following the traffic into the *cursus publicus* and the wider mainland of Italy. Rome never truly slept, no matter what its denizens did. All the better to watch, and plot into the night. For the men inside the *Castra Praetoria*, the dusk was a time to make plans of their own, ruminating on how best they could tighten their grip on the city they inhabited.

As evening turned to nightfall, light faded from the marble roofs and palisades of Rome. It was replaced with illumination of a starker kind, as a multitude of lamps and torches were lit across the streets and skyline. Any living soul that could have looked down upon that skyline from above – in short, anyone with a god's eye view over the metropolis – would have seen the Eternal City lit up like cinders in a fire's heart, a vast colossus of charcoal black, its outlines picked out by a thousand amber embers.

One such ring of embers haloed an immense ovoid structure, its spherical wall as high as its silty grounds were low. Lofty tiers of wooden seating stuck out against the flame-lit night, empty of the day's spectators.

Night had come, but the *Circus Flaminius* knew no sleep.

GLEAMING STEEL MET corroded iron. The latter broke, cracking into two jagged shards.

He smiled behind his brazen helmet. Foolish. Now he had two blades.

The two men broke apart, circling each other across sand bloodied from old fights. He clutched the severed *gladius* in his dominant hand, the broken piece of sword-blade in the other. The shard was nasty enough to cut his palm, blood seeping from his hand to the dirt, the growing pain a soothing anchor for his thoughts.

But he'd shed enough blood tonight already, and there would be more pain yet to come. Right now, he scarcely noticed either.

No crowds clamoured from the stands, hungry for slaughter. No sun shone mercilessly in the sky, burning his skin through his battered armour. The only light came from the braziers that ringed the arena walls, the only sound the crackling of those distant fires. And his own hacksaw breath, harsh and ragged, blasted back at him inside his helm. The *Circus Flaminius* had a different ambience at night. The pain that ravaged him, the abuses heaped upon him... after dark, it all felt that bit more personal.

'Come on, Vinculex!' a reedy voice called from the wooden ramparts. Brassus. 'Finish the bastard!'

The aedile's words jolted him to the here and now. He felt the pressure on him in that moment, building, swelling in his breast. Which meant... No. Damn it. *No.*

The first ripples of pain crept their way down his back, across his chest. It would be running all through him in moments. The fear would start it, with the torches' heat building it up, and the adrenaline of defending his life raising it to fever pitch. For now, it was acid. It would grow to the Fire soon enough.

The other gladiator was running at him now. That alone showed just what a beast of an opponent he was. He was capable of sprinting while wearing a cuirass of segmented bronze, two ill-fitting greaves hewn from poorly-carved oak, and carrying a damaged legionary *scutum* shield.

Focus. He clutched the shard tighter, deepening the cut in his hand. The stinging pain was almost enough to eclipse the caustic agony beneath his skin. Almost.

'*Ja!*' his attacker screamed.

Vinculex took the first blow head on. Quite literally. He didn't dodge, parry or even block. The other man's *spatha* swept down, hammering his armoured face.

It struck true. Hard enough to permanently mangle the helm. And smash against his forehead, breaking skin and bone together. Vinculex couldn't see stars. There was too much blood in his eyes for that.

His fists moved. The halved *gladius* speared against the breastplate. The jagged tip squealed, sliding across the segments. It couldn't find purchase. Couldn't break through. But it worked. The warrior shifted away from it.

Bringing the shield up.

The shard of sword shot upwards. The broken iron crashed through the armour chink, shearing leather. And shearing something else too, if the spurting blood meant anything.

The gladiator screamed, stumbling back. Vinculex tossed the iron fragment aside, his palm bleeding as much as the wound he'd inflicted. He drew his sword-hand back. His foe had dropped the shield, and the truncated weapon was still good for maiming. Or killing.

'Enough!' Brassus' nasal voice called out once more, from the topmost tier of seats. 'He's finished. Let it be.'

Vinculex didn't respond, *gladius* still primed for the killing blow. His prey fumbled on the ground before him, trying to edge away on elbows and haunches. The bleeding hadn't slowed, trickling down the beaten bronze breastplate and into the filthy sand. The screaming hadn't stopped either.

Only... *No. Please, no.* The Fire was starting, well and truly now. Searing, seething, burning every nerve ending. He could feel it, spreading across his back and torso in a gradually rippling wave. *The Fire.* What else could he call it? He'd been burnt with actual flame before. He would take that inferno over this one.

The broken *gladius* felt suddenly heavy.

'*Vinculex!*' Brassus shouted. 'It is over!'

Another burst of Fire washed over him. *Damn it.* The aedile always had this effect on him.

Vinculex slashed. One final blow. But what should have been a mercy stroke was made savage by the sword's new ragged edge.

The two of them screamed as he hacked at him again. And again. And again. They were both equally bloody by the time it was over, a pair of bronze-clad sanguineous twins, each carrying a host of seemingly mortal wounds. Only one was still standing, and the other was gone. What remained wasn't even a corpse.

And the Fire... by the gods, it burned like anything. He thought the kill would give it some release, relieving the moment's tension. He just needed calm. He just needed a cold, empty room, with nothing and no-one to press him. Somewhere his thoughts could grow cold again, and the world could slow down to its familiarly oppressive tempo.

'Damn you!' a familiar, reedy voice snarled, growing closer. Vinculex slowly turned, leaving bloody footprints in the sand. There would be no respite from the Fire tonight.

'*I told you to leave him,*' Brassus snarled, drawing up to him. 'He was *finished. All* you had to do was *leave it.*' It didn't take a sophistic genius to see what had riled him so. Every kill that wasn't witnessed by the *Circus'* devoted crowds was a waste of money. And every gladiator killed in the private nightly entertainments Brassus and the other aediles staged for themselves, as opposed to in the height of day for public spectacle, was something to potentially answer for.

'He was broken,' Vinculex growled at him. 'He was already dead. All I did was finish him.' He gently pulled the helmet off, revealing a face pitted and marred by a lifetime of old, fossilised scars. He wasn't old, by any stretch, but his years in the arena – and his years suffering from the Fire – had aged him in a way time couldn't quite manage. The skin around his eyes was sallow, and his face was raw with more than just heat exposure. His shock of barley-coloured hair clung to his brow with dried sweat and grime.

It was his expression that made him hardest to look at; that dead-eyed mix of hunger and despondence. He might well have been handsome, if he'd been born into a different life.

Brassus looked into that face for a few moments, before breaking eye contact. He was an aedile, one of

Rome's lowermost public officials, charged with organising citywide games for festival days. An unglamorous, servile role, which had lost a lot of lustre under the Emperor's reforms, but an easy one nonetheless. The noblemen's sons who scrabbled over themselves for the posting had a Parthian's trove of family money to call upon, and as long as they were happy to watch it burn, it would take a special breed of imbecile to fail at an aedileship.

Not that many of them particularly gave a toss. For them, the aedile's chair was a birth-right, a lowly stepping-stone into a senatorial career.

Cornelius Brassus was one such man, a venal young blueblood with one eye on the future he believed he was owed. He didn't much like the more practical aspects of the role, though. Such as actually talking to the gladiators who fought in his games. Or dealing with the human aftermath of the slaughters he loved watching.

'He could have been *saved*,' he managed through gritted teeth. 'Ptorchas could have tended to the chest wound. A month in the ice, at most. He could have been ready for the Quinquatria.' He folded his arms, aiming for dignified fury. All he'd hit was childish surliness.

Now that was truly funny. Vinculex knew that, because a fresh flash of Fire slithered its way down his back in time with his amusement. Anything that made his mind race or heart beat faster – in short, anything that made him *feel* – was fair game. The Fire didn't discriminate. It punished every facet of life in the same way.

'You think the poor bastard would have pulled through the cut I gave him?' Vinculex cupped his helmet under one arm, jerking his head back to his dismembered opponent. 'He was dead the moment my blade took him.'

'And you aren't?' Brassus asked him pointedly, glancing at his brow. The stupid little man had a point there, at least. Blood was still pissing from the forehead gash, and Vinculex didn't dare touch it now. Not before he'd come inside the walls. He'd need salt and boiled water to cleanse the wounds, before Ptorchas could even think about tending them. Which meant more pain. Which meant more Fire. How glorious, the life of a gladiator was.

'I'll be fine,' Vinculex tried.

'You might think,' Brassus snarled, refusing to let go, 'that being the best at carving up your fellow slaves somehow exempts you from my will. But know this, Chained One. Your leash is no longer than any of your wretched little friends'. When I bring you to heel, you will–'

The aedile's petulant little rant ended there, cut short by the gnarled hand that had him by the throat.

'I…' he wheezed, his face reddening. 'You…'

Vinculex tightened his grip, cutting off what little air the man had left. He pulled him closer, Brassus' feet dragging along the sodden sand.

'I don't like your tone, senate-boy.' Inwardly he regretted moving so suddenly, as the Fire surged anew down his body. 'And I think it's in your best interest to keep me sweet, no?'

They both knew what he meant. Vinculex was the Gutter Prince. The most murderous, most popular gladiator in the *Flaminius*. Even if Brassus found a legitimate reason to kill or maim him, the fallout for the young aedile could be unquestionably worse. It wouldn't do, to lose the *Circus* so valued an attraction. It would do his senatorial ambitions no favours.

'You're the one who orders this late night... entertainment,' Vinculex continued, inclining his head towards his slaughtered foe. 'I doubt those pretty boys in togas would be too pleased, knowing you've been abusing your station. Ordering us to cross blades each night, for you to enjoy on your own with no-one else to see.'

'It is... practice,' Brassus squealed. 'It... is necessity.'

Vinculex laughed, a throaty Latin bark. 'Go scurry, *Cornelius*. I always enjoy our talks.'

He hurled the aedile to the ground, and the young man did, indeed, scurry. If anything, he seemed more affronted that his toga had been dirtied than the fact that he'd been physically threatened by a man whose life he owned.

Vinculex waited till he was alone, in the middle of the *Circus Flaminius*. The disjointed remains of the gladiator he'd slaughtered were all the company he had, while the only light came from the distant flickering torches that somehow never seemed to go out. He grasped his battered bronze helmet in both hands, regarding the metal face he'd worn for so long. The amber torchlight caught the metal surface, reflecting auric gold from the brazen visage.

And then he made his way down into the Undercavern, leaving his butchered foe to decay in the dirt.

THAT NIGHT, IN the squat little caverns the prisoners called home, he tried to fix his helmet and his mood. He didn't have much luck with either.

Vinculex swore under his breath, trying to hammer out the helm's dents. Bronze wasn't a difficult metal to shape, but this piece of armour had simply been battered and remoulded too many times. More and more of it would need to be cut away, with extra metal sheets fashioned into shape and welded on.

But then, the less structural integrity the helm would have. Vinculex put the hammer down, sensing it was a forlorn hope. More gladiators would die, and there would be fresh pickings of armour and weapons. This wasn't really worth it. And getting too wound up would only rekindle the Fire.

Vinculex's hovel was the most isolated part of the cavern, a cell in the tunnel's deepest stretches. The furthest below the arena grounds, it was bitterly cold when the sun went down. Hence why no-one particularly wanted it, and why Vinculex wanted it so much. Any respite from heat, for a man with his condition, was a blessing.

Right now, the gladiator shared a larger communal cavern with others of his own kind. What little light there was outside streamed in through slit grooves in the walls and ceilings. The *Flaminius'* other denizens grouped around the shadowy chamber, tending to their wounds and wargear.

Vinculex tossed the helm aside, testily. This wasn't getting anywhere.

'Molchis!' he called out across the gloom. 'Get over here, Molchis.'

A figure detached itself from the shadows, coming his way. The newcomer was a strong and spindly man who seemed more at home in this damp little crypt than he ever would topside. He was powerful, if not brawny, built more like a survivor than a warrior. You couldn't tell much more from first appearances, because the poorly drawn tattoos and sigils daubing his face made all that rather difficult.

Some were as infantile as stick sketches – the sort of crude art found on cheap Suburan terracotta – while others seemed considerably more nuanced and intricate. Those markings upset any attempt to discern his age. The man could have been thirty or fifty years old.

Vinculex had seen enough gang markings in his time, though.

'Easy there, Chained One,' Molchis delicately joshed him. 'How was this evening's kill?'

Vinculex brushed that flattery aside. 'Where's Fuscator? Get him here, Molchis. I need him.'

'The pain that bad?' Molchis raised the scarred flesh where an eyebrow had once been.

Even hearing someone talk about the Fire was enough to start it tingling again. The gladiator had long wondered how psychological it really was.

'Just get him here, sewer-rat,' he growled. 'I need his wares.'

Molchis smiled, as if he'd just received a compliment. Three sorts of men wound up on the sands of the *Flaminius*, invariably. Men like Vinculex, who were large or martially talented enough to train as gladiators. Men like the opponents he was forced to slaughter, little more than screaming, mewling wretches who were broken and hysterical enough to die with messy spectacle. And men like Molchis, convicted criminals who were so anarchic and troublemaking that even a lifetime's internment wasn't punishment enough. Even keeping them in the Carcer would have them fomenting havoc each day.

'You do know—' Molchis cocked his head whimsically. '—that Fuscator is not the only... *purveyor* in these parts. I have my own supply of henbane, and plenty of grateful customers.'

Vinculex wrinkled his brow at that. A slight commotion broke the moment, as two of the burly *Circus* guards dragged through a set of bloody bronze armour.

'Your spoils of war await us, gladiator,' Molchis sarcastically crooned, making the leap. 'Nothing you want first grab at?'

Vinculex didn't answer. He hadn't even known his opponent's name, for the other fighter hadn't been here long enough. He was supposed to be good, although to Vinculex that was a fairly brittle claim. He slew them all just the same.

'Stop trying to change the subject,' the Gutter Prince growled. 'And get me Fuscator. I need him.'

Something flashed in Molchis' glance – something impish, charming and murderous. He'd been absently chewing something with his back teeth, and this he now gently spat into his hand.

'If you want some, take some.' He proffered the little seedy obol forward.

'No...' Vinculex was fighting a silent battle with his rising impatience. 'Not yours. Fuscator's. Can you not tell the difference?'

That made Molchis smirk again. 'Of course I can tell. We all can tell. Why do you think there's such a demand for his stash?' He rolled his eyes. 'If I knew how he got it, I'd just slit his throat and claim it for myself. *If* I knew how he got it,' he sighed bitterly.

Vinculex was scarcely listening now, pressing the flat of his unsheathed sword hard against his bruised and battered torso. Doubtless to try and cool him down, but still…

'You have a fine body,' Molchis ventured. For once, he actually sounded diplomatic.

Vinculex felt too bleak to even snort. 'This body is worthless, Molchis. All it has ever done is betray me.'

The former ganger wasn't an idiot. As Vinculex dragged rough fingernails across his back and torso, Molchis wondered just how much pain he was in right now.

The two of them were not friends. People who got too close to the Gutter Prince wound up dead, either struck down in anger down here or bleeding out their last topside. But they found each other useful, on occasion. Vinculex won every duel and contest he ever fought in, and slaughtered almost every other living soul he encountered on the sands. Betting on those near-certain odds had made Molchis a rich man. Rich, at least, for a criminal scraping out a life in the Undercavern's black-market economy.

Henbane, dreamfish, mad honey… many of the scum and fighters in this subterranean world craved those psychotropic crutches and escapes, much to the dismay of the aediles who ran the gladiatorial games. But in Vinculex, Molchis and Fuscator had found their dream patron. A man wracked with such pain that he'd grasp at any alchemical respite, no matter how dangerous the side effects.

As bonds went, it was a tenuous one, based more on utility than fellowship. But still, this common need led them to tolerate each other. They had both been forced into this life, and that had draped an odd sort of camaraderie over them, two damaged men taking what they could to get by in this world of the damned. Of course, that camaraderie was precarious, and could shatter at any moment.

'It made you strong, though,' Molchis continued. 'It made you what you are.'

'*I* made me what I am,' Vinculex replied, and Molchis sensed he'd gone too far.

'*Attention!*' a drearily familiar voice called out from the cavern's gated door. No guesses who. Only one man could sound so authoritative, yet so officious.

The fighters put down their weapons and food, squaring up to the opening gate.

Brassus entered, flanked by four of his personal lictors. That always brought a smirk to Vinculex's face. Brassus never appeared down here, among the rabble, without those hired bodyguards. No doubt his father's money was spent on paying for them, and perhaps it was just as well. Brassus' manner with the gladiators warranted a good kicking, not that it was ever likely to happen.

'Ergot!' he declared with regal awkwardness. 'It has come to my attention – and please, don't ever suppose it wouldn't have – that ergot is spreading through your wretched little ranks.'

'Took him bloody long enough,' Molchis murmured at Vinculex's side. 'Ergot, though? The boys down here crave something more real.'

'The gods only know how you're getting it in here,' Brassus continued, oblivious, as if dragging felons and fighters down here from every corner of Rome wouldn't bring with it its own back-alley trade of narcotics to numb them all to life's miseries. 'But I tell you, right now, that it ends here.'

The was a muffled curse from outside, a few more fumbled bootsteps, and two more of Brassus' men appeared, restraining another prisoner between them. This man was small, diminutive, but with a cunning, rodent look in his eyes you overlooked at your peril.

Fuscator.

Brassus' head twitched fractionally to one side, the sole sign that he was now talking to the lictors. 'Search them all. At once.'

The smarter ones just let it happen, nursing curses under their breath. They knew that resisting would only bring hardship down upon the lot of them. The prouder ones, at least, made a show of bluster. Vinculex stifled his protests, physically restraining himself from smacking the not-so-burly lictor across the room when his turn came. Molchis seemed more pliant as the guards bodily searched him, and that made the gladiator uneasy. What if they found what he'd been chewing?

'Oh, you naughty boys.' Molchis seemed to perversely relish the lictors' attentions. 'If this was what you wanted, you only had to ask.'

'Nothing, sir.' The lead lictor, a gruff, hard-bitten man in his late thirties, didn't seem satisfied. 'They're all clean.'

Brassus did a poor job of masking his displeasure. No excuses to order any more beatings, it would seem.

He chopped the air with his hand. 'Molchis is the other dealer. Take him too. And the gladiator.'

Two leather hands crashed down upon the Gutter Prince's shoulders, each belonging to a different lictor. Their grips were equally vicelike, which struck Vinculex as slightly theatrical. How could he even escape? This cave was too small to run in. It was barely large enough to live in.

'What are you doing?' he snarled. The Fire was well and truly burning now – the pain, the surprise, the uncertainty. It all fed the flames beneath his skin.

'You are coming with us,' the lictor growled.

BRASSUS IMPERIOUSLY PACED through the Undercavern's cold stone corridors, his expensive boots clacking against the old marble underpavings. Here, in the confines of passageways not meant for prisoners and the soon-to-be dead, they had the luxury of light to see by. The odd torch hung upon wall-mounted sockets, silently spluttering through its oil reserves.

'What is this?' Vinculex called out to the young man's back. The three of them were still being pushed roughly behind him. 'Where are you taking us?'

Brassus snorted without turning. 'Your talents are wanted, Chained One. Some wet-eared little fop from the XII Legion came sniffing around, asking about acquiring your sword-hand. You may be the best gladiator in the *Flaminius*, but you're not irreplaceable. I would happily cash the Gutter Prince in, if it meant acquiring four or five Gutter Paupers in return.'

Vinculex had nothing to say to that. A legion of Rome had coming looking for him? How was a man even supposed to react to that? What could be worth plucking him out from this life of senseless slaughter?

'Then where are Fuscator and I going?' Molchis added.

'Because, my tattooed friend, I fancy making a little pocket money.' Brassus sounded uneasily sure of himself. 'I didn't come to the XII with Vinculex. They came to us. Which means their need for a savage fighting man is greater than my need to make money.' He smiled, an unlovely thing that thankfully no-one saw. 'And since they want your gladiatorial friend so badly, then you pair of sordid little troublemakers can go with him as a package.'

He laughed to himself in the torchlit gloom, as if this was the slyest thing in the world.

'I owe it to the XII, I suppose. Perhaps I'll have father arrange them a vote of thanks, for taking the pair of you off my hands. You're off to join the Fulminata, too. You and all your motley little crew. You can be their problem now.'

VIII

AUXILIA

BYDRETH TRACED A dirty finger across the sigil engraved into the wall.

'What does this mean?' he asked. That tone betrayed his burgeoning curiosity; alone of his Ulthaini kinsmen, Bydreth had displayed an as-yet-insatiable interest in the Rome he now lived in, and had devoured every answer the Praefector gave him.

Orbus pulled a pained face when he saw the mark in question. 'Leave it, Bydreth. That knowledge is not for you.'

They were stood in a *Principia*'s open courtyard, not dissimilar to the one in the heart of the XII's own fortress. Only this one lay further off the beaten track, its neighbouring buildings decidedly quieter, for reasons Bydreth was skirting tactlessly close to now.

Orbus put down the piece of whetstone in his hand, holding up his sharpened *pugio* dagger to the light. He blew the stone dust from its steel flat, looking again at the mark that had caught Bydreth's interest.

XVII

'Those lines…' the Ulthaini ventured. He clearly wasn't letting this go. 'They are numbers, aren't they? Like the numbers on your legionary standards?'

'It is *a* number,' the Praefector corrected him with a sigh. 'The number seventeen.' He gestured to the barrack walls surrounding them both. 'This fortress, this *Principia*… it once belonged to the XVII Legion. The Arcadians.'

'Once belonged?' Bydreth repeated, his interest piqued. 'Where are these Arcadians based now?'

'Nowhere.' Orbus smiled ruefully. 'The XVII Legion doesn't exist anymore, nor do the XVIII and XIX. They were wiped out, all three, in one black day of war. Since then, no legion has ever been given those numerics.' He looked away. 'Some tragedies cannot be swept from memory. They have to be commemorated.'

'So that's why this place has gathered dust for so long,' was Bydreth's rather undiplomatic retort. 'No wonder it seems so run-down.'

He had a point. When they'd all first arrived, Orbus and Argias had practically had to break the ancient doors down to let them in. And once inside… half of Bydreth's kinsmen had collapsed in a fit of choking coughs, as well as some of the older hoplites. Such was the dust.

This *principia* had stood alone and undisturbed for a long time. The dust of ages clung to the walls and surfaces, and little of the furniture and fabrics that made a building home had pulled through the decay of time either. Within the central *praetorium*, Orbus had swept the desk of the officer's quarter vaguely clean with the back of his arm, wiping the cobwebs and dead spiders from his tunic sleeve, and wondered just how he was going to raise an army from this long-dead mausoleum.

'And that is why we are now here?' Bydreth asked.

'Partly,' Orbus assured him. 'We honour the memory of the Arcadians, our slain XVII Legion brothers. *In pace resquiescant.*'

Bydreth wasn't sure he agreed. If anything, picking through this long-dead crypt of a fortress had felt more like robbing an old tomb than anything else. In the last few days, the presence of people had admittedly breathed a little life back into the place. The Achaeans' grunted curses had a way of carrying through walls, while Ulthaini laughter echoed quite naturally down the length of once-dead corridors and concourses.

Orbus hadn't chosen this base of operations lightly. The land and building belonged to no Legion's infrastructure, still listed on public record. Which meant it had been technically available to buy.

A fair few objections had been raised when Orbus had made his intentions known to the magistrates – indeed, *sacrilegious* had been the word bandied about more than once – but some smoothing over from Cascana, and a sizeable portion paid from Orbus' dwindling reserves, had put the old *Principia* in the Praefector's hands.

Anyway, as he now ruefully reflected, in a short span of time money would cease to be a worry. He would have to approach Aemilia's uncles soon. There was still so much to do.

But a barracks was still a barracks, even one that had stood empty for decades. Few people of Rome passed through this forgotten subdistrict, and more crucially still, it sat practically leagues away from the XII's own *principia*. Orbus' motley band of followers now had a home. That, at least, was something.

He looked at Bydreth, the younger man trying his hand at sharpening his own *pugio* without much luck. He wondered how long it had been since the tribal prince had had a home to call his own.

'Where are your kinsmen?' Orbus asked him from nowhere.

'With your man Arxander,' Bydreth told him without looking up. 'He took them for a jolly out on the Plain of Mars. I think they were doing spear practise.'

'Field of Mars,' the Praefector corrected him. 'And barbarians of the northern climes use spears. In the legions, we use *pila*.'

Bydreth pulled a face, but Orbus could see he was more amused than annoyed. He looked up again, noting the sun's position. 'Five hours since dawn,' he observed. 'Wasn't that when…'

'Indeed it was,' Orbus nodded, rising to his feet. 'Well remembered. Argias is never anything less than punctual.' He brushed the sand off his *subarmalis*, leading Bydreth inside. 'Come on, then. Let's see what he and Cascana have managed to rustle up.'

THERE WERE BARELY thirty-five of them. It was enough to make Orbus' hopes plummet.

The legionaries stood arrayed in loose ranks, bare of weapons and armour, but still for all intents and purposes spear-ready. It was as if they were putting out their training and battle readiness for all to see, a gesture that went completely wasted. Orbus would have settled for *hastati*, or even *tirones*, as long as they'd undergone some degree of legionary training.

In that regard, he was surprised by how old and jaded these *milites* seemed. But still... thirty-four men? Barely enough to fill four units. The barrel's bottom had been well and truly scraped.

'Your *optio's* search was not in vain. These gentlemen were from the IX Hispania,' Cascana called out, standing at their head, 'and the XXI Rapax.' He didn't need to emphasise the *were*. Orbus knew, instinctively, that if he were to strip these legionaries down and inspect their torsos, they would all bear the same tell-tale scar tissue upon their flesh.

Ritual branding. The marks of shame. These were men of Orbus' own ilk, proven deserters and allotted victims of the decimation; dead men who had somehow escaped their sentence. Cast out from the regimented brotherhood of their legions, thrown together into suicide units and sacrificial maniples, such souls survived on borrowed time.

For these men, falling in battle was more a formality than a fear. All that remained was for that rightfully earned death to catch them up, and perhaps somehow redeem themselves in the act.

And here they were, throwing themselves at Orbus' mercy. These damned legionaries, men who had broken the oaths they'd once sworn, who now came to him as prospective brothers in arms.

'Who here speaks for you?' he called, assuming his booming parade-ground voice.

A greying veteran stepped forward from the first rank. He looked to be about Orbus' own age, with a thin patina of hair that was starting to gently frost over and a pinched, drawn face that seemed more strained than severe. He was a *decanus*, by the rank markings on his tunic, and from the outlines of icons and crests that had once been sown into the Red – icons that had presumably been ripped away following his disgrace – he'd once borne several commendations for valour and swordsmanship.

'Praefector,' he greeted him with a formal Legion salute. Some habits were hard to break. 'I am Gaius Civilius Optatis. Formally of the Quintilian Century, Third Cohort, IX Legion.'

Orbus nodded. He knew that century, and the man who led it. Marcus Quintilius was no easy man to please, but he wouldn't condemn a fellow *miles* lightly. Whatever sin this Optatis had committed to lose his place in the Hispania must have been grave.

'How many years were you with the IX, Optatis?' Orbus asked. Again, the words carried across the *Principia* courtyard.

'Twenty-two, Praefector.' Optatis seemed to slightly bristle, and Orbus fancied he knew exactly why – twenty-two whole years of his life. Just three shy of completing his first full tour of service. From there, he could have re-enlisted as an *evocatus* on a notably higher salary, or retired with full honours as a *veteranus*, living out his days on a comfortable military pension, with his own bequest of private land.

'Why did you take the brand, *decanus*?'

Orbus ignored the way the other men stiffened. There was no way around this question, and an army thrived on trust as much as beer and discipline. It was time to clear the air, to get their sins out in the open.

'I failed, Praefector.' For whatever it was worth, Optatis looked him right in the eye as he confessed. 'I broke, when it mattered. And my fellow *milites* died for it.'

Orbus let the old soldier confess in dignified silence. He had no idea how well Optatis knew these other legionaries, but shouldering such guilt was hard, let alone sharing it with other soldiers. Orbus didn't know the details, but in truth he didn't need to. Here was a man with blood on his hands, and he wanted more than anything to wash it away.

The Praefector nodded his understanding, before looking out over the other legionaries.

'These men with you here,' Orbus replied. 'Were they part of that failure, too? Were they all your comrades from the IX, or have you come together since then?'

Optatis indicated the men behind him with a single sweep of his gaze. 'I cannot speak for all of them, Praefector, but I know many, both within the Hispania and without. Some of them are deserters, who never quite made it away. Others are just men who were caught breaking ranks and fleeing, and were unfortunate enough to be witnessed. A handful of us were men from formations that failed, or disgraced themselves, and were the souls marked in each unit for decimation. For whatever reason, those sentences were never carried out – to make an even more shameful example, usually, without shattering the morale of those who remained.'

Orbus met the eyes of a few *milites* in the frontmost rank. Or rather, he tried to. The soldiers remained stood to attention, their gazes fixed on something a hundred yards ahead of them.

'Quite the menagerie of friends you've made,' he drily observed. 'So how did you come to lead these men here, Optatis?'

'We were left behind, while the IX returned to campaigning,' the *decanus* explained. 'Some of were kept on at the *Principia*, to aid the *evocati* in the selection and training of new recruits.' He snorted, shaking his head. 'At least, that was the cover story. In reality, the drillmasters wanted to make an example of us. Each day, they would parade us before the *tirones*, and have them pelt us with rocks and rotten meat. Ostensibly it was to teach target practice, but we all knew the truth. They wanted to show the fresh meat what happened to those who failed, and broke their oaths.'

A few grunts of agreement came from the other legionaries, no doubt bitterly remembering their own falls from grace and how they'd come to be here. The Praefector took them all in, noting the hunger in their faces, the desperation to be something more than what they'd been.

Time to be a leader, once again.

'The *tirones* were right to do that,' he announced, apropos of nothing. The soldiers with Optatis were far too disciplined and canny to show any shock, but Orbus fancied he saw them tense at his surprise bluntness. 'And their drillmasters where right to order it. That is what happens to an errant legionary. That is what *rightfully* happens.'

The atmosphere changed, in that moment. The former men of the Legions kept their silence, as professionalism dictated. But Orbus could feel the change, as they lurched between confusion and resentment at this picking of old wounds.

'I ran from battle,' the Praefector continued. 'Our camp was ransacked by Gauls, and I had a choice to make, same as you did. I could hold my ground, and die with honour, or I could flee and buy life with my self-respect. I chose the latter.'

Still no-one said anything, although Optatis' worn and weary face began to soften. The veteran *decanus* could see where Orbus was going with this.

'I don't need to know your shame, *milites*. But now you have mine.' Orbus gently reached for the tunic, pulling the fabric right off his torso. The blacked-out tattoos revealed were just as stark as the horrific mess of scarring on his back.

'My *legatus* was right, in his wisdom, to give me the punishment he deemed fit,' he went on, gently turning to give every man present a view of his wounds. 'Just as your centurion was right to expel you from the IX.' He pulled his tunic back down, satisfied he'd made his point. 'For you are right, Optatis. That is what happens to those of us who fail. Those of us who soil their chances for greatness.'

Orbus drew away from the old *decanus*, walking across the ranks of disgraced legionaries he'd brought with him.

'But I'm not interested in how you men soiled your chances,' he called out. 'All I care about is how you're willing to spend your second chance.' He felt his impetus shift, dropping back into character as a belligerent legion officer. 'Because from here onward, I don't give a horse's tit how your sorry arses ended up at my door. Just as you won't care how I wound up standing here. From here on, you are legionaries again. You'll hold your sorry selves as you would in a legion, just as I do.'

He was passing Optatis again, and stayed put this time. 'Whatever orders I give, *you* will obey them without question. *I* will give them without doubt. Nothing more, nothing less. Are we clear, *milites*?'

Optatis snapped another crisp salute in response, and a few of them tentatively called out. 'Yes, Praefector!'

Orbus frowned, taking another step closer. He was practically within kissing distance of the first rank.

'I can't hear you, *milites*!'

'*Yes, Praefector!*' they all shouted this time.

'Are you ready to be a part of this *auxilia*?'

'*Yes, Praefector!*'

'And are you ready to leave your sins behind you?'

'*Yes, Praefector!*'

Good. Very good. So there was still a fire in them to be stoked. That was half the battle won, then. Orbus had faced the task of leading men who had given up on life before, and no amount of training and whipping could make those men what they used to be. These once-legionaries clearly still had some fight in them, and still held fast to their training and experience. They would require little practice and drilling to make them battle-ready once again, and that was good.

The cohort needed a strong, disciplined core, and these men already came with a *de facto* leader in Optatis. No-one had challenged his right to speak on their behalf, despite their varied and scattered origins. That was a good sign. That would make organising and commanding them easier.

'At ease,' Orbus commanded, and the ranks of soldiers finally relaxed a little. For a moment, just one moment, the Praefector dared to believe that building this army might be a little easier than he'd–

'Master,' a familiar voice dragged him back down to earth. 'Master, we need to open the gates. Argias has returned.'

Puli couldn't help but look a little worried as he delivered that news. Orbus knew the whiff of subtext when he smelt it.

'What is it?' he asked the slave.

'It is probably easier to show you, master.'

'WHAT?' WAS ALL Orbus could say. '*What*?'

He'd sent his new recruits away with Optatis and Cascana, dismissing them to one of the *Principia*'s communal gathering halls the hoplites and Ulthaini had been using earlier. If any of them had anything to say about traipsing through the bones of the Arcadians' old fortress, no-one did so.

But that was far from Orbus' thoughts now. The Praefector looked out across the courtyard, just as he'd done scarcely an hour before. But whereas last time he'd been looking at several neatly-regimented ranks of *milites*, this time he'd been greeted by another group of fighters. Only this one was decidedly more… motley.

Bydreth was still standing at his side, where he'd been when Optatis and his men had arrived. But where the Ulthaini prince had been content to silently marvel at ranks of Roman legionaries, now he had a little more to say.

'This is not quite what you'd led me to expect,' he quipped, unwittingly echoing Orbus' very own thoughts. 'I thought it was just one gladiator you sent your boy out for.'

Familiarity breeds contempt, and Orbus had been trying to cultivate a little distance between himself and his growing band of followers. But Bydreth was proving a hard man not to like, so far. And out of all the men who now called this *Principia* home, Orbus somehow found him the easiest to talk to.

'You aren't wrong,' he quietly replied, still looking out over the crowd of new arrivals. 'But I'm sure there's an explanation for this.'

'Praefector,' Argias crisply stepped forward, breaking Orbus' chain of thought. He still sounded like the eager young pup Cascana had introduced him to, and today that felt rather less reassuring. 'Excuse my days of tardiness, sir. Negotiations with the *Circus Flaminius* took rather longer than I'd hoped for, but I'm sure you'll agree that we reached an acceptable result.'

Orbus looked out at the *Principia's* sixty new arrivals. Fully half of them were walking slabs of brutish muscle, with enough scars and flesh-burns to match a whole legion of Roman *milites*. Even without the blocky, bronze armour they were clad in, they were easily identifiable enough. Gladiators.

But the rest... the other thirty or so specimens looked, if anything, more piratical than gladiatorial. Optatis' men had been soldiers. The gladiators, less rigidly-trained but more harshly raised, could be considered warriors. But these criminals? They had the look of backstreet gangers about them.

Orbus could tell, at a glance, that they had been relegated to death in the arena from their prison sentences for whatever crimes they'd committed while inside the Carcer. A few of them had muscle to spare, but most of them were of a wiry, deceptively frail build.

Several of them were tattooed, over their faces and profiles. Not the fading, ancestral body art the Ulthaini wore; these markings were far cruder, and with far less meaning. Some of them even looked self-inflicted, poorly marked scrimshaw ink criss-crossing their faces and features in patterns that were, no doubt, supposedly symbolic.

Most tellingly of all, they were neither silent nor still. They eyed the Praefector less the way soldiers would regard their commander, and more how vultures would hover around a dying animal, wondering how long it would be before they could steal up to it and pick its carcass clean. These men had never been trained as soldiers, and they'd been deemed too weak or devious to shape into gladiators. The only discipline they'd ever known was their own, and Orbus doubted there had ever been much of that.

'Enough,' he called out. 'Silence, all of you.'

They quietened down a touch, though not completely. More eyes were on him now, which he was perfectly comfortable with. But they were still sniggering, and Orbus was fairly sure they weren't laughing *with* him.

'*Silence!*' he shouted, more fiercely. 'I don't know how much my *optio* has filled you in on, but you belong to me now. And that means that *I* give the orders round here.'

Argias flinched a fraction at that. He seemed, finally, to sense that he'd done something wrong. That Orbus wasn't particularly happy with his performance.

The Praefector took a step back, not from fear, but simply to take all the street-scum and gladiators in with one glance.

'Does anyone here speak for the lot of you?'

The mob began to shift and jostle, murmuring and laughing. All around one of the fighters in bronze armour, in particular. He didn't look much different from the others, apart from the enflamed redness of his torso and muscles, and pained grimace on his face.

'He probably does,' one of the gangers jerked his head at the gladiator in question, with a grimy chuckle. 'Although he probably won't admit it.'

Orbus wasn't sure if this newcomer was taking the piss or not. 'And you are?' he replied.

'The name's Molchis.' This crooked little fellow seemed a particularly wretched example of the group, and he wore so much striating ink that it was hard to actually pick out his features. His beady eyes were visible, though, and they conveyed a wealth of emotion on their own. 'And you must be Sertor Orbus.'

'And who do *you* speak for, then?' Bydreth quipped back. He smiled, revealing those rotten gums of his, and somehow the expression came across as charmingly gormless. Oddly enough, Molchis began to laugh again, a little more honestly this time.

'I like your ink, Celt boy. It's better than mine. And I wouldn't presume to speak for anyone,' he replied with theatrical humility. He gave his neighbour's shoulder a pejorative slap, to jeering. 'But Fuscator here will only be *too* thrilled with the responsibility.'

Orbus ignored their banter, moving towards the gladiator. He didn't recognise his face, but there was only one man this could be.

'You must be Vinculex.' He didn't smile at him, or extend a hand. Neither would have sent the right message. 'I'm your new praefector. I have heard of your exploits, Gutter Prince, as have many in my former legion. I am honoured to have your blade in my service. As well as your comrades,' he added humbly, casting that last remark over the other gladiators.

Thankfully, none of Molchis' fellow vagabonds were on hand to witness his sincerity. They all seemed rather taken with Bydreth. To Orbus' irritation, the tribesman seemed to be rising to the moment, joking and apparently bonding with these new comrades with effortless ease. The Praefector tried not to let it annoy him.

'Don't call me that,' was the gladiator's reply. 'I'm just Vinculex.' He had an odd way of talking, giving clipped responses that sounded either hostile, or somehow pained. Orbus wasn't sure which.

'Very well, soldier,' he replied. 'These gladiators. Do they answer to y—'

'*Yes*,' Vinculex practically snarled. 'Whatever I tell them, they'll do. Just get me out of the sun.' And with that, he practically shouldered Orbus aside, swift enough to almost bruise him. For a moment, the Praefector was speechless. In the Fulminata, he'd have had any soldier who treated them like that whipped on the spot, and put on barley rations or docked pay to ensure the sting didn't wear off so easily.

As it happened, Vinculex had simply shifted to the square's shadier edges, tearing off his bronze cuirass and shield strap. Some gladiators followed suit, pulling off their armour and letting their sweat-bathed skin breathe in the shadows. A few of Molchis' seedy little friends tagged along, putting Orbus briefly in mind of blood gnats, swarming around elephants at a Numidian watering hole.

He wanted to roll his eyes. Barely five minutes, and his new charges were already ignoring his commands. Time to make the most it, then.

'Take some time,' he ordered the lot of them. 'Catch your breath. You've had a hard day's march. Leave your kit here.' He took in the whole courtyard with a gesture. 'I'll have it cleared and stowed away later. Two hours from now—' He noted the sun's place. '—be back in this courtyard. I have some announcements to make, and I'm sure you all have questions.'

No-one seemed interested in delving into that, so the Praefector carried on regardless.

'Be there, on the dot. I mean it. Any latecomers will find themselves on latrine duty.' His eyes flashed with cynical charm. 'Optatis will explain what that entails.'

That seemed to puncture the tension, with the new arrivals dispersing to talk amongst themselves. Argias, presumably dismissed, seemed ready to slink back indoors, retreating to his other duties. Orbus dashed that hope with his next command.

'Argias,' the Praefector crisply, coldly, summoned him back. 'With me, *optio*.'

'*GATES OF FIRE*, soldier! What in Teucer's name were you *thinking*?'

The Praefector was rather less composed, now they were out of public view. Alone in a lonely barrack corridor, Orbus had grabbed the young *miles*, pinning him against the marble wall.

'Cornelius Brassus knew well the value of the Gutter Prince,' Argias stammered. 'And the other gladiators. He was canny enough to realise how desperately we—'

'Don't call him that,' Orbus snarled. 'His name is Vinculex. And *we*? He knew how desperate *we* were? You were the only one of us in that room, *optio*. What did he do, ply you with wine?'

'Nothing like that, Praefector.' Argias, now released, dusted his tunic down. He felt glad Orbus didn't have his vine stick to hand. 'Aedile Brassus seemed particularly eager to be rid of Molchis and Fuscator. He realised that we wanted Vinculex, so he wouldn't let him go unless we paid for the two of them as well.'

'Alright,' the Praefector continued, his anger still simmering. 'So why did you take so many of their grubby little cohort, instead of just the two of them? The gladiators I can understand, but those reprobates?'

The *optio* craned his neck to either side, in case one of 'those reprobates' happened to be within earshot. 'We needed bodies, sir. Your orders... weren't the clearest.' He swallowed, regretting his choice of words.

'Oh,' Orbus hit back archly, 'so this is *my* fault, then?'

'Of course not, Praefector. I think there may be something... wrong with them. The aedile practically jumped at the chance to be rid of them, and truth be told the money we paid per head wasn't that much.'

And that brought them to the crux of the matter. Something that, by his reticence, Argias clearly didn't want to talk about.

'How much did you pay for them, Argias?'

'Praefector...'

'*How. Much?*'

Argias, to his credit, looked him straight in the eye. And then he told him.

Orbus took a step back, wiping the stress from his face with one hand. Had he made a mistake, promoting this man to First Legionary?

'Blood of Teucer, Argias... buying the *Principia* damn near cleared me out, and now *this?* That is almost everything I liquidated from Baiae gone. *Gone!*' he snapped. 'Those are my *life's* savings, soldier. *Everything!* What would you have me do now? Slink back to Elysia, and beg a housekeeping job off my brother? Well?'

Argias straightened, regaining a little poise.

'I was led to believe...' he ventured, 'that you would... no longer have to worry about money. Not after a month or two, at any rate.'

Oh, how tactfully put. How wonderfully diplomatic. They both knew exactly what Argias meant.

'The wedding,' he growled. 'Cascana told you, then.' Of course he had. Who else for miles around even knew about it?

Orbus turned around, idly looking about for something to smash. 'By the gods,' he began, 'by the

Penates of my father's hearth, and by Silvanus and Mars who guide my blades, will you *damn* that accursed woman!' He wheeled around, as Argias subtly tried to edge away from him. He'd never seen Orbus like this before.

'*Damn* Aemilia!' he shouted, smashing a fist into the faded fresco on the wall opposite. '*Damn* the brothers Lemnon! *Damn* the Volscani!'

His shouted echoes faded from the stone surroundings. For a moment, all was still – and then Orbus screwed his face up, cradling abused knuckles as the pain caught up with him.

'Varus' balls,' he muttered. 'That hurt.'

Argias, very wisely, hadn't commented on the Praefector's outburst. 'I won't try to defend my choices, sir. If you'd like to pick another *optio*, I understand. I will return with Cascana to the XII, if that is your will.'

Orbus looked at him for a moment, trying to gauge the man's sincerity. 'That's being a little dramatic, don't you think? You're my First Legionary, Argias. From time to time I'm going to end up shouting at you.' He raised an eyebrow. 'If that is too much for you to handle, maybe you should return to your legion.'

'Not necessary, Praefector.' Argias snapped to attention. 'The men are still awaiting us. Your orders?'

Orbus rubbed his eyes. He hadn't slept much in the last few days. 'Send Puli out onto the Field of Mars. I want the hoplites and Ulthaini all back here, in a couple of hours. Pass on what I told the others – I want everyone in the courtyard, two hours before sundown, silent and ready to hear what I have to say.'

The *optio* nodded. 'Done.'

'And one more thing,' Orbus added. 'The doctrines of sale, for the men of the *Flaminius*. Do you have them?'

'I do, Praefector.' Argias nodded. 'They're in my quarters. Locked away, sir,' he hastily added, before Orbus could lose it once again, 'in my strongbox.'

'Get them out,' Orbus told him. 'Leave them on my desk before you go. And get me some lamp oil, while you're at it. And a torch.' He allowed himself a conspiratorial smile.

'Sir?'

'Just do it.'

THE HOUR CAME. Orbus couldn't leave the moment any longer.

Being the only man of rank in this fortress meant he had the whole *praetorium* wing to himself, which in any other circumstances would have pleased him no end. Here, today, in this particular *principia*, Orbus was forced to agree with Bydreth. He felt like an intruder in a long-dead crypt.

He'd ordered Optatis' and Arxander's men to keep the newer arrivals in line. That chafed at him, in truth, because setting one group of his charges over another would only lead to problems down the line. But what else could he do?

He'd even dressed for the occasion, the first time he'd done so since Baiae. Orbus generally disliked the segmented breastplates which had spread through the legions of late. A *lorica segmentata* was fashionable, impregnable, but a bitch to clean and maintain. Unless you actually enjoyed scrubbing every last plate clean of rust. And what it granted in protection, it stole in agility.

His old suit of chainmail was getting on in years, but it had protected him in every war he'd ever worn it in. It had been a little indulgence, when times were better, commissioned especially from a forge at Herculaneum on the day he'd taken the prefect's crest. The rings were cast from steel, rather than lesser metals, and instead of the standard-issue shapeless chainmail meshes worn by most legionaries, this suit had been especially tailored and fitted to his torso.

The suit was past its prime, with its fair share of notches and dents that no smithy could iron out. Several patches of darkened metal striated the steel, replacement rings of iron or bronze where the alloy hadn't been available or affordable. The chainmail wouldn't protect him the way a proper breastplate would – it would stop a slash, or sword point, though probably not a spear thrust – but Orbus trusted his instincts to keep him out of danger, more than his wargear.

Beneath the chainmail he'd tied a *focale* scarf in place, all the better to keep the chafing at bay. He'd strapped on his *cingulum*, the leather waxed and metal polished by Puli until the rivets gleamed from their hanging bands, and donned his best pair of *caligae*, the ones with extend thongs and bootstraps. He hadn't taken his helmet, either, because helmets weren't for making speeches, but he cared enough about this first impression to come armed, belting *Ananke* to his hip.

Orbus rounded the corner, emerging into the courtyard. In one hand, he carried a burning torch. In the other, a sheath of creamy parchment.

His ragged cohort was waiting for him. The Praefector felt a tickle of anticipation catch his breath – something he steadfastly refused to show on his face. This was the first time he'd seen the lot of them together, and the truth of what he'd been building finally hit him.

Nearly two hundred faces stared back at him, enough to fill the whole square. Gaius Optatis and his men held the middle, standing to in impeccably-formed ranks as they undoubtedly had in their old legions.

Almost forty Achaeans thronged them in loose groups, less organised but just as ready. Arxander and the rest of Behemon's old veterans favoured Orbus with their full attention, without standing in regimented lines.

Bydreth held the crowd's head, but more surprisingly Brauda did too. Orbus could sense the trust from Bydreth's gaze, if not his cousin's. Their fellow countrymen had dispersed among the others, mingled with men of different pasts as easily as Bydreth had done. They were easy men to like, with an openness about their souls that invited confidence.

The Gutter Prince's gladiators seemed least committed of the group, ready to begin yet another chapter in their fatalistic lives. They looked no less menacing without their bulky armour and weapons, somehow coming across as both louche and resolute in their bearing. Vinculex's face was a rictus of pained focus behind a line of Optatis' men.

Molchis and Fuscator's sewer-rats somehow filled the most space. They had the look of ravens about them, raggedy black little birds eying their prey from the corners and shadows. Orbus couldn't see Fuscator anywhere, but Molchis nodded at his gaze, the gesture surprisingly sincere.

'And finally, we get to it.' Orbus had been waiting for this, ever since he'd left Sextus behind at Baiae. And now the moment had come.

'If you were expecting a speech,' he called out to the silent horde, 'then I'm going to disappoint you. The army is a place for deeds, not words, and it is my deeds I want you to remember tonight.'

He raised his right hand, displaying the bundle of papers for all to see.

'In my hand,' he continued, 'I hold your doctrines of sale. Over half the men I see before me now, I purchased as slaves. I saw potential in you, and it suited me to have you beholden to my commands.'

Orbus set down the burning torch he'd been holding in his other hand, resting its stand upon the earth. The crowd watched this in intrigued silence.

And then he hurled the papers skyward. They flew into the air, billowing apart as each one sailed down to earth.

It had the right effect, though. Almost two thirds of the doctrines of sale cascaded right into the torch's billowing fires. And began to burn.

The gesture wasn't perfect, but every man present caught the symbolism.

'Manumission,' Orbus explained, driving the point home. 'Whichever master you once served, whatever lives you used to lead… gone. From this moment, you are all now free men.'

The effect was instantaneous. Men who'd never met shared words of shock and congratulations. Bydreth's mouth split in a putrid, charismatic grin, as if his hunch had been vindicated. Brauda seemed to lighten up a notch, but still appeared as guarded as ever.

'But while I have no legal shackles to keep you here,' Orbus continued, 'I think you may wish to stay beneath my aegis. Because it is my intention—' He allowed himself a smile, beginning to walk toward them. '—to pay each and every last one of you a full legionary's salary to remain at my side. Two hundred and twenty-five *denarii* a year. Of course,' he wryly added, 'full board in this *principia* is taken care of, now I own the building. And as with any Roman army billeted at home, expenses for your living, training and equipment will be covered.'

He was practically among them now, a handful of paces between them.

'How does that sound?'

He'd almost expected cheering. Or at least acclamation. But neither came.

'Nobody's biting,' he noted. 'Wise. Because I haven't told you what I want in return.'

He turned, regarding the men either side of him. 'I once ran the XII Legion,' he announced. 'And now, I seek to raise you to those standards. I won't lie, friends. You have all known hardship, but the coming months will test you in ways that you will never have imagined.'

Again, there was no approving hail. This time Orbus had hoped for one. These were his men – at least, he hoped they would be – and a commander owed his men the truth.

'You will fail these tests,' the Praefector told them. 'You will fail each and every challenge I set for you, because these challenges are meant for more than men. They are meant for *legionaries*. You will be broken upon that anvil, again and again... but it shall temper you, make you into something stronger. And then you will pass.'

Another murmur ran through the ragged ranks of freedmen.

'I will break you, and forge you anew.' Orbus felt his own spirits rising, despite himself. 'I will make you into something your old selves would never recognise. It will hurt, but I will make you conquer things you would never believe you could. I will make a legionary out of every man here, and when all is said and done, I will consider it the finest honour of my life to stand shoulder-to-shoulder with you, as my *auxilia*.'

Some of the crowd – Ulthaini, the Praefector noticed – began to grunt in approval, but it wasn't enough. Not yet.

Foreigners, he thought.

'Some of you have been to war,' Orbus noted. 'Some of you know what it is to spill an enemy's blood. But I tell you now, and may the War God be my witness – the life I offer you will be hard. It will change you, more than any test of mine ever could. It will fill you with horrors that no man was ever meant to witness.'

The throng had settled back down to silence, rapt more than sullen, hanging from his every word.

'But it will be your own,' Orbus promised them. 'It will be a free man's life, and no-one will ever take it from you.'

Former slaves and soldiers clustered round him on every side.

'So what is it to be?' he asked them. 'Men... or *milites?*'

IX

THE TEMPERING

THE FOLLOWING MONTHS passed deceitfully quickly, but every man living beneath Orbus' roof counted the days.

Life had trickled back into the decrepit old *principia* with the coming of people, and with each passing night the Arcadians' former bastion felt a little more like a home to its new inhabitants. And they felt a little less like intruders, or grave robbers.

Having slaves about the place had helped with that. Orbus had procured some houseslaves and domestic servants from a nearby fleshmarket – old hands at their game, who knew how to keep a household ticking over without much supervision. Age-old cobwebs were finally swept away from cloisters and lintels, while the last dust was wiped from the floors and billets. Hearths were lit and tended for the first time in years, and warm air billowed beneath the terracotta flooring in gentle currents of convection.

Brauda had scarcely believed such a thing existed at first. 'Warm water, I can get used to,' he admitted, referring to their ill-fated expedition to the Baths, 'but indoor heating? You Romans, and your godless little inventions.' The rest of his countrymen were similarly grudgingly awed.

And that was far from the slaves' only task. The basic duties of keeping the *Principia* fed three times a day, even on basic rations, required a surprising degree of logistical nous, one that dictated a chain of servile command. Puli, in particular, found himself in a position of newfound authority, running the fortress' day-to-day life during his master's many excursions. Even a slave in charge of slaves had a measure of power, and it wasn't long before the *Principia*'s new inhabitants started to realise it too. Before long, Puli was beset by *tirones* desperately wanting to be his friends, all in the hopes of a better meal at day's end, or comfier feathers in their bedlinen.

The old servant never cracked beneath the strain, and never complained about how his daily workload had jumped. His little time free from keeping the barracks running smoothly was spent hunched over carefully scrawled parchments with Argias.

An army thrived on information, and information required records. Each recruit to Orbus' newborn cohort needed a paper record – name, background, age, skills, injuries, even scars and birthmarks to mark out a corpse. All was game. Argias also needed help growing his inventory, expanding it beyond what he'd done for Arxander's men, until every last weapon, piece of armour and equipment had a verbal shadow on parchment. These men were no legion, not in Rome's eyes, but Orbus would damn well run them like one.

'Don't we have tribunes for this crap?' Optatis had remarked, on one of the many occasions he poked his head around the *praetorium* doors. Orbus' resolution to treat each faction of men as equals had fallen short within weeks – some of them had leaps to take, and all some others needed was polish. Optatis, in particular, he came to lean on, as well as some of his most trusted once-legionaries. The former *decanus* knew how a legion worked between deployments, and had already had a little taste of camp duties.

'If you can find a tribune willing to take this posting,' the Praefector quipped back at him, 'in this ancient shithole, with these fine specimens of mankind, I'll choke Ceres with his salary.' He didn't look up from the desk, reviewing Arxander's less than glowing assessment of the Ulthaini's blade-practise that morning.

As if to underline his point, a dribble of damp chose that moment to drop onto the parchments from the ceiling. The *Principia* was well-tended to these days, but it was still old.

'In all honesty,' Optatis mused as he gazed at the reams of chaotic parchment and wax tablets covering the desk and floor, 'you may well have to.'

He had a point, as irksome as it was. In a way, Orbus found himself glad for the excuses to drill the men personally. Any escape from the wax and parchment was something to cherish, and at least out there he felt like he was making an impact.

A soldier was worthless if he couldn't march, but the *tirones* had taken to that punishing skill with unexpected ease; then again, many of these men had had upbringings far harsher and more destitute than Orbus' own. The physical impact of marching for miles to a time limit hadn't bothered most of them, even while carrying dummy weapons, camp equipment and ration packs all twice as heavy as anything they'd bear in real life.

No, what it came down to was discipline. A hundred or so weary men to march was one thing. Getting them to march *as one* was quite another. A unit, a maniple, a century… their power lay not in the number of spears they could hurl, but in their ability to move and act with one voice and one will. That was what made a horde of armoured Romans into a legion, and what set them above the foes they fought against.

In the case of these men, it would come down to repetition. He would march them, and he'd do it again, and again, and again, until their joints cried out for mercy. Until they cursed the day they'd agreed to serve him, and until they all moved in lockstep without even having to think about it.

So far, the Praefector had kept them all at it equally, drilling each group he led out into the countryside with equal zeal. Former legionaries and Achaean hoplites fared far better than Ulthaini circus-slaves and Carcer inmates, but the truth before his eyes didn't matter. Appearances had to be maintained, and the less fairly he treated them, the more likely they'd be to act out, chafing against their newly-imposed discipline.

'Perhaps,' Argias tactfully suggested, one morning the two of them were looking out over the Field of Mars, 'mixing their factions was a little hasty.'

Orbus half-smiled at his *optio*'s hesitancy. A hundred paces ahead of them, a mix of gladiators, Achaeans and Ulthaini were taking turns to leap off the Tiber's banks, swimming the river's flowing width and pulling themselves up the other side. Such a feat could barely be considered testing, if not for the bullion weights belted to their backs and torsos – weights put there to simulate the load of full legionary body armour.

'Come on!' Orbus called out, as he saw one of Vinculex's men begin to slacken. 'The *Batavi* do this every damned day!'

He knew where Argias was coming from. The decision to reorganise them anew, in units irrespective of their background, had been an optimistic attempt at binding them together. To highlight their commonality, more than their differences. And it hadn't particularly worked, to be honest. Off duty, the men congregated toward their own kin anyway.

'Come on,' the Praefector told him. 'We're coming to noon. Let's get them home.'

His haste was understandable. When he led the *auxilia* out of Rome, Orbus usually kept them in the deeper countryside, using the hills and gentle valleys of Greater Campania to practice their manoeuvres in peace. Daring the Field of Mars too often, along the river's length and considerably closer to Rome's beating heart, felt like a needless risk. Too many officers among the legions used it for training and parading, even outside of every calendar day when the Roman people congregated there for festivals and events.

By some miracle, they were yet to run into any men from the XII on their exercises. Truth be told, the handful of times they crossed paths with other legionaries had gone fairly smoothly so far. They'd even formed some decent bonds with the VIII Augusta's *hastati* centuries, whose own infantry training was proceeding at a similar pace. But those men hadn't known who Orbus really was, and before long someone might actually recognise him. Or Optatis. Or any of them.

In time, winter gave way to spring. The sky grew bluer, and the vibrant verdant hue returned to the Italian countryside. But better weather didn't assuage the *tirones'* burdens. Leather and metal hardly warded against cold, but it barely let the skin breathe either. Following their herculean schedules only became harder beneath the sun's punishing stare.

The drilling still happened in shifts, the only feasible way to not leave too many men idle and unsupervised. One morning Orbus would take a few units through their rites and exercises, either in the *Principia* courtyard or on the plains surrounding Rome. Hours later, Argias, or Optatis, or Arxander, or sometimes even Cascana would rouse the next bunch of men, taking them through whichever facet of legionary training the Praefector's intricate web of paperwork dictated. And on it went, until the sun had finally fallen, and the last staggered bands of would-be *auxilia* had finally stumbled back into their billets.

Men frayed from constant hardship had little spark to rebel, and the iron discipline of an army camp had ostensibly prevailed. So far.

Orbus could still recall the most troubling exceptions. Not surprisingly, they'd mostly happened during the first days and weeks of the training. The euphoria of being free men on legionary wages had worn off, and the grinding reality of training to be *milites* had started to truly hit them.

The condemned men had been the worst, even though they'd all had teething problems. During one of Orbus and Argias' first sword drills, two lines of Optatis' former legionaries and Molchis' fellow arena scum had faced off back-to-back down the length of the *Principia* courtyard. The first opponents they were bidden to draw wood against had taken them aback; they'd clearly been expecting something a little grander, or at least more dangerous.

'Posts?' Fuscator could scarcely hide his disappointment. 'You want us to spend the morning hitting *posts?*' He nudged his with his wooden *gladius*, lamely. 'How many ways can there be to strike one?'

Orbus had looked out across the square, taking in the conical wooden stakes that Puli and the slaves had dug into the ground the night before.

'Every legionary who ever fought for Rome began this way,' the Praefector informed him. 'And this—' He rapped Fuscator's stake with the pommel of *Ananke*. '—is the first foe you will ever have to vanquish. Unless you don't fancy your chances against it?' he added with mock gravitas. That did the trick, and got the others laughing and hacking at their own poles with righteous abandon.

'Don't slacken!' Orbus called out after several minutes of this. 'And keep your power. Technique matters, but it's pointless if there's no strength behind it.'

'This is stupid.' Molchis threw down his dummy blade, clutching his palm with his other hand. It was glistening, with sweat and the pus from ruptured blisters. 'What's the point of doing this all morning?'

'You'll learn enough.' Orbus tried to maintain his nonchalance. 'Gaius Marius once said it takes ten thousand hours to master a skill, and ten thousand more to become the best there's ever been at it.'

A few more of the others had stopped hacking away, now. They turned to look at their Praefector, and the ganger whose tone was becoming increasingly challenging.

'That Marius sounds like a right mewling bitch,' Molchis sniggered. 'And this stupid wood is too damn heavy.' He gave the dummy weapon a kick, stepping out from the line of *tirones*. 'What's the damn point? No sword's ever going to weigh as much as that.'

'That is *precisely* the point.' Orbus shifted, so he'd be right in the way if Molchis tried to leave. 'You will train your proficiency with a weapon heavier than metal. And when you pick up a true *gladius*, it will feel as light and nimble as an extension of your arm.' He smiled, not unkindly. 'Believe me, *tiro*, Marius was right. There'll come battles when you have to swing it ten thousand times or more. When that day comes, you'll be thankful you put the hours in.'

'Whatever.' Molchis wouldn't play along. He was already walking past Orbus, towards the small wooden colonnade that ringed the square and led into the *Principia*'s inner chambers.

'*Molchis!*' Orbus called after him. The others had all stopped now, following his gaze. 'You stay right there, soldier!'

The former inmate smiled impishly. Orbus had known this was coming; he'd known all along that beneath Molchis' skin-deep bonhomie and on-paper acquiescence, there lay a man with nothing but contempt for authority. In truth he'd been waiting for the moment that he pushed Molchis too far, and forced him into something he didn't want to do.

There were next to forty pairs of eyes on him now. Orbus' newly-cultivated authority would live or die with whatever happened next.

'Ten lashes,' the Praefector told him, loud enough for the others to hear, 'if you don't return to your rank right now.'

Molchis stayed where he was, his smile daring Orbus to make good on that threat. Then he took another slow, backward step towards the gates.

'Twenty,' Orbus cautioned him through grit teeth. Molchis' smirk deepened, and he actually turned his back on the officer, taking another couple of steps.

'My, my,' the Praefector was talking more to the group now than to him. 'We really are going to be getting well acquainted tonight. *Thirty* lashes.'

Molchis stopped, but made no attempt to come back. What had started as a simple pissing match had grown into a full-blown battle of wills. With almost twenty of his cutthroat comrades from the *Flaminius* watching him, as well as the former legionaries who regarded him as little more than street trash, Molchis suddenly had as much to prove in that moment as Orbus did.

'You think whipping me into submission will work?' the criminal called out. 'I spent three years of my life in that arena. Three years, living when I should've bled out on the sands. I've had more beatings than you've killed Gauls.' He laughed, though quite tellingly no-one joined in.

'Oh,' Orbus gently relieved him of his confusion. 'You're getting your thirty, Molchis, regardless of what you do now. You don't speak to your officer like that. But if you don't get back up here and pick up that cleaver...' His smile was a little less genuine now. 'Then every man here is on barley rations for a month, and latrine duty for two weeks.'

The other men gently bridled in their lines. Orbus' words had the exact desired effect. No physical power could make Molchis do what he wanted, so instead he'd aimed for his one sore spot – his popularity. Orbus knew the sort of man he was dealing with. In the social underworld, renown and reputation were the only currencies worth spending.

Forcing the day's comrades to clean out the barracks' communal latrines, as well as putting them on food scarcely fit for the donkeys, would hardly come back to him in dividends.

Molchis sullenly picked up the dummy weapon, rejoining the others in their frustrated slashing.

'Which brings me on to what today's lesson was about!' the Praefector shouted at them. 'Have any of you had much luck, chopping your foes up like lumber?' He gestured to the lines of wooden posts, each one scored with lines and indents, but no weaker for it. 'You want to split your target in two? Take up your axe, paint your face blue and run screaming to the bogs of Germania.'

A few of them laughed, uncertainly. Molchis was most certainly not one of them.

'Fools and barbarians hack with a sword,' Orbus continued with a laugh. 'And to block an enemy's blade, that isn't a bad way to go. But to kill with a sword, nine times out of ten, you use the damn point.'

Ananke came loose from its sheath with an expert spin of his wrist, before he abruptly skewered Molchis' stake with a gleaming flash of silver.

For a moment nothing happened. Then a fracture line began to spread, and the whole thing came apart with a loud wet crack.

'You see?' Orbus sheathed his sword, grasping Molchis' hands with his own. Callouses and blisters galore, enough for a lifetime. 'You won't forget that now, will you?

THERE WERE THANKFULLY few cases like that in the weeks that followed. It usually came down to simple hijinks, rowdy men's spirits that needed toning down. Few punishments had been corporal, and fewer still as extreme as Molchis'.

In his case, Orbus had used a simple leather whip, rather than the multi-tailed *flagella* used for scourging. The former left a sting and mark, a simple deterrent against acting out again. The latter ruined whatever flesh it touched, and no man who took it was truly the same again. Mercifully, long postings on guard and latrine duty warned most *tirones* off before problems became that dire.

But then, big issues weren't necessarily the worry. Minor infractions, part and parcel of life in a Roman army on or off deployment, were what ate most of his time and effort. Beer, curfews, women in the billets… as the XII's camp prefect, he'd at least had the centurions' backing when he'd cracked down upon the men. These days, as the *auxilia*'s sole disciplinarian, Orbus enforced every rule and shouldered every morsel of ill will that followed.

Bydreth and Optatis had taken him aside one night, after an informal briefing over evening mess had devolved into a shouting match between the Praefector and his men, and Orbus had reluctantly agreed to a few concessions. He still refused to have ale shipments supplied straight to the *Principia*, and was loath to relax the training regime any more than he already had. But he had to give them something.

'Ungrateful sods,' Argias had scoffed at the very idea of concession. 'They don't know how well they have it.'

And he wasn't wrong. On deployment, leaping over the *fossa* ditch that marked the camp boundary was grounds for immediate dismissal. Climbing over the *castra* walls, or entering in any way other than passing beneath the gate-sentry's judgmental gaze, was courting the death penalty. Urbanus had always been a stickler for old Marian discipline. In *his* camps, the rules had been even more draconian.

In the end, Orbus had been forced to compromise. He'd shuffled around the regimen's more staggered shifts, resulting in the latest units finishing their drills a little earlier. He'd also wound the *Principia's* evening curfew back a notch, permitting a few men at a time to step outside on the occasional excursion into Rome.

And he knew full well what those trips involved. The local taverns and brothels had doubtless profited handsomely from a cohort of *tirones* springing up in their neighbourhood. But since none of those places had burned to the ground, and none of Orbus' men had wound up on a court docket or a slave galleon bound for the provinces, he was grudgingly inclined to let it continue.

Some of them were probably absconding from the *Principia* each night anyway. If Argias and Puli conducted a surprise sweep of the billeted quarters, evidence of drink and female company would doubtless be all too obvious. Sentry-watch was a long and punishing duty, one he'd been increasingly forced to dole out as a punishment, and Orbus doubted any man at the gates would feel particularly inclined to rag on his comrades.

And, to tell the truth, he'd thought a few times about summoning Merope to attend on him here in the *praetorium*. Only the thought of a *tiro* discovering him, and blasting him as a hypocrite, had persuaded him otherwise.

'Well, a compromise is a start,' Bydreth had assured him, when he'd made his feelings clear. 'My thanks, Praefector. I'll pass that onto them.'

Argias had raised an eyebrow at the man's familiarity, but Orbus had let it pass. On parchment – in the Praefector's dense sea of parchment, more accurately – the painted man was no more rank and file than the rest of his kinsmen, or any of the criminals, soldiers or gladiators he trained beside. But as with any organisation this size, it all came down to one issue above all. Hierarchy.

Optatis had lost his rank of *decanus*, along with everything else, when Marcus Quintilius had expelled him from the IX. Nothing set him above the other former legionaries, other than the memory of that role, and the respect he once commanded. The other legion exiles looked up to him, following that former lead. The reliance Orbus had started placing on him – for keeping the others in check, helping to lay the paper foundations of the cohort's infrastructure, and simply helping teach the others one end of a *gladius* from the other – had only crystallised that authority.

Things hadn't been quite so simple with the Ulthaini. Bydreth had struck them all, from the outset, as officer material, a fact that, if the Praefector's barrack-room observations were correct, would probably chafe at Brauda no end. And Brauda was, to his credit, a fairly passable contender. The man trained and fought well, and seemed respected enough by those around him. He clearly had a following, other *tirones* somehow magnetised by his gruff and caustic attitude to life.

But, as Orbus reflected one morning as he watched the men share a loud and boisterous morning mess, Brauda was never truly Brauda when Bydreth was around. While Brauda was respected, Bydreth was admired. The loyalty Brauda worked hard to cultivate was something Bydreth effortlessly commanded. Bydreth was an open book, where his cousin was closed to the casual reader.

They loved each other, there was no doubt about it, and together they were far more than the sum of their parts. Only Bydreth seemed to live and breathe that familial proximity, while Brauda seemed all too often diminished by it. All Orbus could do in the meantime was sit back, and see how things played out.

As far as the other *tirones* were concerned, the Praefector's speculation and patience had run equally dry. He resented Molchis and Fuscator's followers, as much as he'd tried not to. Few of them seemed particularly invested in his endgame, and he doubted any of them would have stuck around but for the money and roof above their heads. He was half expecting some of them to up sticks and abscond into the night as soon as they'd pocketed enough wages.

Maybe neither Molchis nor Fuscator would step up to the mark. With everything else on his plate, the Praefector simply couldn't bring himself to care.

Their gladiatorial companions had gone similarly unled, but again there was only one feasible candidate. More from the fear he put into people than any semblance of charisma, but leadership was leadership. Except Vinculex, from the day he'd arrived at the *Principia*, seemed no more interested in leadership than... well, anything. He trained when ordered to. Beyond those stretches, he took his own company. There wasn't much more you could say.

Eventually, Orbus had tried to tackle this *ennui* head on. Whatever malaise was eating away at the gladiator – spiritual, as well as physical – wouldn't be resolved by letting it fester. It was time to get things out in the open.

He'd summoned Vinculex to the square one Februarius dusk. With the drills and mess all done for the day, the only souls still up and about were the slaves going about their duties, gate-sentries beginning their onerous nightshift and a few unlucky *tirones* still scouring rust from their companions' gear. The courtyard was quiet, open to the fading evening air. The occasional sounds of a city nearing slumber washed through on a gentle breeze.

With hindsight, that had been a mistake. He'd planned this meeting with discretion in mind. But looking back, this lonely scene must have seemed all too similar to the gladiatorial arenas of Vinculex's past.

'What am I doing here, Praefector?' was his grunted greeting. He'd arrived first, propping up a wooden pillar by the colonnade.

'We're here to talk. Ostensibly.' Orbus slowly closed the distance between them across the courtyard. 'I've been watching you, these past weeks. You march when you're ordered to. Your bladework stands above any man here. And you've displayed endurance beyond any *tiro* I've trained in my career.'

The Gutter Prince didn't seem particularly moved by any of that.

'And yet,' the Praefector continued, 'you don't seem to care about being here. Like an inert piece of driftwood, buffeted on the tides. You waved a sword around for Brassus, and now you're doing the same for me.'

The gladiator took a few steps closer. 'What are you getting at, Orbus?'

'Do you respect me, Vinculex?'

'You're the Praefector. You're the man that pays my wage.'

'Not what I asked.'

Vinculex took a moment to think on that. Orbus could see how that cost him, right there. This difficult, uncertain conversation had kicked the gladiator's silent malady into life. The way his head and arms twitched, the ghost of a wince in his expression. Subtle. So very subtle. But very much there.

'I can't respect you,' he told the Praefector honestly, 'because I've never seen you fight.'

Orbus nodded. He'd had a feeling it would come to this. And so he'd come prepared.

'Very well,' he told him. And then he tossed the sword he'd brought with him across the space. Vinculex caught it easily, with one hand.

'I've had my fill of training blades, these past few weeks,' he snorted. 'I don't have any use for a blunted sword.'

'It isn't blunted,' Orbus informed him. He pulled *Ananke* free with a rasp of metal. 'Take off the sheath.'

Vinculex did so. The *gladius* revealed was a weapon fit for a *miles*, its ridges and point honed at the whetstone for killing.

'The others respect me because I'm better than them.' He spun the *gladius* in his grip, bringing it up to fighting stance. 'Time to show me that you are.'

Their dance began slowly enough. The two of them gently circled one another, trading a few blows, silver against steel, which rang and echoed around the empty courtyard. But there was little heart in them, for neither one of the combatants was a duellist. Orbus was a soldier, trained to stand in shield walls and break an enemy's charge. Vinculex was a gladiator, and his trade was slaughtering foes in the most spectacular way imaginable.

Neither discipline leant itself to flowery displays of swordsmanship. Getting too arty or creative with a *gladius* in either profession was the easiest way to die.

War, when you boiled it all down, was made from the same stuff. So, at least, old Paulinus used to say. Swordplay, siege work… whatever your first move, the opening salvo was never seriously going to cause your target hurt. All it did was test your opponent's defences, letting you know what kind of fight you were in for.

Orbus and Vinculex swung for each other, each blocking the other man's blows with every attack that followed. Only none of it was really meant to strike true. They were merely testing the waters, getting a feel for each other's fighting styles.

And then it truly began. One of them began to lay right in, and the other stepped up his defensive swings. Simply blocking wasn't going to cut it. Even if his blade came through the onslaught whole, he'd be forced right over into the dirt.

'On the back foot so quickly?' snarled Vinculex, though the taunt felt strangely empty.

'It takes two to dance,' Orbus laconically replied. 'And you lead so well.'

Their duel was only minutes old, but had already carried them far across the square. That, itself, was another basic swordsman's trick. Two fighters could plant their feet on solid ground and hack at each other's blind spots. Before long, one of them would simply gauge the holes in their opponent's guard and put a messy end to things. Moving across your space, never staying in one place too long, simply gave your attacker one more thing to think about other than skewering you.

'I wonder, Vinculex,' Orbus admitted as he feinted for the gladiator's neck, only to retreat and swat away the backswing, 'if you really are the equal of your reputation.'

'You've watched me fight,' the Gutter Prince growled back. He kept up the barrage of sword blows as he talked, a feat of considerable stamina. 'You've seen my tally. You know what I'm capable of.'

Their blades locked together once again, and this time they stayed there, as both fighters braced themselves against the deadlock. Then it was broken – Vinculex dropped his guard, shoulder-barging the Praefector hard enough to send him flying.

'Satisfied?' he hissed.

Orbus took a moment to rally, wiping blood from his nose on the scuff of his vambrace. 'Hardly.'

The gladiator came at him again, and this time, his attack was matched by another. Orbus gave up trying to batter down his guard, simply opting to strike at as many different targets as possible. Face. Crown. Neckline. Sternum. Vinculex's blade couldn't be everywhere at once.

'I'm sure you can beat any man in this fortress,' Orbus told him without lying. 'But can you beat them without hacking them into ribbons? You have power, *tiro*. But I need control, too.'

The Praefector's feint arced upward, hoping an overhead slash could catch Vinculex in another deadlock. No such luck. The Gutter Prince caught the falling blow before it could truly gather strength. He shed it with a simple swish of his *gladius*.

'*I've* never needed control, Orbus.' Sweat bathed his torso, his face twisted with pain as well as effort. 'Do you need control in war? Is there much call for beating your opponents, while leaving them whole?'

'Not much,' Orbus conceded. 'But I need *milites* who can control themselves, no matter their... afflictions.'

Vinculex's snarl was a thing of ursine frustration. He threw a short blow to the Praefector's sternum, fist vertical, little force behind it. It was still enough to throw Orbus back, winded, scrabbling to repel the next flurry of *gladius* strikes.

'You think it makes me weak?' he called to him. 'You think it makes me worse at what I do?'

It was biting now, well and proper. His heart had been racing for too long, too much toxic adrenaline roaring through his bloodstream. The Fire was burning now. Billowing.

Vinculex grabbed the Praefector's wrist as the two of them locked blades again. Orbus tried to shift away, but he wasn't fast enough. The Gutter Prince tried his damnedest to twist his forearm upwards, to armbar him and make him drop *Ananke*. Orbus fought him every inch of the way, but it was a battle he was slowly losing.

Vinculex roared, as the zenith of the Fire engulfed his entire body. Small wonder he hadn't woken half the *Principia* by now.

A headbutt was all it took to end it. Orbus was flung, once again, across the ground. He crashed to a halt, a picture of gritty chainmail and dried blood. *Ananke* lay in the dirt a little way off, close enough to grab. But not yet.

'Have you ever tried to focus, while your entire body is wracked with pain?' the gladiator spat at him. 'Let me tell you, *Praefector*... you get good at it.' A little dribble of saliva glistened at the corner of his mouth. 'When *no* gods-damned wound can match the pain inside you...' He trailed off, tossing the borrowed *gladius* aside. 'Then there's little that can put you in the ground.' His face and torso were flushed with red, and Orbus knew what he'd see if he looked a little closer. A sea of scarlet pinpricks beneath the skin. He could hardly guess how much pain the gladiator was in.

'And none of it matters,' Vinculex continued, returning to the here and now. 'Because I beat you.' He took another step closer, and kicked *Ananke* a little further out of reach for good measure.

'No, Orbus replied, straightening up a little, 'you did not.'

The Gutter Prince didn't react to that at once. His eyes narrowed as the Fire began to slowly subside, his silence inviting the Praefector to elaborate.

'Look how far we've come,' Orbus continued. He craned his head back to the square's centre, where scattered footprints were just about visible in the dirt. 'You died the moment we started to move, Vinculex.'

'What?'

'You aren't a gladiator anymore. You are going to be a *miles*. Soldiers stand in shield walls, protected by their comrades' spears and swords. The moment moved back across the space,' Orbus gestured behind them, sitting up, 'you would have been cut to pieces by the blades of your attackers.'

'That...' Vinculex was momentarily lost for words. 'That is moronic.'

'That is how the legions wage war.' Orbus stood firmly by his claim. 'Think back to your swordplay, *tiro*. Why do you think we train you to stab, instead of slash?'

Vinculex slowly and unwelcomely arrived at his conclusion.

'Because you can't slash with a sword when you're standing in a shield wall.'

Orbus picked himself up, retrieving *Ananke* from where it had fallen. 'I know you're good at what you do, Vinculex. But I need you now to be something more.' He wiped dirt from his armour as he sheathed his silver blade. 'That is what worries me.'

And with that, the Praefector had left him in the courtyard, contemplating the path that lay ahead.

TESTING TIMES, TO be sure.

Orbus couldn't recall the last time he'd been pushed so brutally off deployment. Keeping any camp ticking over and its *milites* in peak fighting condition was never easy, as any camp prefect would agree. But building that corps of men from scratch... that was a newfound nest of challenges.

It was enjoyable, in a way. To throw oneself into a calling that swallowed up your every waking moment. They were days of hardship, but they were also days of laughter, when Orbus could focus on nothing else but the struggle. In that struggle lay simplicity. Here, there was no disgrace. No familial legacy of failure. No rival officers, hungering for his downfall. Just the daily grinding task of holding his new cohort together, pushing them forward, and keeping them on the straight and narrow.

Argias unintentionally broke that spell one morning, leaning over Orbus' chaotically messy writing desk. Cascana's visits had become fewer and further between as the weeks passed, his unscheduled absences becoming increasingly hard to explain to Thracian.

In the First Spear's absence, the *optio* was the only soul who knew what Orbus was trying to distract himself from.

'An auxiliary prefect's work is never done,' he wryly observed. 'It's enough to make you forget about the wedding.'

X
BATTLE LINES

THE SUMMONS WAS always bound to arrive. Rome's was not a peaceful Empire, because it was a growing one. When you pushed, something always pushed back.

Cascana had been the one to drop the news, arriving at the *Principia* in a more hurried, less dignified fashion than was custom. He'd ridden through the streets on a legion horse, something he normally hated doing. But haste was needed, and he wouldn't trust this matter to a courier.

The Praefector was waiting for him in the fortress courtyard, where they'd all gathered three months before. Orbus and Arxander were sat under the portico, a small sheath of parchment between them that both were studiously ignoring. A group of twenty *tirones* filled the courtyard space; more precisely, two teams of ten. Argias and Fuscator led one team, a roughly equal mix of Molchis' street trash and Achaean veterans. Bydreth and Brauda faced them, alongside another eight of the Ulthaini. They battled for possession of the skull-sized leather ball, bouncing it on the gritty earth and attempting to intercept each other's passes.

Commonball, Orbus called it. A loose variant of *epikoinos* still commonly played in Greece, Aruxeia had taught it to Gaius and Sextus as children. Fortunately, Arxander's hoplites knew enough of the rules as well, and so Orbus had encouraged their gameplay to let off steam between drills. Most *milites* in the legions favoured the Italian game of *harpastum*, a rather more brutal variant that resulted in as many fractured bones and smashed teeth as scored points. But Orbus didn't trust his *tirones* with that sort of game, and had thankfully steered them away from it.

'Iulus,' the Praefector gently greeted him. 'All well?'

'It's happened, uncle.' Cascana still hadn't quite caught his breath back. His words barely carried above the sound of twenty sweaty men playing commonball, a fact that was just as well. 'The XII has received new marching orders. War council's in an hour.'

Orbus nodded his head slowly. So, the call to arms had finally happened. Considerably sooner than ideal, but later than he'd feared. Still, he ought to feel grateful there was need of him.

'Thank you, Cascana,' he finally replied. 'I suppose the holiday is over. Back to war we go.'

The commonball chose that moment to crash between them. It thankfully didn't hit either of their faces, but landed close enough to spill Orbus' water goblet.

'Foul!' he shouted, as Klaujan came up to retrieve the ball. 'Free play to Dorthoi, from the centre.' He tossed it over Klaujan's head, and the hoplite caught it with a bounce.

'Today, of all days…' Iulus murmured, shaking his head. 'I'm sorry, Orbus. The timing of this is sickening.'

Orbus waved the other man's concern away. He knew exactly what Cascana meant, but mulling over it wouldn't solve anything.

'What do we know?' he asked, once they'd retreated under the portico where they couldn't be overheard. One of Puli's slaves was scrubbing footprints off the stone. He didn't look up as the officers talked.

'It's Urbanus and Thracian chairing it,' Cascana replied, 'and all five centurions have been summoned.'

'The whole First Cohort?' Orbus raised an eyebrow. 'Must be serious.'

'Must be.' Cascana's uncertainty made him look a decade younger. Orbus hadn't seen that face in a while. Not since the court martial.

'What?' the Praefector asked him. 'What is it?'

'Nothing. Just rumours, about who it is we're fighting.' Cascana couldn't quite meet his eyes. 'Rumours that I hope are not true.'

FIVE OF THEM would go, it was decided. Any more would simply show him up against the other officers, but as a leader of *auxilia*, Orbus felt he needed some strength behind him.

This would be his first official appearance before the Fulminata. Word of his doings had surely filtered through to the XII by now, however discreet Cascana had been. Better to get the first round of mockery swiftly over, before they got down to business.

Argias was a natural choice, as *optio*. Each officer would have a part to play in the duties running up to the mustering, and for those officers' right-hand men, that meant legwork. Arxander too, as the Legion's command echelon was long used to dealing with Achaean faces. Optatis was making his way back from running errands in the *Forum*, and he'd add another touch of respectability to proceedings.

And the last member of his ragged entourage would be Brauda. Bydreth had also offered, but it wouldn't hurt to let Brauda feel he had his own voice. Bydreth had agreed without a fuss, promising to help keep the rest of the *tirones* in line in their absence.

Orbus wisely let him think this was why he was staying. He decided against telling him the truth; that Bydreth's ghastly teeth weren't quite the first impression he was looking to leave.

Urbanus had chosen the Theatre of Pompey to hold the council, a decision that hadn't done much for Cascana's apprehension. The First Spear had left ahead of them, to gather his command staff and make his own way.

'What's got him all riled?' Brauda asked as Cascana's horse had kicked away from the *Principia* gates.

Orbus looked at him for a moment, deciding how much he should say. 'Have you ever heard of Julius Caesar?' he asked him.

The Ulthaini warrior's facial tattoos contorted as he glared. 'I'm a savage, sir. Not an idiot.'

'The *curia* chamber, where the meeting will doubtless be held,' Orbus replied. 'That's where he was murdered.'

THE THEATRE LOOMED up ahead of them, though not especially ominously. A quaint avenue of cultivated gardenwork filled the courtyard, fountains whispering their sibilant songs as their water caught the afternoon sun. The sound of the city barely reached them here, something that put Orbus back in mind of the Gardens of Sallust. None of that surprised him. For a man who enjoyed his own voice so much, Urbanus had a surprising love of the quiet.

'Seems we're not the first ones here,' Optatis remarked as they walked down the avenue, to the covered complex lying beyond. The Praefector nodded – a number of wagons and equine mounts had been left to the tending of slaves at the courtyard's entrance.

'Come on.' Orbus was already setting off ahead of them. 'Whatever this is, it can't be good.'

THEY WEREN'T ENTIRELY the last to arrive, but were thankfully late enough to go largely unnoticed.

Little had changed in the Theatre's *curia* since the murder that had gilded it in infamy. In truth, Orbus was sorry to miss the chance to explore the wider complex, with its galleries of renowned art and sculpture. Still, the *curia* had a bleak majesty all on its own.

An immense granite table stretched from one chamber end to the other, a cloth of ostentatious imperial purple lain across it more fit for a banquet than a council of war. Men had gathered, milling around that central table in a loose group. Some sat at the table itself, pouring over what appeared to be a cartographer's hand-scrawled battlescape as well as other scattered parchment rolls. Others stood around it, studying proceedings from afar or quietly firing ideas off each other.

Cascana stooped over one part of the map, flanked by his *optio*, Hesperon. Manius Pylades and Marcus Scipio stood opposite him, poring over more handwritten intelligence, while Rufus Alvanus remained a little way off from Urbanus' seat at the table's head. The *triarii* centurion seemed unusually taciturn for once, content as yet not to share his thoughts.

It felt oddly reassuring, in a way. Last time Orbus had met with the centurions, they'd all been murderously focused on him. Today he'd arrived and had barely been noticed. That, at least, was one thing to be grateful for.

Thracian was, predictably, the last officer to arrive. The Fulminata's new camp prefect entered not long after Horatian Ardius made his appearance, and he'd brought the largest delegation of them all. Ten men had marched in with them, and Orbus recognised every single one of them as *evocati*. These veteran soldiers took up an at-ready position by the chamber's doors.

'Seems a tad unnecessary,' Argias muttered as they stood to attention. But by then, Thracian himself was stepping from his entourage and bearing down upon them.

'*Praefector!*' he called with deliciously artificial bonhomie. 'I had no idea you had been summoned here.'

Orbus hadn't, and they all damn well knew it. 'When war calls,' he replied through gritted teeth, 'I respond.' He briefly turned to the men around him.

'Allow me to introduce these men from the *auxilia*. Arxander, you doubtless know already. Here is Titus Argias, my *optio*, Gaius Civilius Optatis, one of my *decani*, and Brauda…'

'Brauda ap Uîth,' the Ulthaini briskly responded.

'Charmed.' Thracian barely batted an eyelid, reserving an imperious glance at the painted man before him. Orbus fancied his tanned features had filled out a fraction since their last encounter.

'We've all heard, of course.' Thracian aimed his saccharine smile of his at the five of them. 'Housing your ragged little thieves and wastrels in the XVII's old *principia?*' he tutted theatrically. 'I'm sure the Arcadians are turning in their graves, Sertor.'

He turned away at that, returning to the table with the other centurions.

'What a prickless little inbred,' Brauda grunted.

'I dare say I agree,' Optatis put in. He turned to look at Brauda. 'Ap Uîth?' he echoed.

Brauda's smile was so false it could have been a leer. 'In my homeland, orphans and boys with slain fathers are called *ap Uîth*.' Around them, the others all seemed to be taking their places.

'It means "from nothing",' he explained.

'I HAVE GATHERED you here,' the Legate calmly spoke down the table's length, 'to impress on you the severity of the threat befalling us.'

He briefly cast his gaze along each side of the stone table, taking in the officers and their subordinates staring back at him.

'Here, in this very *curia*, madmen and conspirators committed a foul murder that plunged our city into decades of civil war.' Urbanus' stoic stare barely moved as he spoke. 'And I have gathered you here, in this room, because our empire now stands upon that precipice once again.'

He let his collected centurions and prefects digest that in silence. How many of them had ever heard a war council begun in that way? They all had their bitter share of campaigns, but those were fought outwards, to expand the rule of Rome. Not to preserve its soul.

'I was called to an emergency meeting of the Senate,' Urbanus explained. 'We received a distressing report in the last few days, one which the Emperor himself had us verify as true.'

He met the eyes of each centurion, these officers he'd led and relied upon for so long. And then, as an afterthought, he spared a look at Orbus, his former Praefector's gaze impassively returning the favour.

'The XXV Legion,' he told them, 'has broken its *sacramentum*, and revoked its oaths of loyalty to the Empire.'

From across the table, Orbus watched Cascana slowly close his eyes. Clearly, his dark suspicions had just been vindicated.

He was scarcely able to process it himself. The XXV Legion was legendary. One of the first legions Augustus had personally raised after his victory at Actium, they had blazed a path of victories across the newborn Empire. Gaul, the Germanic outlands... even Parthia. Rich men's sons and honest plebeian boys fought tooth and nail for a chance to join the Ignipotens, as they were known, and the Legion rightfully had their pick of the hardiest or most distinguished youths to be their *tirones*.

'Who else knows?' Scipio asked the Legate. 'Is this common knowledge?'

'It is not.' Urbanus shook his head. 'We have been able to contain it, so far, to the Senate's uppermost echelon. The consuls, the praetors, and their own supporters. But I am not a fool. It will spread through the entire Senate house within days. I expect every patrician will hear the news within the week.'

'And what of their officers?' Thracian followed up. 'Were they overthrown? Do we even know if they're still alive?'

'Oh,' Urbanus gently assured him, 'we *know* they are alive. More's the pity, it would seem.'

Orbus made the leap before the others. 'Their commanders have led them into rebellion.'

'So we hear,' Urbanus nodded at him. 'Reports are understandably mercurial, but it would seem that Legate Ignatian has spat upon his oaths to Rome, and led the Ignipotens, in almost their entirety, into open rebellion. "The Army of the Free." That is how the former XXV has rechristened itself.'

Again, the silence. Legions turning on their senatorial taskmasters was not something that sat easily with any of them. It simply… didn't happen.

'They were given the Right of Settlement, weren't they?' Alvanus' question broke the quiet. 'If I remember rightly…'

'Indeed, they were.' Cascana confirmed it with a nod. 'Some of them, at any rate. The Legion's highest officers, and their foremost cohorts.'

Orbus had a vague recollection, too. This going some years back, but he'd picked up enough Imperial tattle in his time.

'You have the grasp of it, First Spear.' Urbanus told him. 'After their victory in Aquitania, there was talk of granting the legionaries land to retire from service. Gnaeus Ignatian sought to turn the final conquered city into a veteran colony for his *milites*.'

'Arx Agrippum,' Horatian Ardius put in. 'That was the name.'

Urbanus acknowledged that truth with a nod. 'That was the new name, at least. The city's former name escapes me. But the Emperor was reluctant to lose such a potent legion and general. Hypax and Vicinius were the consuls that year, and they urged him to adopt a compromise. Legate Ignatian and the bulk of the XXV were given the Right of Settlement, to rule this new city-state in the Emperor's name without disbanding his troops, or forfeiting his military *imperium*. That way they could be called upon to campaign again, if circumstance required.'

A harsh, braying chuckle cut across the table in answer to that. For his part, Orbus hid his own disquiet, which came from another place entirely. *Aquitania.* Not far from the borders of Narbonensis, where the Gauls' ambush had changed his life forever. So that was why he remembered it.

'Oh, blood of Teucer,' Alvanus scoffed. 'So that means we're marching against a fully supplied and regimented Roman *city*, and the remnants of a *legion* led by one of our best and brightest damn legates!' He took a moment to wipe spittle from his chin. 'How many legionaries can he call upon? Three thousand? Four?'

'It may not be so many,' Cascana tried to placate him. 'It wasn't the entire XXV that took the Right and settled there. Only a number of his eminent cohorts.

And think how many individual *milites* will have died, or taken their *veteranus* pension since then.'

'If he can spit in the Emperor's face,' Alvanus snorted, 'then he can probably find men to fill his ranks.'

Such informality had no place in a *curia*, but Urbanus dignified his centurion's concerns with a nod. Recrimination had its time and place, and this was neither.

'So what exactly are we dealing with here?' This from Pylades, sat a little way further down the table. 'A mad lunge for provincial power? A way for Ignatian to keep his relevance, as the Ignipotens' reputation gradually fades?' And then he dared to voice a darker prospect. 'A play for the throne?'

'It certainly stands to reason,' Urbanus conceded, though not immediately. 'Ignatian courts popularity, across the legions and the Senate house. He was always ambitious, as I remember him, but something like this...' He trailed off. 'Perhaps a legion is no longer enough to slake his appetite. Maybe only a city, or province, will do.'

'Or an Empire.' Thracian let that hang in the air. Orbus fancied the new Praefector seem to enjoy the silence that followed.

'Well, forget all that,' Alvanus blustered once again. 'How many men can we call upon? That's what matters.'

Urbanus coughed to clear the phlegm from his throat. For once, the old man seemed a tad... apprehensive.

'That is why I called this conclave so urgently,' he explained. 'High Tribune Verrinus has sent no word from Parthia, so we can only assume his three cohorts are still embattled against the sand-riders. And the other cohorts? Tyrian still commands the Third and Fourth, supporting the XXI Rapax in Numidia. Valens has another three bound for Germania Inferior. The rest remain under command of their respective *vexillarii*, and we haven't received word that any are ready for immediate redeployment.'

Urbanus didn't seem willing to elaborate any further. The reason for his hesitancy became unwelcomely apparent in moments.

'So this is all we have,' Marcus Scipio sounded even more sober than usual. 'Just us. Just one cohort of the XII, against Varus knows how many legionaries the traitor Ignatian can call upon. To say nothing of whatever levies and local forces he can muster from Arx Agrippum.'

'Can we not call upon any other legions returning to Rome?' Ardius asked. 'I'm sure many others would answer the muster, if we put the call out.'

Orbus was forced to admit he had a point. How many *legati* would jump at this chance to prove their loyalty to the Emperor? Or, for that matter, to launch their career over the broken back of a general as renowned as Gnaeus Ignatian?

'Many would,' Urbanus informed them. 'And, in truth, there are several campaigns ongoing where we could pull cohorts, or at least centuries, from where Legions are embattled, without risking the active fronts.' He drew in a gentle breath. 'But we will not.'

'But that is madness!' Pylades interjected. 'What gain could there possibly be from sending us in so undermanned?'

'The Emperor,' Thracian calmly explained, 'has expressed a desire for knowledge of Legate Ignatian's schism be kept among as few legions as possible. This is a problem that requires a surgical response, as opposed to a sledgehammer. We do not know what the traitor has offered his men. The last thing we want is this insurrection to spread across more than one legion.'

'But if the Senate will know soon enough anyway—' Cascana put in.

'Enough.' Urbanus' will was implacable. 'Our empire – the *heart* of our empire – has known peace since the Civil Wars ended, and I will not be the man to raise that hell again. Not until we have exhausted all alternatives. The Emperor has ordained it so, and we will obey.'

That, at least, Orbus could see the merit behind. Legions supported their legates, even after they laid down their military duties and exchanged their breastplates for togas. Swathes of the Roman military harkening for a change of leadership... that would only serve as a clarion call to any patrician fellow, with legion ties, who fancied himself on the throne. Even if it never came to bloodshed, simply courting the loyalty of any *milites* would automatically embolden their claim, and make any detractor think twice about challenging it.

Keeping the other legions in the dark, for now, was a shrewd decision. Regicide was a dangerous game to play. If the board really needed to be set, then keeping neutral pieces off its surface was the safer bet. Neutral pieces tended to move whichever way they scented blood.

'I have volunteered the XII,' Urbanus added. 'And our lord Augustus trusts in our steel and our loyalty. I will not see that trust go unfounded.' The first edge of iron crept into his voice. 'The First Cohort will muster against Arx Agrippum, and bring Gnaeus Ignatian to heel. And we will do so alone.'

Murmurs passed among the centurions and their hangers-on. Many of them were legion veterans, and had fought in far larger battles than this. But few had ever countenanced these stakes. Civil war was something new, that didn't exist beyond their grandfathers' fearful stories. None of them had ever expected to stand on that precipice again.

'Although,' Thracian wryly appended his legate, 'the XII won't be *entirely* unsupported.' His gaze travelled down the nape of the table, coming to rest on one veteran *miles*. Every centurion, *optio* and legionary in the room followed the glance, until the whole war council was focused on one man.

'Orbus,' Thracian addressed him. 'How many men can you muster from your new *auxilia*?'

'Almost two hundred, give or take,' the Praefector replied.

'And of those two hundred,' Urbanus pressed, 'how many of those are battle-ready?'

What a question. It was a truth self-evident, agreed by generations of centurions and *decani*, that it took at least six months to mould a man into a legionary. And that was a wildly conservative figure, that took little extraneous circumstance into account. Six months of marching, weapon drills, agility practise, and honing battlefield manoeuvres forged a soldier who could deploy to battle and not immediately die to a stray arrow or piece of flying debris.

But from there, months of tailored experience, understanding what it was to mete out death and watch it take your comrades, and the bitter realities of living on deployment in a world that hated you, were required to mould a shiny-armoured *hastatus* into a tempered, experienced warrior of Rome.

None of the *tirones* living on Orbus' dime were anywhere near that point. Some of them had lived hard, and many were well acquainted with spilling blood. But they weren't ready. They weren't an army. Not yet.

But to shy away now… To let this first opportunity to prove themselves pass? If Orbus couldn't muster the balls to fight beside the legion he'd disgraced, how would any other take his cadre of *auxilia* seriously?

'My men are ready for battle,' Orbus lied. 'And we will stand with you in the war against Arx Agrippum.'

None of the officers seem particularly moved by that avowal. Of course they weren't. Here they were, poised to march against a radically larger foe, and all they had to back them up were a couple of hundred extra spears, wielded by slaves and savages.

Urbanus' hand tightened its grasp on his end of the table, a subtle sign of his building fervour. 'Return to your men, all of you. The First Cohort will muster in two weeks at the Capena Gate, equipped for two months' march inland.' He looked out across the men he'd led for years, taking in their faces one last time. By the next campaign, not all of them might be here.

'May the gods be with us all.'

ORBUS JUST WANTED to be gone from here. The shock of what he'd heard – and what he'd agreed to do – was still searing its way into his heart. He just needed to return to his quarters, reach for that bottle of mead and—

'Orbus,' an all-too-familiar voice called from behind him. 'A moment, if you would be so kind.'

The Praefector stopped where he was, leading his four-man entourage through the antechamber before the Theatre's garden avenue. Thracian stood imperiously at the top of the marble steps. Some of the officers had already taken their leave, but others had remained behind to confer some more with Urbanus.

'What can I help you with, Praefector?' Orbus' tone could have turned water to ice.

'Oh, I just wanted to express my thanks to you in person.' Thracian's response was equally glacial. 'On behalf of the XII Fulminata, of how glad we are for some *outside* reinforcements.' He smiled a glass smile. 'I'm sure you and your...' His gaze coldly drifted over the men behind Orbus, Brauda in particular. 'Barbarians, will do their part for Rome.'

'Say that again?' Brauda took a threatening step closer, his eyes alight with something not particularly pleasant. 'I can't say I heard you, *sir*. Come a little closer and say it again.'

'Brauda...' Orbus subtly, oh-so-subtly, moved his hand to block the Ulthaini's forward step.

'Oh, don't bother restraining your boar,' Thracian chimed in. 'I don't know what Sertor here has told you, boy, but the *auxilia* exist for one thing and one thing only. To die, messily, for Rome, and to take the spearheads meant for legionary throats.' He clapped Orbus theatrically on the shoulder, and he wasn't gentle about it. 'For that, you're learning from the best. Good old Sertor Orbus, the saffron-livered coward who ran from the Gauls.'

Brauda looked ready to bite the new Praefector's head off, but Orbus thankfully got there first.

'I wouldn't want to keep you from your duties, Thracian,' he replied. 'A camp prefect on war's eve has much to do.'

Thracian cast one last, imperious glance over Orbus' followers, before abruptly turning and marching back up the stone stairs. His expansive retinue still milled around at the top, clearly listening to whatever more Urbanus had to say.

'Oh,' he called over his shoulder as he left. 'And best of luck for tonight, Sertor!'

Orbus was left to ruminate on that, that final dabbing of salt in an especially sensitive wound.

'What did he mean by that?' Argias asked.

The Praefector shook his head. 'Not a clue.' He turned to look at the others. 'Come on, all of you. Let's go home.'

XI
THE LEGATE AND THE BRIDE

CIVIL WAR BECKONED, for the first time in a generation. And depressingly enough, that wouldn't even be the worst part of Orbus' day.

The bell for afternoon mess rung out across the *Principia*, though he made no move from his desk to answer the summons. A full belly of food was the last thing on his mind, right now, and he had little desire to face the barrage of questions surely waiting for him.

Argias, in his professional zeal, wouldn't say a word about the council, not unless Orbus explicitly ordered otherwise. But the Praefector hadn't ordered silence from Brauda, Optatis and Arxander, simply because there was no real chance of it happening.

Bad news, as a general rule, travelled slower than good, but sensational news spread quickest of all. For all the Emperor's supposed attempts to conceal the XXV's rebellion, the Senate would come to find out. Which meant their followers and hangers-on would know, and in time so would *their* families, slaves, and friends across every alley, temple and bathhouse.

It would be halfway across Rome within days. Halting its spread through the *Principia* was a fool's hope.

Still, it would take time before other legions caught wind of it, the ones abroad on campaign at any rate. That, at least, was something.

Orbus slowly, gently, drained the goblet with his lips. He couldn't dare a second glass. He'd need a little liquid courage for tonight, but anything more than just the one would only end in disaster.

He idly nursed the empty goblet, his gaze on the well-woven and gilded tunic that hung from its dresser on the opposite wall.

It wasn't going to wear itself.

'O Jupiter on high,' the Praefector mumbled, slapping the goblet down angrily. 'O Penates, who guard my family's hearth... forgive me for what I am about to do.'

IT HADN'T BEEN a long engagement, or even a particularly normal one.

The first letter had arrived at the *Principia* one muggy, cloud-ridden morning. Cascana had thankfully intercepted the courier before Puli or the other slaves could get their paws on it, and was tactful enough to keep it to himself until he and Orbus were alone.

'Expensive parchment,' he noted, dropping it on the *praetorium* desk. 'And look at the sigil on that seal. That's from the brothers Lemnon. About Aemilia, presumably.'

Orbus hadn't responded, pretending to be rapt with whatever official document was in his hands.

'Uncle,' the Centurion tried to prompt him. Orbus had finally looked up with a noncommittal grunt, pulling the message a little closer.

'It's a written *sponsalia*,' the Centurion guessed. 'It has to be.'

Weeks later, when Cascana had stopped by the fortress again to check in on training, he couldn't help but notice that same letter, considerably more dog-eared, seal still unbroken, buried under a pile of cargo manifests from local sword and armour smithies.

As well as three other letters, identical in gilt and wrapping but considerably newer. Also unopened.

'I've tried,' Argias remarked from his own smaller desk, by way of explanation. 'He won't hear it.' The First Spear was thankful for Argias' attention. He was the only other soul in the *auxilia* who knew about this.

'Where is the Praefector now?' Cascana eyed Orbus' empty seat, without satisfaction.

'If you're here to talk about the wedding,' the *optio* replied with a touch of exasperation, 'then he's doubtless on the longest camp drill in the history of the army, as far away from here as is possible in a day's march.'

Cascana bit back the urge to swear. 'Blood of... *someone* needs to talk to him, Titus. If this marriage doesn't happen, Uncle's head is going to roll.' He gesticulated around the room with one arm. 'The Volscani girl's dowry is what's paying for all this!'

Argias knew that was true. The day after Orbus' ill-fated Garden meeting with Legate Urbanus – when the Praefector had managed to down a month's supply of Iceni mead in one evening, and Cascana had had to calm him down and sneak him out of the Fulminata's barracks – he'd gone with Orbus and Argias to the great *Aerarium*, the public treasury housed in the Temple of Saturn off the Capitoline Hill.

Once Orbus had made it known he was marrying the heiress to the Volscani fortune, securing funding for the cohort had been insultingly easy. A line of credit had been opened, with little more than Orbus' remaining savings from Baiae as security for the money. *Auxilia*, as he'd discovered, was a very loaded term among the city's financial glitterati, and the *Aerarium*'s prefects were happy to picture a sea of foreign faces ready to die for Rome.

And just like that, the Praefector now had a steady and none too shabby sum of *sesterces* each month, to spend on feeding his *tirones*, repairing and replenishing their armour and blades, and keeping the *Principia* warm and running.

Such bounty had a double edge, however. A guardian could spend his ward's gold with impunity, a husband even more so. But Aemilia's long-dead father had been shrewd. A patrician to his core, and a titan of the lawcourts, he'd had his daughter's fortune throttled and constricted by ironclad laws of probate.

Death or divorce of either spouse would default the inheritance back where it came from – into the pockets of the brothers Lemnon, presumably.

Orbus would have to stay the course, or pay back every last *denarius* he'd spent on his men. After all, it wasn't a wedding that Urbanus was demanding of him. It was a marriage.

Cascana himself had put it most bluntly, on their return trip from the *Aerarium*.

'They're not asking you to love her,' he told him. 'They're asking you to marry her. You're a soldier, anyway. And you have Merope. If it pays for all this… will being married to that girl really change anything for you?'

beautiful in a stately, cultivated sort of way. And she was clearly an entitled brat, too, from the pout in her eyes.

Young, nubile and deluded. Quite her long-dead father's little princess, no doubt.

'Are you for me?' Her mood seemed to brighten a touch, only for Cascana to dash her tentative hopes a moment later.

'Not I, it pains me to say.' He laid a gentle hand on his companion's shoulder. 'May I present to you my comrade and friend, Gaius Sertor Orbus.'

The Praefector swallowed his distaste, forcing himself to fake gentle humility.

'It is good to finally meet you,' Orbus lied. 'But no-one calls me Gaius. You do me much honour, lady.'

'Aemilia of the Volscani,' she replied. 'And the honour is mine.' She held out a pronated hand for him to kiss, only for Orbus to tenderly clasp it with both of his.

Cascana subtly winced at this bungled etiquette, but said nothing. In all honesty, Aemilia didn't seem unhappy with her prospective husband, but Orbus was not a fool. This heiress had clearly expected to marry while considerably far younger, to someone far older.

'Well, then.' This from the *libripens* by the altar, calling them all to attention. 'I do believe we are ready to begin.'

THE CEREMONY BREEZED by mercifully quickly, although to the spectators in the atrium outside it surely dragged on for hours. The reek of cloying incense filled Orbus' nostrils, as the priest's gentle droning chants washed over his ears. After some time the two become one, a single soft melange filling the senses. None of it particularly set him at ease.

The five pairs of eyes on his back weren't entirely welcome either, but after a while they became forgettable. It was far from his most pressing concern right now.

Orbus stood before the *libripens* at Venus' altar, Aemilia Volscania beside him. The young woman gave him a momentary sideways glance, a look that was surprisingly amenable, before her focus returned to the rites.

She *was* a beautiful woman, if he was fair about it. His thoughts drifted, once more, to that morning spent teasing Publius about his betrothal on the Field of Mars. Was this how he'd felt?

Only Publius and Falvia, against all odds, had come to truly love each other, first with youthful passion and then with mellow wistfulness. From that love had sprung young Iulus here, and their *familia* had been one the Praefector had envied as much as he'd felt a part of.

Part of him wondered what Caesula would have made of this, and the precocious young maiden stepping up to take her place.

The *libripens* ended his weary sermonising, slowly lifting up his burnished weighing scales. Orbus felt the men behind him quieten further down, rapt in anticipation. Here they all were at last.

The Praefector reached into the pocket of his exquisite chiton, fishing out two faded golden rings and placing them in the scales' sacramental dish. The opposite dish was already full, holding some incense and a broach that had presumably belonged to

Aemilia's family. The old priest balanced the dishes, weighing each offering up.

Symbolism was everything. A *coemptio* was, as legend had it, the purchasing of a wife, and here the *libripens* indulged the pantomime, playing the part of a cattle market merchant weighing up the amount of money to be spent.

And then he nodded, satisfied.

'*Sponde?*' he abruptly asked, breaking the silence without ceremony.

Deucalios Lemnon smiled, nodding his assent.

'*Spondemus.*' His happy avowal filled the air. *We give in marriage.*

'Good.' The *libripens* lowered the scales, letting his lungs fill with incense. 'Then all we have left are the formalities.'

Orbus and Aemilia turned to each other in the same moment, knowing what was to come. The way he saw it, if he was to sup from this venomous chalice, then he might as well drain it to the bottom.

'Indeed,' he told the priest. 'Formalities.'

And with that, he clasped Aemilia's face in his hands, and kissed her for long enough to seem willing.

DAY HAD FALLEN to dusk as the wedding procession began. The crowd of Aemilia's supplicant well-wishers provided enough of a column, and Cascana and his fellow officers were soon lost in the gently marching throng.

Thankfully, the brothers Lemnon hadn't put them through the full rigours of matrimonial ritual. Orbus didn't have enough guests with him to re-enact Romulus' seizing of the Sabine women, and Aemilia had no mother or father to feign protecting her.

Perhaps the brothers had recognised the groom's reluctance in the weeks leading up to today, and were sensitive enough not to press the issue. In the end, they'd settled for Orbus gently pulling the scarlet veil from Aemilia's head, tying a woollen *cingulum* around her hips in a lover's knot.

The two of them now slowly led the procession, a little way ahead. Further spectators had appeared on either side of the street, stopping to cheer and applaud the column's steady progress. And that wasn't all. Before long, Orbus was wiping lentil shavings and nutmeg from his brow as their cheerful onlookers began to throw nuts, rice, and other organic confetti that signified fertility.

Aemilia actually laughed as she picked out grains from her hair, the first expression of honest pleasure Orbus had heard from her.

'This lot…' He looked out at the random well-wishers on each side. 'Are they all here for you?'

His new wife laughed some more, nodding and smiling thanks as some scattered flower petals billowed down into her face. 'Well, I don't think they're here for you.'

Orbus let that pass. He caught himself looking back at the column a few times, catching occasional glances of Cascana but no-one else he knew. Somewhere in that throng a distaff was being carried, as well as a spindle and yarn. Tradition, tradition. Always tradition.

Their destination wasn't particularly close, but Orbus' unwillingness to reach the end made the journey seem briefer. The procession eventually veered away from its onlookers, onto a quiet street beneath the Viminal dotted with modest yet respectable dwellings.

It was a true homecoming, for Orbus as well as for Aemilia. He hadn't been back here since... since before Gaul.

The procession came to a steady halt outside the house. It was truly nightfall now, and only the torches in the crowd's hands lit the way ahead. Deucalios and Teucris Lemnon had found themselves at the head of the column, turning to look at Orbus with surprisingly kind eyes. Or maybe that was delight, at sealing this little deal of theirs so smoothly.

'You do us great honour, Gaius Sertor Orbus,' Deucalios assured him. 'We could not ask for a finer son-in-law.'

That was a rather coloured view of events, but Orbus tactfully kept his silence. A darkly surreal thought occurred to him, as he watched the *libripens* move to stand before the lintel of the door. Urbanus must have known the war with the XXV was coming, for some time before the council. Was that why he'd thrown Orbus to the wolves like this? Knowing there was a good chance he wouldn't survive the coming fight – that none of them might – it was a rather bleak investment. Having a soon-to-be-slain officer married to some spoilt heiress for a month or so before the end, in exchange for her wealthy guardians furnishing the Legion with siege engines for years afterwards.

'And now, the time comes.' The priest tore Orbus' focus down to earth again. 'The threshold awaits, my groomsman. All now is down to you.'

Orbus drew in a breath, looking at Aemilia. The sooner this was over, the better.

The Praefector briefly rolled his shoulders, and swept the young woman off her feet. For what it was worth, Aemilia had the good grace to wilt in his arms.

'*Quando tu Gaius, ego Gaia,*' she told him, loud enough for the others to hear and start applauding. The ancient bridal salute, custom for as long as Rome had stood. *Wherever you are lord, I am lady.*

And for the second time in his life, Orbus carried a bride over the threshold of his home.

TRADITION DICTATED THAT the festivities didn't end there. A feast of grand proportions normally followed, with the cutting of an immense *mustaceum* and the sharing of its sweetened pastry among the guests. A night of wistful music and drinking then ensued, although in truth Orbus had few enough friends to hold a *repotia* for.

At any rate, Aemilia's uncles weren't fools. They knew they were pressing for a great deal already, and doubtless didn't want to rub the reality in any further. So their procession had delivered husband and wife to the door of Orbus' town house before dispersing and leaving them be.

And here, he awkwardly reflected, they finally were. Alone on the night of their wedding.

Thankfully, they'd gotten the first disappointment out the way before long. Aemilia had promptly run her finger over the carved stone walls, as they'd stopped to pay respect to the household gods. She flicked dust from the small fane with a disgusted sneer.

'You clearly aren't hard enough on your slaves,' she fussed. 'How often are you even here?' She was still wearing her formal *tunica recta*, and in truth it was a real designer's piece. Only now it was sullied with dirt from the procession, and the cobwebs on the floor weren't helping.

Orbus softly laughed, still hovering at a loss in the middle of the first-storey hallway. Merope had never been a houseslave, and Puli was far too busy at the *Principia* these days to be sent here.

'It... has been some time, actually.' And it had. He'd lived here with Caesula, for a while, before he'd been forced to relocate her back to Baiae. Since then, this house had long ceased to feel homely, and it had become easier to let his praefector's duties consume him, living day and night at the XII's own fortress. Or more recently, the XVII's.

'So if this isn't your home,' Aemilia asked, idly peeking through doorways to see what lay beyond them, 'why are we here?' Someone had at least been round earlier in the day to light some torches, and here upstairs there was a little city light from the windows. Argias, maybe. Or one of Cascana's men.

'I don't think I could have brought you to the barracks.' That may have sounded wry, but it was the absolute truth. The thought of this heiress sharing a roof with men like Molchis or Fuscator made his gut itch.

'No?' Aemilia seemed to find that frightfully funny. 'I suppose it wouldn't be particularly proper.' Whatever her flaws, she wasn't as uptight as Orbus had feared. *And how would I even know*, he thought ruefully. *I barely know this woman... and here I am married to her.*

'I thought soldiers weren't allowed to get married, anyway.' She was un-weaving her tied and manicured hair now, letting some of the blonde mass fall down to her shoulders. A bride's hair was traditionally parted and tied around a spearhead – another cultural touch that went back to the Sabines – and this, Aemilia now tenderly removed from her nest of locks. The rest of her hair came down in that moment, as she drew her hands through it a few times to shake it loose.

'We're not, as a general rule,' Orbus replied, trying to keep the conversation airy. He wasn't sure what she was expecting tonight, or, for that matter, what he was. 'Some *milites* do anyway, without telling their officers. Sometimes they are prosecuted for it. Other times, the officers in charge don't care enough, or at least don't pursue the scandal and attention that would follow.'

He walked a little further inside, finding himself in one of the night chambers built for guests. 'For officers, it is a little different. Some only join the legions after they marry, or are betrothed. And some are expected to, depending on their families.' He couldn't quite keep the bitterness from his voice. 'Money has a funny way of talking.'

He sat down on the corner of the bed, acutely aware that Aemilia didn't seem much interested in what he was saying.

'Are you listening to me?' he tried to feign annoyance.

'I'm sorry.' She couldn't help but giggle some more. 'It's just… the way you talk.'

Orbus blinked, uncertainly. 'The way I talk?'

'Your accent.' She tried her best to regain some sincerity. 'You sound like someone scraped you off the Suburan pavement. All stern and stoic, like the whole world's been built to stand against you.'

'And have you heard many men with this accent?' Orbus asked her back. 'How many plebeians do you know, and how many of them are soldiers?'

Aemilia held his gaze for a moment before conceding. 'Fair point.'

'I suppose that comes with the territory.' The Praefector lay himself down on the bed, his back propped up against the headpiece. 'Families like yours. You assume everyone beneath your station is nursing some secret sadness at their own thankless lot.' He snorted, more playful than serious. 'How very soulful of you.'

The girl's reply was halted by a sound from the street outside. A dog barking, somewhere out around one of the tenement blocks. Or maybe a wolf.

Orbus caught Aemilia's gaze in that moment – uncertain, dangerously close to fearful, beneath her delicately precocious mask.

'Not the sort of neighbourhood you're used to, I take it?'

It was her turn to snort, as she came to sit right where he'd been. 'My uncles have a country villa, a few miles up the Tiber,' she told him. 'It has its own private water supply, underfloor vents for every room, and separate dwelling quarters for each one of us to live in, completely undisturbed by our slaves and the outside world.' The thought of that quaint little retreat made her sigh, as if she'd remembered something she shouldn't have. 'Free from it. It might as well be detached from it.'

The Praefector said nothing. Maybe there were more to this spoilt little brat than initially met the eye.

A father or guardian could legally sequester their daughters indoors, to whatever extent they deemed fit.

That could be a lonely existence, depending on the daughter. And Achaeans, he ruefully reflected, had their own attitudes to women.

'Did you want this?' he gently asked her, sitting upright once again.

That actually made her laugh. 'What a question,' she replied, shuffling up closer. 'My uncles are... kind. They treat me as their own blood. But old men don't adopt young women without reason. I've no father, no brothers... what would I ever do in this world if I stayed unmarried?'

Orbus wasn't quite convinced. 'With your private means,' he drily reflected, 'I suspect you could do anything you wanted. In fact, I imagine many young women would yearn to have your lot.'

'Anything,' Aemilia petulantly replied, 'that my dear uncles allow. Does that answer your question, *husband?* No girl ever wants to marry at their family's behest, believe me. But I'm not deluded enough to think I ever had a choice. I knew my uncles would try to find me a man I could take to.' She looked the Praefector up and down.

'It could be worse, I suppose.' She smiled at that, a little rueful, a little mischievous.

Orbus digested that backhanded compliment in silence. Women of the patrician class were a strange breed; in his experience, they tended to act radically different with no fathers or husbands to police them. At least with Falvia, he'd known her long enough to feel like family.

'So go on, then.' Aemilia seemed to move past her earlier wistfulness. As Alvanus was fond of remarking on the subject of tricky women, her shield wall was well and truly up. 'Tell me, Sertor Orbus. Did you really want to be married to me?'

There was little point in lying, and she'd probably see through it anyway. 'No,' he told her, gently but unkindly.

'Well,' she replied, suddenly petulant again. He'd probably been a little too blunt. 'At least in *that*, dear husband, we stand united.' She shifted up from the bed, walking to the oil lamps by the doorway and gently snuffling them out. Did she want to go to bed? After all this?

'So why you, then?' She turned back to look at him. 'What drew my uncles to your name?'

Orbus began to chuckle. 'Nothing at all. It was my legate's idea, as a way to punish me for defying him. And because he seeks to court your uncles, to design war machines for the Legion.'

Aemilia took a moment to make sure she'd heard right, seemingly dumbstruck.

'To... punish you?' She drew her *tunica*'s sash across her chest, folding her arms. '*You* think that? That *you're* the one being punished tonight?'

Orbus was, all things considered, a little rusty at dealing with the fairer sex. This was probably why he completely missed the rising danger in his wife's tone.

'What else would you call it?' He raised an eyebrow, expecting Aemilia to join him on his hill of laconic self-pity.

'You...' The young heiress was choked with indignation. 'You... *man.*'

'Is that the blackest curse you have for me?' Orbus quipped. That, too, was a mistake.

'You think *you* are being punished here?' Aemilia cried. 'You're a soldier! You'll be off all year on your bloody wars, you iron-headed plebe! How will this affect *your* life in any way? Oh…' She cocked her head in mock-resignation. 'Oh, I do apologise. I suppose there's the burden of how you'll spend my inheritance, eh? I suppose that is a mighty weight upon your shoulders.'

'Now look here…' the Praefector began, but the floodgates were open now.

'And what about *me?*' the woman shrieked. 'You think being carried over your threshold is *freeing* me? All I'm doing is passing my yoke from one vile old man to another… till death do us part, after all! Or more likely, till your ghastly little offspring rips me open from the inside and—'

'*Enough!*' Orbus slammed his fist down on the bedside plinth, hard enough to shake it. That seemed to get through to her. She stopped with her semi-tearful tirade, wondering perhaps if she'd touched some nerve.

'You think this is easy for me?' Orbus snarled. 'I've been married before, Aemilia.' He felt his voice catching in his throat, a sign of weakness that he'd never bring himself to share. 'Did you ever stop to consider that? Or are you still lost in your petulant princess's tale of woe?'

'Well, it's good to know I'm in company!' she retorted. 'You should have sent her my way. I could have taken notes on how to fade away within four walls, while my brute of a husband sails off to slaughter savages and fuck camp wenches!'

And with that, she stormed out of the bedroom, finally succumbing to her histrionics.

Orbus stayed where he was, on the bed. At least that particular part of the night's obligations was off the cards.

'Blood of Teucer...' he swore. What a day it had been.

He rose, leaving the bedchamber and walking down the stairs. Whichever room Aemilia had fled to, he couldn't care less.

A few steps later, he was out in the open air of Rome. The ambience of the city at night was that much closer out here, and the mix of barking urban strays, smashing bottles and dolorous drunken braying felt as homely to Orbus as any *principia*.

And then he was off, melting into the streets, headed in the vague direction of Merope's apartment.

XII
DELIVERANCE

THE MOOD IN the *Principia,* a fortnight later, was hard to define. Evening mess tasted better after a hard day's training, and the ale and wine certainly helped. That didn't happen often beneath Orbus' roof, so the *auxilia* enjoyed it while they could. There was enough going around to make them raucous, if not troublesome.

But those *tirones* with some self-awareness fancied they saw this for what it was.

A valediction.

Achaean hoplites jostled shoulders with gladiators, Ulthaini circus-slaves and Carcer inmates, tearing into their meat and bread. Jars of pickled fish and olive oil were cracked open for the last time in many months.

For tomorrow they marched. The *auxilia* would muster alongside Urbanus' five centuries of the XII, for the long march to Aquitania. Arx Agrippum waited, at the end of months of gruelling travel.

For all they knew, this could be the last thing they ever did together. That cast a certain pall over the merriment.

Argias and Optatis made their way down a lonely corridor, the echoing cheers and jeers from the mess hall still in earshot. They weren't hurrying. An unwelcome duty lay at their journey's end, and a particularly unpleasant conversation. But then, the cohort mustered tomorrow. There might never be another chance.

'He won't hear it from us.' Those were Brauda's words, when he'd taken the pair of them aside to ask this of them. 'It has to come from you two.'

Optatis hadn't been comfortable with the suggestion. In the ranks of an actual legion, this was military treason, plain and simple. But desperation had driven them to this place. He'd already lost his place in the IX, anyway. How much further could a man fall?

'I don't know, Brau...' Bydreth had responded at the time. 'Is it really our place to say?'

'*My* place, you mean?' Brauda snapped back with surprising vehemence. 'Stay out of this, Byd. You weren't at the council.'

Bydreth had shot him a disparaging look, but silently relented. How sadly commonplace, this friction between them had become.

'He does have a point, my friend.' Optatis tried his best to sound conciliatory. 'We *were* there. Our opinion will ring truer.'

'Aye,' Brauda had growled. 'And the muster's tomorrow. We can't take our sweet time about this.'

And so the former *decanus* of the IX found himself approaching the *praetorium* with Argias in tow, the two men appointed to have this difficult talk with their commander. While the others drank and stuffed their faces, the two legionaries steeled themselves for what was coming. All their lives could well be riding on this.

Orbus was exactly where he'd said he'd be, something neither surprising nor welcome. Wedged behind his writing desk, goblet in hand, he was still wearing his praefector's gear and uniform. How long had he been here? When had he even last left the *praetorium*?

'Praefector,' Argias began in his clipped yet officious tone. 'We're sorry to disturb you, sir, it's just that—'

'We wanted to talk to you.' Optatis was a touch firmer. 'About the war council.'

Orbus started to chuckle without irony. That was when they realised he'd been drinking. Not necessarily drunk, but certainly onto his second or third goblet. The telling odour of old British mead had become depressingly familiar to them all over the last week, with the Praefector turning to the bottle as an increasingly frequent crutch.

His desk looked surprisingly tidy today, with all its papers in apparent good order. Meaning Orbus had probably not even started dealing with any of it, preferring to ruminate in semi-drunken solitude.

'What a day that was,' Orbus gently slurred. Argias and Optatis looked at him uncertainly across the desk. 'I can picture it now. Our two hundred eager children with sticks and swords, against this insurmountably superior foe… truly, this will go down in the annals of the Fulminata.' He smiled indulgently at his own wit. 'Strain your ears, boys. Out to the Appian Way. You hear that noise? That is Gaius Marius himself, spinning in his own funerary urn.'

In that light, the Praefector's drunken wallowing was perhaps forgivable. Neither man really knew how to respond to that.

'Mark my words, men.' Orbus concluded his self-pitying ramble. 'If we follow the XII to Arx Agrippum, and stand against Ignatian and his rebels... we are all going to die.'

And here, they came to the heart of it. This was exactly what they'd come to talk about.

Orbus wasn't alone in that belief, and enough men beneath his command felt strongly enough to voice that fear. Brauda had outright told him so, asking Optatis and Argias to intercede.

Did the others lean the same way? Vinculex? Did he and his men particularly care about another day dancing with death? And what of Arxander? Or Molchis and Fuscator?

Still. The Ulthaini counted for a lot of sway, as did the former legionaries under Optatis' influence. And whichever way Bydreth leant, plenty of other men would surely follow.

Argias and Optatis shared a momentary look. Here they were, then. Now or never.

'Of course,' Orbus idly cut their building courage short, 'if you think the council was bad...' He snorted, reliving the memory. 'What about what came after?'

THE ATMOSPHERE INSIDE *the great command tent is stiflingly opulent. Torches and oil lamps ring the gathering, kept fed by an army of slaves and helots. In one corner girls play lutes and lyres, while more carry and pour* amphorae *of wine into* kylix *cups in the Greek style. In a general legionary mess, this would probably lead to bawdy chaos, with the smartest slave girls letting the* milites *have their rugged way with them.*

Here, tonight, in this exclusive symposium for the officers, it merely makes them feel cultured.

The Praefector lounges back on his couch, trying to enjoy the wine that is not mead. None of the other officers around him seem to mind. Maybe their tastes are simply more acquired.

No men stand guard around the borders of the tent. Out here, at dusk, on the Field of Mars, there is little that can feasibly worry or challenge them.

In Urbanus' absence, Thracian is holding court above the cohort's centurions and their trusted men. Dinner couches ring the former First Spear's in loosely concentric rings, naturally pulling all eyes onto him. Orbus' couch is nearer the back than the front, and away from those of the Fulminata – nothing less for a legion exile, the scarcely-tolerated ghost at the feast. This does not bother him one jot. This symposium is an extension of the war council, nothing more. Here, at the back, he can get away with finishing his dinner and drowning his sorrows, without having to mingle tediously with his fellows.

In the Legate's absence, Thracian believes himself the emergent face of the XII Legion. In reality, Urbanus cares little for day-to-day matters, content to leave his legionaries' ongoing training to the officers beneath him.

'Where is he?' a familiar voice suddenly snarls. 'Where is that treacherous bastard?'

Horatian Ardius storms into the tent, brow creased and eyes full of fire. He is out of armour, still wearing a centurion's basic panoply – the practical, stripped down style of uniform worn on deployment or the training ground. More eyes, however, are on the man behind Ardius. The ratty, beady-eyed little man he has dragged along with him.

Fuscator.

The music-slaves have stopped their lutes and lyres. The officers, optios *and veterans abruptly cease their yammering, their attention drifting over to this brewing confrontation. Even Thracian seems a little affronted.*

'Whatever is the matter, Horatian?' he coolly asks.

Ardius hurls Fuscator, one-handed, to the ground. Slaves cry out, scattering from his wrath. The hastati *centurion cares little for commemorative feasts and celebrations, so no-one had expected him to show his face tonight. But here he is, billowing with a temper Orbus can scarcely remember witnessing before.*

'This inbred little stray from the auxilia,' *he spits. 'My men caught him at the nearest tavern. He just stuck a knife in two of my boys!'*

The entire gathering takes a collective breath. Eyes not fixated on Thracian have now turned to face the other praefector.

'Are you... sure of this?' Orbus neutrally replies.

'S— am I sure?' Ardius looks ready to tear him in two. 'Typical, coming from you. Once an oathbreaker, always an oathbreaker,' he growls, striding menacingly closer to Orbus' couch. 'Can't you control those rabid dogs of yours? Or are you enough of a mongrel to put him up to this?'

A hairpin could be heard dropping in the silence that follows. On the floor, Fuscator slowly straightens where he has fallen, not daring to pick himself upright. He gazes at the officers around him, his face pleading for mercy, his eyes somehow still full of bile.

'I think,' Orbus begins, 'that we should talk this through in private.'

OPTATIS COULD SCARCELY believe his commander's words.

'Varus' *corpse*,' Argias swore. 'And it was Fuscator? There wasn't any doubt?'

'I wish there had been.' Orbus drew a hand through his greasy hair. 'They found the bloody *pugio* on his person, not twenty strides from the bodies. Some of our men were out drinking with the *hastati*, during the symposium. Ale was flowing. They were playing cards, gambling for high stakes.' He snorted. 'However the hands were dealt, our friend from the Carcer must not have liked the end result.'

'I know the man's a felon,' Optatis conceded. 'And he's certainly brazen... but this?'

'He was a ganger and a murderer,' Orbus reasoned, 'even before he went into the Carcer. I don't even know why I'm surprised. Him, Molchis, all those sewer-rats who walk in his shadow... if anything, I'm surprised it's taken this long for them to cause a headache like this.'

He took another long swig of his mead, seemingly content not to delve any deeper.

'Ardius would never let something like that go,' Argias prompted him.

'No,' the Praefector replied. 'He would not.'

'I WANT HIS head!'

Ardius paces back and forth across the grassy ground, moving like a starved panther on the sands of the Circus Maximus. *'That lapdog is dead. No arguments. Though frankly, deserter,* your *head would be the more fitting forfeit.'*

Orbus *chooses not to rise to that, more from lacking a particularly suitable rejoinder than any self-control.*

'I'm sure,' Cascana sardonically intervenes, 'that we can settle this without coming to that.'

The three of them have taken their grievance outside, in the growing night of the Field of Mars and out of sight and earshot of their contemporaries. Fuscator awaits, a little way off from them, the spears of two of Ardius' hastati *resting at his throat. They have taken him alive and relatively uninjured, something that Orbus and Cascana could scarcely believe at first. A testament to the martial discipline their centurion prizes so dearly.*

'If it is restitution you want,' Orbus maintains, 'then you are welcome to the vagabond's head, right here. If that satisfies your principles, and wipes the stain from your personal honour, then so be it. I am truly sorry for what has happened. Fuscator is a liability, and while I do not have an excess of men to lose before Arx Agrippum, I am happy to wash my hands of him. Fuscator is clearly the sole guilty party in this sorry episode, so have him. Take your blood price from him, and let's be done with it.'

The night is dark and deep, and what little light emanates from the far-off tent barely catches the Centurion's face.

'You think this is about honour? My honour?' Ardius looks angrier than Orbus has seen him in years. 'I'll tell you what this is about. This is about my milites, *and their wellbeing. They are* my *charges.*

Every single one of those sorry little shits is my *responsibility. They are under my protection. That is the first responsibility of an officer, Orbus. To protect his men.'*

Memories of Gaul flood back behind the Praefector's eyes, memories of his beloved legionaries hacked to ribbons as he'd fled, weaponless, into the smoke and shadows. He cannot fault the other man's priorities.

This is a side of Ardius he's never seen before. The brutal, demanding taskmaster of the cohort's hastati *century, who brutalises and subjugates the Legion's newest recruits as he trains them… finding this fiercely protective man beneath that merciless façade is a surprise, to say the least.*

It doesn't change the facts, though.

'If you're expecting me to throw my neck upon the chopping board… over this*? One regrettable moment of blood, between a non-citizen and a file legionary? I'm afraid I must disappoint you, Horatian.'*

At his side, Cascana winces, and the other two see it just fine. Orbus' words are ill-chosen.

'That is Centurion Ardius *to you, deserter. And are you really so without shame? Without any semblance of accountability? Or did you leave that behind in the Gallic woods as well?'* He *contemptuously shakes his head. 'The first principle of leadership, Sertor Orbus. Have you really forgotten what that is? That a fish rots from the head down.'*

'Not necessarily,' Cascana interjects. 'That is a lazy leap of logic. Do you really think the Praefector would sanction something like that?' He slowly *squares up to Ardius, drawing level with Orbus' shoulders. 'I don't want to have to order you,*

he still had his wits. He could read between the lines of what Optatis was suggesting.

So *this* was what they'd come to talk about. Others in the cohort felt strongly enough to send spokesmen on their behalf... and these two, as well. Not Bydreth and Brauda, their more vocal and popular counterparts. Optatis and Argias, two Romans, two articulate legion men who supposedly had their praefector's ear.

Orbus inwardly swore, holding Optatis' gaze. This had implications.

'You know,' he started pouring himself some more mead. 'After the council, I honestly thought this was the Legate's intention all along. That the last *caliga* had finally dropped.' Another glugging sup of drink. 'He must have known this war was coming. Half the Senate must have known. An Empire does not fracture overnight.' He smiled without mirth. 'So here we come at last. Now his axe can finally fall, and my sentence be completed by an enemy's sword. I believed, in my naivety, that this could be my atonement. I was wrong. It is simply the last of my dues.'

'The men are not ready,' Argias pressed. 'They are not legionaries. Not yet.'

'The men are as ready as I can make them,' was Orbus' retort. 'I have done all I can for them. You know how this works, First Legionary. Training will only take us so far. We need battle, *real* gods' honest battle, to temper them. To whittle out the chaff.'

'It still isn't too late,' Optatis continued. 'The men will only march upon your say so. One word from you, and this entire cohort will down arms and refuse the muster.'

The Praefector smiled, not unkindly this time. 'No, my friend. It isn't that simple. I gave Urbanus my word we would stand with him.'

'Then withdraw it.' Argias seemed to have recovered his voice. 'The Legate cannot make us follow him.'

'He cannot,' Orbus gently agreed, buoying the *optio*'s hopes... 'but he will not have to. Because I do not intend to go back on my word.'

Neither of the others said anything.

'I broke faith with Urbanus once before,' he quietly confessed. 'And it cost me everything. And now, whatever shreds of honour I have remaining to me... I will not make that mistake again.'

'With the greatest possible respect,' Optatis replied, 'I don't think the men in this *principia* care about your personal honour. They care about surviving this war.'

'That is not their choice to make.' The Praefector didn't seem particularly moved. 'They knew what they were agreeing to, when I offered it. You all did. Men die in war, Optatis.' He almost wanted to snigger. Maybe that was the mead talking. 'What did you think would happen here? You've been under this roof for long enough, man. You know I'm not this sentimental.'

Argias cleared his throat. One last try.

'It is not just our lives on the line,' the *optio* tried his best. 'It is yours, Praefector. To invest all this time, coin and effort into us... do you really wish to see it wasted so soon?'

Orbus' eyes had lost their light. Maybe it was the drink. Maybe not. 'I am dead already,' he admitted. 'I have been dead for months. Since Gaul.'

He went back to his goblet once again, and the others sensed that the window of receptiveness had closed. They had tried. For whatever it was worth.

'I want all the men drawn up in ranks tomorrow,' Orbus announced, apropos of nothing. 'In the courtyard, an hour after sunrise. Make it happen, both of you.'

He didn't see their faces harden as he drank. The die had been cast, for good or ill.

'Dismissed,' he slurred, draining the last of the goblet.

Optatis had the grace to leave quickly. Argias was a little more hesitant, hovering in the doorway, watching the man he'd pledged his life to get gradually more drunk.

'The *Principia* had a visitor, yesterday,' he noted. 'It was your wife, Praefector.'

That got his attention. Orbus' gaze flicked up to where his *optio* was standing.

'She needn't have bothered,' he snorted, pulling up an opened letter from his writing table. 'Her uncles have been on the case to me already. Apparently, I'm spending too much of her precious dowry on feeding you sorry bastards, and cladding you in armour.'

Argias shook his head. 'That wasn't why she came, sir. She hasn't seen you since your wedding night. She wanted to make sure you were alright.'

Orbus shook his head, showing just what he thought of that... and reached to pour himself another goblet.

'She was worried about you, sir.' Argias wouldn't be ignored. 'She cares enough about you to be concerned.'

Orbus looked at him archly. Whatever point the *optio* was trying to make, his acid glare dared him to go about it.

'Change is a terrifying thing, Praefector. There are no two ways about it. But you don't have to just give up. You can embrace it.'

Sertor Orbus, in his prime, had been a man who commanded easy confidences. A leader of men, with allies and comrades at every turn. People who believed in him. People he could trust.

How he'd fallen since then. To this damp, dark corner of a fortress of ghosts, sharing shadows with the grimiest and most benighted specimens of man. Men he could scarcely bring himself to care about, who felt just the same about him.

As it happened, his talent for driving away his devoted few was one thing he'd yet to lose.

'Get out my sight, Argias.'

'LOOKING VERY THOUGHTFUL there,' a familiar voice chided him.

Brauda screwed his face up, putting down his stoned bread. He hadn't retreated out here, to the courtyard, because he wanted company. And yet here it came anyway.

'Steady on,' Bydreth added, lightly. He moved to playfully slap him on the shoulder, but instead ran a brotherly hand through Brauda's thinning mane.

Only he didn't, as his cousin pulled away.

'Something I said?' Bydreth raised an eyebrow. Night had fallen, and the courtyard's solitary torch was the only light to see by. Orbus was still in the *praetorium*, locked in discussion with Optatis and Argias. The others were still having their fill of evening mess. Out here, in the dark, the two Ulthaini had a little privacy.

'The others are right,' Brauda finally replied. 'About talking to Orbus. You didn't have to undermine me like that.'

Bydreth bit back a sigh. 'I didn't *undermine* you, cousin. I just think you should trust him a little more. You, and the others.' He took a proffered piece of bread from Brauda, chewing it thoughtfully as he looked up at the stars. The view out here certainly wasn't bad.

'You find it so easy, don't you?' Brauda quipped after a few moments. 'You just surrender to the journey. You never worry about the destination.'

'I'm sorry?' Bydreth was bemused by that, but they both heard the edge of challenge in his tone. 'Is that what you think?'

'I do. That such a surprise?' Brauda's tone rose to match his cousin's. 'I guess it might be. How many times have we talked, in the last few months? We've trained and trained and trained, thrown together with all these other freaks and strays, but how many times since winter have we *actually* talked?'

Bydreth stopped. Here it finally was.

'So, this is what's riled you these past months?' the painted prince growled. 'That we've got more playmates in our circus tent, and now you've got more people to share me with?'

'No,' Brauda smiled, not hiding his ire. 'The fact that you're happy to just fall into this life, without thinking through the consequences. *Legionaries*,' he pressed. 'Orbus wants us to be *legionaries*, cousin. Just think about that. We're not soldiers! We're Ulthaini. And then this man swans in – whose past we know nothing about, who still won't tell us why he left his legion – and seduces us with a shady manumission into doing his bidding!'

'Cousin…' Bydreth began.

'Don't *cousin* me!' Brauda sneered with bared teeth. 'Maybe if *I* had a tongue of silver, I could charm the rest of our troupe into liking me, or to stop asking questions about what comes next.' He was snarling now, his blood well and truly up. 'I was *there*, Bydreth. I was at that council. We're going to be marched into a slaughterhouse, *cousin*, and no-one will bat an eyelid over our corpses! Not Orbus. Not that copper-arsed legate of his.'

The two Ulthaini looked at each other as Brauda's rage evaporated, mutual disdain written plain across their faces. Bydreth was the one to break the silence, clapping a condescending hand on his kinsman's shoulder.

'You know, I thought for a moment you really had something important you needed to share.' Now it was his turn to sneer. 'But just listen to yourself, *cousin*. You're whining like an infant, shorn from his mother's teat.' He let go, shaking his head. 'It doesn't suit you.'

Brauda opened his mouth to speak, but Bydreth wasn't done.

'*We are Ulthaini*, you always say. How often have I heard you bleat that since we arrived? Puff yourself up on that legacy. If that's what gives you strength, I won't knock you for it. But you can't be so boneheaded. We *are not Ulthaini* anymore. We lost that years back, when the slavers took us. We are… we are who we are now. I'm sorry, cousin. But you can't let that past hold you back. It doesn't exist anymore.'

A droplet of rain tickled his brow, a droplet of a droplet. It wasn't a guarantee of rain to come, but Bydreth wasn't optimistic. They were due some summer rain, if Optatis was to be believed.

'We were who we were,' Bydreth continued. 'And we are who we are now. We've committed to the Praefector, and we have to own that commitment.'

Brauda couldn't speak for a moment. He'd never heard his cousin talk like this before.

'And you really don't think you've surrendered to the journey?' was all he could manage.

'Life is change, Brauda.' Bydreth wouldn't be swayed. 'And Fortuna is a fickle partner. If you can't take her hand, the dance will leave you behind.'

The younger tribesman idly tossed his bread away. He'd never had Bydreth's way with words. Never when it mattered.

'*Fortuna*,' he echoed. 'You sound like a bloody Roman now. Being Ulthaini,' Brauda maintained, 'is something more than flesh and blood. More than the colours on our skin.' The fading blue and crimson of his ancestral ink was still visible through his scarlet army tunic. 'It's a bond of kinship. Does that mean so little to you? They *took* us from that world, and put us in theirs. Forget the semantics, Byd… does that past not matter to you anymore? It is the only piece of us we have left.'

Somewhere, out in the dark, a bird called out. Both cousins tried not to see it as an omen.

'Of course it matters to me, Brau.' For a moment, their mutual bitterness was forgotten. A tenderness had replaced it, something each man knew the other felt for them. 'But it isn't all I am. And it doesn't gatekeep what I can be.' He looked Brauda right in the eye. 'Change, cousin. Not the most comforting word there is, but what else have we got?'

Brauda snorted. 'That still sounds like hindsight to me. You believe those things because of where we are, not the other way round.'

And just like that, the moment was lost. Tenderness turned to flint in Bydreth's soul, as he tried not to rise to Brauda's childish provocation.

'You pledged your agreement to Orbus, just as I did. He was hardly opaque about what he offered. What were you expecting *auxilia* service to be? Basking in the sun's rays while other men did the fighting for you? And yet, for the last three months you've lived beneath his roof, taking his coin. If you want to leave, I can't stop you. But what work can you see yourself getting that doesn't kill you faster?' He shook his head in amusement. 'A little late to go back on your word, kinsman.'

'*Shynnach shar!*' Brauda cursed. '*We* didn't agree anything, Bydreth. *You* agreed, and just expected me to follow. Like you always damn well do!' Small miracle he hadn't stirred the whole *principia* with his shouting.

'Do you really believe in Orbus?' he continued. 'You should have been at that damned war council. The way the others talk about him, the men in the Legion…' He trailed off, anger giving way to cynicism. 'You have more faith in him than I do, Byd.'

'I trust him, cousin, if that's what you mean.' He wouldn't be drawn into Brauda's gossip. 'And Orbus trusts me. And you know what? Argias trusts me too.

And Optatis. And Cascana. Even that mewling dog Molchis.' He raised a dirty eyebrow. 'Do you think those things are unrelated?'

Brauda turned away from him, looking back into the fortress. 'I remember you used to trust me.'

HE WAS STILL drinking sometime later when he started seeing things.

How much mead had he had? Now, his vision swimming, pores perspiring, he fancied he saw someone he knew. A thin, sparely built figure, wearing a saffron gown that hugged her body and hips.

'No, Sertor. You are not imagining things,' Merope assured him. 'I am standing here.'

Orbus snuffed air through his nose. Had he spoken out loud?

'You should think about easing off on the mead,' the courtesan continued. 'I can smell it on you from here.'

Privately, Orbus thought that was a fair assessment. Still, he felt his maudlin mood threaten to lighten, and didn't try to fight it.

'I...' he began. How hard it was, to bare his soul before his faithful few. 'I am glad you're here, Merope.' And that was the gods' honest truth, however hard he found admitting it. 'It's been one hell of a day,' he wistfully added, reaching for her waist.

Only for her to swat his hands away, eyes full of delicate scorn.

For his part, drunken shock was written plain across Orbus' face. The shock was twofold; he was too arrogant to bank on such reticence from Merope, of all people. And no slaveowner would ever countenance their property denying them anything – even anything as small, or great, as human contact. Consent to touch didn't exist between slaves and masters, and Orbus owned Merope for nothing else.

'That is what you said to me, master, the last time I saw you.' That openness about her, that tender receptiveness, was all gone now. 'And that is what I came to talk to you about.'

Orbus took a step backward, gently leaning against his writing desk. He was glad for its presence, as his legs were feeling a little wobbly.

'How did you even get in here?' he asked. 'The gates are always under watch.'

'It might help more if those men on watch were sober,' the courtesan replied, dragging a lock of chestnut hair back from her face. 'I don't know what sort of revel you've got going on, master, but your men certainly seem to be enjoying it.'

Something in Merope's demeanour stopped him from laughing. 'I'm clearly not making guard duty punishing enough,' he half-joked.

He reached for the goblet behind him, ignoring the woman's judgemental gaze as he did so. It was thankfully full.

A part of Orbus had known this moment was coming. A larger part of him had assumed – had hoped, if he was being truthful – that it wouldn't arrive before they left for Arx Agrippum, an unwelcome boil to be lanced on his return. *If* he returned.

'How do you think it made me feel, master?' Merope didn't waste any words or time. 'You left me without a word, before you returned to Baiae, after

organisation. Maniples, centuries and ultimately entire cohorts of *milites* were built up from each tent-party or *contubernium*, men who would fight, eat and ultimately sleep together in the shared tents of the temporary camps.

In an ideal world, each '*bernium* had two non-combatants to carry kit and tend their needs, but Orbus hardly had men to spare. Squabbles to lead these new units as *decani* had been fierce, if a little petty, and after much deliberation with Bydreth and Optatis, both Praefector and *optio* were largely content with each *decanus* who'd been chosen.

'Today is the day, *tirones*,' Orbus called out. 'As we speak, the XII Legion's First Cohort is mustering upon the Field of Mars. We will join them, and from there we will march for two months to the city of Arx Agrippum, to make war upon Gnaeus Ignatian and his Army of the Free.'

His words washed over the gathered men in uneasy silence. They had tried their best to dissuade him from this cause of action, and they had failed. He knew it as well as they did.

'But we have some formalities to observe before then,' he continued. 'We may not be a legion, not at least as Rome sees it, but I told you the first time we gathered that I intended us to work like one. And I stand by that promise now.'

No-one said anything, because no-one knew what to say.

'From this moment, you have all completed your training,' Orbus announced. 'You are no longer *tirones* anymore. You are now *milites*, and I consider you all to have earned that name.' He paused, letting that sink in, before offering an accompanying riposte.

'Training is hard, but the life of a *miles* is harder. This cohort will suffer many fatalities in the battles to come. War is hell. It will take many of you, and the ones left behind will be changed. Coming to terms with that change is what makes you a *miles*.'

He took a breath, feeling two hundred pairs of eyes on him. 'Bydreth. Vinculex. Optatis. Arxander. Molchis. Step forward, all of you.'

The named men did as he bid, still holding their military poise. Orbus found himself smiling, as Argias handed him a small woollen sack.

'Some of you may recognise these,' he announced, pulling the thin wooden objects out and holding them up for all to see. Every man knew a vine stick when they saw one, for so many of them had had a lash or beating from one during their training. But they were more than just tools of discipline.

'This,' he continued, 'is the symbol of office for a centurion in the legions, just as surely as the crest upon his helm. And while we may not be a legion...' He trailed off with a half-smile. 'I will have centurions in my cohort.'

He walked down the first rank of men, where the five champions were standing. And with no more ceremony than that, he began pressing vine sticks into each of their disbelieving hands.

'This is more than symbolism,' Orbus went on. 'Because like it or not, each of you leads the men you arrived at my gates with. You represent the best, and worst, of your companions. And a centurion, no matter where he hails from, leads a century.'

He turned to Optatis, the former *decanus* running disbelieving fingers over his new staff of office.

'Your men, my IX Legion friend,' he told him. 'From this moment forth, shall be known as the Branded.'

That was irony, of a kind, for no shortage of Optatis' men did indeed bear brands for cowardice or escaping the decimation.

'And yours, Bydreth,' Orbus continued as he handed him the vine, 'shall be the Painted.'

The Ulthaini prince accepted it with a smirk. Clearly, that choice of name had gone down well. Brauda noticeably didn't share his cousin's mirth. Nor did he seem particularly pleased with Bydreth's sudden promotion.

'Arxander!' the Praefector called as he reached the next man in the line. The Achaean warrior took his new wooden trinket without fuss. 'As you once served beside the Fulminata, you honour me with your service now. You shall be the Riven.'

Arxander snapped a crisp salute, fist against sternum. The Praefector had expected nothing less.

Orbus reached Vinculex next, the former gladiator at the head of his respective '*bernia.*

'What in Erebus would I need that for?' the Gutter Prince muttered. 'If I want to beat one of mine I'll use my damn fists.'

Orbus' hand remained outstretched. 'Just take it,' he sighed. 'And as you're so keen to keep hold of your roots,' he added for the others to hear, 'your century shall be the Brazen.'

He walked away before any of them could protest, bearing down upon the final array of men.

'Molchis,' he greeted the ganger coldly, sparing a particularly venomous glance at Fuscator a few '*bernia* away. The murdering bastard had somehow wound up as a *decanus*, something that Argias and Bydreth had both objected to when they'd heard. But Orbus had reluctantly signed off on it, knowing the reprobate was too damn popular with his friends. And saddling him with responsibility would hopefully douse his capacity for mischief.

'Your men,' the Praefector abruptly thrust the vine stick into his hands, 'will be the Creedless.'

That got some sniggers from Arxander's and Optatis' men, but Orbus' cold glare stopped them dead.

'Take heart in those names,' he called out, walking back down the frontmost rank. Two hundred gazes followed him as he moved. 'These centuries you belong to now… they will be your family. You obey your centurion's commands as you would obey mine, as you would follow the gods-damned Emperor himself. Your centurions can honour or discipline you, with every ounce of authority I have. But on the other side of that coin…' He smiled bitterly. 'Your Centurion is accountable for everything you do. Every triumph, and every failure. That shit all lands on your *caligae*, my friends.'

'So, what does that exactly mean?' Bydreth asked. 'Do we get *optios* then, and all that rubbish?'

'Entirely up to you, Centurion.' Orbus didn't seem bothered. 'They are your men. Run them as you see fit.'

A few of the troops had begun to laugh, mixing among themselves. For a moment, they seemed to forget the terrifying odds they would be walking into.

'Enough,' he crankily shouted. 'It's not just me you answer to now. Centurions, draw up your '*bernia* to march and reconvene on the Field of Mars. We will rendezvous with Legate Urbanus, Praefector Thracian and their five centuries of the XII there, in full battle panoply.'

'There is also the matter of equipment,' Argias added his voice to Orbus'. 'As you may know, it is against the laws for Roman legionaries to bear arms within the city, past the *pomerium*'s sacred boundary. Our weapons and armour are being conveyed by carriage to the Field as we speak. We will don our wargear and prepare for full armoured march alongside our allies in the Fulminata.'

More Volscani money down the sinkhole, Orbus thought ruefully. Or, more precisely, down the expense ledger. The thought of Deucalios Lemnon firing off another letter of expletives almost made him smirk.

'That will be all, *milites*,' he formally gave them notice. 'Dismissed.'

He tried not to meet their gazes as they filed on out past him. This image – of all his charges, united, marching out to face the world as one – was not something he wanted in his mind's eye.

For all he knew, it could be different faces next time.

PART III
TIROCINIUM

BLOOD AND IRON

'SHE ISN'T A *bad girl, from what I hear,*' Cascana tells him, softening. *'Her name's Falvia. From the Rutuli.*'

Orbus whistles low. He has heard of that family, even before he began the training.

'Maybe not,' he replies. *'But that isn't really the point, is it? She'll never be what Caesula was.*'

Cascana looks at him with Caesula's face. And speaks with Aemilia's voice.

'How could you say that to me?'

Orbus is dumbstruck, frozen with fear. *'Publius?*' he stammers.

And Cascana screams *at him, his wrath like molten lava.*

'NO!' ORBUS BOLTED awake, his loved ones' screams fading from his ears.

For a moment, he was helpless. His eyes saw black, his nose full of the odour of unwashed men.

'You're alright,' a hoarse yet familiar voice growled into his ear. Bydreth. The Praefector reared himself upright from where he'd been sleeping on the ground. Men stole respite while their comrades kept watch, tending their gear. Sometimes for moments, sometimes for hours. As much, out here in no man's land, as they could take.

Orbus swallowed, pulse gradually dying down. He always got like this while sleeping on deployment, even back in camp. Shallow sleep was an unwelcome shadow. You couldn't rest deeply in enemy territory, in a land that wanted to kill you. It was like living with a *pugio* pressed into your backbone.

They'd taken a forest clearing for the night. Several of the others – Painted, all of them, from Bydreth's two most trusted *'bernia* – were similarly stirring from rest, waking to another day of being hunted. They had clustered together, like sleeping wolves, to take up less space and protect each other better. Anything different was a needless risk, and Orbus and Bydreth wouldn't take needless risks.

He rose, wiping away sleep with dirty fingers. Not a lot came away so he couldn't have been out for long. Three or four hours at most. His weariness confirmed that guess. The sky had just a touch of light to it, so it was either dawn, or dusk. He couldn't remember which.

Fighting and travelling through the night, stealing sleep irrespective of the shining sun above them, made the days lose their arbitrary boundaries.

'Time?' Orbus called out through a dry throat. He splashed a few drops of water onto his face and tongue, all that was left from his stoppered jar. If nothing else, he relished the coolness on his face, taking away the taste of long-dried sweat.

'Half an hour till sunrise,' Drygg's young voice answered him. 'On the fifth day.' Drygg alone of them seemed able to keep his sense of time, something the others had come to rely on.

'Blood of Teucer,' the Praefector muttered, dusting grass and pine shavings off his tunic and *lorica*. Five days? It felt like twice as long.

Still, it hardly mattered. They were late back to the *castra* anyway, and had missed their expected rendezvous by quite some margin. 'And how long since last contact?'

'Can't have been more than a day,' Bydreth muttered, slapping himself awake even as he yawned. He jerked his head at Drygg, too tired to even point. 'He'll know.'

Orbus waved that response away. 'Doesn't matter. It's been long enough. I say it's time to move again.'

'Aye, Praefector.' The Centurion of the Painted sniffed the air as he nodded. 'I was getting tired of the scenery.' Twigs snapped, withered greenery was crushed by *caligae* and a few birds were disturbed from their treetop perches as the *milites* readied themselves to move out.

Around the clearing, the curling knots of tree trunk stretched out into the forest, casting inviting shadows through the thickets. Beyond that, great conifers gave way to more open grassland, and gentle hills reminiscent of Greater Campania.

In the open, even if the enemy picked them out at once, they could get a good way upcountry before breaking into cover once again. The foe's greater numbers would count for nothing in the dense lattice of trees, and Orbus' little band had reconnoitred his ground already.

'You really think we've shaken them off?' Brauda asked from a little way off. He clutched his *optio*'s staff as he helped the others pack up for the march. Orbus had to suppress a smile – even now, months since they'd set off from Rome, he could still hear the ghost of a challenge in the Ulthaini's tone.

'We'll never know for sure,' the Praefector replied, tossing Bydreth his travel sack. 'But it's been a week, my friend. Near abouts. There's too few of us to be worth chasing for much longer.'

'And if you're wrong?' Brauda replied.

Orbus grinned as he buckled on his helmet. 'Then it's time to earn your keep, *optio*. I'm not paying you for your brooding good looks.'

ONCE THE FULMINATA and their accompanying *auxilia* had dug their foothold into Aquitanian territory, a rather unwelcome truth had become evident.

Gnaeus Ignatian's occupation of Arx Agrippum was not, in fact, an occupation. He hadn't simply holed himself up in the city's highest tower, using his legionaries to keep brutal order on the streets.

Ignatian had led the XXV Legion into revolt, and the entirety of Arx Agrippum had gleefully followed him.

Ending his treacherous reign would take a bloody fight at best. Or a long, punishing siege at worst.

Bringing the rebellious legate to battle wasn't proving a simple task, either. The Army of the Free had numbers on their side, so a pitched battle was out of the question. Attacking Arx Agrippum head-on would only lead to a long, protracted fight, even with the siege engines such an assault would demand.

It hardly mattered, anyway, because until now the legionaries of the former Ignipotens had yet to appear on the field of battle.

'Bastards are holding back,' Alvanus had grumbled one morning as his *triarii* returned, dejected, from yet another aborted sally. 'They won't face us head-on. Just let us cut our teeth on the levy, and waste our mettle on them.'

The levy. The bastard levy.

Calling upon a city's worth of resources and volunteers had a way of prolonging a war. The menfolk of Arx Agrippum, given weapons, shields and training that were all equally rudimentary, had proved surprisingly effective in large enough numbers, deploying in crude formations and maniples.

Against a full legion, it would have hardly been an issue. But one depleted cohort and a band of untested *auxilia* could only spread themselves so far. Anything else would only provoke the Army of the Free to attack in force – which could actually help, as it might well have ended the war faster. But without a solid plan to even the odds, such an attack would only end one way.

No legionaries of the Ignipotens had even shown themselves so far, and why would they? Their comrades in the levy could take the brunt of the XII's anger, breaking like the intentionally brittle anvil that they were, while gradually bleeding them from a thousand cuts. From there, the bruised Fulminata would be easy prey for Ignatian's true soldiers to hunt down and slaughter.

Urbanus had been largely content to delegate the war's prosecution to Cascana and Thracian. The *Legatus* oversaw preparations, chaired the increasingly fraught war councils and ran the central *castra* in a fashion so draconian that it made their previous campaigns feel breezy in comparison.

'I have no easy salve for our problems, men,' he reluctantly confessed to the centurions one evening in the cramped command tent. 'The enemy possess the advantages of numbers and home ground. Even with the hourglass running dry, overextending ourselves will only lead us to disaster.'

And so this grinding, tedious stalemate had crawled on. The XII struck out into the Aquitanian countryside, daring how close they could come to Arx Agrippum before the city's levy hit back in force.

Their attempts to break that deadlock had only raised the pitch of battle, and brought pressure down on all their heads.

And it had brought Orbus to this point, living off the land like a dog, trying to keep his men a step ahead of danger.

'WELL, THIS LOOKS promising,' Bydreth had remarked as they scrambled towards apparent safety.

They had forded the river at the glade's edge, the forest now far behind them. From there, they'd crested the hill's gentle slope, emerging out onto a flatter heath further up above. Ordinarily, this wouldn't have been safe, not with the possibility of pursuit. But they'd set a good pace, and all those weighted marching drills from Orbus and Optatis had clearly paid off.

'Always the optimist,' Orbus gently chided his centurion as the *'bernia* crossed the heath, coming to another lighter wooded area. 'You really think we've lost our pursuers?'

He had a point. *Auxilia* usually got the dirtier jobs wherever a legion set foot, and this campaign was no exception. While the XII played their game of cat and mouse with Arx Agrippum, Orbus' men hunted down and broke key centres of resource throughout the surrounding countryside. An inglorious role, to be sure, if an important one. Storehouses and granaries were torched. Horse-borne convoys were set upon. Wells were collapsed with rubble.

Bands of the citizen levy still roamed the countryside, and Orbus' men, even marching as one, were far too few to stand and fight them. As it happened, neither side seemed willing to muster in large numbers anyway. Orbus divided his new soldiers into bands, following their objectives with their own noses, and that was that.

Some struck gold, finding and crippling the enemy supply lines. Others came up short, retreating back to the *castra* empty-handed.

And some, like Orbus and Bydreth's group today, were caught out in the open by roving levy. The lie of the land could hide them, going to ground until they were safe enough to break for their own lines.

Safe, or merely desperate.

The band following them now had numbered almost forty men, at last count, and the Praefector was daring to think that their days on the run had paid off. But if the enemy didn't get them, at this rate, thirst and starvation would.

'I've no wish to tempt the Fates,' Bydreth murmured from the column's other side, 'but we rarely make it this far unmolested.' Bydreth's hand unconsciously drifted to the small *signaculum* hanging from his neck, and Orbus noted some other Painted do the same with their own corpse-markers; yet another superstitious touch he'd allowed to spread through the cohort. Another echo of the legions they sought to emulate.

Orbus raised an open hand, bringing them to a halt. They weren't marching in tight formation – a hasty flight from enemy lines wouldn't allow that – but his *auxilia*'s manoeuvres came more naturally, entire *'bernia* moving with one mind. Even with full-scale battle out of the question, this baptism of fire had sobered them all nicely, something reflected in their weathered and tarnished armour. Orbus could scarcely remember it gleaming on the Field of Mars.

'Sirs,' an older Painted caught their attention. Graufh. He was standing by a long-dead tree, pulling an ashen branch down to eye level. The Praefector and the Centurion saw it at once. The small piece of torn red cloth, tied to the branch, was hard to miss.

Army red. From a military tunic. Orbus' pulse quickened. They were in the right place, then.

'What did I tell you?' Bydreth cocked his head at the Praefector cynically, and a few of the others laughed. Even Brauda cracked a smile. Orbus mimed slapping him, his backhand gently cuffing the Centurion's metal helm. 'What's next then, sir?'

'You can set your packs down again, *milites*,' Orbus told them, brandishing the crimson rag. 'We've got incoming.'

HE WAS RIGHT. Eventually.

It was almost midday when they made it. First arriving in ones and twos, until a full *'bernium* had melted out from the heath's edges.

'Took you bloody long enough,' Klaujan growled with a smile. 'Well met, lads.'

The lead figure smirked back at him, his crudely-etched filaments of black facial ink a far cry from the curling claws of blue and red that painted the Ulthaini.

'Nice to see you're not all dead,' Molchis replied. 'You've kept us waiting long enough. Another hour or so and we'd have left you for dead.'

Orbus stepped towards him, clasping his wrist in a warrior's greeting. 'Sorry to disappoint you, Centurion.'

Molchis conceded with a throaty laugh. The former gang lord seemed to have thawed a little, presumably following the incident with Fuscator. Around him, the other Creedless bustled in among Bydreth's men, swapping greetings and parting with what little water and grain they could spare.

'Praefector,' a familiar voice drew Orbus' attention. 'It is good to see you, sir. We bring news.' The voice belonged to Argias, and the *optio* stepped out of Molchis' shadow to greet his commander. Once, Argias would have balked at even talking to Molchis' benighted followers – let alone living and travelling among them – but that time was now past, another fact of life the *optio* had left behind in Rome.

Argias had hardened, just like they all had. He'd gone into the fire, and come out tempered.

'News?' Orbus cocked an eyebrow.

'Good news,' Fuscator put in from behind them. He was still smirking – indeed, Fuscator never seemed to stop smirking – but it didn't detract from his sincerity.

'Wagons!' Molchis hissed with gutter glee. 'Two of them, headed this way from the northwest. Minimal guards, and they're not hurrying about it either.'

'And what's more,' a greasy little urchin in army red added, one of the Creedless Orbus didn't know by name, 'they're open-topped. Shrouds and sailcloth pegged in place, but they aren't sealed. Cargo needs to breathe, whatever it is.'

Bydreth and Orbus both made the leap at once. 'Food.' The Painted Centurion snapped his grimy fingers. 'Headed for their garrison. It has to be.'

'Headed that way, for now,' Molchis retorted. The breeze had started to shift, giving the trees around them a sylvan rustle. 'I'm sure we can change that.' A few of the men, his and Bydreth's both, shared a malevolent chuckle.

Inwardly, Orbus shared his *milites*' optimism. The *auxilia* could burn and salvage what they wanted from the countryside, but this was far too good an opportunity to pass up. If they extracted the food, then it could go to fill the *castra*'s dwindling stockpile. Otherwise they could at least torch it, and deny it to the enemy.

The goddess Ceres, up on high, might object to such a wanton sacrifice, but Orbus had more on his mind right now than superstition. Any officer would see it as a win, either way.

'You say it's practically unguarded,' the Praefector noted. 'Are you sure that isn't the point? A juicy prize like that, perfect circumstances... sounds ideal fodder for an ambush, Centurion.'

Molchis' reply was a particularly nasty grin. He reached for the *pugio* at his belt, lifting it half out of its sheath. A few of his Creedless did the same, and Orbus was resigned to see carved serrations in the steel, with trinkets and fetishes tied to the hilts.

'What do you think we've been doing these last two days?' Fuscator snorted. 'All these hills and forests. Oh, the fun we've had scouting them out, hiding... melting from the shadows.' A few of them grunted cruelly. 'We've had some good sport, Praefector. This convoy's out there all alone. Have no fear of that.'

Orbus and Bydreth shared a sardonic glance. The criminals and street warriors who followed Molchis weren't the most natural soldiers, but they had other, darker talents.

Stealth operations, shadow-play, daggers in the night... they'd been plying this trade long before they'd come to Orbus. Whatever doubts he had about their loyalty, he couldn't afford to waste those gifts. He'd need sharp blades wherever he could find them.

It was something he'd gradually started to accept, about all his men, since they'd left Rome. He couldn't change their nature, but he could harness it.

'Alright then,' Orbus' voice hardened, making it clear that much was riding on this. His hand drifted to *Ananke*'s pommel. 'Lead the way then, soldier. Let's see just how much you've really done.'

THE ATTACK DIDN'T last longer than a dozen frenzied heartbeats. Molchis' men clearly knew how it was done, and endless weeks of drilling and rough living had made the Painted into something just as deadly.

Two guards were down before the charge even hit home. Orbus didn't see who made those kills. Brauda, probably. Or Fuscator. They each had one hell of a javelin throw.

The Praefector roared a battle cry as *Ananke* tasted air. Silver flashed. Blood arced. The unwashed brute before him screamed an oath to Mars as he died, exalting his worthless soul to the War God. Or maybe that was Orbus. He wasn't sure which. Blood was thumping in his ears.

Bydreth had grabbed another guard from behind, crushing the man's neck in his oaken arms. The rest were already dead or dying; one tried his luck sprinting for the forest's cover. Orbus watched him run for a few moments, before an arrow shot him through the neck. Drygg, still in position in the woods, swept the area for more runners with his shortbow. Tuggi and two more Painted went about equally bloody work, hamstringing the asses with slashes of their *gladii*.

And just like that, silence fell over the moor. Sweat cooled, and hearts calmed. The horses brayed a little, unable to flee, as the pain of their wounds sunk in. A man groaned, shifting in his death pose, before Molchis sneered and put a boot on his windpipe.

'What a dignified end that was.' The Praefector's unimpressed gaze bored into him for a moment. 'Alright, *milites*. Let's see what we're taking home.'

Brauda and Graufh were already getting to work, daggers slicing the canvas sheets and pulling them away to reveal the cargo. Orbus didn't bother watching, instead unbuckling his helm and running a hand through his greasy tufts of hair.

Long nights in the field made grooming a challenge. Those who were even bothered used their blades to shave their faces and scalps. *Pugios* made for decent grooming tools, though Orbus and Argias hadn't proved particularly gifted at cutting each other's hair.

'Praefector,' Bydreth's voice hauled him down to earth. 'You need to see this, sir.'

Orbus walked over to join him, standing with a handful of his men at the second wagon's rear. 'What are—'

And then he saw it.

The cargo hold wasn't full of food. It wasn't carrying food at all.

'The other wagon?' Orbus asked Molchis.

'Full of the same,' a Creedless put in. 'We've just been through it.'

Orbus swore. How could he have been so blind?

He jumped up into the wagon's *carruca*, fishing through a sea of assorted leather items. Halters, bridles, reins... even a selection of wooden and metal stirrups, fashioned specifically to accommodate armoured boots or *caligae*.

Legion equipment, of a kind, but not commonly fielded en masse by infantry cohorts.

'Cavalry,' he spat, hopping back off the *carruca*. 'So *this* is what those traitorous curs are planning. This is why they've been avoiding open battle all this time. Hammer and anvil. They hole up in their citadel and let their mounted forces sweep us away.'

Few of the others seemed quite so perturbed. But then, few of them had faced a mounted charge of the *equites* before. Few who did lived long enough to talk about it.

'You're sure that's what this means?' Argias asked. He alone of the gathered men had some appreciation of the danger, but he didn't seem particularly convinced.

'Look at it.' The Praefector threw a leather halter at his *optio*, perhaps a little too hard. 'In these quantities? With all that manpower behind them? How else could you explain skulking behind their city walls? They're going to sally out and hit us with hoof and spear. You mark my words.'

He rounded on Molchis, who was still picking the dead clean for coins. 'You and your men have been out here longest. Have many convoys like this came this way? Have many that were too big, or well-guarded, to risk attacking?'

The sun chose that moment to manifest, light shining through the clouds to glint off their armour.

'More than you'd hope for, sir,' was the Centurion's glib reply.

Orbus gnashed his teeth, tossing another leather bridle to Brauda.

'*Varus*,' he swore. 'Take that one with us. Urbanus and the others will want proof.' He snorted air through his nose, locking his helm in place. 'Bydreth, set this all alight and we can be away from here. There are no winners here today.'

'Sir,' Argias cut in. Orbus didn't acknowledge him.

'Painted! Back to the *castra*. To the abyss with stealth. Molchis, fall back the same way going southeast. We'll be less conspicuous in smaller groups. I'm done playing games out here in the wilds.'

'Sir,' Argias repeated.

'Look sharp, lads.' Bydreth clapped a younger *miles* on the back as they went about their orders. 'Something tells me we're getting our *gladii* wet soon.'

'Sir!' Argias exclaimed.

Orbus finally turned to his ragged-looking *optio*. For a moment. And then his gaze travelled over Argias' shoulder, to the lip of the horizon. To what the younger man had seen.

Shapes, growing in his field of vision. Not even the sunlit background could obscure their forms. To any infantryman, those silhouettes were unmistakable. Hunched. Sinuous.

Equine.

'Form up,' the Praefector snarled, drawing *Ananke* and dropping back among the Painted. Out ahead, the wing of mounted figures drew closer.

'Ciringe frontem.'

THEY CLOSED THE distance fast. Like a *pilum*, hurtling from Gnaeus Ignatian's own hand, its broad-bladed tip seeking out throats to pierce.

Orbus' grizzled paranoia had probably been justified this time. Legions generally suffered against mounted enemies, a problem that no general of Rome had ever truly resolved since the Republic. No reform of Gaius Marius's had ever truly protected earthbound *milites* from a stampede of four-legged shock troops.

Many Legions fielded their own corps of mounted soldiers; men of the *equites* class themselves, those families who could afford to own, tend to and train a horse, as well as an able-bodied son to ride it.

These wings of cavalry were a force to be reckoned with, and one that had made its mark in battles across the Empire. Orbus had no desire to face them head-on. Such a clash would only end one way.

The traitor Ignatian had been canny with his forces. As a former legate of the Roman army, he knew too well the strengths and weaknesses of the legions he'd once fought in. The amassing and rearing of this many cavalry couldn't possibly be coincidence, rather an all too deliberate ploy. All the better to crash into and confound the legionaries sent against them.

A handful of unblooded *auxilia* would be sport for the equestrians' blades. They would barely even slow their charge.

'SHOULD'VE BROUGHT OUR damn shields!' barked Brauda, spear over his shoulder and sword ready to draw. None of them had objected to leaving their *scuta* back at camp for this week of shadowy reconnoitres, but here, right now, the Praefector didn't particularly feel like reminding him.

'Typical Brau,' Bydreth grunted to forced chuckles. 'Always a bloody genius with hindsight.'

The *milites* had formed a rather crude line, spearpoints up. With *scuta*, or just more men, they could have mustered a vaguely passable shield wall, or even a half-decent *testudo*. *That* could actually stand a chance of fighting back, or at least not getting slaughtered to a man. Most horses couldn't be goaded into charging a densely packed phalanx of enemies, even if the very threat of a mounted charge was enough to scatter their prey anyway.

'What are they doing?' Fuscator asked suspiciously. The throng of cavalry had formed two wings, each haring off to one side, flanking the *auxilia* by a wide, wide margin before gradually turning in their stampeding path. They roughly passed each other some distance behind the Praefector's little band, neither wing stopping, but going on with their arcing charge like the moving paths of a sundial.

Orbus saw through their plan at once. 'They're cutting us off,' he growled. 'Two wings, each one circling us. They can trap us like this till Vesta's hearths turn cold. We'll never get clear in time.'

'But why?' Drygg piped up from somewhere behind him. 'Why not just attack?'

Brauda was about to cuff the lad's head for his impudence, but Bydreth thankfully got there first.

'I think we're about to find out, son.' The Painted's centurion pointed into the distance with his *pilum*.

A handful of cavalry had parted from the nearest wing, drawing up to the *auxilia* at a gentle canter. That last detail made the Praefector raise an eyebrow. These new arrivals, whoever they were, weren't looking to storm or charge him.

They were coming in peace.

Orbus found himself smiling, chiding his leaden mind. They didn't want to kill him. They wanted to talk.

The sound of thundering hooves briefly filled his helm as the two wings lapped them all again, still content to circle their prey from a long way off. Orbus lowered his *pilum*, pushing Bydreth gently to one side as the new arrivals drew closer.

'Well, they've got our attention,' the Praefector drily reflected. 'Time to hear them out, I think.'

Bydreth wasn't quite as ready to let him face them. 'Sir, do you—'

'*Move.*' There was no arguing with that tone. Orbus abruptly threw down his spear, knowing the cavalry would see, uncaring if anyone bothered to retrieve it. He sucked in a vaguely ashen breath before finally stepping out from between Bydreth and Brauda's shoulders. Out from behind his comrades' protective huddle, he couldn't help but feel a touch exposed.

Still. No going back now.

Orbus drew *Ananke*, its feel in his sword-hand going some way to soothe his nerves. The three arriving riders had slowed to a leisurely amble, and at this distance he could make them out a little clearer. Two of them were guards, clearly. Decorated, veteran legionaries, judging by the ornamental touches to their armour and uniforms. But legionaries, nonetheless.

The third rider, leading his two companions onward, was no rank-and-file *miles*. The extra slash of heraldic colour in his Red, as well as the ragged crest adorning his battle helm, told that truth. This man was a decurion, a cavalry commander. Or at least, he had been before the XXV Legion had spat on its oaths to the Principate.

Orbus reversed his grip on *Ananke*, holding it down across his body. The gesture was plain to see, its meaning unmistakeable. He wasn't looking for a fight, but was more than ready for one.

The three cavalry had halted where they were. None of them greeted him, or even spoke. For a moment, Orbus' helm echoed once again with the pounding crashing of hoof-falls as the mounted wings lapped them all yet again.

'Hail,' he called out, raising his free hand in greeting. 'I am Gaius Ser—'

The Decurion didn't interrupt, but didn't give Orbus time to finish either. Instead, he did something that caught the Praefector off guard.

He dismounted from his horse in one fluid motion. Level to level, he seemed unmoved by the need for formality.

'We know who you are, Sertor Orbus. Former Camp Prefect of the XII Legion. Now an auxiliary prefect, with no legion to speak of. Those rabid dogs in Red can only be *auxilia*.' The cavalryman cast a cold and judgmental gaze over the Painted, still trapped behind them and thankfully out of earshot. 'And you are the only officer to be found in their ranks.'

Orbus had to hand it to him. It was hardly a titanic leap of logic, although this decurion still seemed alarmingly well-informed for a rebel hundreds of miles from Rome.

'Then we're at odds,' the Praefector warily replied, 'for you know me, and I don't know you.'

One of the horses gently snorted as his rein was tugged, before the Decurion pulled his crested helm free.

'I am Septimus Graecillus,' the mutilated man informed him. Orbus knew a sword wound when he saw one, and whatever *gladius* blow had fouled this man's face must have been savage indeed.

Graecillus had clearly hoped revealing his ruined face would give his opponent pause, and he wasn't disappointed.

'Once, I was First Spear in the XXV's foremost cohort. Now, I am Marshal of the Army of the Free.'

Orbus didn't dignify the other man's newfound calling with a reply. Instead, he simply frowned as he lowered *Ananke*.

'Your name,' he conceded. 'I know it.'

'Indeed, you do.' Graecillus' unskinned, ruined visage twisted in amusement. 'We've met, only briefly. And it was a long time ago.'

'Bithynia,' the Praefector confirmed. The Fulminata and Ignipotens had campaigned together there, for a handful of months. This was going back some years now, but Orbus knew what he remembered.

'Aye,' Graecillus agreed. 'You were just a centurion then, and I was a recently-raised *decanus*. I remember you there. You and that witless braggart Publius. I didn't much like either of you, to be honest.'

Orbus' jaw tightened, as did his grip on his sword. 'If you have something to say to me, *Marshal*, spit it out and let's be done with it.' He paused, cocking and aiming a wry half-smile. 'An entreaty for mercy, perhaps? Legate Urbanus is not a cruel man, but I can't promise he's in the mood to dangle *clementia* at your feet. I can carry your prickless master's pleas to him, at least. You never know. Maybe I can talk the old man round.'

The two wings stormed past them once more, still holding fast to their lapping paths. Graecillus smiled, a lipless thing of icy magnanimity. He didn't rise to the Praefector's puerile baiting, seeming to share the joke with him instead of bristling at it.

At some unspoken signal, the other two riders began to gently trot forward alongside him. They each drew to one side of Orbus, drawing their *gladii* menacingly without descending from their mounts. Graecillus did the same, his longer *spatha* coming free with a hiss of scraped metal.

'Nothing so brazen, Praefector. Today, our only objective is you.'

Orbus didn't react. He *wouldn't* react. If they wanted him dead, why bother with all this pageantry first?

Graecillus snapped his fingers, pursing his lips together and whistling a note. His forsaken steed took that cue to saunter a little closer, its leather-bound head dipped in equine subservience.

'Mount up.' Graecillus didn't waste a single word. 'You are coming with us, Praefector.'

Orbus tried his best to feign a little nonchalance. He hadn't been expecting this. 'As what? A prisoner of war? A hostage to be bartered?'

'As an esteemed guest.' The former First Spear pulled his horse closer still, leading it by its leather bit. 'We need an officer, a man of rank, to hear our message and carry it back to your legion.' His gaze drifted over Orbus' shoulder, to where the rest of his men still stood at guard, back-to-back with spearpoints out. Graecillus' two wings of cavalry still haloed them at a steady distance, sauntering now where once they'd charged. 'If it helps, I will have my *alae* slaughter your friends to the last man if you refuse.'

'And if I go with you?' Orbus snarled. He was a man of action. He would not be dictated to.

'Then your men will remain here,' the Marshal explained, 'under guard by mine. When you have heard our truth, I will return you to this spot, and you can all leave at your leisure.' He smiled, a viciously reasonable smile. 'We are busy men, Praefector, much like yourself. We shan't keep you for more than a couple of hours.'

Orbus took a moment to think on this, though he was mainly playing for time. What choice did he really have, anyway?

He spared the Painted and Creedless a glance. Molchis and Fuscator would doubtless be content with this sudden twist of fate, but Bydreth and Brauda wouldn't take this lying down.

'Why me? What's the value in an auxiliary prefect?' he asked Graecillus.

The other man snorted unkindly. 'Absolutely nothing. We'd hoped to find ourselves a *true* officer, a proper legion man, after all these months of cat and mouse. Maybe even your legate himself. But plans change, Orbus. You're the one we caught. You'll do.'

Fair enough. Orbus chided himself inwardly once again. 'My men will need to be appraised of the... situation, before I go.'

'Naturally,' Graecillus assured him. 'My riders will take care of everything.' Then he inclined his head at the horse, giving its rump a slap for good measure. Here they were, then. No more prolonging the inevitable. 'Now up you get, Orbus. And hand me that pretty sword of yours, while we're at it. You should be honoured. You're going to be the first man of the Empire to enter Arx Agrippum.'

Orbus sighed, relinquishing *Ananke* to the Marshal's hands and pulling himself onto the horse's saddle. He'd always hated riding, and he'd never had any talent for it. He was dimly aware of distant shouts from his men, no doubt confused by this strange turn of events. They'd find out shortly.

'I have to tell you, Graecillus,' he offered, 'that based on these feeble attempts of yours at posturing, I doubt I'll give a shit about anything you've got to say.'

The other man mounted up with considerably more grace, taking front position and grasping the reins. 'Very droll of you, Praefector. I may not change your mind, but Gnaeus Ignatian will. And when he's done with you, you'll be the one clamouring to spread his message.'

And with that, he kicked his horse into life, the two of them galloping off into the noonday sun.

We'll see about that, Orbus chose not to reply.

XIV

ROME'S LAMENT

THE BREEZE FELT cool on his face, a long and lingering kiss that soothed his weathered features. The cooler weather in Gaul agreed with him more than Rome's, and he always took a little time each day to savour it. But then he'd never felt at home in the capital, whatever the weather was like.

The view from his mountainous spot was unrivalled. Arx Agrippum, in all its rustic glory, stretched out for miles in each direction. Dark smoke curled from the chimney-chambers of smithies and potters' kilns, while the occasional waft of burnt fat and spoiled meat drifted home into his nostrils. It was a feast day, although the exact god and festival in question escaped him. The temples would be thronged with supplicants as priests slaughtered heifers and commended their steaming offal to the heavens.

The streets would smell of blood and burnt meat. Auguries would be divined from the sacrifices, immortals would be appeased by the offerings, and life would, as always, go on.

Little had truly changed in Arx Agrippum with the dawn of his new order. Banners once proclaiming the glory of the XXV had been torn down from towers and balustrades, and the Legion's old *signae* and holy eagle had been melted down in sanctified fires. Statues crowned with the likeness of Caesar Augustus had had their heads forcibly removed; heads that, he recalled with a rueful smile, were already designed to be fully and readily detachable. A sad relic of the Civil Wars, a time when every day could bring a new lord to pledge your life to.

His own face adorned those statues now, freshly carved in imperfect circumstances. He hadn't felt comfortable submitting to that, and the feeling hadn't improved each time his own stony visage met his gaze across a square or courtyard. But his people had needed a figurehead. Such were the burdens and sacrifices of leadership.

But beyond that? Life in the great colony-city continued with little difference. If anything, he counted that as a victory. He'd led them to a state of freedom, of breaking the fetters Rome had chained them with, and his ironclad will to govern had given them… if not *prosperity*, then perhaps *continuity* was the more appropriate word.

They'd come so far, but still had so far to go.

The throne's vengeance had arrived, just as he'd known. The Emperor's reach was long. An entire legion, no less, and one he knew well. It had been some years since he'd last seen Decius Urbanus, and even if Fortuna decreed they meet here as enemies, it felt oddly reassuring. The thought of seeing his old friend again.

'Lord Ignatian,' a clipped voice brought him down to earth. 'Marshal Graecillus has returned from his sortie.'

The voice belonged to Alcius, a man who'd once served as one of his tribunes. But Alcius no longer wore that rank, for he had left those days behind him. They all had.

Gnaeus Ignatian, once *legatus* of the Emperor's XXV Legion, took one last look across the cityscape of Arx Agrippum. The wind had changed, and his once-ceremonial robe started billowing in the breeze.

'He has brought a prisoner, my lord,' Alcius added. 'They await you in the Temple of Perfidy.' He paused, knowing his master would wish to greet the new arrival in person.

Ignatian's smile was a thing of stately mercy. 'Lead on, my friend.'

HE'D ALWAYS ADMIRED the Temple. No-one in Arx Agrippum remembered its true name. It was Greek in its build, from the ancient Ionic columns and statuary. The Temple's more recent history had shrouded it in infamy – it was under this painted, frescoed roof that Gnaeus Ignatian had first declared his renouncing of the *Pax Romana*, and the forsaking of his oaths to Rome's Empire.

Men had objected, blades had been drawn, and blood was spilt. And so, amid all the tumult that followed, the new name had stuck. The Temple of Perfidy.

'I don't know what I was expecting,' the prisoner confessed. And he was truly a prisoner, no matter how magnanimously Ignatian claimed otherwise. 'Maybe a little round table, in a pit. Hunched men in hoods mewling their craven fears to one another in the dark.'

Ignatian forced himself to smile, somewhere between pity and disgust. 'I'm sorry to disappoint you, Sertor Orbus. Although I've no doubt that you'll hear every word from my mouth as something craven. The perils of clinging too tightly to one's beliefs.'

The other man smiled thinly, not taking the bait. 'No danger of that, traitor. I don't really believe in anything.'

They were seated across the Temple's central atrium, a chamber that long since fallen into disrepair. Ignatian's makeshift seat was hewn from old Gallic granite, parked at one end of the hall, overlooking the steps and walkway. His deputy, Graecillus, occupied a similar seat across from him.

A rank of armed guards – former legionaries of the Ignipotens, all – stood across one wall, armoured up and arms held in utter stillness. They were their only friendly company.

Their prisoner had found a more sacrilegious seat. Perched atop an ancient, untended sacrificial altar, Sertor Orbus didn't cut a particularly heroic figure. The former camp prefect leant back, noting the bruises and scrapes he'd taken over a fortnight of life on the run. He wasn't favouring his captors with a great deal of attention, something surely meant to convey a lack of fear.

Even years after the Temple's deconsecration, sitting on an altar struck Ignatian as a trifle disrespectful.

'That seems a rather pitiful way to be,' the former legate offered, as kindly as he could. 'To live one's life without a purpose.'

Orbus smiled, and to Ignatian's eyes it was an unlovely thing. 'I didn't say that now, did I? Maybe I was put here to kill traitors.' His gaze slid over to Graecillus. 'Or to skin their running dogs dry.'

The former decurion looked ready to settle that account right now, moving to rise from his granite throne. One move from Ignatian was all it took to still him. One gentle motion of his hand, and Graecillus grudgingly relaxed.

'Septimus Graecillus is no man's dog,' he maintained, 'yours or mine. And your choice of words betrays you, Praefector. When the ideal a man is sworn to serve is warped beyond recognition… is it an act of treachery to turn your back on it? Is it truly? Or would the greater betrayal be to follow that purpose doggedly, as it twists and mutates ever further? Would breaking faith with it, in fact, be truer to that first ideal than ever?'

The prisoner groaned, his head leaning on his hand. 'Oh gods… another talker. You're worse than Thracian.'

An uncomfortable silence fell upon the chamber, and Orbus didn't seem much inclined to break it. Time for a slightly different tack.

'Are you not curious,' Ignatian offered, 'to know why you are here, Orbus?'

The Praefector snorted. 'Your thuggish little horsemen were fairly clear on that score.' He shifted position on the altar, trying to ignore the judgemental gazes of Hellenic statues all around him. 'You didn't want me at all, traitor. You just wanted a legion officer, and I was the closest thing you found.'

Graecillus lowered the goblet he'd been drinking from. Both his and his master's were filled with water, while the goblet offered to Orbus was full of Falernian red. A canny tactic, although the prisoner's choice not to drink was, frustratingly, cannier still.

'You aren't wrong,' Ignatian conceded, gently sipping from his own glass. 'And perhaps an actual man of the XII would have been better...' He trailed off, lowering the drinking vessel. 'But then again, the gods do move in mysterious ways. Perhaps you and I can find some common ground.'

Across the chamber, Orbus eyed the traitor general curiously. 'I somehow doubt that is going to happen. Because from where I'm sat, you and I are nothing alike.'

Graecillus smiled his lipless smile, as if they'd both been gambling on that exact answer.

'Are you so sure?' Ignatian countered. 'We each once belonged to a legion, only for each of us to evolve past its stifling bounds.' That smile again, disconcerting for its apparent lack of mockery. 'And I know that you lie in your bed each night, wondering if you're stronger or weaker without that bond of happy brotherhood. Just like I do.'

Silence followed that gentle confession. Orbus abruptly shattered it with a charmless chuckle.

'How poetic of you, *"Legatus"*. Then again, maybe I'm just a worthless coward, and you're a treacherous bastard. Not so alike, after all.' He actually took a swig from his goblet then, wiping red wine from his mouth with the back of one hand. 'And if we lie awake in bed each night, then I fancy we each wonder when we'll get what's coming to us.'

Graecillus gave the prisoner a dutiful glare, but made no move to cow him this time. Ignatian didn't seem much impressed by Orbus' response, but quite tellingly he didn't challenge that claim either.

'I didn't have you brought here to spar with words, Gaius,' the former legate tried to mask his rising impatience. 'I brought you here to extend an offer to the XII Legion.'

'No-one calls me Gaius,' the Praefector drily corrected him. 'And what, on Pluto's acrid shores, could you possibly offer the Fulminata? What could you have, that could come between our *legatus* and his sworn duty?'

The sunshine chose that moment to reappear, streaming in through unintentional windows where the walls met the roof. As much as Ignatian cherished this place of quiet reflection, the Temple of Perfidy fulfilled no functional purpose in Arx Agrippum. Which meant he couldn't justify squandering the colony-city's resources restoring it.

'Very well then, Sertor Orbus. But can you truly not guess my intent, from everything I've said to you thus far?'

'Everything you've said thus far,' Orbus levelly replied, 'has been a pile of roiling shit.'

The fingers of Ignatian's left hand tightened on his armrest. Slowly, subtly, but enough to be noticed.

'I have no wish to fight your friends, Orbus. I didn't have you brought here to punish you. I did it to extend a hand.'

The prisoner didn't say anything.

'I'm serious,' the Castellan of Arx Agrippum added when no reply was forthcoming. 'The blood shed between our two forces has been regrettable, but not nearly enough to constitute a *casus belli*. Your fellow officers have doubtless wondered why I won't face your forces head-on, despite holding the advantages. Have none of you stopped to think why?'

For his part, the prisoner still hadn't quite digested Ignatian's claim. 'You truly are serious,' he finally managed. 'You want us... to join you?' But then his hacking laughter blasted through the moment, the sound ugly. Almost ursine.

'I'm sorry,' the Praefector tried, stifling another fit of choking laughs. 'You... you expect us to *join* you? The very army sent to punish your treachery, and haul you back to Rome in chains... and you would make *allies* of us?'

'Lose the laughter,' Graecillus growled, his ruined face darkening. 'You haven't heard the Castellan's offer.' He seemed about to go on, but a murderous glance from his master stopped him dead.

'What could a rebellious *legatus* offer us?' Orbus countered. 'What prize, or *gratia*, could outweigh spitting on his oaths to the Empire?'

'My, my.' Ignatian's pity seemed achingly sincere, and that just made it harder to stomach. 'Your stubbornness no longer does you credit, Praefector. A man of your standing cannot afford to be this obtuse.' He gracefully rose from his granite throne, his most expansive moment since he'd arrived. 'You think this rebellion is some pitiful lunge for power? Nothing so crude, Orbus. I had power, once. I wielded full *imperium* in the Emperor's name. No, Praefector. I have no quarrel with your Emperor. My quarrel – *our* quarrel – is with the throne he sits on.'

No-one said anything for a moment, as the legacy of those words sunk in. Orbus, for his part, shifted a fraction on the antiquated altar, watching his captor with new eyes.

'You are a Republican.' He let that comment hang in the air. Then he laughed again, but briefer, hollower. 'You seek to turn back time.'

The Castellan begun to slowly walk towards him, his steps drifting near-silently across the decaying stone floor.

'Are you finished?' Ignatian had halted, about ten paces from the altar. 'You seek to paint a radical portrait where none exists. In truth, I had little love for the Republic That Was, before the coming of the Empire That Is. I am not a nostalgic man, Orbus.'

'Then what?' the prisoner asked him.

Ignatian walked over to the altar's abandoned basin, pausing to gently dip his forefinger into the murky rainwater. This had the exact desired effect, and oblique as it was, Orbus fancied he knew the point he was making.

'Every great decision creates ripples, Praefector. Ripples that spread and grow, far beyond the locus of their origin. A cicada can beat its wings in Rome, and somewhere off the coast of Britannia or Pictland, a storm will break.' He pulled his hand from the water, disturbing the surface even more. 'Every decision, that echoes both ways, every precedent you set in stone… it all has consequences, Orbus. It all adds up.'

Ignatian gently walked up to where Orbus still sat. On the altar, they were roughly of a height. Orbus didn't move, favouring his would-be captor with a noncommittal sideways glance.

'An Empire needs a leader,' Ignatian continued, more quietly. 'A figurehead. A man who can rule with an unchallenged grip. The Principate functions, where the Republic once floundered.'

Orbus raised a dirty eyebrow. 'But?'

'But,' the Castellan effortlessly rose to the moment, 'just what ripples have spread out from the *Palatium*, since our Imperial majesty set forth his dreams of conquest? What precedents has our beloved Emperor carved into Rome, as his power and reign grow more eternal?'

The Praefector allowed himself a moment before answering. This wasn't how he'd expected this meeting to go. None of it was.

He'd expected degradation. Torture, even. He'd expected a drooling, self-serving despot holding Graecillus' leash, a craven lord clinging to his delusions, who would simply have him killed for sport or carved up for information.

He hadn't expected to be treated as an honoured guest. As a supposed equal, even if his freedom was the price. He hadn't expected to have his loyalty courted, rather than mocked, by this self-declared iconoclast who seemed more a preacher than a general. A demagogue, who ardently believed in every word he spoke.

'You're just talking in loops and riddles.' He tried to sound as self-assured as Ignatian. 'Caesar Augustus has given us years of—'

The Castellan was already chuckling, dissolving whatever point Orbus was going to make.

'Augustus, indeed. Therein lies the problem, Praefector. People hear that name, that self-conferred title, and they stop thinking. All the people remember is Augustus, that golden lord who rewrought Rome in gleaming Syrian marble. Scarce few men remember Gaius Octavian, the blood-soaked soldier who slew his way to the state's heart.'

Orbus didn't feel like being drawn into this. He felt he was standing on shaky ground, and following a fanatic onto shaky ground seldom ended well. 'It was a time of strife,' he begun. 'He ended the Civil War—'

'He was the last man standing from the Civil War,' Graecillus spat from far across the atrium. 'That's all. Lepidus? Mark Antony? Cicero? He simply outlasted them all.' His snort was a far uglier thing than his master's. 'Octavian, cloaking his past sins with a glittering new name. Proud to wear it. Ashamed of how he got it.'

Orbus' gaze flickered between Ignatian and his lackey. 'You're going to let him do your talking for you now? I didn't come here for a history lesson, traitor. What? So you think our *Princeps* an unsuitable ruler of Rome?' He almost wanted to laugh again. 'I'd say you're about forty years too late to lodge a grievance. No, "*Legatus.*" I wouldn't stake my *denarii* on it. You're just a snapping dog off his leash, like your pet over there. You want to rebel, and you seek a righteous reason for doing so.'

He started to shift off the altar, wanting to pull away from his captor.

'Sertor,' the Castellan began.

'*No.*' Orbus stood up, making to walk away. Anything to get away from this man's forked tongue. 'I'm done playing house with you, traitor. Either let me go, assuming my men are even still alive, or just kill me now and end this moronic charade. I honestly don't care which.'

He stopped, slowly, uncertainly turning back when he realised Ignatian wasn't following him. The former legate of the XXV remained where he was, informally sat upon that very same altar, looking at him with disconcertingly soft eyes.

'I am a man of my word, Praefector,' he gently confessed. 'Your men have not been touched. They will return to your comrades in such a fashion, when we are finished here. As will you.'

'They will?' Orbus didn't bother hiding his surprise. Prisoners of the legions seldom walked away unscathed. They almost always lost a hand or finger, or simply had their wrists broken. All the better not to wield a weapon for months to come, effectively ruling them out of any coming battles. At the very least, Orbus would have had their weapons and armour stripped in Ignatian's place. All the better to humiliate them, as well as leaving them useless on the field of war.

If Ignatian was really willing to let his *auxilia* escape the ambush intact...

'You're serious, then.' The Praefector kept his tone neutral, conceding nothing. 'You are serious about this overture of alliance.'

The smile that bloomed across the Castellan's face was horrifically genuine. 'I knew you would understand. Urbanus is a man of reason, Orbus. I was right to pray you would be too.'

Orbus raised a hand, forestalling any more compliments. 'Enough honey, traitor. I am not committing to anything. But what is it you want from us, exactly?'

Ignatian somehow managed to look vulnerable, but resolute, at the same time. For a man as old as Urbanus, his face had the openness of someone far younger.

'All I seek, Orbus, is for your comrades to examine their consciences. To ask themselves if theirs is the banner they truly wish to march beneath. I

- 345 -

cannot make that decision for you. So meet me halfway, Praefector. Tomorrow, at three hours past sunrise, Graecillus here will muster four cohorts of our army before the Ionys Depression, on the borders of the River Garumna. That is where your fellow legionaries are encamped, is it not? So meet us there, Orbus. Bring Urbanus and his officers to our table. Let us talk. Negotiate. Share with you our vision. From there, your paths are your own.'

The prisoner and the Castellan held each other's gazes for a moment, before Orbus spoke again.

'And what do you hope will happen, if we do this? That we will forget our orders to break you on the field of battle, our gods-sworn Imperial mandate, to embrace you as brothers in arms?'

Ignatian said nothing. Which said it all, really. Suddenly, the quiet stillness of the Temple felt deafening.

'And what then?' Orbus found himself perversely warming to this whimsical train of thought. 'What happens after that? Will the XII and XXV march across Europe, swatting aside any other legion forces that dare to cross their paths? Until what?' He gestured in the air, inanely. 'Until you come to Capena Gate, somehow bear arms across Rome's *pomerium*, and settle this... this *grudge* of yours, with the Emperor himself and his very own Praetorians?'

'So naïve!' Ignatian took another step closer, the first edge of temper creeping into his voice. Or maybe it was just his burning passion. 'Who says it would even come to that? Think of it. Consider, if you will, the matter of appearance. *One* Legion, at the arse-end of Imperial shores, sloughing off its loyalty and crying out for regime change? No, Praefector. It would only reek of regicide, as men with less cynicism than you would doubtless see it.'

He took in a gentle breath. 'But *two*? Two legions, with scarcely a single bond of brotherhood to connect them, and another legate who shares share my conviction? Think of it, Praefector.'

Orbus did, and to his chagrin, he saw the Castellan's point at once. If Ignatian could sway even one other legion to his cause – the very legion sent to stop him, no less – the ripples, as he'd put it, would surely spread. More legions could well follow. If other legates decided they shared his beliefs, then the power beneath his banner could swell further still. Suddenly, the Senate's fear of civil war didn't seem quite so remote.

And even then... Orbus remembered that first council, when Urbanus had been so reluctant to let any other legion lend support to the Fulminata for this war. Power blocks grew through momentum. Any senator who'd ever held military command, who felt a slain Emperor was opportune to their fortunes, could simply throw their weight behind Ignatian. The bigger the faction grew, the less inclined anyone else would be to challenge it. And on, and on, the momentum would grow. If Ignatian had his way here in Aquitania, then he may never need to fight another battle.

'There.' The once-legate had read the realisation on Orbus' face. 'Do you see now, Sertor? Why it is so important that our officers talk?'

The Praefector smiled, rueful and vulpine. 'Maybe you're not as clever as you think, Castellan. The way I hear it, we don't even need to fight you at all, to truly subdue your treachery. All we need to do is shut our ears to your pleas, leave your followers at the negotiating table with their pricks in their hands, and this delusional dream of yours never even leaves Gaul.'

'Gods…' Ignatian actually turned around in that moment, trying to master his exasperation. 'You and your moronic *pride!* What sort of legionary are you, Orbus? What is it that truly matters to you? Orders? Or the world they leave behind?' He looked ready to spit in disgust. 'I have the full power of the Ignipotens at my disposal, Praefector. The *Ignipotens!* Not to mention the entirety of Arx Agrippum. Do you think I *couldn't* have annexed half the country from here to the Gallic coast if I'd wanted to? Or slit the throat of any messages or couriers carrying word of this to Rome?'

Orbus didn't try to respond. Once again, he felt the ground beneath his feet grow less firm.

'Because I *wanted* this, fool.' The Castellan cleared his throat. 'For the exact same reason that your legion-mates have been playing seeker with my levies, rather than breaking themselves against the shields and spears of my true army. Because I *wanted* a legion here, in the shadow of my city. Here, and unopposed. I made sure that word of my deeds reached Rome, and that the path to my door would lie clear for you. I *wanted* this, Orbus. And I wanted an officer here, a man I could speak to face to face, to begin the good work and wrench those channels of communication open. You're not here to start a war with me, Orbus. You're here to do so much more.'

The prisoner was silent for a few moments. He had no witty or scathing retort, and why would he? He'd read this all wrong. They all had, right back to the Theatre of Pompey. Orbus had stumbled into this situation half-blind, and what was more, he'd taken the exact line of argument his captor had been expecting to hear.

He needed the advantage back. Hanging back now would solve nothing.

'Alright, then.' He found himself walking back to where the altar was. The hollow gazes of marble Achaean heroes followed him as he sat again. 'Say I can convince them to come to the table, weapons sheathed. How can you convince them to share this fool's dream, and betray the Red—' He leant back. '—if you can't even convince me?'

This time, it was Ignatian's turn to pause. For whatever it was worth, he didn't presume any familiarity this time. Or any fellowship. They'd passed that point now.

'I have no desire to sit in Augustus' throne,' he confessed as he drew closer, trying to ignore how Orbus scoffed. 'I've no desire to see anyone fill it. I want that throne destroyed.'

'So, we come to it at last,' the Praefector replied. 'You *are* a Republican.'

Ignatian frowned. 'No, Sertor. I am a pragmatist. An Emperor,' he spat the word, as if distasteful, 'is a bleak necessity of the world we live in. The world we *once* lived in.' He started walking back towards his own seat, next to where Graecillus still sat obediently silent, like an overly loyal hunting dog. 'Think back to the Civil Wars, Sertor. Of what you know of them, at least. Crassus, Pompey, Caesar, Lepidus... that chain of dominoes falling, all the way to Octavian's victory at Actium.'

'Get to the point,' Orbus growled, renewing Graecillus' frown.

'Think of those battles,' the Castellan pressed. 'Think of the anarchy between each one. That dreadful breathing space, each time the provincials cowered behind their borders, wondering who or what would rule their world. Each time the people of Rome braced themselves for the Republic's end, not knowing how their city would look each passing morning. My father fought at Actium, on the Emperor's side. He knew what he was fighting for. If one man, with a grip of iron, was needed to set the ship of state back on course, and to extinguish that cancerous fire… then so be it. But no more.'

'And is that what you want, then?' Orbus almost sighed. 'To restore the Republic?'

'The Republic is *dead,*' Ignatian snapped. 'Julius Caesar murdered it. Softly. With kindness, perhaps. The Civil Wars were merely the kindling of the funeral pyre. And perhaps it was just as well, Praefector. I'm no starry-eyed lover of the Senate. There was a reason Caesar was able to snuff it out.'

He half-smiled, ruefully like a child. 'Because it was broken. Riddled by flaws. When the enemies of Rome came knocking at our gates, we didn't cower behind our consuls and senators. We appointed dictators, to rise above the politicking and steer us through the storms. We gave them the *imperium* to do what was needed. Not an honour. A burden. A burden of duty, to be duly discharged.'

Orbus thought it best to at least interject. How easy it came to him, to talk of treason and civil war with his sworn enemies.

'And the Emperor is what, then? Another burden? Another means to an end, in need of discharge?'

Ignatian favoured him with another wistful smile. Pity, for a lost cause. Orbus fancied the Castellan would wear the exact same expression if he'd slaughtered him on the field of battle. A pitiful glance spared for a deluded fallen foe.

'The Emperor,' he replied from across the Temple hall, 'is a relic from a time that needed him. A time of strife, which we should have truly left behind. Rome can never again be a republic. History has taught us this. But to throw the discus right the other way... to let one man wield such godlike power, over so many souls, for so many years? How long before he forgets what it even is to be without it?' He didn't seem to take pleasure from laying this revelation bare. 'The kings of Rome sleep ill in their graves. We have seen where that road takes us, Sertor. We all have.'

Orbus made a show of raising one eyebrow. Anything to avoid actually considering the other man's words.

'And what? You think you're the man to change all that? With nothing but one city, one decaying legion and some empty, honeyed rhetoric against the weight of an empire?' He shook his head, hiding none of his mockery. 'And you still haven't answered my question. Augustus has ruled for almost four decades. Why now, Gnaeus Ignatian? Why now, when your star has finally begun to wane, are you suddenly filled with this noble impulse for treachery?'

'*Insolent cur!*' Graecillus shouted. He actually rose from his throne, but came no further. 'How can this braggart be so blind?'

'Peace, Decurion.' Ignatian seemed to have a talent for soothing tempers. That, Orbus had to concede. He continued as Graecillus sat once more.

'The air in here grows stifling, don't you think?' The Castellan rose from his seat once more, more slowly this time. And more deliberately. 'The stench of so much death in these four walls. Come now, my unwilling friend. Let us walk and clear our heads.'

THE VIEW FROM up here was astounding. Another claim of Ignatian's proved frustratingly true.

'I come here quite often,' he'd confessed as they'd climbed the mountainous steps. 'It isn't a bad place, when one needs to do some honest thinking.'

And Orbus had silently agreed. In terms of grandeur, Arx Agrippum's skyline could hardly match Rome's. Even one district of Rome's. But the solitude... up here, looking across the once-great city-colony, Orbus could scarcely recall a sight so hauntingly still, from a view so wonderfully aloof.

This great, mountainous hill of slate and rubble was perfect, as a viewpoint or a resting place. This was where a god would come to die.

'What does a leader do, Orbus?'

It was the first time Ignatian had broken the silence since they'd arrived. The Castellan had busied himself by gutting an apple with his *pugio*. Half of it he tossed through the mountain air, for the Praefector to warily catch with one hand.

'I said no more riddles, traitor. You want to parley with my legion? I'm not walking out of this city without a straight answer.' If he ever left at all. Back in the Temple, thousands of feet below them, Septimus Graecillus still waited, still surrounded by armed legionary guards. However haughty his master's intentions were, the former decurion was patently waiting for an excuse to slit his throat.

'A leader's role is to govern,' Ignatian answered his own question, as he diced the apple further and ate a piece off his dagger. 'As any *scholam* master or street sophist would tell you. But what does it truly mean? To govern?' He chewed a piece of fruit intently, fixing his companion with intent eyes. 'Have you truly given it much thought? The etymology of the word is fascinating.' He lowered the *pugio*, and the skewered apple fragments with it. 'To our cousins in Achaea, a *kubernetes* is a helmsman. A man who steers the ship.'

Orbus could see the other man's point already. 'The ship of state, you mean. The man who keeps it on its course.'

'Indeed.' Ignatian smiled, equally pleased that Orbus was eating the fruit as grasping his line of thinking. 'And what would you deem the mark of a *good* governor? A man whose influence maligns every part of his citizens' lives, invasive and insidious, like a bindweed of Imperial purple?' He helped himself to another mouthful of apple. 'Or a man whose gentle touch is all that's needed? A man whose efforts to steer the ship are so minimal, so subtle that Rome can breathe every bit as easily for his velvet-masked hand?'

The Praefector actually threw down his apple shards in that moment, something that couldn't have sat well with his host. This was hardly the blindsiding rhetoric Ignatian had promised.

'Jupiter on high... is there *anything* you have to say that isn't totally devoid of meat? You're so gods-damned empty, with every word that leaves your silver mouth. You keep insisting, you keep on lamenting that your hand has somehow been forced. That this is some noble crusade you've undertaken, a solemn duty that gives you no pleasure... but all I hear from you is hot air. Do you genuinely believe your own lies? Or are you that poor of a charlatan that you—'

'*Enough!*'

That stopped Orbus in his tracks. It was the first time he'd heard the Castellan raise his voice.

He looked out across the distant city beneath them, the towers and tenement blocks crowned by banners and chimney smoke. The breeze up here wasn't as cold or as biting as he'd feared, and the faint aroma of burnt fat and incense wafted into his nose.

'Must be a feast day,' he muttered.

'That's one thing from Rome I'll never miss,' Ignatian confessed. 'All the streets full of sacrificial sheep and cattle, every festival and market day.' He started chuckling at the memory, though it barely carried over the growing wind. 'Brings all the accursed hoof traffic in the *Forum* to a standstill. And always when you've got somewhere pressing to be.'

Orbus wasn't even looking at him. For all his anger and exasperation, for however ridiculous this whole situation truly was, he found himself smiling in sympathy.

'The stench of it...' he agreed. 'I'll swear by my own Penates, that it never damn well fades. Even fully opening the Great Sewer never makes it much worse. Do the *vigiles* just stop noticing it, do you wonder?'

Ignatian held his gaze as the Praefector trailed off. It was a rather uneasy moment to draw out, this odd shadow of camaraderie, a sense of fellowship that could have been. How similar these two outcast officers were, how similar and yet how different. One twist of the Fates, one altered deployment or secondment, and Ignatian might well have fought together with Orbus and Cascana the Elder as tentmates. Or might Orbus in fact have stood at Ignatian's side, and helped lead the XXV Legion against the Emperor they'd once fought for?

Ignatian dared come a little closer, laying a tentative hand on his prisoner's shoulder. The first raindrops chose that moment to fall, and Orbus didn't need to be superstitious to see that for the omen it was.

'A good governor steers the ship of state,' the Castellan pressed. The rain wasn't stopping, and there would be no escaping it on this mountain summit. 'He steers it as little as can be, as little as needed, affecting the lives of those aboard as little as possible. He doesn't cradle every aspect of those passengers' fates in his hands. He doesn't dictate the things we can write, the things we can say, the people...' He looked away for a moment. 'The people we can love. Those things are not for a consul, a ruler, to decide. Whatever remits an emperor even truly has, not that it's ever truly been agreed... that is too far.'

'But an emperor is... is the thing that binds all those people together,' Orbus weakly countered. 'Sometimes he must require... unity. Unity and fealty, from those who would serve him.'

That actually made Ignatian laugh, gently and honestly. 'Which one of us believes his own lies now? A ruler's role is to serve his people, Sertor. Not the other way round.'

He drew a hand through his rain-washed hair, pulling his robes together as the deluge gently grew. 'Think back to the ripples, my friend. Precedents, that erode themselves into Rome. Even if you consider Augustus a good emperor. A master of statecraft, as well as war, who chooses to exercise his *imperium* with grace... What of the man who follows him? Do you really think it won't get worse? Do you really think a man who rules the known world won't grow deeper and deeper into that tainted throne? *That* will be when we pass the point of no return. That will be when the die is finally cast.'

Sextus had said something similar when Orbus had returned to Baiae all those months before. *Mark my words, brother. It will be when Augustus dies that I will be proved right. That's when we'll know we've brought a king back, at the head of his own foul dynasty.*

'You asked me why now, Orbus?' the Castellan finally concluded. 'Why, after forty years of an emperor, am I doing this now?' He smiled without any real emotion at all. 'Because forty years have passed, Praefector. Because our noble *Princeps* nears the end. He will die, Orbus, and then there will be one final precedent set, one that I cannot allow to stand. A line of emperors. If that happens, than the battle is lost. If Rome accepts a second *Princeps*, to follow in Augustus' bloodstained footprints... then we've as good as admitted to ourselves that tyranny is our choice. That our empire is ready to enthral itself to one man. Not simply *this* man, the man who put the Civil Wars behind us. But to one man, *whoever he may be*.'

A peal of thunder cracked across the sky, before Ignatian had even finished speaking. Whether divine providence or an unfortunate twist of fate, it was enough to make the Praefector smirk as rain began beating their clothes and armour.

'And do you think it will be as simple as that?' the traitor continued. 'Do you truly think the next Emperor will be chosen with words, instead of weapons?' He grasped Orbus' metal *phalerae* of office, hanging on their chain beneath his red tunic, holding them up to the rain. 'This is where Rome's true power lies, Orbus. Here, in the legions. Not the Senate house, or even in the *Palatium. This* is what a man needs to be Emperor. Augustus will die, and whoever controls the most legionaries will succeed him.'

He let go of Orbus' *phalerae*, giving the other man an almost brotherly touch on the shoulder. 'You think there will be a civil war if I continue on my path? For all we know, there may be a bigger one if I *don't*. By striking now, and ending this menace of tyranny before it starts, I am simply sullying my hands to ward off something far worse.'

He smiled once again, and this time he almost looked… sad. Defeated. Like he'd been truly forced to this point, and knew that whatever choices lay ahead would only make the world fouler.

'I won't pretend I have all the answers, Orbus. Maybe I do not know what is truly best for Rome. We cannot be a republic once again. But this tortuous descent into kingship… that, I cannot tolerate either. Whatever we are meant to be—' He turned to shield his face. What was that? Rainfall, or shame? '—we will be.'

The storm was beginning to die, as quickly as it had been born. A little bit of sun found its way through the caul of cloud, pale rather than golden, and without warmth. Rain still fell, although it was harder to notice by now, catching what traces of sunlight were there to catch.

'All these months of rebellion,' Orbus ventured, emptying his helmet of rainwater before fastening it back in place, 'of ruling this worthless little city. You've had a lot of time to repeat these claims to yourself, until they ring true in your own ears.' He turned away from Ignatian, walking towards the point where he could begin the climb back down. 'We are done here, traitor. Graecillus can take me back to my men.'

And he really was about to go, to leave this arch-traitor to his own devices on top of this mountain. Only for the man's honeyed voice to halt him once more.

'I meant what I said, Orbus.'

The Praefector turned again slowly, regarding his captor with hawklike confusion and suspicion.

'What I said to you in the Temple,' Ignatian gently clarified. 'Living, fighting, with nothing to truly believe in. That cannot be a life you wish to lead.'

Orbus had had enough of this. 'Whatever.' He made to turn his back once again.

'What do you fight for, Sertor Orbus?' What do you truly fight for?'

'I fight because I'm paid to.' The Praefector didn't feel shame, feel pride, feel anything at all as he confessed the truth of it. 'Because it is my life.'

'Is that all?' Ignatian's incredulity was palpable, even from a distance. 'Maybe that is what you believed, when you took the ink as a *tiro*. But what now?'

Orbus' own words came back upon his tongue, once again recalling that night with Sextus. 'That's what being a soldier is.'

'Perhaps,' the other man conceded. 'But no, Praefector. I don't think you truly believe those words. Not anymore.'

'And why is that?'

The traitor *Legatus* smiled wanly. 'Because I saw how your face changed, when I spoke of the Battle of Actium.' There was no glint in his eyes now, no wry self-awareness. 'Not an especially common surname, 'Orbus...' He studied his guest's face, the last vestiges of doubt leaving him. 'Ah, *yes*. I fancied I'd heard that name before, after Actium. Your father fought there, just as mine did. Only yours, if I remember, didn't quite pick the right side. One of the lucky ones, no? Granted *clementia*, when the ashes had finally settled.'

We're Republicans, Gaius. We always have been. We always will be.

'Are you sure you're on the right side, Orbus?' Ignatian folded his arms with stately patience, as the last raindrops sloughed off his clothes and face.

'I am leaving,' the Praefector neutrally replied. 'Muster your men at the Depression tomorrow, if that is what you truly wish. I don't care if you truly mean what you're saying, but our response will be the same. Your traitorous kinsmen can come with *gladii* in hand, or open arms. The XII will meet you head-on, regardless. We will put every last one of your followers to the sword. And then we'll bring you back to Rome clapped in irons.'

And then Gnaeus Ignatian did something most unexpected. Scarcely ten paces from his unwilling guest, he completely, utterly, lost his façade of calm.

'Have you *truly* no wish to fight for what is right?' he thundered. 'How dark does the world have to be, Orbus? How much wrong can you stomach, before you step out from your regimented ranks and make a stand?' He was snarling now, snarling and shouting. The stately, silver-tongued equivocator had evaporated. In its place stood a wild, zealous demagogue. 'I come before you with open arms, but do you think that is my only choice? Marching to Rome with the Fulminata at my side will send one message. But rest assured, *miles*. Making that crossing over your broken backs will send another.'

'Goodbye, Legate Ignatian.'

'*I will not yield!*' He bellowed through the diminishing rain. '*I will not take the knee before the tyrant!*'

Orbus was already leaving, making for the top of the winding walkway they'd ascended up from. 'We are Romans,' he drily replied as he took his leave. 'We were born to do nothing else.'

XV
CONVERGENCE

'ALRIGHT,' OPTATIS SIGHED, smiling shyly as he toyed with the *signaculum* hanging from his neck. 'Just three guesses, so use them well.'

The hilltop, overlooking the babbling River Garumna and the conifer glades that hugged its banks, gave them a decent view of the valley further down, and the military camp nestled in its base. The bustle of an active *castra* on enemy soil was visible even from here, and across the ridges and dips lookouts scoured the surrounding landscape for any hints of an oncoming attack.

'I can get this.' Bydreth clapped his hands together, clearing his throat. After the week they'd all had out in the wilds, even a few hours of friendly company back at camp was enough to rejuvenate him. 'Did you...' He paused, with that trademark glint in his eye. 'Did you walk in on your centurion getting his prick out for some camp wench?'

At his right, Molchis rolled over in a fit of hoarse laughter, and then some rather phlegmy coughing. A life lived in the *Subura*'s smoggy slums did that to your lungs. At Bydreth's other shoulder, Argias turned aside to suppress a *scholam*-boy's smirk.

'Ah,' Optatis finally replied with a twinkle. 'How amusing, is the mind of a British savage at work. Alas no, my dear Bydreth. If catching your officer in... *questionable* company was all it took to be discharged, then the IX would run out of men. Goats, those officers were.'

That made them laugh even more, and Optatis tried not to show how much he enjoyed that. Two guesses left.

'My turn,' Molchis growled roguishly when he was done coughing up phlegm. 'Did you have your *'bernium* hijack your cohort's ale shipment, and sell it back to your friends round the campfire for a greasy backhand?'

'Gods below,' Optatis replied after a stunned silence. 'Are you a misunderstood genius, Molchis?'

More laughter, not quite so hard this time. And only one guess remained. The former *decanus* took a long look at the youngest man among them, giving the *optio* a fatherly smile. 'Go on then, Argias. Last man standing.'

The First Legionary looked at Optatis, choosing his words. He'd seen the maelstrom of faded scars adorning the Branded officer's back, and although he'd always known better than to ask, he couldn't stop himself from speculating. They reminded him of Orbus' own disfigurements, only these ones seemed a little more... deliberate.

'Were you...' He found himself hesitating. Molchis and Bydreth were watching him intently, oblivious to his internal machinations.

'Jackal got your tongue?' the Painted Centurion asked him wryly.

'I'm sorry,' Argias sheepishly replied. 'What I meant was... were you caught bedding some tribune's mother, perhaps?' He tried to make the joke sound more convincing. 'I've seen the marks on your back, sir. I know some kittens like to scratch.'

That was enough to send the other two howling. Optatis watched him through the laughter, looking ready to say something more, before giving in to a conciliatory smile.

'Bad luck, my friends,' he finally replied when the others had settled. 'That's three guesses, all spent. Looks like you'll never know why the IX exiled me.'

The others were far too busy ribbing Argias for such a sordid suggestion. Bydreth had pulled him into a crushing bear hug, rubbing his knuckles through the younger *miles*' hair as they continued to boyishly tease him.

'Just think how prim and proper you were, when we came to you,' Bydreth laughed. 'Our little *optio* is growing up so fast!'

'Isn't that the truth.' Molchis darkly chuckled. 'I think we've been a bad influence on you, boy.' He stopped for a moment, before quietly pulling out a stoppered flask from his belt and twisting it open for a sip.

The other three men just stared at him, united in naked shock. Even Optatis seemed taken aback.

'Where, in the name of Rome's Emperor, did you get that?'

Molchis shrugged, trying to look nonchalant as he took another swig of ale. 'It's all above board. The quartermaster signed off on it last night. Came from the camp inventory.'

'You lying git.' Bydreth grinned, and soon the two of them were wrestling like street brats, playfighting like boys yet to take the toga of manhood. The Ulthaini prince's raging thirst was forgivable, all things considered. Running a *castra* in wartime required an ironclad devotion to discipline. Thracian, as ranking camp prefect, was hardly going to go a different way on his first official command.

Out of the cohort's dwindling stockpile of food and provisions, what little alcohol Urbanus permitted wound up in the XII's hands more often than the *auxilia*'s.

'Aha!' Bydreth snarled triumphantly, brandishing the half-empty flagon at last. 'Victory is mine,' he declared, before throwing his head back and promptly downing the whole draught. A good amount spilt down his neck and tunic, but he didn't seem to mind.

'Really?' Optatis asked with dry exasperation.

The tribal prince flashed one of his grins, giving his mouth a crude wipe. His friends had a glimpse of blackened, rotted gums and discoloured teeth before he replied. 'I just think if our light-fingered friend from the Carcer is going to go raiding, then we should all get to share in the spoils. Those haughty bastards in the XII aren't exactly sharing with us, are they?'

Molchis pulled a face. 'You're worse than Arxander.' He stuck his chin out, aping the hoplite's coarse Achaean accent. '"*You hold your drink like a Persian boy...*"' It wasn't particularly convincing, but it made them snigger all the same.

Bydreth's brow wrinkled as he thought some more. 'On second thoughts, maybe keep your hands out of the stores from now on, eh? If those boy-clerks find *anything* missing, no matter who's been at them, you can bet we'll be the ones who get the blame.'

He had a point. Even when the two armies had joined forces on the field, relations between the Fulminata's First Cohort and Orbus' cadre of men had remained frosty, at best. The *auxilia* largely kept to their own corner of the *castra*, a situation that suited both parties. None of the *hastati* from Ardius' century would even deign to speak to them following the incident with Fuscator back in Rome.

A part of Bydreth actually relished the recent escalation in the fighting. Soon enough, these XII Legion bastards would have to set aside their distaste and embrace them as allies of desperation.

If they wanted to live, at any rate.

'Whatever,' the Creedless' centurion testily replied. He didn't seem much given to the idea. 'I'll leave it be. Unless I get thirsty again.'

Emboldened by the other men's rough familiarity, Argias dared to risk a little more banter. 'I could report you to the Praefector, Molchis.' He tried to sound as officious as he could. 'Either praefector, come to think of it.'

'Steady on,' Optatis chided him. 'First of all, there is only one praefector we answer to. And secondly, the old man's got bigger things on his mind right now. They all do.'

He hardly needed to elaborate, for the other three *milites* had all been out today with Orbus. Upon being released, unharmed, by Graecillus' riders, they'd returned to the *castra* as quickly as they could. News of the ambush had spread through the *auxilia* and Fulminata, and was doubtless all over the camp by now. Orbus, however, had immediately left to convene with Urbanus and the centurions, debriefing them on whatever had transpired on his foray into Arx Agrippum.

And there they still remained, hours later, in one of the campaign's longest and most secretive war councils. The troops had been forbidden to disturb it, on pain of death. Bydreth found that needlessly theatrical, but Optatis and Argias had convinced him they meant it.

'We ought to be getting back,' Argias told them. As if on cue, a loud crash from down the valley drew their eyes back to the *castra*. A few burly shouts followed. Another cache of legion weapons, presumably. Or armour. Either way, dropping them was probably punishable by whipping.

The four of them got up, getting ready to walk back to whatever duties were waiting for them.

'I left Brauda in charge of weapons inspection,' Bydreth admitted as they descended from the grassy knoll. 'I haven't heard from him since, which means he's almost certainly got into a fight with the armourers.'

The others chuckled as they followed him down the ridge. Below them, the *castra* waited, cold yet welcoming.

VINCULEX WATCHED THEM return to camp from his vantage point on the overlooking hill.

The other three centurions hadn't noticed him, and neither had that little pup Argias. The Gutter Prince had decided against joining them. He had little truck with his fellow *auxilia*.

Months of marching for Aquitania, and weeks of guerrilla war hadn't done much to change that.

The burning beneath his skin held his attention. Flesh and muscle cried out for relief, as incendiary poison roared its way through his bloodstream.

Vinculex leant forward, over the hilltop. All the way forward. And let himself fall.

For a long and agonising second, the Garumna rushed up to meet him.

And then he hit the surface.

'AND THERE WE have it,' Orbus concluded, drinking in the eyes boring into him. 'That is where we stand.'

The other seven men around the war table had no immediate response. Although they'd interrogated every part of the Praefector's account as it unwound, the full impact would take time to sink in.

And time was one thing they didn't have.

'Well.' Urbanus gently reclined back in his curule chair. 'This rather puts paid to trying to break them down piecemeal. So they aren't merely rebels. They are fanatics.'

'You were a fool,' Ardius growled, eyes fixed on Orbus. 'You were with him long enough, without the presence of armed guards. You could have just broken the bastard's neck and ended it.'

Orbus had had his fill of pissing matches lately, and not even the prospect of a decent argument could fire his blood today. 'Do you really think he would be that lax?' he retorted across the table. 'He was surrounded by guards, the whole time we talked. And he had a *pugio* on him. If I'd tried anything, it would have failed.'

'Craven as ever,' the *hastati* centurion quietly retorted. Orbus didn't even grace that with a reply.

'Gnaeus Ignatian's greatest strength is his voice.' The Praefector was addressing them all again now. 'That is how he has a city dancing to his tune. He believes every word of what he says, however deluded. And that belief is infectious.'

His grim gaze bore into them as he continued. 'Killing him, alone, will not end what he stands for. Only scattering his army to the winds will do that. Like the Hydra of Lerna,' he ruefully added. 'Cut off one head, and more will simply grow.'

'Never mind the hordes of unwashed trash he can summon from Arx Agrippum,' Alvanus cantankerously agreed. His words agreed, but his tone was still challenging. 'We've got eight hundred men. *Barely.* The traitor can call upon… well, the gods know how many. What do we have to do? Hurl back everything he sends against us, march across the country and raise that damn city to the ground?' Alvanus smiled grimly, trying to pass the idea off as a joke. But then, every joke is half-meant. Therein lies the essence of humour.

Urbanus locked eyes with the *triarii* centurion, silently weighing up his words. 'Something to consider,' he finally replied. 'But not the only consideration, I'm afraid. We can only stretch our mandate so far, my friends.'

No-one spoke, for the Legate's meaning was entirely obvious. Urbanus had a fairly wide remit to put the rebellion down hard, as quickly and smoothly as could be. But there were limits to that authority. To go too far in his zeal would be hard to explain to the Senate, especially if he had any particular enemies in those hallowed ranks.

Even a legate as renowned as him, who'd held command this long, could not afford to overstep his bounds. An enquiry, no matter how many years later, could well blow back on him. And nothing like that could be allowed to touch the Emperor.

'At least we are not totally without options,' Cascana added, trying his best to sound hopeful. 'With the *ballistae* provided by the brothers Lemnon, an attack on Arx Agrippum's walls isn't out of the question, if it truly comes to that.'

'Indeed,' Thracian agreed, and Orbus subconsciously groaned as he realised what would follow. 'We must thank our esteemed guest from the *auxilia*.' He waved a hand at the other praefector with faux magnanimity. 'So noble of you, Orbus, to whore yourself out for our benefit. How fares the good lady Volscania, in her bridegroom's absence?'

The other centurions shared a low chuckle, while the Praefector silently ground his teeth. The multiple letters the *castra* had received, inscribed with Aemilia's unmistakeable scrawl, still sat beneath a pile of old tunics in his billet. Not a single seal had been broken open.

'There is one other matter worth considering,' Orbus added once the sniggering had faded. 'Gnaeus Ignatian believes we have brought the entire XII to bear. As far as he knows, the whole legion is being arrayed against him.' He paused, breathing out gently. 'And I did not correct that belief.'

Urbanus leant forward, his fingers steepled against his right temple like a king weary of kingship. A part of him wanted to chastise the Praefector for muddying things further. Another wanted to contemptuously wave the issue aside, supposing that the traitorous general would have simply brought a larger force anyway. The rest of him simply wanted to scream, regardless of whose fault it was.

'The right decision,' Scipio interjected, more for decorum than to assuage Orbus' doubts. 'It is not our place to feed the enemy intelligence.'

'Numbers, we can do nothing about.' Urbanus was done ruminating on his fears. Practicalities were what mattered now. 'The levy shouldn't give us a great deal to worry about. Not now we can march out in force, without an incentive to hold back. The legionaries of the XXV, however, will be the true threat. Years have passed since they last saw active service, but those men were born soldiers. And they'll die like them, too.'

No-one argued. The Legate paused, before he dared make his next inquiry.

'Orbus,' he began. 'From everything you saw and heard... how serious do you think the traitor was about that offer of alliance?'

It must have taken some fortitude to ask that question. To even contemplate asking it. Orbus couldn't help feeling a stab of sympathy. It was a brave commander who voiced an idea like that before his subordinates. The Praefector didn't doubt Urbanus' loyalty for one second, but the point still stood.

'In all honesty,' Orbus levelly replied, 'I think he would truly make allies of us if he could. Reluctant allies, at least. Even if he had to break us on the battlefield first. He may strive to be magnanimous, but it'd be a choice between joining his army, or facing destruction.'

'How merciful,' Alvanus snorted.

'You didn't let me finish,' the Praefector added, shaking his head. 'Gnaeus Ignatian might have loftier goals in mind than conquest, but I doubt Septimus Graecillus does. He was practically chomping at the bit, the whole time I was there. No matter what games his master plays, I can't see him walking away from this. Not without a slaughter.'

Marcus Scipio's face darkened even as he raised his eyebrows. 'And if this Graecillus is the marshal of the massing army…'

Orbus nodded. 'Exactly. If Ignatian hands command of the Ignipotens to his attack dog, then there will be no quarter given. Not until one side lies dead.'

No-one in the tent seemed eager to jump on that. And who could blame them?

'So.' Alvanus cleared his haggard throat, all formality forgotten. 'Just another day at the coalface, eh?'

A few of the others snorted, Orbus and the Legate included. Whatever the *triarii* commander's faults were, when the devil came knocking, he was a man you wanted in your corner.

And that knock was set to come sooner than planned, as the tent's mouth flapped open. Daylight briefly painted the length of the war table, before the flaps fell shut again.

'*Legatus.*' The young tribune, assigned to Urbanus' own command staff, was the only soul in the *castra* not forbidden to disturb their council. And there was only one reason he would.

'Our last scouts just returned to camp,' the Tribune reported. 'Yours too, Prefect,' he added, nodding to Orbus. 'Five different '*bernia*, all arriving from different paths, each one telling the same tale.'

'Go on,' Urbanus replied.

'Enemies draw near,' the Tribune informed him, and the others all seemed to tense in unison. 'In numbers we've yet to witness. Down over the moors, through the forests, as the crow flies instead of sticking to the paths. And not just the levy, either.' The young man paused, and they all saw the fear pass over his face. 'Nothing is confirmed, *Legatus*, but there are reports of legionaries.'

So it was finally happening. Orbus almost felt like spitting. Ignatian had promised him another day, more or less, if a traitor's word was ever to be believed. Or maybe Graecillus had forced his hand, straining at his leash.

'Time of arrival?' Cascana asked.

'About two hours, First Spear. Perhaps three.' And then, dismissed with a perfunctory nod, the Tribune was gone.

'Well,' Thracian commented in the pause that followed. 'I suppose this rather expediates things.'

'Let us focus on what we know.' This from Cascana, already rising to his feet. The other centurions around him were gradually doing the same. Outside, voices were being steadily raised. Steel rasped as armour was buckled on and blades were drawn and sheathed. The scouts' ill tidings had spread through the rank and file, and the *milites* knew this old dance well. They readied themselves for war even as their officers drew up plans. Whatever orders were headed their way, the men of the Fulminata would be ready.

Orbus doubted his own charges would be quite so disciplined.

'No legion can move that swiftly,' Cascana maintained. 'Not as one body.' He pulled close one of the maps that lay before Urbanus – a rough topographical sketch of the Ionys Depression, and the area around it. 'Which means they'll be moving as centuries. Or at the very least, as cohorts,' he added, pointing to where an 'X' marked the XII's *castra*. 'The logical route of attack would be here.' His finger moved. 'From the southwest. The ground is kindest to them there.'

'True enough,' the Legate conceded. 'But to negate the Depression's treacherous footing, and have their numbers actually count for something...'

Ardius had seen it too. 'A pincer deployment, from the north. With a full-frontal attack to draw us out. And while we engage the first column of traitors head on...'

'The trap's jaws swing shut,' Pylades finished for him, for want of anything better to say. 'So how do we counter such an attack?'

Whatever Urbanus was going to say, Alvanus got there first.

'There was me, thinking it was the young bloods whose veins were full of piss and wine.' He seemed to enjoy where he'd found himself, perversely. 'Where's your fire, boy? Do you whine like this every time the odds are against you?'

Pylades simply pouted, peering at the battle map over Cascana's shoulder.

'It would seem,' mused Thracian, moving to join them, 'that the simplest way to avoid falling into the snare is to break it open. To crush the first prong, before their jaws close around us.'

'That makes sense,' Scipio nodded, pointing to the map from his side of the table. 'It breaks us free from the deadlock, if nothing else. At best, though, it robs them of their coordination.'

'Exactly.' That seemed to pique Pylades' spirits again. 'Their commander – whoever it turns out to be – will have to take to the vanguard, if he hopes to coordinate his men with any grace. Which gives us as an opportunity,' he added with unashamed relish. 'A chance to put their leader right in the earth. How's that for piss and wine, Alvanus?'

'Easy, young man.' Alvanus seemed pleased with what he heard, but they weren't there yet. 'It's as we said from the outset. This battle – this war – won't end with a princeling's severed head.'

'Maybe not,' Ardius thoughtfully murmured. 'But it will certainly affect how this ends. What is easier? Facing one almighty horde, that moves and strikes with a thousand eyes and one voice?' He smiled grimly. 'Or a number of fractured, smaller forces, shorn of their orders and reeling in disarray?'

'Valid words.' Thracian, still at Urbanus' side, graced them all with an elegant smirk. 'And that, my friends, is a fight we might actually win.'

THE CENTURIONS CONTINUED to plot and plan, growing more animated as they milled about the war table. Pegs were pushed across the crudely-drawn map to showcase troop movements and potential manoeuvres. This plan they'd hit upon – to break the first phalanx of Ignatian's troops before the remaining bodies could flank them – seemed to be going down rather well.

And it didn't stop there, either. All talk now was of turning the tables on their attackers. Leaving a tantalisingly small and weaker force to meet the Army's first column head on, and draw out the attacking pincers, was a gambit the officers yearned to exploit.

From there, their other forces could pour out from the Depression, and beat the flanking forces at their own game. This time, they would be the ones springing the enveloping trap.

At best, it could succeed, dividing the enemy and destroying them piecemeal. At worst, it could allow the traitors to do the very same, and grinding their outnumbered foes down through wrath and weight of iron.

Orbus didn't particularly share his comrades' enthusiasm. Privately, he doubted the veterans of the once-XXV would be rattled by something as symbolic as the loss of their leader.

And, as he silently met the Legate's eyes across the war table, he had a feeling he knew where this was going.

'Who will be the lure?' Thracian asked, the question pointed enough to gently silence the others.

'I wouldn't peg your hopes on volunteers,' Alvanus snorted with a light belch. 'Whoever's picked to stand in that sacrificial line... well, you'd better put the cohort's funeral club on standby. The butcher's bill will be dear.'

'It always is,' Cascana smoothly shot back. 'We're not earning our keep otherwise. And anyway... that seems a quaint thought for a *triarius* to have, no? Some of us have to stand at the front of the battleline, instead of anchoring the rear.'

'Now, now.' Thracian raised a conciliatory hand, patting the map with one of his satisfied semi-smiles. Orbus had never liked that look. 'As right as you are, Alvanus, maybe we can take the burden off our troops entirely, while still lining the trap with bodies.'

And here, at last, they came to it. Had Orbus suspected anything else?

'Some soldiers, perhaps,' Thracian idly went on, 'who are not part of the Legion?'

Orbus met their expectant gazes, acutely aware that he wasn't saying anything. The only sound came from outside, where the preparations for battle were growing louder and more fevered.

'All things considered,' he finally recovered his tongue, 'are you sure this is the wisest cause of action?' The words were meant for Thracian, but his gaze drifted over to the largely impassive Urbanus. The *Legatus* said nothing, seemingly content to let his underlings thrash out the minutiae of this plan for themselves. 'My men are the least tested of our forces. This is quite a burden to place on them.' He cocked his head. 'The *triarii* would be better suited to this task, in my opinion.'

'That is not for you to decide,' Urbanus finally snapped. 'And the blood of legionaries is never spilt lightly, Orbus. Whatever the odds of victory. In this respect, Praefector Thracian is correct. If *auxilia* can die in place of legion stock, then they have fulfilled their career's purpose.' For whatever it was worth, the old *legatus* didn't seem to take any pleasure from admitting that. 'And you assured me that your men were ready for a true war. Was that a lie, Praefector?'

Orbus swallowed his bile and his misgivings. 'No, sir. It was not.'

'It is settled, then.' Thracian nodded. 'Praefector Orbus and his *auxilia* will hold their lines, taking the brunt of the traitors' first push. Alvanus and Scipio's centuries will join the attack from the east and west flanks, respectively. The other three will be the ones to finally spring the trap. Once the enemy's foremost cohort is broken asunder, any of the rest that do not flee – well, we will fight them as one.'

Orbus had to hand it to him. He could come up with a score of battle plans that suited the moment just as well, right off the bat. But none quite so expedient. And none that put his men in such peril, while keeping the others in the clear.

That opinion was purely academic, however, for he wasn't legion anymore. His presence here was merely by invitation, one extended as a dubious courtesy. He had no real voice at this table.

But it didn't matter, thankfully. Not today. Someone else had yet to weigh in on the matter.

'As noble as your intentions are, Praefector,' Cascana archly cut in, fixing Thracian with a pointed look, 'I'm sure we could adhere to the spirit of this plan, if not the letter. Without getting our allies slaughtered to a man, if the inference is slipping beneath your notice.' The saccharine smile that followed put all the others on edge. Few men in the XII were brave, or foolhardy, enough to challenge Thracian so adroitly.

'I'm sure there is,' the Camp Prefect replied, with tranquil, murderous charm. 'Iulus Cascana, the tireless voice of sentiment.'

'Not this time,' Cascana amicably retorted. 'I am First Spear of this cohort, Thracian, just as you once were. You may rule this legion in our legate's absence, but the First Cohort answers to me, first and foremost. And let me tell you, Praefector, through the lens of any future command aspirations you secretly nurse—' He let that hang in the air. '—think how it will look, the next time you seek to enlist the aid of auxiliaries. Or court another legion to fight at your side. Think how it will look, to have recklessly thrown away your only allies' lives during your first true command.'

Grumbles broke out from around the table, but Cascana paid them no heed. Thracian's icy gaze thawed a notch, which was what mattered. He saw the First Spear's point. Urbanus, for his part, said nothing, and shorn of his legate's support, the only way for Thracian to save face was through concession.

'I hear you, and I heed you, First Spear. But what do you propose, in that case? Will your century take Orbus' place, in the mouth of the trap?'

'Not quite.' Cascana had been counting on that very suggestion. 'We will join the Praefector's men, standing shoulder to shoulder. And I say this,' he added. 'If our *legatus* permits, of course.' He favoured Urbanus with a respectful nod. 'I say that each centurion at this table should be given the option to join us. If he so wishes.'

For a moment, it looked like Thracian would laugh that idea off the table. 'Do you...' he began, looking to Urbanus for support that was not coming. 'If that is your wish, First Spear. Well then.' He slapped his hands together, locking eyes with the closest other centurion. 'Time to hear your answers, men.'

Manius Pylades pretended to think for a moment, avoiding Orbus' gaze. 'I sympathise with your aims,

First Spear,' he began. 'But the more legionaries who spring the trap, the more likely we will all live. No.'

Cascana swallowed. No surprises there. Thracian still knew how to pull his old *decanus'* strings, clearly.

'If you think I'm letting any of my *hastati* die for that traitor,' Ardius growled, 'or his mongrel soldiers, then you're mistaken, First Spear. Not a chance.'

Orbus winced, though no-one saw it. To be honest, that had been gentler than he'd expected.

Rufus Alvanus, true to form, was as affable in his bearing as he was crude in his reasoning. '*Auxilia*'s lot, Orbus. Your throats for our lives. Those *triarii* of mine, their lives and records are worth their weight in *aurei*. Can't waste them, Praefector. Not on a whim.'

'I appreciate your rationale, Centurion Alvanus.' Cascana had the dignity not to challenge him. 'I only w—'

'I will stand with you.' That final avowal cut over whatever Iulus was going to say. 'I will stand with Orbus and Cascana.'

For a moment, uncle and nephew were speechless. But one look at Marcus Scipio told them his mind was made up. There was no arguing with the look on his face. 'You will have my sword, First Spear. And my men.'

Orbus stretched a hand across the table, clasping the Centurion's. 'Thank you, Scipio. You honour me.'

'Look at you.' Urbanus startled the nearest men with his voice. 'Working as one without my guiding hand. I would say our work here is done, gentlemen.'

WITH COUNCIL ADJOURNED, the officers emerged to a camp at war. Men at arms shouted readiness at each other, drawing up into *'bernia* and centuries. The ring of hammers on steel carried over even this ruckus, as the cohort's last few weapons and suits of armour were readied for battle.

The clamour, the chaos – they could have been at war already. Such was the noise.

The centurions strode out into this maelstrom of industry, barking orders and making their *milites* ready for the coming fight. The Praefector was already leaving, making his way toward the *castra*'s southern quadrant where the *auxilia* were billeted. He could smell incense in the air; one of the pre-battle Martian rites, probably. Something involving the Legion's *aquila* and the *signae* born aloft in each century. Neither Orbus nor his men had been invited to join the rituals, but by now he knew better than to nurse that grudge.

Cascana broke his train of thought as he passed, sending his *optio* away with orders even as he buckled on his leather vambraces.

'Iulus,' he called to him. They'd barely spoken since their row on the Field of Mars, and although things had thawed since then, they were still far from warm. 'What you said in there—'

'Later, uncle.' Cascana simply slapped his shoulder, the gesture more soldierly than affectionate. Regardless, it was the warmest, most familial thing Orbus had felt in months. 'We'll talk later. When the battle's done and won.' Around them, the riotous racket of the *castra* grew louder. 'I'll race you to the traitor's feet.'

And then he was gone, one man amid a shoal of legion red. Orbus watched him leave, pride wrote plain upon his features. As the lure, both their forces would be hit hard. Perhaps irrevocably. And yet Cascana hadn't thought twice about standing with him.

Orbus turned, to see a trail of running legionaries in specialist uniform. *Immunes*, making their way to where the *ballistae* had been planted. They had no particular orders for the coming battle – indeed, none of the other officers had factored them into their plans – so by default, they would pull their siege engines back to the camp, out of harm's way.

An idea came to him, in that moment. The unwelcome ghost of an idea, a daring idea that wouldn't survive scrutiny. But one that might even the odds for all of them.

'You there,' he called out, setting off after them. 'Where's your *decanus*?'

'FORM UP, SWORDS and spears. Very good.'

Marcus Scipio barely glanced at his *triarii* as he trooped by. All seemed in readiness, but then he ran a tough ship in his century. He was known and respected for it.

A rough crest was painted over his tent's side, marking it out as an officer's personal *praetorium*. Within he'd find his weapons, his *optio* and a keg of better-quality ale he'd secretly imported from Rome to keep him going through the summer. Without a backward glance at his veterans, he threw back the flaps and went inside.

'Hello, Centurion.'

The voice made Scipio start, against his pride. He'd been taken off guard. A centurion in the Roman army didn't get taken off guard.

'Thracian,' he ventured, eying the Camp Prefect with suspicious respect. They were the only two people in the tent, which was odd. Scipio's *optio* and armoury-slaves were nowhere to be seen.

'I won't keep you, Marcus.' Thracian was holding Scipio's trusted *gladius*, idly weighing up the weapon in his hand as he affected a lack of interest. 'That was quite the stand you took back there, throwing in your lot with Orbus. You are a brave man.'

Scipio didn't reply at once. Brave for agreeing to help bait the trap? Or brave for defying Thracian's wish to have the *auxilia* stand alone?

'Not that it matters,' the Praefector continued. 'Because you're not going to go through with it. You will take your place with Alvanus and Pylades' men, as was the original plan.' He smiled malevolently. 'A last-minute change of deployment. Such is war.'

At first, the *triarii* centurion thought he'd misheard. 'With respect, sir, you agreed before the Legate to give us all the choice. And you heard me make mine.'

'I did,' Thracian conceded with a shrug. 'But with any truly free choice, a man has the prerogative to change his mind. And right here, right now…' Thracian's eyes raked Scipio's face. 'I believe you've just changed yours.'

A pause followed, heavy with the weight of the implicit. For all the cacophony outside, the tent suddenly felt very alone.

'And why…' Scipio matched Thracian's conspiratorial tone, 'why, precisely, would I do that?'

'Because of our earlier conversation, Marcus.' Thracian was smiling again now. 'Our little talk, at the *Circus Maximus* back in Januarius. I am sure you can recall what we discussed.'

Of course. Scipio silently cursed himself for a fool. What had he been thinking? Thracian still had that dirty little secret of his, a tool of blackmail to dangle at will.

'I gave Orbus and Cascana my word.' Oh, how impotent he must have sounded now. How helpless. 'The others all heard it, Urbanus included.'

Thracian nodded, mock-sagely. 'Indeed you did. Tragic.'

'They will curse me for a coward. An oathbreaker.'

That actually made the Praefector snigger. And *that* set Scipio's fingers gently curling, on their way to becoming fists. 'Perhaps, Centurion, you should be a little more politic with your words. You never know when you'll be caught out.'

'You utter shitting bastard.'

From sniggers, came laughter. 'Now, now, Marcus. That's precisely what you called me last time. At least try to expand your repertoire.'

He made to leave, turning his back on Scipio and throwing the *gladius* down upon the tent floor.

'One day, Thracian,' Scipio spoke to his back, 'the tables will be turned.'

'One day, perhaps.' Thracian seemed to genuinely agree. 'But for now, I need men I can rely upon. Show me you are one of those men, Marcus. We still have a war to win.'

XVI
THE BATTLE OF ARX AGRIPPUM

HE LOOKED OUT across the wilderness with the patience of a god. But for the hundreds of soldiers marching in drudging lockstep far behind him, and the armed and armoured guards flanking him, he could have been a travelling nomad.

'Well?' he asked, without turning.

Septimus Graecillus gave his horse some soothing clicks as he dismounted. 'Our outriders all tell the same story, my lord. The enemy have retreated through the Depression, no doubt hoping our numbers will count for nothing in the narrowed confines. A small rear-guard has been left behind, presumably to stall our advance and give their brethren time to regroup elsewhere.'

'Naturally.'

'Naturally,' Graecillus continued. 'Numbers are not on their side, however. The rear-guard barely amounts to five hundred men, if our reports are accurate.' He shook his head. 'The gods only know what they're trying to achieve. They must know our reinforcements are barely a day's march away. And most of *their* strength must have already withdrawn. There were scarcely less than a thousand men encamped here, even before we mustered out.'

There was an unpleasant light in the former decurion's eyes, kindled by the prospect of bloodshed. 'We could break them right now, even just with what's behind us. The scouts mentioned siege engines in their camp, as well, but I'm not worried. They just sound like *ballistae*. Wall-breakers. Nothing to threaten us on the ground.'

Gnaeus Ignatian nodded, unbothered by anything he'd heard. 'And the rear-guard themselves?'

'Some legion, apparently,' the Marshal told him. 'But *auxilia*, for the most part. Ragged, ill-disciplined, the lot of them.'

'Orbus.' Ignatian breathed the name like a confession. The wind breathed in their faces with nothing to break its flow. 'More's the pity, Graecillus. I'm going to regret slaying him, more than any other man in that army. He would have made a fine soldier for the cause.'

Graecillus chose not to dwell on that, screwing up his mutilated face as he thought. 'And Urbanus, Lord Castellan? Do your plans for him still stand?'

Ignatian smiled. 'They do, my friend. A legate of Rome, as our prisoner. Our spoils of war.' The smile deepened, entertaining the prospect. 'Think of the symbolism, Graecillus. Think of the shockwaves it will send. Think how the Senate will baulk, to see one of their wretched little cabal so humbled.'

The Marshal smiled too, savouring that mental image. 'Let them cower in their lofty little curule chairs. Let it shake them to their corrupt little hearts. We are coming for them, my lord. We are coming for all their kind.'

Ignatian didn't quite share his follower's relish. Nothing about this calling, or the bloody places it brought him to, gave him relish. It was duty. The self-appointed duty of a man who knew he was right.

Rome would be reborn once again, the purple and gold of the Imperial sham torn asunder. But you couldn't slay an empire with words and ideals.

Gnaeus Ignatian drew his sword in one smooth motion, pointing the gleaming falchion into the air.

Behind him, a thousand similar blades caught the sun's afternoon gleam as the Army of the Free raised their *gladii* in emulation.

'Here we are again,' the Castellan of Arx Agrippum murmured, sheathing his weapon and pulling his horse's reins. 'Onwards. Let us get this sordid slaughter over with.'

'HERE WE ARE again,' Orbus unwittingly echoed his traitorous counterpart, some miles away. 'Part of me didn't think I'd stand in a legion battleline again.'

Chuckling answered him from both sides. That was a half-truth, quite literally. Cascana's warriors had broken down into maniples, small groups of his men interspersed between each century of the *auxilia* to make a line with no weak links. Such was the theory, anyway.

Cascana himself commanded one such group a little way off, east of the Branded. His *optio*, Hesperon, had taken charge of another to the west, holding position with Brauda and the Painted. And Orbus himself had taken command of one further group of them; a handful of *'bernia* nestled between the core of his and Cascana's defensive gauntlet.

The Praefector's own centuries were equally arrayed for combat, each man and unit finally knowing his place in the order of battle. On the line's eastern flank, Arxander and the Riven stood as resolute as ever.

Vinculex and his Brazen formed the next corps of *auxilia*, the former gladiators close enough to the battleline's heart to assuage their master's ego. Orbus hadn't let it bother him, in the end. Cascana's unit of *principes* hugged their flank, and the First Spear's watchful eye gave him some solace. Besides, Orbus had sent Argias to reinforce them, just to be sure. The *optio* had to stand somewhere, and in a legion, his traditional role as 'second in the century' meant watching from the rear and stopping any men who tried to run away.

'With the Brazen?' Argias had originally asked. 'Do you really trust Vinculex so little?'

'I trust him to fight,' Orbus explained. 'I don't trust him to keep his head. Cascana's out that way, but he'll have enough to worry about. Besides,' he added, 'it's either that or Molchis. Your choice, *optio*.'

'Point taken.' That had shut Argias up. Any excuse to steer clear of the Creedless.

And nearer the centre, sandwiched between Orbus and Cascana's *principes*, lay the true and tempered core of the *auxilia*. The Branded, standing proud with Optatis, were the closest the Praefector's followers came to true legionaries. Nothing drove a soldier's pride like redemption. Nothing spurred on a broken man like the chance to be whole again.

Orbus had clapped Optatis on the shoulder as they'd taken their places. 'How are you feeling?' he'd asked.

The former IX Legion officer had shrugged. 'Like a freshly-minted *hastatus*, about to piss his breeches for the very first time.'

That had made Orbus smile. 'You're an old hand at this game, Gaius. Think how the others must feel.'

'Hear, hear, Optatis. Imagine how we must feel,' a guttural, accented voice agreed. Both Orbus and the Branded's centurion turned to look.

'I'm serious,' Bydreth added. 'Don't let the ink fool you. I've never fought before. Not like this.'

Orbus had actually laughed at that. Of all the cohort's lieutenants he could have picked to stand with him, he was no longer ashamed to admit he trusted Bydreth the most. It didn't feel forced, taking him away from the Painted. Bydreth was the cohort's beating heart, and he damn well knew it. With him and Optatis anchoring the line's core, Orbus had his left and right hands right where he needed them.

The Praefector looked to his left, where the Creedless stood in near-silent maniples. He thought he could see Molchis among the line of helms, but couldn't swear to it. Not that it mattered. He'd put that century on the middle left specifically, so he'd be close enough to take command if anything went wrong. Jupiter knew they'd given him enough reasons to doubt them. And Hesperon had their other flank, along with more of Cascana's men.

So here they were, at last. Standing as one, an army of men Orbus had made into *milites*. On the precipice of the first true battle since his disgrace and fall, he really ought to feel something.

He turned to look at Bydreth, casually joshing with some of Cascana's *evocati,* somehow making even the hoariest among them grin. Optatis was gently smiling at the Ulthaini prince's jokes, even as he whispered some steadfast words of comfort in a younger Branded's ears.

Then Orbus turned the other way, to where the Creedless and Painted held their own positions, too far away to gauge their thoughts or faces.

Yes. Perhaps he should feel something. But what would be the point in admitting that?

Orbus buckled his crested helmet on, his last piece of battle gear to be donned. His newly-relinked chainmail had been bound too tightly into place, enough to make his recent scars ache, while his tunic and red leather *cingulum* gently idled in the summer breeze. That same breeze pulled and twitched at the wreath atop Cascana's century *signa*, standing proud but aloof among the *principes* a little way off.

Ananke slept in its sheath, belted to Orbus' hip. His sword hand clutched an immense javelin headed with iron. As did every last man in the line.

Out on the plains, the vague forms of the enemy begun to crowd the horizon. Around him, unblooded soldiers stood ready to follow him into war.

What more could a doomed man ask for?

'I RECOGNISE THAT *signa*.'

Graecillus pointed into the distance. There, indeed, the vague form of a military totem stood proud above the enemy lines. Ignatian spurred his horse a little closer, following the Marshal's finger and frowning as he tried to pick out the heraldic sigil adorning it.

'From Bithynia,' Graecillus continued. 'Publius Cascana. That's his iconography. I'm sure of it.'

Ignatian let it go, not particularly moved by this update. 'Are we ready to begin, Marshal?'

Behind them, the throng of Graecillus' cavalry had already parted in two, knowing the order that was coming. And behind *them*, the XXV's former legionaries could be seen ready to march, as well as…

'The levy,' Graecillus observed. 'They are ready.' His ruined face furrowed as he raised his longsword, only to dramatically slash the air with it.

'Oppugnate!'

ORBUS HAD NEVER forgotten this feeling. The gentle susurration of the ground beneath his *caligae*, growing to a staccato thunder that shook the earth in anger.

It was the sound of several hundred men charging at you.

Orbus' whole body tensed as the tell-tale stress of combat engulfed him. His palms grew gradually sweatier as his grip on the *pilum* tightened. He'd already dropped into fighting stance, shoulders arch, centre of gravity low.

Every man in the line had done the same.

'Spear-ready!' he bellowed.

ACROSS THE RANKS, almost four hundred javelins were lowered into place, levelled at the oncoming horde.

The *signa* wavered. Prayers were murmured. Breath sharpened.

THE DUST.

Whatever the battlefield – open plains, autumnal tundra, desert canyons – a thousand pairs of charging feet always brought the dust with them. Enough to feel on your face. Enough to choke the air.

If Fortuna turned her fickle gaze from you, it could even shroud the sky.

The mass of men charged closer.

ON THE RIGHTMOST flank, the Riven eyed the oncoming foe with murderous focus. This was far from the Achaeans' first slaughterhouse, after all. Their spear-hands barely even wavered.

'Levy,' Arxander growled, eyes never leaving the horde. 'Nothing we haven't carved up already.'

'But this many?' Dorthoi grunted, at his right. 'How many is that? A thousand?'

The Centurion rolled his eyes behind his helm's visored faceplate.

'What were you expecting, man? A fucking market queue?'

THEY ATE UP the distance. When a charge begins, momentum grows.

Hearts thunder within muscular chests. Strides lengthen. The power behind them roils and grows. Adrenaline deadens the nerves and senses, corrupting thought, drowning fear... all of it sacrificed on the pyre of *more speed*, *more rage*, *more power*.

Five hundred feet to go. Barely.

ARGIAS' BLOOD FLED his stomach. The tide of flesh drew nearer.

Around him, the *milites* of the Brazen grew more and more tense. Their cherished love of bloodshed robbed them of what little discipline Orbus had hammered into them.

In the first rank, Vinculex's helmed head was curled downward, rivulets of perspiration streaming from his weathered face.

He'd never known Fire like this before.

'*CIRINGE FRONTEM!*' ORBUS roared.

The effect was instant. Across the formation, nearly four hundred metal shields crashed together as one. Legionaries and *auxilia* alike held fast, forming a line – a wedge – of unbroken red and bronze. Sunshine pooled in golden bossplates, glinting and shining from helms and chainmail.

The Praefector dug his heels into the ground. Not long to go now.

ON THE LEFTMOST flank, the Painted raised their shields to answer Orbus' order.

Brauda breathed heavily, his helmet blasting it back in his face. Around him, his Ulthaini kinsmen muttered paeans and whispered orisons to their scarcely-remembered gods, steeling their souls against the doom that was coming for them.

Part of him had chafed at Bydreth's singling out by Orbus, but Brauda needed this. A chance to stand alone, from out beneath his cousin's shadow.

A chance to show he was more than just Bydreth's *optio*.

They were all with him now. Tuggi. Graufh. Falwyn. Godruga. Klaujan. Even young Drygg, his head barely big enough to fill his battle helm.

'*Shynnach,*' they silently chanted. *The Otherworld be praised. The Otherworld be damned. Shynnach shi. Shynnach shar. Shynnach shi. Shynnach shar.*

Brauda gripped his javelin tighter. He didn't intend to die today.

THEY WERE ALMOST on them now. Close enough to hear the screaming.

At the gauntlet's heart, Orbus bared his teeth, raising his spear a fraction. Not far away, Bydreth and

Optatis did the same, unconsciously bracing themselves for the barrage to come.

Fifty feet down the line, Cascana raised his shield a notch.

Fifty feet the other way, Molchis and Fuscator inched backward.

On the eastmost flank, Arxander drew breath to shout a battle cry.

On the flank opposite, Brauda spat into the earth for luck.

Then Orbus shouted three last words. The last thing anyone heard, before the world plunged into hell.

'*Here they come!*'

And then, with a crash like the War God's hammer, the levy hit the Roman lines.

BYDRETH'S HEAD RUNG like a gong.

What had hit his helm? An arrow? A spearhead? A throwing axe?

Whatever. It hit hard enough to concuss him, sprinkling blindness across his vision and making his lungs heave.

Or maybe that was the screaming. He'd roared his lungs ragged, as had every man on either side. The cacophony – the rage, the agony, the percussive boom of swords meeting shields – was so loud he could scarcely hear his own screams.

And his other senses had deserted him too. Vision? Gone, shrunk to what little existed above his shield's rim and the gaps between his neighbours'.

Touch? Too much, from all sides. The tide of Arx Agrippum's levy had crashed against the shield wall like one great creature, and the battleline had anchored its feet to meet it. One horde of men threw everything they had into pushing the wall down. The other side pushed with all their might against them, refusing to yield an inch of ground. Bydreth was glad he wasn't in the first rank. Even here, three or four men deep, he felt like he was being crushed alive.

Even smell had been thrown to the wind. The sun-baked odour of sweat, faeces and rancid breath shrouded them all like fog. Bydreth had actually pissed himself when the charge had hit home, something Optatis had warned him would happen. At the time, he'd laughed the idea away.

If the reeking stench of sulphur meant anything, someone behind him had vomited.

And taste? Well, the front ranks got a face full of copper each time they—

'*Spears!*' Orbus was shouting again. '*Iacite!*'

IT WAS A scene playing out a thousand times or more across the gauntlet. Javelins were thrust over, or through, the line of shields. They couldn't miss. There were too many foes, pressed too tightly together, to miss. Every thrust hit flesh. Every blow ended lives.

Occasionally, the weight of skewered dead would bear one such spear to the ground. Like boars impaled on hunting pikes, each time pulled free from grasping, sweaty grips.

Still. Plenty more where they came from. The defenders had spears to spare, and the attackers were hardly lacking in manpower.

It just meant blood. Spilt, shed, free to fill the air, as much as the dust and the shouting.

Among the Creedless' part of the line, Molchis swore as he spat some of that blood from his mouth.

He wasn't sure whose it was – his own, or someone else's.

'Fanatics!' he bawled to his men over the roaring din. 'Can't break them. Can only kill them!'

CASCANA DROVE HIS shield forward with all his might, refusing to give any ground before the crush of levy. Spittle strung down from his mouth and chin.

'*Push. Them. Back!*'

His legionaries all around him were straining, heaving, grinding their strength up trying to do just that. Every spear-blow was a win, a skewering risk that cleared some space before them before new foes swarmed to fill the gap. But each win was also a gamble, a moment of lowered shield that risked a sword or knife in your face.

None of the *principes* had fallen yet, but those at the front were taking the brunt. Cuts, flesh wounds; nothing that could kill. But it added up.

The scrum of attackers seemed no weaker for losing so many; hands, blades and faces still pressed forth with equal impunity. Cascana was surprised more of them hadn't trampled each other underfoot, or simply crushed each other to death in the scrambling morass. An enterprising few had tried an over-the-top attack, clambering over their frenzied comrades and vaulting clean over the wall of shields.

They'd made it, but hadn't lived long to savour it. Cascana's second rank had seen to that.

'Brace!' he suddenly yelled as he saw the danger. A *gladius*, flying end over end into the men behind him. Presumably from the death throes of its wielder.

The legionary behind him threw his shield up, just in time. The sword crashed, point first, hard enough to dent. It cartwheeled away, deflected, spent.

Not too far up the line from him, a couple of Branded had gone down. Optatis' helmed face wasn't among the slain, but Cascana couldn't pick him out in the ranks either.

A worry for later, then. More frenzied levy were hurling themselves, breaking themselves, on his portion of the line.

A surge of men pushed his shield back.

One kick, to throw them back. One sweep of his *gladius*. One screaming, falling foe.

Block. Blow. Block. Repeat.

To Iulus Cascana, this was simply the ebb and flow of life.

THINGS WEREN'T MUCH better beyond the First Spear's patch.

Neither side seemed to have the upper hand, but only one side seemed to feel it. It didn't matter how many levy died to the wall of spears. It didn't matter how well the Imperials spent their strength, giving all they had to shield friends and slay foes.

Because Graecillus' plan, callous and methodical, was still working.

Gradually, inch by harshly-conceded inch, the defenders were being forced back.

It was as if two thunderbolts had been loosed against each other, each one as potent and reactive as the other, with no outlet for the power of their collision. One was a train of enraged humanity that could cascade its way through anything. The other was the most disciplined, harshly trained fighting force the world would ever see.

There was no apt metaphor to grasp the moment, no pithy turn of phrase. They were two unstoppable forces going head-to-head. Two immovable objects, each as timeless and implacable as the other.

But time was one thing neither side had. Whatever grew weaker, could buckle.

And anything that buckled could be broken.

ORBUS' *PILUM* SHOT out one last time. The crowning iron shaft had crumpled beyond repair – as they always did after enough solid blows – but it was potent enough to bore through one final skull.

Enough of this. The Praefector wiped sweat and grime from his brow as a trio of *principes* closed ranks in front of him. The back of his hand came away with drying blood.

'Want another?' the legionary to his left hoarsely offered, brandishing a fresh javelin. Orbus barely heard him over battle's din, but read the man's lips well enough.

'Don't bother,' he replied. 'I've had enough of this.'

The Praefector grabbed the wooden bugle hanging from his belt. Most Legion formations had a dedicated *cornicen* whose duty it was to sound the horns. Orbus did his own trumpeting, however, and trusted his centurions to do the same. They made the decisions, after all. Theirs were the voices that mattered.

He blew the bugle long, hard and clear.

Nothing changed anywhere around him. The battle raged on. Men threw, hacked, and spat against the straining line of shields.

But Orbus had their ears, now. He knew they were ready.

'*Contendite vestra sponte!*' he roared, hurling the worthless *pilum* clean out into the enemy. '*CONTENDITE! VESTRA! SPONTE!*'

And in that moment, the killing truly began.

FROM THEIR MOUNTED vantage point, the Marshal and the Castellan took stock of this new development.

'And finally, he bites.' Graecillus' malignant grin made him uglier still. 'I was beginning to think he'd never give the order.'

The sounds of slaughter still carried to them here, in fragments. The clashing of blades. The rending of flesh wounds. Screams of the dying, from pride and anger as much as pain.

'It matters not,' Graecillus hastily added. The rise of his master's left eyebrow was reproach enough. 'We needed them to commit, Lord Ignatian. They cannot now recover their defensive poise.'

A dash of his cocksure certainty returned to him. 'Our Imperial friends have played their hand.'

'NOW *THIS*,' BYDRETH howled, 'this is more like it!'

Orbus was too busy killing to reply. He heard his centurion, even as he felt them crash back-to-back. And then Bydreth was gone, chasing another foe.

Ananke arced left, taking off a forearm. Orbus' shield hammered back another enemy. The silver blade leapt back, stopping the falling axe head. One twist of his sword hand disarmed the man. Another was enough to disembowel him.

This damned longsword. *Ananke*'s blade was always too long for a shield wall. He should've taken a *gladius* instead, like the rest of them.

'They're not breaking!' a *miles*, painted head to toe in sanguine gore, called out in Optatis' voice. And he was right. But it wasn't the entire truth.

'No,' Orbus gasped in agreement. Gasped, as clearly as he could, as he tried to dislodge the gauntleted hands around his throat. A headbutt sent his assailant tumbling into the muck. Three *gladii* followed the poor bastard down, sticking and dicing him like a prize sow. One of them belonged to Optatis.

'But they're dying faster,' the Praefector added. 'That's what matters.'

He'd already swung *Ananke* at another foe. All the men around him – Bydreth, Optatis, the Branded, and his swathe of Cascana's century – were doing the same. The shield wall had served them well till now, as had the longer yet less precise reach of javelins.

But at Orbus' bellowed command, all that had changed. The *auxilia* and Cascana's legionaries had drawn their swords now. And instead of pooling their strength into forcing the levy back, now they began to hack them down.

The effect had been immediate. The dishevelled fanatics of Arx Agrippum's citizenry had been corralled, whipped up, worked upon like a coiled spring, and spurred into this suicidal act of bravery. They had been drilled and indoctrinated in arms and murder. They'd had their feeble little skulls filled with Gnaeus Ignatian's honeyed poison, dark promises dangled just one battlefield out of reach.

But against legionaries, against *auxilia*, against regimented soldiers that Orbus had spent his whole career training and shaping, they were horrifically outclassed.

Bydreth was laughing. Laughing as he killed. Whatever he'd told Optatis beforehand, he was fighting like a man born in the Red. Battle-joy – that treacherous, nebulous feeling that could make a corpse or hero of you with similar odds – flowed through him, guiding every strike and fall of his *gladius*.

He'd lost his shield somewhere in the mêlée, something that hadn't dampened his spirit for the fight. All those lessons in swordplay from Orbus and Argias had sunk in after all. Bydreth killed with the point, took blows on the sides and flats, all the while weaving the path of his footwork on a merry dance that no attacker could even follow.

And damn him to Pluto, he was loving every moment of it.

'Come on!' he urged, exhorted, championed the *milites* all around him. '*Come on!*'

The Praefector couldn't quite share the sentiment. He'd stumbled over a group of corpses, trying to pull back from the latest charge.

Friendly corpses. These men had all been Branded. That was the other, double-edged consequence of opening up the shield wall. It was easier to kill. And to be killed.

A mass of furious levy bore him earthward, filling his vision.

'More fool you,' he growled. His *pugio* flashed.

The first attacker gurgled, dagger in windpipe. Orbus had already kicked him aside. His *caliga*'s iron toe took the next bastard in the face, even as he lunged for *Ananke*'s hilt. Sword and dagger carved down with equal malice. Flesh parted. Blood, dark and venous, pissed in his face. The stream was hard enough to make him flinch.

Another booted foot crashed down. A windpipe shattered.

'Get up,' Optatis grunted. 'Can't hold this rank on my own.'

And Orbus did, shield recovered. He chose not to inspect himself as he rose, knowing what he'd see. Army red blackened by sweat patches. Tanned skin painted by wounds and vitae. Iron-dark chainmail corroded by dirt and sand.

Here, a rank or two behind the first line, at least they could see a little way across the wider battle as they fought.

'What are they hoping to achieve?' Optatis called out, booting a not-quite-corpse back into its former kinsmen.

Orbus shook his head, spitting muck from his mouth as he raised *Ananke* once again. An earlier spear-blow had frayed his helmet's leather strap. Much more of that and he'd risk losing it.

'Good question!' Bydreth yelled as he split another man in two. The Ulthaini was so bloody you could scarcely see his ink. '*You there!*' he roared at one of the levy, free hand grabbing him by the neck. '*What are you hoping to ach—*'

A surging wave of attackers swamped him as one, throwing him crashing into Cascana's *principes*. The rebels' reward for exposing themselves so valiantly was death. Steel flashed and reddened as Orbus helped the Branded butcher them all.

'Idiot,' Optatis laughed. The tide of battle had swept him further off, some distance up the line from Orbus with more of his own century. No matter. Optatis could look after himself.

Orbus took a moment to catch some breath, studying the shifting, deafening seascape of clashing forces. A new maniple of Cascana's legionaries pushed past, taking their place on the first rank.

Bydreth had a point, the reckless fool. The levy must have lost... what? Six hundred men? Seven?

Yet here they were, still hurling themselves against the *auxilia*'s defended ground like a horde of rabid bacchants, unable to see sense or doom. Still, they hammered on, beating themselves bloody against a line of swords and—

'Oh, no,' the Praefector rasped, throat haggard from shouting orders all afternoon. He'd been a fool. A proud, blind, fool. How could he have missed it?

'Oh please, by Mars' brazen veins... no.'

THE HORIZON WAS moving.

Any of the Painted or Creedless who looked up in that moment – those not currently imperilled by the maelstrom of blood and iron around them – would have seen the danger too.

They'd been out with Orbus on the wilds, the first time the cavalry had come.

Those unmistakeable silhouettes grew darker, and more defined. They weren't sauntering up to them this time, for prisoners and crossed words. This was a full-on battlefield charge.

It came down to the horses themselves, in the end. A more loosely-trained steed would shy away from even approaching a fully-rigged wall of *scuta*.

But a harsher-trained one? They would simply hit it like a cannonball.

The Praefector swore in back-alley Latin. He slashed a wounded foe's throat out with *Ananke* even as he watched the oncoming wave of *equites*.

He wasn't a betting man. But he wasn't a particularly lucky one either.

'*HNNH!*' GRAECILLUS GROWLED as he spurred on his horse. Behind him, almost fifty of his mounted comrades did the same. '*Hnnnh!*'

FAR BEHIND THEM, Ignatian watched from atop his own beast of burden.

And smiled.

THE CAVALRY CLOSED the distance, swift enough to be unmanning. They bore down upon the clashing battlelines – more precisely, one battleline and the shifting tide of flesh trying to flood it away.

There were still hundreds of Arx Agrippum's levy breaking themselves against Orbus' men. Hundreds of men getting themselves slaughtered for the chance to pull down the odd few legionaries and *auxilia*. And hundreds of men, as Molchis and Optatis had both surmised, who weren't going to break and rout before every last one of them was slain.

No matter. Their lives were ten-a-*sesterce*. And they'd already fulfilled their purpose.

'*CRUSH THEM!*' GRAECILLUS roared.

His followers hardly needed the encouragement. Iron-shod hooves and flashing *spathas* made short work of most grounded opponents – not to mention huddled, poorly clad and bloody-minded ones. The cavalry blazed a path through the mass of levy, crushing and hacking any too slow or foolish to clear their path. They barely even slowed in their charging stride, reaving a path through their own allies to their true target.

This wasn't cruelty, or even spite, though some of the *equites* themselves might have felt differently. It was cold, naked pragmatism. The levy was expendable, and the cavalry needed to reach the enemy. Those men had done their job – wearing Orbus and Cascana's men down, sapping their strength, breaking the odd sword and shield.

And exposing the one part of their line that was weakest. The century whose ranks were buckling most.

The most vulnerable place to strike.

ARGIAS WAS SCREAMING his lungs inside out.

'*Vinculex!*' he bawled, trying to push his way through the ranks to him. '*We have to close the line!*'

If the Brazen officer heard him, he didn't react. The Gutter Prince stayed resolutely focused on his place – at the vanguard, of course. Where else would he be?

He hadn't stopped hacking his foes apart, a sword in each hand, as unconcerned with his own safety as he'd ever been in the arena. By Argias' reckoning, Vinculex must have slain almost thirty men since the attack had begun – and the *optio* hadn't even been watching him the whole time.

'*Vinculex!*' he shouted over the battle's roar. '*Come back, Centurion!*'

He was pushing his way up to him, shouldering aside other Brazen and carving up the odd foe still stupid enough to draw near. Vinculex was a little way ahead of the first rank, surrounded by a sanguine trail of slaughtered bodies. And still, he fought, on and on through a sea of knocks and flesh wounds.

'*Vinculex!*' Argias screamed. He'd finally got the warrior's attention, for whatever the hell it was worth. It was too late anyway. The line of cavalry was crashing through towards them. Even the War God himself couldn't have turned it back in that moment.

Vinculex's head snapped up, blood and sweat spilling from his face. Just in time to see it happen.

'*NO!*' ORBUS BELLOWED from the centre of the line. *Ananke* swung like a reaping scythe, as he tried, vainly, to start cutting his way eastward. '*Vinculex!*'

GRAECILLUS' HORSES SPLIT the line apart.

The Brazen hadn't bothered keeping a defensive formation. They were gladiators, first and foremost, no matter how much soldierly training had been thrashed into them. Vinculex hadn't cared much the shield wall's discipline, either – as soon as Orbus had given the order, he'd set about slaying, with little thought spared for his own safety.

His men – who hadn't received much leadership from their centurion since leaving Rome – had all followed that example.

And right here, right now, they would pay for that failing.

Argias knew there was no turning back this charge. The Brazen were going to get mauled. All that mattered was containing the damage.

Vinculex was still killing. Perhaps he hadn't seen the oncoming cavalry, the cavalry that was *seconds* away. Or perhaps this was, quite literally, the hill he was ready to die on.

Not on Argias' watch, though. He wasn't about to fail the Praefector so gravely.

'*Come on!*' he yelled one final time, ploughing straight into Vinculex and knocking him out of the line of attack.

'*DAMN!*' GRAECILLUS SPAT as his mount thundered past. The warrior with two swords – an officer, only an officer would be so brash – had been thrown clear by his little lackey.

Out of sword range.

No matter.

'You upstart cur,' he swore, reaching for the *pilum* locked over his back. Around him, his riders were crashing into Orbus' men. Any who weren't cut down or trampled would scramble in all directions.

A tug on the reins pulled his horse around. He wouldn't be denied that easily.

'Come here, you little wretch…'

VINCULEX SPAT MUD. His eyes flicked open.

A warhorse's braying whinny snapped his wits into place. The Fire was burning him senseless now, but he couldn't give a damn.

He pulled himself upright, a static island among the routing chaos. The rest of the cavalry were haring off, cutting his Brazen down or crushing them beneath their iron hooves.

Half the century, gone in seconds. How would he look Orbus in the eye after this?

He looked up just in time to see Argias. The stupid, loyal little runt had risked his life to get him clear of the charge.

'Fall back!' the *optio* shouted, pulling himself upright a little way off. He'd lost his helm in the fall. He looked so young without it. 'Get clear, Vinculex! Fall ba——'

And then the spear hit him, thrown hard enough to gore him right through. It had barely even slowed on entry.

'GOT YOU!' GRAECILLUS laughed. He barely spared a backward glance as his steed crashed onwards, pounding the young man's body into bloody pulp underfoot.

'*COME HERE!*' THE Gutter Prince screamed. He still had one sword. One sword was all he needed. '*Get off that fucking mount and fight me!*'

He didn't even wait for a reply. He was running, sprinting, faster than a legionary wearing a *lorica segmentata* had any right to move. His body was lashing itself with burning, alchemical agony – and he couldn't give a flying shit.

Four levy, and one grounded cavalryman, stood between Vinculex and his prey. And those five enemies died without him even slowing.

'*Ja!*' he roared, with all the frenzy and wrath of a rabid beast. His *gladius* hurtled through the air, end over end.

And hit the Decurion's horse, blade first, point embedded in one equine eye socket.

GRAECILLUS CRIED OUT as he was thrown clear.

Ground became sky for the shadow of the moment. Then he hit the ground, hard. His helmet broke. His head was bleeding. And something in his neck had cracked.

It hurt to move his head. Blood of Teucer, it hurt to even move his *eyes*. That didn't bode well.

The sword. Where was his fucking sword?

VINCULEX HADN'T EVEN stopped running.

He didn't feel unarmed. Even without a sword, cudgel or boulder to hand, the Gutter Prince never felt unarmed. For the gods' sakes, he'd probably killed more men with his hands than with blades.

He vaulted the fallen horse with one almighty leap, rolling back onto his feet before the fallen decurion. The bastard had butchered Argias for nothing more than spite. And he was going to pay for that right this very m—

AN IRON-SHOD HOOF hit him square in the forehead, as the steed's back leg spasmed in death.

Vinculex had lived in pain every day of his worthless life. He'd endured wounds on the sands of the *Flaminius* that would have killed a lesser man, and he'd forced himself to fight past the point of human endurance countless times before.

But none of that conditioning, stamina or stubbornness could prepare him for a horse's kick to the head.

The Centurion went down like an axe-felled piece of lumber. Graecillus could only watch in supine disbelief. At best, the rabid bastard was dead. At worst, he'd been knocked unconscious, with a mark he'd carry for the rest of his days.

The Marshal of Arx Agrippum pulled himself upright, fighting the swaying blur of his own vision. Standing straight was enough to make him vomit, bloody and phlegmy, pouring down his chin and cheek like the victim of a poisoning.

He retrieved his fallen sword, and looked around for something to kill.

EVEN AS HE butchered the last of the levy, all Orbus could do was watch as a century of his best killers were torn to pieces.

The charge had done its job. It had hit Vinculex's part of the line like a thunderbolt, and while the dispersing cavalry had lost that weight of momentum, they were still a force to be reckoned with.

The surviving Brazen had scattered. That part of the gauntlet was broken. The sizeable troop of *equites* had split legionaries and Riven off from the rest of the Praefector's forces.

And now those riders were carving themselves westward. Towards the core of Orbus' defensive line.

'Praefector?' A bruised and bloody Bydreth looked to him for guidance. 'How do you want to play this?'

Orbus ignored the men looking at him now. Legionaries, Branded, Creedless… it didn't matter. He had command here. It was up to him to spend their lives.

'Those cavalry won't stop driving this way,' the Praefector surmised. 'The Brazen are gone, which mean's Cascana's section is next in line.' He turned to look at Optatis. 'Centurion, take the Branded east and push back at them. Iulus is going to need all the help he can get. In fact——' He gestured to the legionaries of

Cascana's century who were standing around him. '—
you can take this lot to back you up. I'm not sticking
around here, anyway.'

'Sir?' a bloody *miles* asked.

'We're going to have problems of our own,'
Orbus pointed out. He nodded his head out towards
the horizon.

More specifically, towards the glinting ranks of
men marching towards them at battle-pace. There was
no mistaking the sheen of segmented steel armour.
Nor the red *scuta* that reflected the falling sun's light.

'Ignatian's legionaries are finally joining the fray,'
Orbus grunted. 'Bydreth, you're with me. We're
taking the Creedless and the Painted upcountry.
Hesperon's men, too.'

Bydreth eyed the oncoming enemy. He gauged
their numbers in a heartbeat, then tried not to think
about the figure he just reached. He'd never been
much good at mathematics, anyway.

'Brauda will be pissed,' he offered. 'Thinking
he'd get to fight without me over his shoulder.'

Orbus spat, hawking bloody phlegm into the dirt.
'He'll get over it.'

He reached for the horn at his belt once again.

'*Auxilia*,' he boomed, raggedly. His parade-
ground voice had seen better days. 'Men of the
Fulminata. Your officers have their orders, and from
the moment I blow this trumpet you'll damn well
follow them. But here—' He stretched his arms wide,
Ananke pointing out into the distance. '—right now,
you've faced your first gods-damned enemy charge!
And that, *milites*, is the hardest fucking thing you'll
ever have to do in your sorry little lives.'

A few of the younger, less exhausted Branded risked a little whoop at that. The feeling didn't carry.

'The hardest,' Orbus continued, 'and the darkest, no doubt. But probably not the bloodiest.'

The Praefector pointed his sword out towards the advancing ranks of legionaries. At slightly closer inspection, the differences between the Ignipotens and Orbus' men were more obvious. Parts of their red had been replaced, either dyed or painted black, with any insignia alluding to Rome burnt or scoured away.

'And let me tell you, lads.' Orbus' grin had a madman's joy. 'This day's only just beginning.'

XVII
LEGION VERSUS LEGION

'KEEP MOVING!' ARXANDER snarled as the Riven took flight from the ground they'd held. He'd switched tongues to Attic Greek; his warriors all knew the dialect, and this way the enemy couldn't hear what they were saying.

'Onward!' he loudly added in Latin, for the benefit of the remaining legionaries of Cascana's that were following him.

'This is madness,' growled Dorthoi as they covered the ground. As hoplites of Achaea, they were all well-used to advancing at speed in crushingly heavy battle armour. 'You saw what those horses did to the Brazen. Cascana and Optatis are choking with them. They need us.'

'You heard the bugle.' Arxander hadn't even stopped running. None of them had. 'Praefector's orders. We push on ahead.'

'We have to help them!'

'*Praefector's orders.*'

A listless gaggle of levy – leftovers from the opening slaughter – had found themselves in the Riven's path. And they paid for that, quickly and bloodily. The *auxilia* set about them in moments, *gladii* hacking into them or hammering deep into flesh.

Most of them died then and there. And the hoplites hadn't even stopped running.

'Push on ahead,' Arxander repeated, raggedly, over his shoulder. 'More of them are coming, so we create another beachhead up ahead with Orbus and the others. We form another line. One they can't break. That's our only chance of winning this.'

And then he turned back round, and saw what had appeared in front of them, forming ranks and readying *pila*.

'Shit,' he breathed, waving the Riven to a gradual stop.

'Well,' Dorthoi remarked in his thickly-accented voice beside him. 'I guess we won't be joining Orbus after all.' He pointed his spear – an ornate, viciously bladed *sarissa* wielded quite widely across the Achaean lands – at the advancing enemy.

'And I'm no expert,' he added, 'but they don't look like levy.'

IGNATIAN SLID DOWN from his horse, forcing a respectful smile upon his face as the new arrivals drew near.

'Castellan,' the first of the three officers greeted him. 'I trust you have need of us?'

His name was Servius Vitreus – a regal, unsmiling veteran cut very much from Ignatian's own cloth – and together with the other two men following at his heels, he made up the remaining command echelon of what had been a full cohort of the XXV Legion.

'Good of your men to finally join us,' Ignatian coolly replied, as if there wasn't a grinding industrial slaughter unfolding behind him. 'Any later and we'd have lost the cavalry. Your timing is apt, gentlemen.'

'I'd hazard a guess,' one of the other officers, Gaius Ullitor, ventured as respectfully as could be, 'that you might lose them anyway. Our friend Graecillus doesn't believe in holding back, does he?'

Only Ignatian, it turned out, wasn't in the joking mood. 'How many men behind you now?' he coldly enquired. 'And how long before we see any more?'

'We've about five hundred *milites* ready to fight, Lord Castellan. *Principes* and *triarii* both.' The sounds of marching feet and squealing armour carried from far behind Vitreus, as did the tell-tale clamour of battle from up ahead. 'Couriers from Proculus and Thestia crossed our paths along the way. They're making good progress. We should have their combined strength with us here, battle-ready, by sundown.'

Now that finally thawed Ignatian's spirits. Even rounding down, that equated another eight hundred men en route, on top of Vitreus' own forces. And not just men, either, but *milites*. Bona fide legionaries. Ignipotens.

More than a match for a gaggle of untested, slum-raised *auxilia*, and a disgraced camp prefect with a grudge and a death wish.

'As ever, Vitreus, I'm lucky to have you at my side.' Ignatian laid a hand on the former centurion's shoulder, letting the three officers bask in his radiance. 'Well, don't waste any more time talking to me. Prepare for immediate attack, all of you.'

'BRANDED!' OPTATIS ROARED as he braced with his shield. 'You will stand your ground!'

Even that had become a sickening joke. There was no real ground to stand on, no notion of rank unity left. Each man waged their own war, bracing themselves against the storm of equine steel, swords and shields raised against the enemies swarming around them.

The Branded had been well-trained, first as *milites* of their legions, then by Orbus and Optatis. In a fair fight they'd put their detractors to shame, selling their lives and final moments in blood and plunging themselves into the Underworld with pride.

But this fight, today, was far from fair.

Cascana was at his side a moment later, cursing beneath his breath as he slew his way to guard Optatis' flank. He had enough legionaries at his back to give the Branded some backbone, as well as the ones Orbus had left behind. The *principes* fought beside their cousins in the *auxilia*, and likewise did their officer proud. But they were all just infantrymen. There was little they could feasibly do against cavalry.

'Spears!' yelled a legion veteran as another horseman crashed through his *'bernium*. 'Where are our damned *spears*?'

Optatis had scarcely time to shout an answer before it hit him. Cold, hard and metal, it slammed his temple hard enough to put him in the dirt.

Sword pommel. It had to be. He was already moving; rolling faster than his mind could move. He was down. He'd move, or he'd die.

Optatis rolled back onto his knees, scrabbling for his filthy *gladius*. All around him, men loyal to Rome and treacherous riders fought each other to the death, but this one particular attacker seemed in no hurry to close the kill.

He was landbound, too. He didn't ride, though from his leather greaves and stirrup-boots he certainly had been.

But the crest on his helmet, with its ruby-red plume, and the gilded *phalerae* hanging from his neck... if he'd been the one to lead this mounted attack, than there was only one man this could be.

Septimus Graecillus. The one Orbus had told them about. Ignatian's bloodstained right hand.

'You look important,' the Marshal slurred, nodding at Optatis' own helmet crest. That didn't sound too coherent. Had he taken a head wound?

'Already killed one of Orbus' mongrel officers.' Graecillus raised the longsword. 'Want to make it two for two?'

Optatis had no quip to follow that up. No cutting remark to bolster his courage, or give the moment some élan. He simply hurled himself at the other man.

Gladius met *spatha* as the two officers tumbled over each other into the mud. Optatis' red was looking more brown, even counting the bloodstains. His sword came up, just in time to block the downward sweep of steel coming for his neckline. They remained locked, like a pair of feral Suburan gangers, before the Branded Centurion threw his attacker off.

He rolled back up, in time to be kicked clean in the larynx. He sprawled again, choking air through his bruised windpipe.

'Get back here,' the traitor snarled. He picked himself up in time for Optatis to get his own bearings. Both men had their blades to hand. Now neither one of them had the advantage.

And then, from that hanging moment, their two-man war truly began. Steel on steel, fists against armour, trading blows and weaving around each other like god-sired heroes of myth.

They danced. They fought. They bled. They swore. Both men fought to kill. Neither fought to keep themselves alive.

Around them, the *equites* of the former XXV drove themselves against the Branded and Fulminata's remaining infantry, either crashing onto their swords and javelins, or risking coming in close to crush them under hoof.

The Imperials were going down, but they were going down bloody. And here, on this part of the shattered line, they had numbers on their side.

Optatis threw himself to one side as another rider galloped past. The jump left him safe, but thwarted. Another raging horse blocked his path for a moment, and by that point Graecillus was further off, blade to blade with more of the Branded.

'*Silvanus!*' the Centurion swore. 'He's mine!'

Only more of Cascana's legionaries were filling the breach now, driving back at the remaining riders who hadn't deserted their mounts to join the fray hand to hand. It was brave. And a colder-blooded assessment would call it prudent. But neither sentiment was riding high in Optatis' wrath-addled mind.

'*Mine!*' he bellowed.

Graecillus was reeling back now. He'd killed his fair share, but he couldn't take them all.

'That bloody *signa*,' he barked, jerking his gaze at the totem standing in the legionaries' midst. Ragged, but still very much standing. 'I'm going to ram it up your fucking arse!'

The Marshal didn't get a chance to elaborate. A legionary shield, thrown like an *onager* missile, hit him straight in the face.

Graecillus went down, crushed, bloody and howling his misspent rage. He spat blood, a lot of blood, bright and arterial through the stumps of shattered teeth. Somehow, against all rhyme and reason, the blow had made him uglier.

'P-Publius?' Graecillus' broken mouth tried to garble, as he locked bloodshot eyes with his slayer-to-be.

'Not quite, no.' Cascana spun the longsword – Graecillus' own longsword – round in his hand to a reverse grip, before ramming it clean through the traitor's palette and brain. 'But I suspect we'll muddle through.'

IF THE FEW surviving cavalry needed a sign, then that was it. They'd lost the element of surprise. And they didn't have the numbers left to break the *auxilia*'s line a second time.

'*Ha!*' the *signifer* for Cascana's century, Flavius Altex, jeered as the last riders broke off and retreated. 'Down to Charon's Boat with you, devils!' He'd lost an eye in the first attack on the shield wall, and a lot of blood in the fighting since then. But he hadn't lost the *signa*, and that was what mattered.

Nearby, a calmer Optatis accepted Cascana's grubby hand to help him up.

'Is that it?' he asked, recovering his shield as the younger officer tossed him back his *gladius*. 'Did we really rout them that easily?'

'We saw them off, sure enough,' Cascana laconically replied, jabbing a finger toward the retreating *equites*. 'But they're still in the game. And see where they're headed.'

Optatis followed the First Spear's gaze. What he saw didn't make him feel better.

'ORBUS!' MOLCHIS SHOUTED as the dashing hooves drew closer. 'We're going to have company!'

The Praefector turned, as did several men around him. He was neither pleased, nor surprised, with what he saw.

'More bloody horses,' he growled. 'Still, not many of them. If we close ranks and keep our damned heads, we'll prevail.'

'Maybe,' Brauda offered, eying the approaching ranks of rebel legionaries ahead of them. 'But the horses don't need to attack us head on, do they?'

Orbus swore. The *optio* was right.

'What does he mean?' Drygg piped up.

'They'll herd us,' Bydreth explained. 'They can drive us onto their comrades' spears. Or just keep us from forming ranks if we try to move.'

'No.' Orbus growled. 'I'm not giving them that chance. Here,' he jabbed a finger at the war-churned earth, turning to face the others. 'Here is where we make our stand.'

'There is better ground back afield,' Molchis offered, looking uneasy. 'Or my *milites* could link up with—'

'Here, Centurion.'

Bydreth's gaze drifted to Brauda, and then to the battered figure of Hesperon, standing stiffly to attention with his surviving legionaries. This was as good a place to die as any.

'What's it to be, then?' Bydreth asked. Only he would speak to Orbus so informally. 'Do we draw up ranks? Or we've enough room for a half-decent *testudo,* if they're bringing missiles to the party.'

'I admire your optimism, Centurion.' The Praefector smiled grimly. The plan he'd set in motion before the battle's start – the covert orders he'd given the *immunes* – drifted back to him.

Maybe here was a decent place to stand after all.

'*Orbem formate*,' he ordered them. 'Give me a ring of iron.'

'OH, NO...' ARXANDER breathed, almost to himself. The other Achaeans were forming up, all the better to attack or defend. The enemy legionaries up ahead were doing much the same, only with more dolorous roaring and jeering.

Neither side had formed a wedge, which meant neither side was planning a head-on charge any time soon. Still, that could change on a *sesterce*, and a devious commander might bank on Arxander making that very assumption.

'What is it?' asked one of the *principes*, a unit leader by the name of Curio. The rest of his '*bernium* was backing up Dorthoi and the other Riven, trying to make their frontmost ranks seem as solid and threatening as could be.

'Orbus and his men.' Arxander pointed out into the further plains, toward the distant red and chrome figures of the Painted and Creedless. 'They're forming a ring.'

'They're not forming ranks?' Curio asked. 'Or bracing for an attack run?'

'They're forming a ring.' Arxander had nothing to soften that blow. Both soldiers knew at once what it meant.

'Then they don't think they can win,' Curio grimaced. 'Not, at least, without throwing down the gauntlet.'

'Aye,' the Riven's Centurion nodded, turning back to face their own foes. 'One last stand, for the Ignipotens to break themselves on. Orbus must not think there's another way. Not unless each side plays all their cards.' He sucked in air through his filthy, gritty teeth. 'One hell of a gamble.'

The clashing of spears on steel clawed back his attention. Repeated, rhythmic, like a metallic drum. Or the pulse of an iron god. The warriors of the once-XXV clashed their *pila* on their shields, punctuated by roars and subsonic growling.

'They're goading us!' Dorthoi warned them. Regardless, tension was building among the Riven just as steadily. Neither group could ride it out much longer. No matter their discipline, sure enough, one side would be driven to make the charge soon. Such was the pressure.

'Shame Cascana isn't with them.' Curio mused, jerking his head towards Orbus' circle of *auxilia*. 'The *signa* would have made a fine rallying point.'

Arxander spat into the ground, pulling his shield over his back. 'No. I'm not playing into their hands.' He looked around, at Achaeans and Romans psyching themselves up for the attack. 'Men, break ranks. We're quitting this vantage point. I'm taking us west, to help Orbus.'

'What?' Dorthoi snapped. 'No!'

'*Yes.*' Arxander's patience was running perilously low. 'Are you going to question every order I give? If they cut us down here, there was no point in leaving the Brazen to their fate. And we can't help the Praefector either way.'

'We can break them!' Dorthoi protested. Part of his nerve must have frayed or broken. What else explained this idiocy? 'If we take their momentum now, we can break them!'

'*Silence!*' the Riven commander shouted. 'Break ranks, I said! *Tecombre*, you XII Legion whelps. You're with me too. Westward. We join the Praefector's ring.'

Curio looked defeated, but clearly didn't have any better ideas. Within moments, he was giving clipped orders to his surviving *principes*, adding his voice to Arxander's.

'They could charge us as we retreat,' he risked pointing out. 'And if we're not in ranks, we'll be hit harder.'

'That's a blood-price we'll have to pay,' the Achaean snapped back. 'Some of us surviving to reach Orbus is better than none.' He turned to his erstwhile subordinate, a warrior he'd known and fought beside for years. 'Dorthoi, I'm taking our comrades west. Either come with us, or stand here, and take your death as it comes.'

That did the trick, sure enough. The younger hoplite gracelessly turned his back on Arxander, joining the other Riven as they prepared to move.

'I hope Orbus' new wife has got some sizeable coffers going spare,' the Centurion sniggered. 'Rebuilding this cohort when we're done is going to cost a lot of silver.'

'You Greeks,' Curio snorted, when Arxander was out of earshot. 'Always fleecing us Romans for silver.'

GAIUS ULLITOR COULD scarcely believe what he was seeing.

'They're… *leaving!*' he exclaimed, not even a question. His disbelief was palpable enough to make the *triarii* around him edge away.

And they *were* leaving. The mongrel unwashed Achaean auxiliaries, that had until moments ago been arraying themselves for a shield war, were fragmenting before his eyes. They disengaged in decent order, that he granted, peeling off spear-ready, '*bernium* by '*bernium,* to cover their comrades' steps. But Ullitor knew a hasty retreat when he saw one.

Still, no matter. More of Ignatian's troops were en route. Thestia and Proculus would be here within hours, and whatever else remained of the XII Legion off this battlefield clearly wasn't coming back to help its abandoned legionaries.

Their victory was merely a matter of time.

'Ferratian Century!' Ullitor barked. 'Let your *pila* fly. Keep the pressure on them as they scuttle away. Romulan, Helican and Flavian Centuries! Break ranks, full march. Military pace! You can see where they're headed. Let's bleed them dry for the trouble.'

ARXANDER, SON OF Lammachon, had many failings. He considered them to be varied, and over a wide spectrum. But whatever his faults, he had no shortage of courage.

Fitting, then. In a way. The blow that finally killed him came on a treacherous breeze, sinking into his spine and shoulder blade. Or more exactly, thrown. Hurled, by a strong arm with an aim that was terribly true.

'Centurion!' a younger Riven shouted, a lad of seventeen years. Arxander didn't respond. The *pilum* had gored his torso through and through, impaling him face down in the mud.

'Leave him be, son,' Dorthoi snarled, grabbing the youth and hauling him after the charging *auxilia*. 'You can't help him now.'

Dorthoi's baroque Achaean helmet covered most of his face. Right here, right now, he was glad of that.

IGNATIAN WHEELED HIS mount about, turning his back on the hardening circle of enemies far below. This charge, this fight, would be the fulcrum. He could sense it.

The tide was about to turn.

'Ignipotens!' he shouted. 'Former legionaries! Army of the Free!' The newly-arrived soldiers, many of whom had once belonged to the XXV Legion, looked on from their loosely-drawn ranks. 'You have all suffered, and sacrificed, for your loyalty to me. You have shed blood, and cast your own hopes and dreams aside, in service to the ideals we share. But here, today, is when that toll shall strike hardest!'

'On this field of battle, I would have you take your final steps on the path I have carved for us. Before us, *milites* of the XII Fulminata – servile lapdogs, who toil at the whims of our foes – have amassed to destroy you. Honourless waifs and strays from the Empire's conscripted *auxilia* have been pressed into service, all for a chance to feast on their betters' table scraps.'

Growls of agreement and derision greeted this last acclamation, and the Castellan knew he'd struck the right chord.

'Sever these last links to your past! Fight, with me, against these lackeys of a corrupted Rome! Push back these dregs in purple and gold, who seek to punish us for captaining our own fates! Forget who you are, and how you came to my service. Legionaries. Citizens. Militiamen. I care not!'

Those growls and rumbles were rising in pitch, dangerously close to becoming cheers.

'Because here, tonight, I see nothing that sets you apart. You are the Army of the Free, and with my words, and your deeds, I wash you clean of your past! Forget the ranks you once stood in, or the paths you once walked. The XXV Legion died in shame and ignorance, and the folk of Arx Agrippum no longer answer to Rome's blithe demands. Forget the Legion That Was, fed with nostalgia, shackled by ignorance. Look around you, at men bound by ideals instead of blood, and see the Legion That Is!'

There was no denying the cheering now. In spite of all the bloodshed ensuing behind them, Ignatian couldn't help feeling a twitch of pride. He'd made them this way. He'd taken these broken souls, and he'd given them the meaning and guidance they craved.

'To war, my brothers!' he avowed, raising his unblooded sword to mark the moment. 'Follow your officers' lead! Protect your comrades' backs! And fight for whatever those deluded fools would take from you!'

THAT WAS WHEN they heard the horns. They were too far downfield to see, but they hardly needed to.

'Those bugles aren't ours,' Optatis reasoned. 'The pitch is all wrong. It must be them.'

Cascana nodded without looking at him. The Branded, and his own remaining *'bernia,* had enough problems of their own. The arriving mass of armoured enemy veterans, for one.

Whatever could send Arxander and his Achaeans packing was an enemy to fear.

'I could use some help, Optatis!' the First Spear's voice was run thoroughly ragged, but somehow even his impatience sounded dignified. 'Help me draw up ranks.'

The other man was barely listening. His gaze was held further afield, where the distant figure of Orbus, along with two of his cohort's centuries, had marooned themselves in a formation that gave them no quarter to turn to, and nowhere to run.

Perhaps the Praefector knew something he didn't. Or perhaps he'd just given up, and wanted to make a stand worth remembering.

'Oh, gods above and below,' Optatis murmured. 'This won't be good.'

'WHAT HAPPENED?' ORBUS asked, as the gaggle of bruised and bloody men drew nearer. 'Where's Arxander?'

'Dead,' Dorthoi spat as the Praefector's ring begun to part. 'Along with half the century.'

Orbus knew better than to probe any deeper. That loss had clearly turned Dorthoi sour, but twenty more men was twenty more men. 'You're here now. Get into the ring before they attack again.'

Not that they needed reminding. Galloping hooves heralded the last of Graecillus' riders, still doing their passes around the Praefector's circle. They were too few to attack the *orbem* head on, and too far away to intercept the arriving Riven. But at least they could deter them from trying to move again.

'No Optatis?' Dorthoi asked.

'He's still tied up with Cascana,' Bydreth told him, 'and they've got company.' The Painted jerked his head down the shallow valley, right back where they'd all been drawn up at the battle's beginning. 'They may make it upcountry, but it won't be soon. The traitors can't seem to resist them.'

'The *signa*,' Hesperon cut in, a little way across the ring. 'That's a prize worth risking some blood for.'

And savaging our own morale, Orbus chose not to add. More was the pity – even while Cascana and Optatis had their own enemies to deal with, the Army of the Free continued to swell and grow. He'd given up looking at the northern horizon. The amount of red and black coalescing in his vision was getting more disheartening with each glance.

'Where even is the First Cohort?' Molchis asked. 'The Fulminata should be here by now.'

Orbus and Bydreth shared a pointed look, but wisely neither gave voice to it. Delaying their planned entrances would give the enemy ample time to tear the *auxilia*'s strength from them, and still be able to spring the trap. The thought must have crossed Thracian's mind, even now.

As it happened, the Praefector's more immediate problems were taking centre stage.

'Prefect Orbus!' a voice shouted over the growing winds and distant sounds of death. 'The Castellan is extending you one last chance. This is your final opportunity. Throw down your blades and *scuta*, and I give you my word you will all be treated fairly.'

Within his ring of iron, hidden from view by shields and helms, Orbus almost wanted to snort. However dire the situation was getting, and however greater the numerical odds were shifting in the traitors' favour, this timid little officer was still afraid to make the first move. He didn't think he could break the *orbem* and keep his life.

'Who am I talking to?' Orbus shouted. Time for a little fun.

There was a pause, and if silence could sound officious, here was the proof.

'Servius Vitreus,' the voice replied. 'Former centurion of the XXV Legion.'

Orbus held his mischievous tongue for another few moments, letting the tension boil over. And then, looking back at the men clustered all around him, he whispered his next command.

The ring of men locked their shields together, with not even a shard of daylight coming between them. Unbroken bronze and scarlet gleamed out in each direction, daring this nearest band of enemies to try their luck running the gauntlet.

'There's your answer, Vitreus.' Orbus barely even needed to shout. 'Your move.'

'BREAK THEM!' GAIUS Ullitor screamed. 'Push them hard! Don't let them regroup!'

After having their fill of slaying the Riven's stragglers – and, more pointedly, failing to stop the rest of them linking up with Orbus – Ullitor's corps of *milites* had set their sights on the smaller remaining group of Imperials. Slaughtering them and taking their *signa* would be far easier than backing up Vitreus' faltering assault on the enemy's largest formation.

In theory.

The reality had, sadly, been a little different.

The fight, at least, had given Ullitor time to reflect on his error of judgement. Not that he'd used the time to reflect. Instead he'd just bemoaned his legionaries' apparent lack of martial skill, and cursed the enemy officer's skill with a blade.

That blade took him high in the chest, below the collarbone.

Optatis gasped in triumph as he threw the rebel centurion's body down in the dirt. That was far from the end of it, however. Ullitor's men were still standing and fighting. And he'd lost enough Branded already.

'Did I ever tell you,' he wheezed, as he crashed back-to-back with Cascana, 'how I got exiled from the IX?'

The First Spear couldn't turn, occupied as he was with the press of remaining traitor *triarii*. His *principes* were holding their own, as were the *auxilia*, but they didn't have many men left to lose.

'Go on,' he replied, hammering back a wounded foe, blocking another with his *gladius*.

Optatis spun on his heels, taking advantage of a lull in front of him. Cascana's attacker hadn't counted on that, and the Branded officer's sword hit him right where it was least expected. One centurion was challenge enough; two together was asking to be slaughtered.

'I was taken,' he told him, breathing heavily. Even speaking coherently while blade to blade was a trial. It took a man with stamina, as well as skill. 'In Parthia. I was captured by those sand-loving devils. They had their fun with me for hours. Cutting me. Burning me. Trying to milk me for my secrets.'

Cascana kept fighting as he processed this revelation. In his lightweight chainmail, outmanoeuvring the enemy legionaries was a promising, if dangerous, game to play. Mail didn't protect perfectly, but what *triarii* gained in plated protection, they forfeited in agility. Cascana's *gladius* weaved an intricate dance, hacking and hewing at any man who went for Optatis' back.

'What happened?' he asked.

Optatis took the next attack on his *scutum*, smashing the metal shield into two more attackers.

He riposted with his sword before they'd even recovered their wits. And neither of them got the chance.

'I broke,' the old soldier confessed.

Cascana cursed as a *pugio*'s tip caught his forearm. The retaliatory *gladius* blow severed that daggered hand.

'It's been an honour serving with you, Centurion,' he called, as the remainder of Ullitor's men pressed in for the kill. 'And you didn't break this time.'

'MY LORD?' ONE of the freshly-arrived troupe dared break his concentration. 'Do you wish us to engage?'

Still observing proceedings from his horse's back, Gnaeus Ignatian looked uncertain… and suddenly thunderous. But then, the rank and file were allowed to ask questions. He was no despot.

'Forgive me,' he finally replied. 'A moment's distraction. Return to your men, legionary. I will send word when the time comes.'

The Castellan's true source of ire lay out below him. Hours were passing, and more of his army was arriving as the sundial turned. And yet... the Imperials were holding.

The Fulminata's pitiful remnants weren't breaking, and neither were Orbus' auxiliary rabble. They were dying. But they weren't breaking. Even with the wallowing weight of numbers at Ignatian's beck and call, this battle was sliding further from the crushing, decisive victory he needed to give his troops.

It was instead devolving into a grinding, demoralising bloodbath. The Army would still win, there was no doubt. But this fight was only ever meant to be the start, the easy win Ignatian needed to convince them they could take on an Empire. Not crush them upon the anvil right away, mangling them before the next inevitable war.

His teeth found themselves grinding together. Enough of this.

'Soldier?' Ignatian called to the man he'd just dismissed. The legionary was still within earshot, thankfully, and came running back.

'Lord?'

'How many men, in your band that just arrived?' the Castellan asked.

'Two hundred, sir. A little under.'

Ignatian smiled, reaching for the sword sheathed at his right hip. Although he'd drawn it a few times already for pageantry's sake, he'd yet to wield it in combat today.

A fact he now intended to rectify.

'Bring me your officer, would you?'

'PRAEFECTOR!' SOMEONE SHOUTED. Orbus couldn't even tell who. 'I hear the horns again!'

Orbus couldn't look up, because he was still holding his place in the *orbem*. Looking up wouldn't help anyway. The ring of *scuta* was as unyielding and resolute as ever. The only spaces existed between one shield and another, and the outside world only existed through those gaps. Until Vitreus' men were packed close enough to truly strike at, there was no real incentive to open them any further.

'Out there, sir.' That was Bydreth. At least, it sounded like Bydreth. 'The rest of Ignatian's men. They're deploying.'

The Praefector snarled, half-growl, half-laugh. *Ananke* shot through the gap he'd pretended not to notice, and on the other side of his *scutum* a legionary crashed back, screaming.

So here, it was finally happening. He'd put up enough of a spirited defence – as had all his men – and he'd finally inspired the traitor to deploy the bulk of his amassed forces.

And amassing they were, already numerous enough to wipe Orbus and Cascana off the map.

'*Auxilia!*' he shouted. Foul breath blasted back at him from inside the baking ring of shields. 'Men of the XII! You have fought with courage. You have bled with dignity. And right here, right now, is where we make our stand.'

The pressure on the iron ring was growing. Whatever Vitreus thought about his *milites'* chances, they had numbers on their side, and that advantage was only growing. The *orbem* wouldn't hold forever.

'If this is the last price you take from our Empire's foes,' Orbus continued, 'if this is the moment you send your souls into legend, if these are the final deeds our ancestors above will—'

He broke off, acutely aware his words weren't having the reaction he'd hoped. Even taking combat stress into account, even taking stock of their precarious position ... the men were laughing.

Gently, at first. But it grew. The laughter spread, around the *orbem*, as inexorably as wildfire. First from the southern corner, where Molchis and the Creedless held the line. Then through the Painted, and what remained of Cascana's men who'd followed them. Then the Riven survivors.

And *then* the officers who led them. Bydreth, Brauda, Dorthoi... even Hesperon, the surly old legion veteran, was scarcely able to contain his laughter.

'Something I said?' Orbus called out, archly. Something had changed, something in their shared atmosphere, and he fancied himself the only man who hadn't picked up on it.

'You can spare us this woeful bardic valediction,' Bydreth assured him. 'Look to the east, Praefector. It's the Fulminata. The Fulminata are coming.'

XVIII
INTERFECTUM

IN TRUTH, BYDRETH wasn't quite giving his legion comrades their due credit.

The remaining four centuries of the First Cohort weren't coming. They were already here.

For all the Praefector's nihilistic predictions, Urbanus and Thracian had deployed the remaining Fulminata as close to the Depression as was feasible. Any closer would have given their position away to Ignatian's forces, but much further would have meant that they genuinely wouldn't arrive quickly enough to affect the battle. Or worse, give the traitorous legate time to escape.

The delays they'd experienced had been entirely genuine, no matter what Orbus would later think. Hugging the shadows of hills to hide their presence had slowed them, as had manoeuvring the cohort's heavier equipment and armaments. But they were here now, arriving at the battlefield's eastern and western flanks even as their enemies' reinforcements continued to pour in from the north. That was what mattered.

That level of tactical nous required – to coordinate four entire centuries of a Roman legion, without bugles, and keep them hidden for long enough to

and another of the Creedless put temporarily out of action.

'Come *on!*' Molchis swore as he tried to wrench the spear from his attacker's grip. Old Graufh's blood was sprayed over half his face. '*Give it up!*'

'Let them have it,' Orbus hoarsely ordered from across the ring, wiping viscera off his face. 'Not worth your life.'

He'd just finished vomiting. He normally lasted longer before it happened, even in bigger battles. Maybe it was combat shock, bona fide from his first true fight in months. Maybe it was trauma from the day's blows and scrapes catching up to him.

Someone in the ring had shat themselves, too. Orbus wasn't sure who.

'They're nearly here, lads.' That was Bydreth, nursing his broken arm, keeping his stolen shield pressed up into the *orbem*. 'Just keep the ring tight. Keep it locked.'

And then Brauda crashed back in a haze of blood and profanities. By some miracle, the men either side of him had closed the ring the moment he'd fallen, but that ring was getting smaller and smaller. They couldn't keep this up.

'*Hnnnh,*' the Painted *optio* grunted. 'Bastard thing. Can't shift it.' The broken shard of spearhead jutting from his side confirmed that theory.

And that was when they struck. The defenders barely saw anything at first. They felt it, though, the pressure against their ring suddenly melting away, as more and more of Vitreus' renegade *milites* turned from their attacking mass to counter this new threat.

'*Roma gloriana!*' the cry began to go up, from within the *orbem* and without. The legionaries of the

XII's First Cohort. Who else could it be? '*Fulminata in excelsia!*'

Orbus started laughing, mirth spilling from his mouth as easily as sweat and vomit. He realised he was shouting the battle-cry too, as were the *auxilia* around him. They weren't even part of the Legion, but here they were, crying that ancient chant as one.

Roma gloriana. Fulminata in excelsia. Fulminata in perpetua.

They didn't even need to hold the *orbem* anymore. Not truly. They kept the wall going, but there was enough relief for them to break the circle and give the rebels a proper greeting.

'*Ja!*' Even with one arm broken, Bydreth could fight like a demon. One hand curled around an enemy's de-helmed face as he smacked him with a broken spear haft. 'Drygg! Get Brauda clear.'

'I'm fine…' the other Ulthaini croaked.

'*Now!*' Bydreth snarled.

Orbus flung another man's shield wide, slamming *Ananke*'s point through the neck of an important-looking legionary. The man gurgled as he fell, but Orbus had already moved on.

'That's it!' he huskily roared, although there was little more for him to direct. 'Take the last of them. And get ready to reform the wall!' His caution was understandable. They'd broken the enemy formation, and they'd earnt this lull. More of the enemy were coming, but with the arrival of the First Cohort they had a fighting chance now.

And, far more importantly, they were still far enough north.

Ignatian.

The silver-tongued bastard was in their sights now.

'If you have *pila*,' the Praefector called, 'then now will shortly be the time. Reinforcements are arriving. Take whatever arms they can spare.' At Orbus' feet, Servius Vitreus gurgled more sanguine muck from his mouth, as his savaged lungs begin to drown in blood.

'Sir?' one of Hesperon's *principes* called for him. 'Up on the ridge... are those *ballistae*?'

Orbus was too exhausted to even look at the *miles* talking to him. He just smiled, wiping some of Vitreus' blood off *Ananke* onto his shin.

But the man was right. They'd only just appeared at the lips of the battlefield's flanks, some way north of where the Fulminata's reinforcements were joining the fray. Considerably closer to the enemy, for considerably more gain.

'They are indeed, legionary.' Orbus' smile, crooked and one-sided, stayed right where it was. 'I'd hoped they'd be here sooner, but there we go. Wedlock has its perks.'

The last of Vitreus' maniple was dying to a man, polished off by the Creedless and the Fulminata's new arrivals.

'I was there when the centurions gave us orders,' the legionary insisted. 'They said nothing of *ballistae*, Praefector.'

Elsewhere, almost five hundred feet to the west where the cohort's remaining centuries had arrived to spring the trap, the first of the *ballistae* begun to move. Its immense wooden arm sunk as it prepared to fire its brutal payload.

'They wouldn't have,' the Praefector replied. 'I gave the *immunes* my own orders. It was the last thing I did before we deployed for battle.'

Bydreth didn't say anything for a moment, trying to silently process what he'd just heard.

'Why do you think we're holding ranks so close to the enemy lines?' the Praefector snarled. 'Out of the Depression, out of formation, they're most vulnerable. We needed to venture north to draw them out. We needed to bait them.'

The *ballista* fired. A shadow crossed the sky, blotting out the sun's punishing gaze for a snatch of a second.

'*Bait* them?' Bydreth cried as he nursed his twisted arm. 'Orbus... what in the gods' name have you done?'

THEY WERE HUGE. Immense, wooden monstrosities, larger than any artillery Orbus had ever seen. The brothers Lemnon had honed their craft well. The Praefector fancied these immense machines could shoot a payload further than any *ballistae* the XII had ever deployed.

Siege engines like these could lay waste to cities. Immense stone projectiles, unleashed from wooden limbs powered by torsion springs, could sunder the hardest city walls into ruin. Leaving them easy meat for the advancing legionaries.

Urbanus and Thracian hadn't factored them into their plans. Not here. Not today. Perhaps, later, if subjugating Arx Agrippum itself was what it took to end the campaign. But nothing on this open and infantry-laden battlefield warranted that kind of artillery.

Or so they thought.

Orbus hadn't agreed with that assessment. A *ballista*'s destructive payload, while primarily designed to send walls crashing down to earth, was no less mundane when turned upon smaller, more living targets. It wasn't the siege engine's primarily intended use, but any weapon, however ill-fitting, was worth something in the right warrior's hands. Or so Gaius Marius had once taught.

The Praefector hadn't expected to leave this battlefield, and in truth nor had many among his men. Even if Thracian had been true to his word, and brought the First Cohort's other four centuries to battle in time to save them, Ignatian's army could well have wiped them out by that point anyway.

And so when Orbus had chased after the *immunes* right before he and Cascana had deployed for war, he'd given them his own orders.

Something he'd regret doing for the rest of his days, that would shape his life more than he'd ever truly comprehend.

'TAKE COVER!' SOMEONE was shouting. 'Fall back! *Fall back!*'

From any other's mouth, Ignatian would never have believed it. If Orbus' earlier tactics had been an exercise in recklessness, *this*... this was insanity. Insanity, masquerading as pragmatism.

A *ballista*'s colossal stone ammunition could tear through infantry like a *gladius* through milk curd. What use was armour against a behemoth of stone hurled like the War God's spear?

They were devastating weapons, true enough. But they were also haphazard. You couldn't be precise when you were unleashing a rain of rock. All you could do was trust in your aim.

The first volley had pulverised almost forty of the Army's newest arrivals. The second had barely glanced one of Ignatian's veteran '*bernia*, and had carved a deep furrow into the earth as it gradually ground to a halt.

He didn't plan on guessing where the next ones would land.

The Castellan of Arx Agrippum wheeled his mount around once again, trying to spur it as far away from here as he could.

'*Retreat!*' he screamed at the top of his voice. '*All ranks! Retreat!*'

IT WAS A scene repeating itself across either flank of the battlefield, as the rows of *ballistae* fired, strenuously reloaded, and kept on firing. Crews of *immunes* ran their digits bloody, as they lifted ammunition into place, coiled back their engines' immense springs and cranked winches into position.

Several of them injured themselves doing so. One crewman even lost three fingers. But by the gods, they lost no time. The barrage continued, unabated.

Some of the *ballistae*'s payloads just went wide, scarring the earth for dozens of feet but not hitting any living souls. Others were more fortunate, crashing into enough rebel troops to warrant such a reckless and unexpected deployment. Ignatian's more recent reinforcements were still tightly packed enough. They were devastated by this change in fortunes. Still arriving from the wider country, some of them scarcely even ready to fight, they were easy prey.

On the foremost engine, Marcus Galvio nursed his skinned knuckles as he barked orders at his fellow *immunes*.

'Come on!' he shouted. 'Arm's loaded! Pull our aim further south!'

'But *decanus*,' one of his younger crewmates squealed. 'Our own lines are embattled with the traitors. If we aim too far south we'll—'

'*Do it!*' snarled Galvio. 'Or I'll have you back in ranks!'

'We'll hit our own men!'

'We'll hit the enemy too. That's what matters. Those are our damned orders!'

INDEED THEY WERE. Crushing Ignatian's arriving reinforcements proved simple enough, as well as scattering those far enough off to get away.

But those enemies locked in combat against the *auxilia*? And Cascana's Century of legionaries? That wouldn't go quite so smoothly.

Not without some collateral damage, at least.

Fortuna, alas, is a fickle goddess. No man can judge or divine the way she turns, or the methods in her madness.

'WHAT'S GOING ON?' Optatis asked. He could see what was happening, see the catapults on either flank unleashing hell, but couldn't make hide nor hair of it. 'What in *Pluto's blasted shores* is going on?'

Cascana had no answers for him. 'Disengage,' he ordered him, still fending off a pair of rebel legionaries with his sword. 'Pull everyone back, *now!*'

Not that there was much further to go. The Branded lost no small amount of men pulling back from the remnants of Ullitor's veterans, as did Cascana's remaining *principes*. He shuddered to think how many men Hesperon had left.

'They're firing!' someone was shouting.

The men retreated, and did so quickly. It was nearly enough, to their credit.

It was so nearly enough.

'*Go!*' the First Spear screamed, as something briefly blotted out the sunlight. He jumped, he *leapt,* anything to propel himself far enough clear of the impact path.

Gates of Fire. He so nearly made it.

PRAEFECTOR? PRAEFECTOR, CAN you hear me?

Someone was caressing his cheek. The touch was silken, gentle. Almost sylvan. It could've been Caesula.

Praefector!

The blow slapped Orbus awake, making him gasp as his lungs reached out for air. Pain was the first thing he noticed, that and Bydreth's rotten gums as the Painted officer knelt over him.

Orbus recoiled upright. New blood trickled from his scalp, down his face through hair matted with sweat.

He drew in a breath to ask *what happened, Centurion?* But the pain stabbed him in the chest before he could get the words out. Whatever had hit him, had hit him hard.

And there was no point in being coy. He knew exactly what had happened.

'One of your little *ballistae,*' Bydreth filled in for him. He didn't seem particularly pleased with this tactical development, or the fact that the Praefector hadn't shared it with any of them. 'Trying to hit the bastards in front of us. Looks liked it worked, for the most part. But not without its costs, *sir.*'

Orbus looked around, seeing the crushed and broken remnants of Vitreus' reinforcements, as well as the Painted, Riven and Creedless who'd been caught in the line of fire. Enough of his men had survived, at a preliminary glance. But the Ulthaini had a point, damn him. At what cost?

'The payload,' he breathed. 'On impact, it must have fragmented and...' He trailed off as Bydreth's gaze pierced into him. As if any explanation was going to get him out of this now.

The Praefector looked across the field of battle, seeing a similar story playing out around them. Rubble streaked the plain – the *ballistae*'s discharged ammunition, which left bored gullies and dead men in its wake.

How many rebel legionaries had been wiped out by the barrage?

And, more crucially, how many of Orbus' own men had been caught up in it too?

'Was there something you forgot to tell us, sir?' Bydreth asked. Orbus knew him well enough to sense his hidden anger. Not that it was hidden particularly well.

'What do you want me to say?' Orbus snarled. 'Ignatian's men outnumbered us, even with the First Cohort on side. And I had no way of knowing if Thracian would even try to relieve our men, instead of going for the throat himself.' He reached for *Ananke*, where she'd fallen in the mud a little way off. 'I don't answer to you, Centurion. I did what I had to do. For the good of us all.'

'Aye, Praefector.' Bydreth watched the furthermost *ballista* on the opposite flank discharge the last of its load, crushing some of Ignatian's stragglers and a stretch of empty plain with equal impunity. The ground shook, for a moment, with the impact. 'For the good of us all, indeed.'

Orbus tore his eyes away from Bydreth's judgemental glare, jogging over to help the others to their feet. 'Look sharp, lads,' he called, wincing from his wounds as he tried to ignore Hesperon's mangled corpse. 'Barrage has evened the odds, but this day's not over yet!'

Drygg spat out some alarmingly red saliva, checking to see his helm was still clasped in place. 'We're actually going to win this, sir. We're actually going to beat them.'

That made the Praefector smile, despite everything. 'Don't tempt the Fates, my boy,' he replied. 'But we're still here now, eh?'

Orbus took one last look at Bydreth. Around them, the rest of their comrades – the ones who still lived – were getting to their feet, recovering their arms and shambling into vague ranks. Brauda, Molchis, Dorthoi, Fuscator… they were worse for wear, and they'd all lost comrades, but thankfully no-one else more senior had bitten the dust. Orbus had lost enough lieutenants today already.

The Army of the Free still survived, but they'd been shattered. Those who remained were in disarray. Before the barrage, they'd held the cards of greater numbers and structured command. Now they possessed neither.

'You see them?' Orbus shouted, pointing his sword at the oncoming XII. Pylades' century, by the look of things. With the odds now levelled by the *ballistae*, there wasn't much for them to do. '*They* don't care about you, Bydreth. Not a jot. If they'd been in charge, you think they'd have done any different?' he snorted, pushing his helmet back into place. 'If anything, you can bet their plans for you would have been bloodier still.'

'Of course, Praefector.' Bydreth took a moment to help Brauda stand, his damning glare never once leaving Orbus. 'Thank you, sir, for this clarity.'

THE BATTLEFIELD WAS emptier than it had been in hours. The dead on either side outnumbered the living.

The day's events had been a tragedy. But while Gnaeus Ignatian still drew breath, it was a tragedy that could be put right.

The Castellan gave his horse another kick, willing the beast to *move, move, move*. He'd ditched his bodyguards – the few that remained following the Fulminata's sudden reinforcement, and the artillery strike that followed it – seizing the moment in the chaos to get himself north. However valorous his guardians' intentions were, clinging to his shadow would only see them killed too.

And the more of them that died to Orbus' vengeance there, on the battlefield, the better chance he had of escaping to Arx Agrippum.

'*No*,' he snarled, as the horse came to a halting, whinnying stop. 'Damn you! Don't give up now, my friend.'

But the beast was having none of it. Ignatian was far enough away now – far north of his army's original lines, almost at the thin stretch of forest that crowned the lower hills. He risked dismounting, leading the steed closer to see what the fuss was about.

'Ah. Of course.' He reached down, working his fingers into the cracked, mangled horseshoe. It must have happened in the final charge. No wonder the damn animal didn't want to move. 'Let us see if we can –'

He looked back. Down the way he'd come, his horse's travails momentarily forgotten.

His escape hadn't gone unnoticed.

'We're being followed,' the Castellan remarked to the apathetic steed. 'Apologies, my friend. But it's me they are after, not you. I'm going to have to leave that hoof of yours a little longer.'

'IT COULD ONLY have been him,' Curio affirmed, turning back to Orbus' men. 'I have the best eyes in my century, sir. That rider was wearing a legate's ceremonial helm.'

The Praefector grimaced, not even deigning to look at the newly approaching arrivals. Men from Pylades' and Scipio's centuries. He had better things to do than stroking their egos for simply following their damn orders.

'Bydreth? Brauda?' he asked. 'How many of your men are still battle-ready?'

The Painted looked a sorry bunch in that moment, even those who'd survived the *ballista* attack. And several of them were carrying other injuries.

'Twen… around fifteen, at most.' Bydreth's hostility had dialled back a notch, but only a notch. Now it was replaced by uncertainty. 'Why?'

'Gather them up.' Orbus slid *Ananke* into her sheath, checking his *pugio* was also strapped in place. 'Dorthoi, you're in charge here. The other centurions will come asking questions, or whatever bollocks they'll want to know. Tell them the battle's over, and I'm going for the traitor's head.' He paused, wiping more mess off his palms onto his tunic. 'And will someone check on Cascana? I don't trust Thracian to do it.'

'I'll stay,' Brauda offered, something that definitely caught the Praefector off guard. 'I'll be no good at a speed pursuit, not like this.' He gestured to his side, and the nasty gash from the *pilum* earlier. 'Take them, cousin. Finish this.'

Bydreth didn't know what to say. 'This is *your* victory, Brau. All of ours. *You* held our kin together today, as much as I did. Come. Bleed the traitor dry with us.'

A rather obnoxious clearing of the throat slew that moment of familial tenderness.

'This is all very touching,' Orbus put in. 'But while you two gaze into each other's eyes, our man is getting away.'

Bydreth swallowed his rage, turning to address the other Ulthaini.

'Alright,' he declared. 'Three groups of five, to split up when we reach the forest's mouth. We've scouted this area enough times. There's no quick way out of there.' He smiled, properly, for the first time since the *ballistae* had rained death from the skies.

'Let's march up there and kill the bastard.'

THIS TIME, BYDRETH'S assessment was on the mark. The tangled thicket of fern trees allowed a clear path into the wood, but little deviance from that path.

With a little luck, the Castellan could hide. But he couldn't run.

'So he's here, then,' Bydreth offered, when they reached the opening. Ignatian's horse – forsaken, presumably, to allow hastier passage on foot – was still waiting, gorging itself on arid grass.

'Kill it,' Orbus ordered, not even stopping to look at it. 'I don't want him doubling back and getting away.'

'But Praefector –'

'I won't ask again, Klaujan.'

TUGGI KEPT FIVE of them back to hold the entrance, while Brauda took the second group the long way round, seeking to cut off the only viable possible escape route from the forest's far side.

Orbus led the rest of them in, *Ananke* drawn for one last kill. Perhaps slaying the traitor would rob his words of their resonance. He'd found himself revisiting their past conversation, overlooking Arx Agrippum, too many times. The subject matter was something he'd happily lay to rest.

Bydreth had suggested they split up, to cover more ground. Any excuse to get away from him, Orbus fancied.

He found himself grimacing. The sting of that betrayal was still raw. It would take time to win the Centurion's trust back.

But he had other things to worry about now. Alone, hiking his way through the forest's cloistered greenery, Gnaeus Ignatian seemed to haunt his every step. And yet the traitor had never felt further from him.

The Praefector froze, *caliga* snapping a twig underfoot. What had he heard?

He turned, silently, to face the wooded path he'd taken. The breeze was his only companion, gentle enough to make the treetops whistle and whisper. How pure the silence was, now the clamour of battle and death had finally passed. How cleansing.

Ananke was a sweaty weight in his hand. What had made his pulse start to rise?

Guided by something faint and ephemeral – not quite instinct, not quite foreboding – Orbus stepped off the beaten path, making his own way into the wood's deeper depths.

'COME ON, YOU bastard...'

Bydreth was running hard. There couldn't be much wood left to cover. But by the Otherworld, *he* wanted to be the one to end this.

He'd trusted Orbus, ever since that day he'd crashed into their lives. He'd leashed the tribe's fate to him, putting their fortunes in the Roman's hands... only for this. To be treated like worthless cannon fodder, at the whim of a master little better than their last one.

To the abyss with Orbus. The Ulthaini were free men now, thanks to his vanity. And they'd been pocketing legionary wages for half a year. Once the day's bloodletting was over – once they returned to Rome – Bydreth had no intention of staying in the Praefector's service.

He'd go his own way, and he knew he could talk the others into following him. Freedmen all, with physical strength, legionary training and experience of an actual military deployment... yes, they would do well for themselves. Wrangling entry into another *auxilia* wouldn't be difficult, provided they could get a needy or sympathetic officer on side.

A rasp of drawn metal tore Bydreth's focus down to earth. As did a cry of strangled pain.

ORBUS STUMBLED INTO the clearing a little too late. He'd followed the guttural scream when he'd heard it, but by then the damage had been done.

He crashed to a halt, *Ananke* held *en garde*, to the sight of three people.

Drygg, lying supine in the bushes, youthful face frozen by whatever had slashed his throat.

Brauda, in the middle of the clearing, unable to move a muscle despite his every thought and nerve ending screaming otherwise.

And Ignatian, stood right behind him, eyes fixed on Orbus as he held a bloody *gladius* to Brauda's neck.

'I mean it!' the traitor spat. 'Drop the weapon, Praefector. Enough men have died today, wouldn't you say?'

'It's over, Gnaeus.' Orbus tried his best to keep his voice level. 'Your army is broken. Whatever reinforcements you still have are being hunted down as we speak. And we have the forest surrounded.'

Ignatian didn't move. In his grip, Brauda was sweating enough to make his face and forehead glisten. His blue and crimson warpaint caught the sunlight, blazing in the shimmering haze.

But he was shaking his head. Slowly. Ever so slowly. The movement was so subtle Ignatian hadn't noticed.

'We can't let you leave this battlefield, Gnaeus.' *Ananke* stayed right where it was, its grip buried in Orbus' right fist. 'There's been enough death, aye. But I can't let you escape off the back of one less.'

Ignatian's brow furrowed. His grip on the sword tightened. He clearly hadn't expected that response.

A flurry of crushed bracken heralded Bydreth's arrival. Looking back, it was probably a miracle Brauda didn't die there and then. But Ignatian, whatever his flaws, was no fool. This painted savage at his mercy was the only thing keeping him alive.

Bydreth stepped out of Orbus' shadow, hand on the pommel of his own weapon.

'Back off, auxiliary!' Ignatian took another step back, dragging Brauda with him.

'You want to think about this,' the Centurion hissed, equal parts incensed as worried. He didn't step forward, but didn't back away either. 'More of my boys are coming. Nowhere left to run, traitor.'

'I think I'll be the judge of that,' Ignatian retorted. All the time, the blade at Brauda's throat never wavered. 'Is this really what you want, Orbus? All this blood on your hands? Is this truly the penance you've hungered for?'

For a moment, the Praefector was tempted to close his eyes. *Penance.* What a word.

How many months had he spent in self-imposed mourning since his last trip to Gaul? How many people had he looked in the eye – quite honestly – as he'd used the word *atonement* to describe his life's mission and purpose? Urbanus? Argias? His brother?

And had he really wanted, in honesty, to survive the battle he'd just lived through? Half the Fulminata wanted him dead since his disgrace. Several of them had tried to make it happen. Had he really expected the remaining four centuries to ever appear over the horizon's lip, or just take the chance to rid themselves of their unwelcome canker?

The *auxilia* had been thrust upon him by obligation. When Urbanus had first made the declaration, he'd seen it as little more than a collar of shame. A millstone, to drag him beneath the waves. All that time and effort he'd spent building them up, shaping them into something worth leading... had that been for them? Truly? Or was that just vanity, a way to propel him into Erebus' halls with pride?

Was that really all the cohort was to him? An underfoot prop, to form the capstone for his pathetic legacy?

Only they'd pulled through it. They'd been tempered on that anvil, and while they hadn't exactly prospered, who even did? They'd endured. That was what mattered.

Orbus' old life was gone. He was no longer a legion officer. He no longer had a legate to take orders from, centurions to work with, a busy *castra* to run and orchestrate.

He no longer had an Urbanus, a Cascana, a Scipio or an Ardius. He no longer had the aegis of a legion to live under.

But he had a Bydreth. A Brauda. An Optatis. A Dorthoi. And a Molchis, for whatever it was worth. He had a home, that was theirs and theirs alone. He had men, *milites*, who followed him and no-one else. Who followed him out of loyalty, as well as duty.

And here was Orbus, willing to let an arch-traitor keep drawing breath, if only to keep one of his own alive a little longer. A painted man who didn't even particularly like him. A painted man ready to die anyway, if that was what it took.

That loyalty, that selflessness he'd kindled. That was worth protecting. That was something worth fighting for.

Funny, how things turn out. The Fates had a strange knack for bringing you home, as old Ascanius had once told him. Even if it wasn't quite the home you expected.

'This is not penance,' the Praefector finally replied. 'There is no penance here.'

Ignatian's face contorted, his confusion obvious. This was a change of tune from the Orbus he'd confronted in Arx Agrippum. His *gladius* lowered a fraction, weighing up those enigmatic words.

And that was all the opening Brauda needed.

The *optio*'s head shot backward. The metal helm hammered the Castellan's face, smashing his nose and teeth bloody.

The *gladius*, most crucially of all, slipped from his grasp.

And that was when it happened.

ORBUS AND BYDRETH were already moving, blades drawn.

Brauda had wheeled out from under Ignatian's grip. But he wouldn't get away that easily. The traitor caught his blade before it even finished falling, lunging after Brauda with a frothing roar and spurting blood.

'*No!*' Bydreth screamed as he and Orbus knocked Ignatian to the ground.

HE WAS ROLLING. Earth was sky. Sky was earth. The blow to his head hadn't helped.

Somewhere behind him, Brauda was gasping in pain. So no help from him, like as not.

Orbus rolled over, reaching up to tear his helmet off – finally ripping the frayed straps – as Ignatian's bloody maw loomed in his face. He didn't block the fist as it streaked down towards him. He was too stunned to even try.

'*Ruined!*' the traitor shouted, pummelling the Praefector a second time. And a third. '*All* we could have been! All we could have *done! Ruined! All of it!*' The grace, the patrician dignity, was gone from his bloodstained face. That intricate mask had finally slipped. All that was left was fury. White hot, finally bursting free.

Orbus spat blood trying to roll clear. *Ananke* was gone, fallen too far from reach. He still had the *pugio* in his belt, but— *Damn!*

Ignatian laughed, crushing fingers beneath his boot. The dagger fell from a nerveless grip. Or at least, he tried to laugh. What came out was merely a sanguineous gurgle.

Orbus was choking too, from ribs bruised into mauve oblivion. And he wanted to laugh, as well. So much for his grand epiphany. He'd finally found something to live for – and here he was, about to die anyway.

He had to admit, that was funny. That was irony enough for the Fates to gorge upon.

A booted foot hit him, again and again. Enough to roll him over once more.

It wouldn't exactly be a dignified end. But then again, what soldier of Rome ever got that?

BRAUDA STIFLED THE urge to cry out as he tried to push himself upright.

The *gladius* had given him a glancing blow, but a glancing blow still hurt like shit. And if he couldn't purge the wound of corruption in time, it could do much worse.

Blood leaked down his sternum as his vision swam back into focus. There was Orbus, laying prostrate, the traitor prince engrossed in kicking him to death.

Brauda's weapon was gone. His armour was a mess. Even his helm, lying in the mud before him, looked mangled into ruin.

Orbus had pissed away his chance to kill the bastard cleanly, all to save Brauda's life. He couldn't leave that debt unpaid.

Brauda pushed himself forwards, towards the accursed helm.

A little further, gods damn it. Just a little further.

ORBUS HAD FINALLY raised his hands, anything to ward off the barrage of blows. A little late, now.

He hadn't known pain like this since Gaul. Since Urbanus had leashed his back into bloody ruin.

He smiled again, through red-stained teeth and lips that were starting to swell. This was Fate come round at last. His dead man's journey ending right where it had started.

He was dimly aware of Ignatian's cruel visage, just as bloody as his own, leering down at him through his watery vision.

And then a battle helm smacked the back of his head. The traitor wavered on his feet a moment longer, as awareness fled from his gaze, before toppling, inert, into the undergrowth.

'NICELY DONE,' THE Praefector mumbled through split lips.

He spat out some grass he'd inhaled by mistake, which came out disturbingly red. One of his back teeth felt a little loose, too. He dared not test it with his tongue.

And that stabbing, burning stitch… had he taken a chest wound? Or just broken a rib?

Brauda sank back against a nearby tree trunk, eyes clasped shut. One hand was still clutching his sternum, with more blood swelling out between his fingers. Throwing the helmet had taken damn near all his strength, whatever he'd had left anyway. As wounds go, it didn't look too serious, but Orbus doubted the Painted *optio* would be fighting again any time soon.

'Feels strange,' Orbus slurred, 'now it's finally over.' And it did. The *auxilia* had triumphed, against all odds, with only a sliver of help from the Legion. Ignatian was dead. Orbus, somehow, had won.

And then he looked over, and saw the price he'd paid for that victory.

Bydreth lay in the bracken, where he'd landed in their tumble. Orbus and Brauda's focus had been stolen by the fight. So they hadn't seen him.

Or the *gladius*, now buried halfway to the hilt in his chest.

The blow that had glanced Brauda – the blow *meant* for Brauda – had struck the mark, after all. It had simply hit the wrong target.

'Brauda,' Orbus growled as he limped toward the stricken officer. '*Brauda!*'

The *optio* had opened his eyes now. He'd seen what was wrong.

'*Get help!*' Orbus roared, choking on his own bloody bile. He spat a load of it out into the grass. '*Tuggi.* At the mouth, with the others. *Go!*'

THE PRAEFECTOR TORE away the ruined chainmail, ripping Bydreth's tunic and *subarmalis* into shreds of leather and scarlet fabric. Anything to stop the bleeding.

'Stay with me,' he wheezed, he whispered, he *begged*. 'You *stay awake,* Centurion!'

Bydreth's eyes were open, but they weren't aware. They were hooded.

That wasn't a good sign.

He clamped down on the wound with his makeshift rags, and he clamped down hard. Bydreth moaned, wordless, soundless – a cry of agony in all but name, from a man with no air left to scream with.

'Come on!' Orbus gasped.

The Painted's eyes drifted open once more, slowly narrowing as he tried to focus on his commander's face.

'Get...' he breathed. 'Get your... *hands... off me.*'

For a moment, Orbus was dumbstruck.

'Thought… I knew you,' Bydreth's breath was running more ragged. Dry and rattly, like an old man's. 'Thought… we could… trust you.'

Somehow, that was the limit. After everything Sertor Orbus had braved and beaten today, every last thing the gods had thrown at him on this accursed battlefield… somehow, this was the rock that set the avalanche rolling.

'What are you saying, Bydreth?' His eyes were blazing with molten agony. Tears, dirt and crippling injuries weren't a happy combination. 'Bydreth? *Bydreth? What are you saying? Bydreth?*'

The Ulthaini's only response was silent vindication. A stare, long and piercing, just like the one he'd given Orbus on the plain.

Only it wasn't. Bydreth's eyes weren't staring into his soul. They weren't staring at anything.

They would never stare at anything again.

THREE COUGHS FROM the man nearby broke Orbus from his reverie. He'd been thinking about his choices, and the thoughts had been dark.

He wasn't sure how much time had passed. Not long, presumably, as Brauda hadn't come back, with or without the help he'd gone to find. None of the other Painted had found them, either.

'So, not quite dead.' The Praefector lowered his fallen comrade to the earth, pausing only to close his eyes. But for the sword embedded in his side, Bydreth ap Uîth might well have been sleeping.

Orbus didn't even bother retrieving *Ananke*. Such a noble weapon was unbefitting for this task. It felt good to have the *pugio* in his hands again. This wasn't a blade for duelling, or beating down shield walls.

It was a tool for murdering.

'On your feet,' the Praefector spat as he limped closer. Blood of Teucer, he was going to enjoy this.

Gnaeus Ignatian, former *Legatus* of the Emperor's XXV Legion, self-proclaimed Castellan of Arx Agrippum, made no move to rise from his knees. Orbus wasn't sure he even could. The traitor limply raised his hands to his head, pulling off the crested helm of office he'd worn into battle. It tumbled once free from his numb fingers, landing in the brush with barely a sound.

'Whatever you're about to do...' he croaked through a desiccated throat, 'won't be necessary.' He didn't even look at Orbus, instead extending an upward, open hand. 'Give me your *pugio*, Praefector.'

A flash of memory from months ago crossed Orbus' mind. Thracian's glib suggestion, as the First Cohort's officers had duelled over his fate. *Honourable suicide. By hemlock perhaps, or falling on your own sword. It would grant the end of your career a dash of Stoicism.*

Ah, so the traitor believed he was owed an honourable death. Orbus' filthy visage twisted in a half-smile. *How quaint.*

'Have no fear, Castellan,' he began, seeking to get the bastard's hopes up. 'If that is what you want history to say – that Gnaeus Ignatian drove a blade through his own breast, rather than surrender to the inevitable victory of Rome – then that is what history shall say.'

Orbus brandished the *pugio*, with an air of menace that would have made Thracian proud. 'But right here, between you and me... I'm afraid that won't be happening.'

Ignatian gave the Praefector one last, beleaguered look. But then he nodded, rising first to one knee, then standing haggardly upright. He knew when he was beaten, and he was in no place to make demands.

Orbus walked towards him. Around him. Behind him. Close enough to smell him.

'Extend your arms,' he commanded. Ignatian did so.

Orbus took the *pugio* – holding it by the blade, not the handle – and placed one of Ignatian's hands over the dagger's round pommel.

And then he placed the other hand over the first. And then his own hands, over Ignatian's.

And there they stood, one behind the other. The *pugio*'s point rested, just rested, over the torn and battered tunic, right above the traitor's heart.

'Think on what I told you, Orbus.' Even here, even now, the Castellan had some final honeyed venom to share. 'Everything I told you is true. You know, Sertor. You know the reasons I did this.'

The Praefector clasped his hands tight over Ignatian's. And with one final gasp, he drove the *pugio* right into the other man's breast.

'The true hell of life,' Orbus confessed, as the light faded from Ignatian's eyes, 'is that every man has his reasons.'

XIX

AFTERMATH

IT WOULDN'T END there, of course.

It didn't matter how one-sided the battle was, or how decisive the victory. No campaign ended in a day's fighting. No war ended with the fall of one sword.

Clearing the battlefield alone would take days. And that was before dismantling the *castra* even came into it.

The plain before the Ionys Depression was littered with death and detritus, organic wreckage of men and beasts, to say nothing of the sea of sundered arms and armour. Bodies lay, more pronounced, among the waste like flesh among rib bones.

And *the smell...* The *auxilia*, for the most part, weren't accustomed to death on such a massive scale, but the stench of slaughter was all too familiar to the Fulminata. It was inevitable, coming on the heels of each and every war. That coppery odour of blood long shed, spilt from savaged veins and arteries, which gradually soured into a pervasive, cloying aroma of rot and decay.

Legionaries of the XII roamed through the sea of bodies, looking for potential prisoners or slaves and mercy-killing those men too wounded to ever truly live again. Fires had been lit around the battlefield's flanks, small and weak, for the task of burning whatever spoils the victors were happy to part with. The rags of Army tunics, the wooden hafts of spears... even enemy corpses. And so a reek of charcoal and spoilt meat drowned out the stench of rot.

For the survivors, a similar conflagration of sorts was waiting. And this one felt just as painful.

'What's going on?' Molchis had asked at one point, as the groups of *auxilia* and Cascana's surviving legionaries were corralled into meandering queues. 'What's this all for?'

'Saltwater,' Curio told him. 'What did you think was in those barrels? All those wounds and cuts we've all taken? Need to purge them of infection somehow.' A throaty gasp cut them short from the line's head, where a *triarius* of Scipio's was trying to treat the gash in his side. A pair of *capsarii* from the Legion's medical contingent continued wiping him down with soaked cloth, heedless of the legionary's agony. None of the *capsarii* looked much older than any of Ardius' men, with the more grizzled medical staff off treating the more seriously wounded legionaries.

'Hurts more than the wounds themselves,' one of Curio's men chuckled, relishing the *auxilia*'s discomfort. 'Necessary evil though, lads. Unless you want infection clawing after you.'

The Fulminata's men weren't the only souls prowling the fallen. The crows had begun their inevitable descent, fluttering down in ones and twos to have their gruesome way with the dead – or not quite dead – of Arx Agrippum's soldiers. A few of the

mean, that's what *auxilia* are for, right?' He slapped Orbus one final time on the back, before returning to the nearest source of beer.

The Praefector watched the Centurion leave. He weighed up Alvanus' words for a few moments, feeling the sudden urge to bathe himself head to toe.

Another figure had detached itself from the *triarii*, a figure Orbus had no time for. He was already making to leave, walking back to where he spied some Branded huddled around a fire of their own.

'Praefector,' the figure tried. The amber light caught the *phalerae* hanging round his neck, marking him out as another centurion. 'Orbus, please. At least let me explai—'

'Get out of my way, Scipio.' Orbus didn't even stop. He simply shoved the other officer aside and kept on walking. Scipio knew better than to try pursuing him. Which was fortunate, for he'd have only gotten a punch in the face for his trouble.

'Sir.' Even at ease and half-intoxicated, Optatis' straight-arrow nature never seemed to waver. 'Is all well?'

Orbus' gaze coldly drifted back to the drunken *triarii*, carrying on heedless. 'I'm fine,' he lied. 'Anything worth reporting?'

Optatis shook his head, taking another sip of ale. Thankfully, the *auxilia* had been allotted a meagre share of it too. Or maybe they'd taken it for themselves. 'Brauda's men haven't come back yet. And Ardius must have pulled a face at the Creedless, as none of them are daring to loot the dead anymore.'

The Praefector snorted. He took the flagon of drink from Optatis' hands without asking, downing a long draught. For his part, the Centurion didn't seem remotely perturbed.

'No-one's started a fight yet,' Optatis wryly observed. 'Which is a surprise, given how poor some of ours are at holding their beer. But then, the night is young.'

Orbus smirked again, touching his own *phalerae* for luck as he handed back the flagon. In truth, proceedings were unfolding more gracefully than he'd dared hope. Some of the *auxilia* – Branded, mainly, and a few Riven – were even mingling with the groups of Fulminata, sharing drink and terse reflections on the day's brutal events.

To the XII, the Praefector's straw men were something of a curiosity, even if that 'curiosity' had proved it could pull its weight on a battlefield. It wasn't respect. Not truly. But it was the start of respect.

Orbus allowed himself a half-smile, although not even Optatis was close enough to see it. He could work with that.

'You've heard about Cascana, I presume?' Optatis asked, apropos of nothing.

'Indeed I have. Small mercies, given how many others died.'

The Branded officer nodded. 'Aye, and all. Didn't seem to take any serious knocks, either. Wish I could say the same,' he half-heartedly grumbled, giving his shoulder a rub. 'No, that isn't fair. He fought well out there. He did you proud.'

'I'm sure.' The Praefector's gaze trailed back into the darkness, deliberately away from the fire.

Optatis just looked at him searchingly. Orbus' mercurial moods never seemed to settle, whatever was happening, but he fancied he was getting better at reading them. And he had a vague idea of where this latest disquiet was coming from.

'You should talk to him, sir.'

Orbus gave his centurion a look. 'Meaning?' he guardedly asked.

Optatis clearly had no wish to elaborate, taking refuge in his ale.

'I just... I really think you should talk to him.'

BY MORNING, THE battlefield looked a little less devastated. The bodies that littered the plain were, for the most part, hungover and postcoital rather than slain.

The familiar icy caress of Roman military discipline straightened that out, and no mistake.

In the cold light of day, the Legion's next orders of business became a little more sombre. Broken '*bernia* and formations recongregated in ranks, and the butcher's bill for each unit was finally tallied.

The dead and injured were recorded and earmarked, the former stripped of wargear and prepared for the journey back to Rome, the latter catalogued and reassigned, to either temporarily lighter duties or a permanent and unwilling discharge from military service. Arrangements were made with the cohort's funeral club, and the units in direst need of reinforcement were put on notice.

Tribunes set the spinning cogs and gears of the administrative machine turning. Scribes and *immunes* worked with Praefector Thracian to take stock of every change in personnel and inventory. Centurions and *decani* oversaw arrangements to repopulate, or even merge, the '*bernia* beneath their command.

Promotions were doled out in name only, ready to be ratified back in Rome and marked with proper ceremony. Battlefield commendations were handed out to legionaries most deserving or prudent to receive such notices.

And, more predictably, officers who deemed their men's performance as subpar made brutal examples of penance and censure. Punishment duties were given out, and privileges of camp and rank were revoked.

And then, of course, came the rites. There were always some ceremonies to conduct at a battle's end, some auspices to assuage and appropriate deities to thank for their good fortune. Incense was lit around each century's sacred *signa*, as chanting invocations gave thanks to Mars for guiding their blades in battle, to Ceres for the bountiful pickings they had reaped from the land to feed themselves, and to Fortuna for granting them victory.

Heifers were even sacrificed, 'liberated' from a nearby farmstead during a supply raid, and the libations of their steaming blood marked the end of a fruitful week of war.

Orbus and his *auxilia* watched these rites from a distance, having predictably not been invited to partake. And truth be told, few among their number were particularly bothered.

There was far more interesting gossip in the air.

URBANUS' OFFICIAL PROCLAMATION, from the mouth of his favoured tribune, had spread through the *castra* like a plague.

Gnaeus Ignatian, it was reported, had committed suicide rather than be taken by Orbus' men. His army's remaining reinforcements – those that either hadn't arrived at the battle in time, or were far enough away to get clear of the legion reinforcements – had scattered. Or so the scouts had reported.

They couldn't be discounted, not by any stretch. They were still a threat. But shorn of their leadership, and their support, they were no longer a force to be feared. They were piecemeal, divided, and Urbanus was confident they could be picked off by the Fulminata's forces without much stress.

Orbus was inferring that confidence, admittedly. He hadn't so much as seen the old man since the battle had ended, engrossed as he was with plans for the campaign's next stages. And Orbus wasn't legion, anyway. What business of his was it what the XII's commander was thinking?

Nor had Urbanus' announcement ended there. He had plans beyond the slaying of Gnaeus Ignatian, far beyond it. The XII – with the aid of their artillery detachment – would strike at Arx Agrippum next.

Laying siege to the city itself, upon consideration, didn't look to be particularly demanding. The Army of the Free had lost so many men before the Ionys Depression, as well as innumerable hordes of the levy's fittest and strongest citizens, that four centuries of the Legion's First Cohort would have little difficulty in breaking and bringing their stronghold to heel.

Four, not five. Having borne the brunt of the battle that passed, Cascana's century had been exempted from taking part in the coming siege. The First Spear's part in the war was over, having discharged his duty with full honour.

And, of course, the *auxilia* wouldn't be taking any further part in the campaign either. There was wisdom in that – they, too, had taken far too great a mauling to provide any meaningful support to the Legion's other centuries. But Orbus' rabble had, reputedly, done what they'd been brought here to do – to die in droves, and let the XII finish the job with all the glory and little of the cost.

Urbanus had allowed the *auxilia* to take whatever spoils they wished from the Ionys Depression, but the Praefector knew better than to read any respect or gratitude into that thrown bone. If anything, it was probably a snub, more coins and table scraps scattered on the street for his mongrel soldiers to fight over. And no doubt the unquestionably richer pickings from Arx Agrippum would be divided among the Legion itself, as recompense.

In truth, Orbus tried not to think about the coming siege too much. The citizens of this once-proud colony had openly defied the Emperor's *imperium*. Only a grim fate awaited them, whether they lived or died.

Few others seemed to share his foreboding. For starters, another rumour had begun to circulate among the camp – that Urbanus, when word of his men's actions came back to Rome, would be nominated for a Triumph. Perhaps that was why the *Legatus* was so keen to raze Arx Agrippum to the ground. If he was to enter Rome in all the pomp and ceremony of a *triumphator*, with a paraded procession to proclaim his might and glory to the heavens, then a long line of yoked prisoners to display before the thronging crowds would doubtless go down perfectly.

Short of being elected to the consulate, or serving as governor of one of the Empire's more opulent provinces, there were few higher honours in Rome.

The fact that victory had come off the backs of other officers, and men not even belonging to his legion, didn't come into it. Urbanus had command here. Any glory earned was his to claim.

ORBUS CHOSE NOT to think about all that now, as the host of familiar faces began to fill the clearing.

He'd chosen the wooded glade to do this, though the place's resonance wasn't exactly welcome. Bydreth had died less than a hundred paces from this spot, as had Gnaeus Ignatian.

Neither shade the Praefector had any wish to disturb, metaphorical or otherwise. But he needed the open space, and more importantly, he wanted the privacy. This coming moment was going to matter. It wasn't something for outsiders, especially not the judgemental souls of the Legion.

This moment was for them, and them alone.

The most able-bodied *auxilia* appeared first, the ones who had only taken minor or superficial wounds, or had come through the slaughter unscathed. The more injured took their time, limping or helping each other hobble their way to this conclave. The most grievously wounded came last, carried or borne on ragged stretchers by their fellows.

It was a hassle, and it certainly took time. But they all made it, one way or another. The only ones not to heed his summons were the dead.

Orbus' feelings as his *milites* congregated before him were mixed. So many had fallen, both in the battle and the grievous way he'd been forced to end it. The Praefector had brought over two hundred men from Rome to Arx Agrippum. Even if none of the other injured succumbed to infection or died on the journey home, he'd be lucky to return with sixty-five.

They weren't just numberless faces to him, or merely names on a wax tablet. So many good men, so many capable, promising souls, had perished before the Ionys Depression.

Argias. Arxander. Bydreth. And the gods knew how many others. Just looking at their depleted ranks and '*bernia* made his heart sink.

Seeing his remaining officers arrayed before each century gave him a little heart, at least. Molchis and Optatis looked by and large the same, beneath the cuts and bruises they'd accrued over the last twenty-four hours. One of Molchis' arms hung in a makeshift sling, while Optatis' left eye was far blacker in broad daylight than the cover of darkness had let on.

Beside them, a scarred and battered figure still insisted on standing alone and unaided. Vinculex, alongside his few surviving Brazen, had come through the Battle of Arx Agrippum worse than almost anyone else. His face, torso and midriff were all scarred and bruised, because the Gutter Prince had never once shown his back to a foe. A rough crescent on his forehead – where the dying horse had laid him out – was conspicuous even among his other marks, and Orbus doubted it would ever truly fade.

Not far from Vinculex, the cohort's two newest centurions stood to attention. Dorthoi, son of Phillipos, had been the foremost hoplite in the phalanx after Arxander and Behemon. There was no better candidate to lead the Riven now, and none of the surviving Achaeans had taken issue with his elevation.

And then there was Brauda. Loyal Brauda. Bitter Brauda. Brauda, who'd only ever wanted to escape his cousin's shadow. Brauda, who'd just wanted a chance to be Bydreth.

And now, standing as centurion of the remaining Painted, that was precisely what had happened.

The Ulthaini warrior looked surprisingly stoic in the sun's morning rays, something that had taken the Praefector by surprise. Orbus could scarcely reconcile that with how he'd howled his broken rage over his cousin's corpse, or the defeated, dejected look in his eyes as they'd borne away Bydreth's funeral bier.

But then, if Brauda still needed to grieve, Orbus wouldn't be the man to see it. Brauda wasn't Bydreth, and the Praefector didn't know if he'd ever have a bond like theirs again. Perhaps he and Brauda would find a similar common ground. Perhaps not.

It was certainly a sobering thought, one that hit him harder than expected. A wave of sepia nostalgia caught him out of nowhere – of long afternoons in the *Principia* courtyard, of raucous mealtimes in the mess hall, even the occasional drunken expedition into the *Subura*'s seedier taverns.

Looking at the Painted survivors standing to ragged attention, Orbus realised that Brauda wasn't the only one who'd lost a brother in arms.

'*Auxilia,*' he called out to the clearing, when the moment had finally passed. Orbus put thoughts of Bydreth from his mind, his closest soldier, who had died despising him. 'All those months ago, when I gathered you in the bones of that old fortress, I told you that the life I was offering would be hard. That it would test you, and change you, in ways you couldn't conceive.'

None of the assembled *milites* said anything. Though this time it was discipline, not confusion, that held their collective tongues. The Praefector let the moment hang a little longer, before puncturing the tension with a dash of humour.

'I mean, it wasn't *that* bad, was it?'

A few men in the foremost ranks chuckled, despite themselves. Optatis and Dorthoi joined in, though Brauda and Vinculex predictably didn't share the feeling. Neither did Molchis, which came as a surprise.

'We have bled,' Orbus continued, regaining his gravitas. 'And we've been tested. Each and every one of you has lost comrades. Many of you doubtless look on our depleted numbers and see this as defeat.'

A pause.

'You are wrong,' the Praefector continued. 'We donned the arms and trappings of legionaries, even if we are merely auxiliaries. We waged a war of spite and shadows for months, harrying the traitorous foe at every turn, slitting throats and raiding hearths. We fought against an army that outnumbered us many times over – an army of warriors who would have been the match of any legion, never mind us – and we survived. We endured. We *triumphed.'*

A few of them made some noise – a rumbling, susurrating prelude to a cheer. But the tension hadn't quite broken yet.

'There is no denying it now!' Orbus shouted. 'We *fought* beside legion, *against* legion, and we *proved* ourselves equal to that standard! We showed them that we *deserve* to be here! That we are *worthy* of treading their ground!'

And *now* the men were cheering. Not altogether, not coherently, but scores of men shouting in triumph couldn't always be set to a beat.

'The XII can't deny it!' he went on with a roar. *'They saw it! They saw what we are made of!'* Despite everything, Orbus found himself swept up in the moment too. *'They saw men the equal of their own!'*

More cheering. More exaltation cried to the sky. They weren't a disparate horde of freedmen, criminals and mercenaries. Not in that moment. They were a cohort. They were men with one voice and one vision.

'We will return to Rome,' he told them. 'We will take stock of our losses, and we will begin recruiting again to replenish our ranks. Shackle your fear, any who look at the holes in our lines and feel themselves exposed. This cohort will stand at full strength again, and I will not stop there. Our numbers will soon be greater than ever before.'

The *milites* were quieter now, their rapture having passed, but Orbus knew contented men when he saw them.

'But there is one further matter to discuss.' He stepped a few paces forward, drawing close to his five centurions even as his words carried to the whole clearing.

'In every legion cohort, one centurion stands before the others. A First Spear, who speaks for his other officers, and the legionaries at his back.'

Orbus turned his head, taking in each of his lieutenants with a glance. 'While we are not a legion in truth, I see no reason to treat you any differently. And so I, too, seek a First Spear. A man responsible for this cohort in my absence.'

He turned, slowly, to face the Centurion he'd chosen.

'Brauda,' he declared. 'I ask this of you. Do you accept?'

For a second, the Painted officer seemed actually lost for words. Orbus cherished that unguarded moment. He fancied it wouldn't easily come again.

If the other centurions were at all surprised at this choice – and they surely, undoubtedly, would be – they were wise to hide that sentiment. Orbus' word in this cohort was law, and since no legion officers cared enough about these men to give them any damned oversight, that situation wasn't going to change.

'I... am honoured,' Brauda finally replied. 'I accept.'

Orbus smiled. 'I'm glad to hear it, First Spear.'

His gaze travelled up to the sky for a moment, pleasantly, piercingly blue.

'Dismissed, all of you. Take this evening as your own,' he decided. 'Before long we'll have a *castra* to disassemble.'

'I say we just tear it down with our swords and spears!' shouted Molchis, to a few more laughs. He was already filing out with the Creedless. 'We've proved we can do it, after all. Break iron, as well as men.'

Orbus found himself snorting. But that wasn't the thought that had occurred to him.

'Ironbreakers...' he murmured, loud enough for them to hear. 'I quite like that.'

DUSK FOUND HIM still there, some time later. The sun had sunk on its path to the ground, but still cast enough light and warmth through the trees. Less auric, more amber, the clearing still had quite an ambience. It felt like a pause. A threshold between now, and pastures new.

Orbus still relished the look of surprise on Brauda's face, all these hours since. Perhaps Optatis would have been a more realistic choice, or maybe Bydreth or Arxander if they'd survived. It had been a move, but a calculated one. His first two choices were dead, and the Branded weren't a century he was particularly worried about.

He needed to court Brauda's loyalty, and that of the Painted. Without Bydreth's calming guidance, he was bound to become a problem soon enough. He couldn't do with one of his strongest bands of men chafing against him, or wanting to leave.

And anyway, he had a good feeling about Brauda. The man might never be a friend, or even a comrade. But, given the right guidance, he could still be a leader.

A snapped twig broke his train of thought, killing the summer spell. The clearing was just a clearing. With open space, few places to hide and enough damn trees to block any line of sight.

The Praefector felt his hackles start to rise. His eyes snapped back and forth, hand on *Ananke*'s pommel. He was armed, but unarmoured. Hardly a difficult target.

'Thought I'd find you here,' a familiar voice stumbled. Slurred. Orbus recognised it, but it sounded a lot less assured than he was used to.

The figure stepped into view, from behind its evergreen hiding place.

'Cascana?' Orbus felt more foreboding then surprise. He knew the conversation that was coming, and this wasn't remotely how he'd hoped to have it.

Here we go, then.

'I couldn't help overhear your little speech,' Cascana added, sauntering up to actual talking distance. The young officer seemed a little unsure of his footing, to Orbus' eye. 'It all sounded very *fine*, Praefector. Very high and mighty, indeed.'

He was drunk. Blazingly so. How had Orbus not spotted it at once? Cascana was a measured, self-controlled soul at the best of times. He rarely indulged in drink at all.

That didn't bode well.

'Iulus…' Orbus tried to say. 'Look, I know what happened out there was—'

Cascana cut him down with a punch. Whatever he'd drunk, it wasn't enough to dull his reflexes. Or his aim.

Orbus rolled over backward, spitting some blood aside. Somehow, he felt that blow harder than any he'd taken in the battle.

'You little sh—' he begun, before stopping, and looking back up at the younger man with guilt writ large in his eyes.

'How could you?' Cascana spat, hands balled into fists like a child. A gesture that should have been comical was somehow tragic. '*How could you?* I stick my neck out for you, *yet again*, to join you in the muck and dirt, and give you a chance of living through this. And you do *that!*'

The Praefector rose, as quickly as he dared. One hand still rubbed his mouth and jaw.

'Ninety-eight legionaries dead!' Cascana thundered drunkenly. *'Ninety! Eight!* Out of one hundred and forty-three! *Your little stunt cost me my gods-damned century!'*

Orbus' voice caught in his throat. *Ninety-eight men.* He'd known the figure was high, but he hadn't dared guess how much.

'All those men dead!' Cascana spat, lolling briefly on his feet. 'And *why?* Because Sertor fucking Orbus can only win alone!'

Now *that* was enough to raise the Praefector's ire. He stopped feeling angry at himself, and decided to redirect it. 'Are you *mad*, Iulus?' he shouted back. 'We were done for. There were too many of the damned enemy, pouring in from the north. *We didn't win,* Iulus. We held the line, but we didn't win. It would have been a massacre, no matter how valiantly you and I fought!'

'No!' the First Spear bawled. 'No, it *wouldn't* have been! There were four other centuries in the cohort, uncle. *Four! Centuries!* Who just happened to arrive at the *same damn time* as your fucking artillery!' For a minute, the Praefector thought he was about to get punched again. Cascana the drunk's rage came in peaks and troughs, it seemed, more from intoxication than control. 'Yes, maybe it would have been close. Pyrrhic. But we are *soldiers* of *Rome*, uncle! We take those odds when we take up the ink!'

Orbus shook his head without much spirit. He'd made the call, and it had been the wrong one. What else was there to say?

'It wasn't that simple, Iulus,' he retorted. 'Are you really so blind? For all I knew, *nobody* was coming at all.'

Cascana's anger briefly froze, replaced by confusion.

'Do you seriously think Thracian would try to arrive in time to save *me?*' Orbus continued, regaining his fighting spirit. 'Or you, for that matter? You've been a thorn in his side these last few months, just as much as me.' He clapped his hands together, taken by the absurdity of Cascana's innocence. 'He was going to let us *die*, Iulus! I know he was! Hell, it would have been *easier* for him to hold the men back, springing the trap *after* the Army cut us to pieces. The perfect gods-damn opportunity! Hit Ignatian's dogs while they're exposed, and then to hell with you and me!'

'But he *didn't!*' Cascana spat through clenched teeth. '*Thracian, Thracian, Thracian*. That's all I've damn well heard from you these past six months. He's a bastard, uncle. But you're *obsessed* with him! And now look!' He threw his arms wide. 'Look what you did, all to scupper some imaginary fucking plot inside your head. Because *he didn't try it*, uncle. The others *arrived*. In the *nick of bloody time!*'

'And *why* do you think that was?' Orbus thundered back, his fury ungovernable now. 'Because Urbanus made him do it, that's why! Why the hell else?'

'*No!*' the First Spear screamed. '*He didn't! I spoke to Scipio and the others! Urbanus wasn't even there! Thracian had command of the whole march! He didn't betray you at all!*'

For a moment, they both were speechless. Wheels turned inside Orbus' head, as he processed what he'd just heard.

'So there.' Cascana was folding his arms now, almost petulantly. 'Whatever your accursed reasons were, you were wrong. Thracian didn't try to sell you out. *No-one* sold you out. Your hell's gambit was for nothing.' He spat in the earth by Orbus' feet. 'So that's all you can say, is it? A hundred of my boys dead, to slake your damned paranoia?'

'My…' The Praefector was almost lost for words. 'Last winter a gang of legionaries tried to beat me to death! And you *know* he was behind that. You're calling *that* paranoia?'

'And who saved you, uncle?' Cascana countered. '*Who saved you?* Is your memory really that poor? I saved you from Urbanus' wrath. I saved your life on the Field of Mars. I put myself on the line when Ardius wanted your head. I helped you build that filthy cohort of shits!' For a moment, he softened, and his eyes took on a sheen Orbus prayed was from drunkenness. 'I did those things to… to protect my own. Like you'd do for me.'

The moment passed in a blink, so fleeting it could have been imagined. 'And my, *how* you repaid me, *uncle*. You *trusted* me, took me into your confidence about your final gambit… Oh. Wait. You *didn't*. You lied to me, and when our backs were to the wall, you thought my men's lives were worth risking to claw back a win.'

Orbus had nothing left to riposte with. He was defeated. Cascana had him dead to rights, and he knew it.

'*One word*, uncle. *One* single moment of trust would have sufficed.' The First Spear trailed off. 'If only father could see us now.' He snorted. 'He always said you couldn't stand losing.'

'Is that what you think this was?' the Praefector warily replied.

'Oh, I *know* what this was,' Cascana replied with bladed dejection. 'You lost everything. The Legion cast you out. The officers turned their noses up at you. The men kicked you to the roadside, and Thracian got to strut around with your prefect's crest. And after all these months of bashing auxiliaries together and wading through shit, Sertor bloody Orbus wanted to make a gods-damned point. *That's* what this was.'

Sertor bloody Orbus chose not to answer that, raising one thin eyebrow instead.

'Yes,' Cascana continued. 'Sharing victory with the First Cohort wouldn't do, would it? Doing all their donkeywork, fighting and bleeding by my side just for the other centuries to roll in and save the day? No, no, no. Why do that, when you can wipe the damn battlefield clean in one stroke? What a victory. What a *daring* move. Show the XII that you and your little lost boys can win the unwinnable, and who cares if poor little Iulus' men pay the price for it?' He was slurring his words again, seeming to lapse out of lucidity. 'Or your own?'

The Praefector looked at his wayward kinsman for a moment, letting the words sink in. Blood of Teucer, but Cascana knew him well. He'd torn insight from his soul that he could scarcely admit to himself.

'Well?' Cascana spat. 'Nothing to say?'

In a moment of almost suicidal courage, Orbus risked reaching for the younger man's shoulder.

'Iulus, this wasn't my—'

'*Shut up!*' Cascana's hand was a blur, grabbing Orbus' own and twisting it round to armbar him. He shoved his uncle to the ground, already backing away. '*Don't touch me.* Don't *Iulus* me. I am First Spear of this legion. *First Spear!*' Somehow, against all rhyme and reason, the young man looked as if he would burst into tears. 'You're not my damned uncle anymore, Orbus. You and me... this is over. All of it. You and I are finished.'

Cascana was already walking away, paying the broken man behind him no heed.

And then he was gone, leaving Orbus alone in the evening light.

XX
THE TYRANT'S ECHO

THREE DAYS AFTER that, as the men were stripping down their *castra*, the envoy arrived.

Scouts from Ardius' *hastati* were the first to spot them coming, billeted in the southmost rank of tents. Specks of black dust on the horizon resolved themselves into more defined shapes, in a rather provocative echo of how Graecillus' cavalrymen had appeared before their crashing charge.

Only these newcomers were moving much more slowly, and clearly came in peace instead of war.

That didn't put the officers' minds at ease, though. Their response was prudently, understandably guarded.

'Cascanan, Ardian and Alvanan Centuries! *Cuneum formate!*' Thracian barked, from his place in the camp's central courtyard. 'Quickly, you dogs! *Hastati* and *principes* in the foremost ranks, *triarii* anchoring the rear. Spear-ready!'

It took a tortuous few minutes for the wedge of infantry to come together. Most of the men weren't remotely arrayed for battle – the majority of each cohort was engrossed in disassembling and packing up the *castra* – and half of them weren't even armed.

But they were legionaries, first and foremost, and they were trained to exacting standards. A good soldier didn't whine about the odds, or being caught off guard. He simply did his duty as best he could.

The *cuneum* came together, eventually, but it was a *cuneum* nonetheless. At an officer's command, it could make an attack run or break into defensive lines at will.

It all depended on what was coming.

'What is happening?' Urbanus had asked as he emerged from his *praetorium*.

'Unknowns inbound, sir. From the south,' Thracian reported. 'Too far away to determine allegiance, but they don't look like the traitors. And they're not moving in formation.'

'Indeed,' the Legate murmured. By this point, even Orbus and a gaggle of his *auxilia* had emerged into the open. Naturally, no-one had the courtesy to fill them in.

The new arrivals were a little closer now, and the reason for their tardiness was revealed. The frontmost horse was in fact an ass, yoked to a shambling wagon. A few other figures hung back on horses, but they kept pace with their languid leader.

They were military men, that much was obvious. But they weren't legionaries. They were...

'No,' breathed Thracian.

'It cannot be,' Urbanus was similarly bewildered.

A good way off behind them, Orbus put a hand to his eyes, trying to pick the newcomers out. Their arms and armour resembled those of the Fulminata, but for the heraldic white markings that adorned them more liberally, as well as the icons of the goddess of Victory that festooned their shields and helms.

Most tellingly of all, however, was the immense *signa* borne by one of the riders. The emblem on its ornate boss plate, depicting a curling black scorpion upon a pale background, proclaimed their identity for all to see.

'The Praetorian Guard,' Alvanus grunted. 'What are those sorry bastards doing here?'

Thracian, belatedly, made the hand gesture to *tecombre*. As one, the legionaries broke into ranks, more for appearance's sake than to ward against potential attack.

The Praetorian convoy clopped to a halt, about twenty-five paces from the half-stripped *castra*'s outer wall. The lead rider's *signa* stood proud, gently buffeted by the wind's current, just as the wagon's sole occupant emerged into view.

He looked a little clean-cut for a soldier – a sure testament to the dearth of action the Praetorians saw these days – although his square-set jaw and muscles pointed to a combat veteran. He wore a crimson cloak of office that seemed more suited to Rome's palatial corridors than a frontier province.

And most curiously of all, a sash of regal purple hung from one shoulder, slung elegantly over his cuirassed torso.

'Legionaries of the XII Fulminata,' he called out in a curiously elegant accent that nevertheless sounded brutal enough for a *castra*'s grounds. 'We come from Rome, bearing an urgent missive for Decius Urbanus.' He paused, ominously. 'From the hand of the *Princeps*, himself.'

'I am here.' The Legate stepped forward, warily, hesitantly. He made no move to welcome these outsiders, or to encourage his *milites* to do likewise. 'I must say, gentlemen, that your presence here is... unexpected. The orders given to me were quite specific. What manner of Imperial missive requires armed carriage by the Emperor's personal guards? What change in my mandate could have happened so quickly?'

The envoy produced a bound roll of parchment sealed by wax from within his cloak. 'I am Lucius Aemilius Sejanus, tribune of the Praetorian Guard,' he declared, not that anyone had asked. 'I was charged to bring these orders to you, Legate Urbanus. For your urgent consideration.' He proffered the bound vellum.

Behind Urbanus, Thracian and the drawn ranks of legionaries, Orbus screwed his face up in disbelief. *Tribune?* The man barely looked old enough to be a line soldier. Let alone an officer.

Urbanus had broken open the seal, eyes digesting the written words with murderous focus. His lips moved as he read, but he said nothing. No-one else broke the silence, either, but from the shifting expression on Sejanus' aquiline face, this message was clearly going to make some waves.

'We... we are being reassigned.' The Legate lowered the scroll, not quite able to hide his bewilderment. 'What madness is this?' he snapped, taking a step forwards. 'The bulk of the enemy is broken. The arch-traitor lies dead, by his own hand. If we push on now, we can crush Arx Agrippum and uproot this canker of disloyalty for good.'

Sejanus smiled, a little too slick to be trustworthy. 'The Praetorians speak with the Emperor's voice, *Legatus*, and I'll thank you to remember that. But here, today, we are merely messengers. Do not seek to prize any more insight from us, for you will find none.'

'Messengers...' Urbanus echoed scornfully, on the edge of his temper. This slimy little Praetorian knew what was really going on, no doubt about it. 'And what is this?' He stabbed a finger at the rest of the scrawled missive. '*Damnatio memoriae*? Is this some jest?'

Sejanus' gaze went past the Legate for a moment, taking in Thracian and the ranks of legionaries around him. His voice travelled to all of them, too. 'Our lord Caesar's will was quite clear. The treachery of Gnaeus Ignatian will not merely be uprooted, as you say. It will be erased and expunged from time. Every mention of his name, his former legion, the city he presumed to rule, and this treasonous, poisonous movement will be struck from all records and histories. His seat in the Senate will be given over to another. His stone likeness will be cast down from every statue and fresco.'

Behind Urbanus, the legionaries of the Fulminata absorbed this news in sombre silence. Practically half the cohort had appeared from their tents and duties, bearing witness to this unfolding change of plans. The other officers, too, were here to see what all the fuss was about.

Sejanus looked back at the Legate, his smile now all the more unnerving for its apparent warmth. 'You know your history, Urbanus. You know how the *damnatio* works. From this point on, the traitor never existed, nor did any of his mongrel followers...' He trailed off, the implication obvious.

'And this battle never happened,' Urbanus finished, bitterly. 'And this is why we're being pulled out of Gaul? And who will take our place? What legion?'

'Called back to Rome, actually.' In victory, the Tribune seemed perfectly reasonable. 'And as it happens, more of your own Fulminata will take your place. That was the point of deploying just one legion cohort, was it not?' he smirked, pettily. 'To keep news of the insurrection from spreading too far. Not that we need worry about that, now. But as it happens, three more cohorts of the XII are making the passage here. They are about ten miles or so behind us.'

Sejanus' reticence, for whatever it was worth, seemed truly heartfelt. 'For now, Urbanus, your command has been terminated. Upon your return to Rome, you will relinquish your military *imperium* and resume your senatorial duties until you are next allotted a command. Marcus Rubinius has been appointed *legatus* in your absence.'

Orbus was still a good distance away from the confrontation, but he could physically feel the discontent passing through his former comrades. *Damnatio memoriae* was an uncompromising sentence, the path of silence it carved in its wake more unforgiving still.

If all mention of Ignatian and his deeds were stricken from the histories, if every last trace of his life wiped clean from Rome's memory... then there would be no glory. No commemoration. Not even a new name on the Legion's roll of honour.

Hardly a fitting reward for months of death and warfare.

Urbanus was still not satisfied, but knew better than to push back anymore. The same couldn't be said for his underlings, however.

'It's only been days,' Alvanus challenged, stepping forward, 'since we put the traitor bastard in the earth. The journey here from Rome—' He nodded in the direction of Sejanus' wagon. '—takes months. Even for a courier or dispatch. So when did this happen, Tribune? When did the Senate make this call?'

'Do not concern yourself with the minutiae, Centurion.' Sejanus wasn't about to be baited. 'In a few days' march, the new reinforcements will be here to take up your mantle. Your cohort is finished with this war, gentlemen. Continue stripping down your *castra*, and make arrangements for the journey home. This is now Rubinius' theatre of war.'

Only the former legate of the XII wasn't quite pacified yet. 'So, you're saying we were being pulled out of here anyway?' Urbanus asked. 'Even if the war was still ongoing? Why rotate the men, mid-campaign? What can Senator Rubinius be trusted to do, that I cannot?'

But Sejanus was already walking away, returning to the Praetorians on horseback around him. Disconcertingly, they seemed to be dismounting, throwing down their gear and travelling packs as if intending to stick around.

'All is in hand, senator,' the Tribune called over his shoulder. A pair of slaves, descending from the wagon's *carruca*, were carrying out the first of his personal effects. 'And I have twenty men here. Our mandate is broad. By all means, allow us to help dismantle the *castra* and pack you on your way.'

Again, that disconcerting smile. 'We are all on the same side, after all.'

FROM THAT POINT, the air changed. And it had nothing to do with the weather.

The men of the First Cohort went about their final preparations for departure, with the camp broken down into portable equipment or perishable rubble. Sejanus' small clique of Praetorians made themselves useful, doing their fair best to help with the carrying and heavy loading. Not that their efforts were much appreciated. Or called for.

The Tribune, for his part, abstained from getting his hands dirty, a decision that surprised exactly no-one. He remained aloof from the work around him, appearing only to talk in hushed tones with Urbanus. Whatever passed between them would remain a mystery, as no-one else was in earshot, but whatever was said didn't seem to improve Urbanus' mood.

Orbus found him a little later that evening, as the lion's share of the preparations were wrapping up. His own *auxilia* had been geared up and ready to march hours before – his cohort, after all, was far smaller numerically – but he wasn't about to let this go. Not until he had some answers. His men had bled for this day, after all, and now the fruits of that sacrifice were being ripped away from them.

'Tribune,' he neutrally greeted the Praetorian officer as he drew near. 'Quite a stir you caused earlier. Care to elaborate on any of it?' Around them, some legionaries from Pylades' century were busying themselves pitching the armoury's final wooden foundations out from the earth. Or, at least, trying to seem busy. 'Man to man?' he finished.

'Gaius Sertor Orbus,' Sejanus smoothly replied as he turned. 'Former Camp Prefect of the XII Legion.

Now auxiliary prefect of your very own cohort. Good day to you, Praefector.'

'You're certainly well informed, I'll give you that.' Whatever Orbus meant to say next was thrown off-kilter. Something about this Sejanus resounded in his memory. That coiffured hairline, that oily smile…

'I knew you,' the Praefector finished. 'In the *Castra Praetoria*. You were there.'

'Well remembered,' the Tribune replied, 'deserter.'

Somehow, even months on, that judgement still hit Orbus hard. He couldn't even speak for a moment, as the weight of his past misdeeds seemed to pummel him all over again.

'And I would think twice, Orbus, before trying to play the jaded hero with me.' Sejanus stepped a little closer, fixing his prey right in the eye. 'You were lucky not to be executed, in my opinion. That sort of cowardice would never fly in the Praetorian Guard, let me tell you.'

'I am no coward.' It sounded as pathetic as it felt to even say it, but somehow Orbus had no better answer than that. His pride, his authority… all was stripped from him by the tribune's icy gaze.

'Oh, I know exactly what you are,' Sejanus countered. 'The Praetorians' reach is long, and little is hidden from our eyes. You are known to us, Sertor Orbus. Your family, and its… history. The shadow of your Republican father must rankle.' He came in even closer, invading the other man's personal space. Close enough to smell his oaky breath.

'It would seem that treachery runs in your blood, old man.'

IT WOULDN'T BE long now. A day, at most.

The *castra* was all but gone. Cracked and broken earth, bone-dry in the summer heat, was all that was left of wooden walls and foundations. Charred patches of black scarred the ground at random intervals, marking the shadows of firepits and braziers.

But there was work still to be done, and Iulus Cascana never shied away from work.

A couple of his veteran '*bernia* – the veterans among his few surviving legionaries, at any rate – scoured the cauterised remains, performing final checks on what was being left to rot and organising what cargo still needed to be loaded onto wagons. As First Spear, the lion's share of the organisation and oversight rested on his shoulders, though he suspected Thracian had let a fair few of his praefector's duties by the roadside for Cascana to take up.

Still, duty was duty, and in truth he welcomed the distraction. The rest of the cohort were returning home cheated of spoils and glory. He was leaving bereft of a father figure.

The splitting ache between his ears didn't help, one compounded each time Cascana turned his head. Blood of Teucer, he'd forgotten why he never indulged on the beer. This hangover was going to last half the journey home.

'As diligent as your father ever was,' came a voice from behind him. 'He clearly didn't raise a quitter, that much I see.'

Cascana turned to face the new arrival, not sure what to make of his presence.

'Tribune Sejanus,' he replied, unsure of where this was going. He had no issue with the man personally, but nothing in the last two days had changed his feelings about the Praetorians as a whole. 'What can I do for you?'

Sejanus stepped forward, relaxed and nonconfrontational. 'Nothing so formal, First Spear. My men had some time on their hands, and it seems you're a little short on manpower. Anything we can do to help.' He gestured to the blasted *castra* remains around them.

Cascana looked suspiciously at the Praetorian for a moment, but then relented. 'Thank you, Tribune. There isn't much more to do, I fear, but more hands will make lighter work of it.'

Sejanus was already summoning his Guardsmen, whistling with a thumb and forefinger.

'I had the distinct displeasure,' he confessed, 'of meeting your friend from the *auxilia*.'

That piqued Cascana's attention. Part of him – a part drowned out by grief and alcohol – would have seen such an obvious trap from a mile off. But right here, right now, protecting Sertor Orbus was not a worry that plagued him. Not anymore.

'That man,' he replied, 'is no friend of mine.'

Sejanus cocked his head as if contemplating. 'He is certainly… divisive,' he finally settled for. 'The fact his career has survived his mistakes, both now and in the past… it certainly lends him an air of, how shall I phrase it? Messianic arrogance. As if none of us mere mortals can comprehend his thoughts.'

Cascana snorted ruefully, as he helped one of his *milites* lift some rubble clear. 'In all honesty, Tribune, he's had that trait long before his disgrace. I've known that man my whole life. Believe me. That is simply who he is.'

Sejanus thought on that for a moment, reassured by the First Spear's rising to the bait. 'I feel we've all had a camp prefect like that, at some point. I came up in the Fifth Legion, before I joined the Praetorians. The Alaudae had this wizened old goat of a praefector.' His tangent dissolved into chuckling. 'I'll never forget him, to my dying day. Damn prefects. They train you all up from the *tirones*, and think they then own you forevermore.'

'Oh, yes.' Cascana slapped his hands together to shake off dust, joining in with Sejanus' repartee. 'Orbus certainly fits that bill.' And then he stopped, hesitant, as if he didn't know how to finish the thought.

The pain of the last day came to the fore, and the vulnerability must have bled off him. Sejanus was by his side a moment later, a hand, firm yet fraternal, on his shoulder.

'I'm sorry,' Cascana confessed. He made no effort to move the Tribune's hand. 'Orbus... I trusted that man with my life. I had no idea how badly he'd repay that trust.'

Sejanus' tone grew gentler still. Brotherly. Understanding.

The perfect honey to bait the trap.

'Talk to me, First Spear,' he soothed. 'I am listening.'

A WARM AND quiet night later, the moment finally came.

Civilians and camp-hands ran back and forth along the completed baggage train, the lines of straddled mules braying at the return of their cumbersome loads. Spoils, materiel, even the cohort's heaviest equipment – everything too impractical to be borne by legionaries on foot.

Sejanus' Praetorians had only left hours before, on their seemingly faster return journey by horseback. The smaller the group, the faster they would travel, and Orbus had little doubt they would arrive home weeks before he did.

The Praetorians had departed with as little fanfare as they'd arrived. There had been no prolonged goodbye, or any sort of ceremonial nod from the Fulminata – hardly surprising, given the unwelcome tidings they'd been sent to bear. Most of the officers had followed Urbanus' surly example, sparing the departing Guardsmen little more than gruff nods and barebones pleasantries.

All except Cascana, who seemed to favour Sejanus with a little more warmth as the two men parted ways.

And, more disturbingly, Thracian. Orbus wasn't sure what to make of what he'd seen, but from the way the Praefector and Tribune had embraced like kinsmen, they were clearly men who shared a history.

In the end, he'd chosen not to waste time worrying about it. This war had proved his men to the Legion, and himself to them. But it had taken so much from him, too. All he wanted was to go home. Maybe there, things would seem a little clearer.

Only the Fates weren't quite finished with him yet. Fortuna had one last drop of spite left in her horn.

'Master,' the voice broke him from his administrative reverie. Orbus was standing near a cluster of mules at the lines' end; his *auxilia*, and their meagre reserves of equipment, were all ready for the journey home. But that didn't stop him checking their readiness, again and again.

'Merope,' the Praefector replied. 'I sent you to the slaves' wagon with Puli. What is wrong?'

Perhaps, if Orbus' opener had been a little gentler – if that first question had concerned the young woman's wellbeing, instead of why his favoured possession was out of its allotted place – then the following conversation would have run along smoother lines. But then, perhaps not. The seeds of this confrontation had been sown a while before, and the Praefector's manner with Merope in the months since hadn't helped. In that regard, Orbus was only reaping what he'd sown for so long.

'I heard,' Merope gently confessed, too quiet for others to overhear. 'About Cascana. Puli and I both heard.'

Orbus inwardly groaned. He didn't want to get into this. Not now, and certainly not with her.

'And?' he archly replied. His tone dared her to take this further.

'And...' Merope swallowed, gently brushing hair behind her ear. 'Are you not going to seek him out? To apologise, and make amends?'

Far ahead of them, a bugle begun its reverberating cry. Shouts went out along the baggage lines, and whips cracked across the backs of mules as the train's frontmost part began to move. Here he was again, leaving Gaul in shame and loathing for a second time.

'And why would I do that?' Orbus testily replied. 'I empathised with his loss – a loss I suffered too, mind you, and far greater – and admitted that maybe I made the wrong choice. What more can I do? If he can't see past all that, then this is no longer on me. It's on him.'

Merope took a moment to digest that. 'You really believe that, don't you?'

Orbus screwed up his face, turning back round to the wagon he'd been checking. Yes, the halter and reins were still very much secure, tied to the ass still waiting for its beleaguered driver.

Of course it was his fault. But what good would admitting it do, if Cascana wouldn't even deign to hear his voice? What more could he give the man, beyond that confession of guilt?

'It doesn't matter anymore. It's over. Now get back to your carriage. The march is beginning. We'll be leaving soon.'

Merope let out a silent breath. Decision made, then.

'When we get back to Rome, master,' she began, surprised by how little her voice was shaking, 'I would like to buy my freedom from you.'

How strange it felt, to finally speak the thought she'd kept hidden for months. How simple it seemed in retrospect.

'You've been generous in the allowance you give me,' Merope continued, realising Orbus wasn't going to say anything. 'And I have been saving it, diligently, these past few years. I appreciate you may not have been expecting this request, and in light of the sum you originally paid for—'

'Whatever.' Orbus waved his hand, turning once again. 'Whatever you want to pay, just pay it. I'll have the papers drawn up when we return to Rome. In the meantime, consider yourself manumitted.'

The courtesan took that in, struggling to accept this sudden capitulation.

'Go on, then,' the Praefector snapped. 'Unless you want to get left behind here. Go!' He waved his hand again dismissively, still trying to appear less perturbed than he surely felt.

'Don't you... don't you want to ask me why?' Merope ventured.

'Does it matter?' Orbus wasn't even looking at her now, briefly sticking his head into the *carruca* of a wagon carrying arms and armour. 'No doubt you have your reasons, and frankly I can't say I truly care. If you want to leave, then so be it. No need to stand on ceremony.'

'Oh, for...' Merope didn't even know how to begin. This wasn't how two adults who cared about each other moved on. Hitching her skirt and tunic up to avoid the muck, she made her way over to where her master was standing.

'Well maybe I should tell you anyway,' she began. 'Because I can't watch you do this to yourself anymore. I asked you, back in Rome, remember? I asked you if you wanted to die. And we both remember what happened next.' She even laughed. 'And now, instead, you risk all your lives on a battlefield you *chose* to join, and somehow drive away your closest friend in the process.'

She stopped, hoping to see any understanding or remorse in the older man's eyes.

'I can't watch this happen.' She looked back down the train of baggage, where the last few slaves and attendants were joining their comrades' wagons or the steeds of their masters. 'I cannot watch this self-destruction.'

Would anything have swayed her, in that moment? Would any pledge or promise Orbus could make, any admission of how he'd truly felt these last six months have stopped this final bond from breaking?

'I can't play nursemaid to your demons,' Merope finished. 'That is far, far more than anything I could give you. I'm sorry, master. But I cannot help you anymore. You have to face them on your own.'

And with that, she was leaving once again. Finally out of sight, Orbus allowed himself the luxury of burying his face in one hand. Argias. Bydreth. Cascana. Now her.

'Don't bother coming back to the *Principia*,' the Praefector called after her. 'Take whatever allowance you're still owed and leave. I'll have the damned manumission filed in your absence.'

The courtesan – the closest thing Orbus had to a true partner anymore – turned back to him one last time.

'These new soldiers… I thought it would be a new beginning.' She shook her head, more heartbroken than her former master would ever realise. 'But I don't know what you've started here. Or how it could ever end well.'

And with that last confession, she was gone. Truly gone.

Gaius Sertor Orbus took one last moment to reflect on her departure. And then he put it from his mind, same as everything else. He'd spent enough time lately looking backward. There was nothing he could change there.

Time to go. The journey home was long. And there was so much still to do on his return.

EPILOGUE

IRONBREAKERS

THE SUMMERS IN Baiae were always long and lingering. Even in autumn, the pleasure town's grounds and hillsides remained baked and parched as ever before the occasional coming of rain. The water lapping against the beaches of the Gulf remained tepid, the evening air still thick with warmth and cicada-song. September had yet to break that seasonal spell.

Even after sundown, Elysia had all the rustic charm of a crypt in summertime. In the midst of the Gulf's busiest months, the decaying resort still attracted few visitors.

'Neptune's briny bollocks.' Sextus Orbus put his empty goblet back down on the study room desk. 'That is one raging inferno of a story, Gaius. You couldn't have made that up if you'd tried.'

Across the desk, his brother eyed him curiously over his own goblet of mead. His face and torso were a kaleidoscopic melange of mauve, viridian and brown; a tapestry of bruises and injuries, only now starting to fade.

'Those damned Praetorians,' Orbus ruminated, more to himself than Sextus. 'All that menace and intrigue, dripping off the Emperor's robes. Trouble blooms wherever they walk.'

'How did they know?' Sextus asked, fixing his brother's gaze peculiarly hard. 'How did they know all that about our father? I mean, it's hardly a secret,' he clarified, pouring some more mead from the glass tankard, 'but how did they match that knowledge to your face? Everyone who even knew Ascanius is dead. Did they seriously pore through the records of every officer in the Legion? Or...' He trailed off, savouring his mead's aftertaste.

'Or someone told them.' Orbus' voice was grim. 'Someone close to me.'

Something called out in the distance outside, the sound carrying in through the open wooden shutters. Most likely a seabird.

'I can hardly believe the rest,' Sextus went on. Orbus had a feeling this topic was coming, but his brother didn't seem particularly preachy tonight. Best to keep the mead to a minimum and get it over with.

'I mean,' Sextus continued, 'a whole legion, crying out against Imperial rule?' He seemed more than a little smug, something Orbus had frustratingly foreseen. 'And such a concerted effort to sweep it under the carpet? I mean, the *damnatio* just proves it, surely? If our glorious emperor wants to obliterate this from Rome's memory... well, that reeks of fear, no?'

'Perhaps.' Orbus was uneasy, but not for that reason. Passing a sentence like that didn't sit well with him, whatever the reason. Ignatian's words in the Temple of Perfidy came back to him, unwelcomely befitting.

The kings of Rome sleep ill in their graves. We have seen where that road takes us, Sertor. We all have.

'I killed you,' he caught himself muttering.

- 509 -

Sextus slapped down his goblet again. 'You what?'

Orbus shook his head. 'Nothing.' Killing a man was simple enough. But killing what he stood for, extinguishing an ideal, wasn't so easy. Not once it took root in the mind.

And in *his* mind? Well, Ignatian would never be dead there.

'You seem changed.' Sextus brought him back to himself. 'From when I last saw you, I mean. Still not sure of yourself. But not quite as… condemned.'

That crude assessment made him chuckle. 'When you put it like that…' Orbus replied.

'This new cohort must be doing you some good, at any rate,' Sextus decided. 'Whatever happens with you and the XII, it must be nice to have a purpose again.'

The Praefector nodded. Even if he wasn't quite sure what that purpose was.

Sextus gave him another searching look, trying to discern what was bothering his brother, before just sitting back and folding his arms.

'You're thinking about Cascana, aren't you?'

'I am.' Orbus had pushed away his goblet. No good would come from drinking any more tonight. 'Do you think I made the wrong choice, brother? Putting his men at risk to win the battle quickly?'

Sextus blew air through his half-closed lips. 'Are you really asking *me* for military insight, "Praefector Orbus"? Times really must be dire.' He started sniggering at this self-referential wit.

Orbus' scowl cut through the older man's levity. 'Brother,' he replied, 'you know what I mean.'

'Ah.' Sextus crudely shook his goblet, displeased with its lack of sloshing contents. 'Why is my cup always empty when you start talking shit?' he half-joked. In the end, he slapped it down on a nearby tray instead. A houseslave would retrieve it later.

'It doesn't really matter, I suppose,' he finally decided, 'which one of you was right. You shafted him, Gaius. You're like family to that man. I should know. The Cascanae always treated you like their own. I should know. It used to drive me mad.' He snorted. 'And you pissed that loyalty back in his face. It doesn't matter if you were right to do it. What matters is if he'll ever get past it.'

Orbus scowled, closing his eyes. 'I had a feeling you would say something like that,' he confessed.

'And sorry to hear Merope's skipping out on you,' Sextus tactlessly added. 'The nerve! You know, brother, you really aren't hard enough on your slaves. I'd have taken the brand to her, in your position.'

The Praefector's disapproving silence showed just what he thought of that. Maybe Sextus had a point. But then again, Sextus hadn't bedded any of his own slaves. And had certainly never started sharing all his darkest secrets with them, either.

'Nowhere I can turn, these days, without people fuming at the sight of me,' Orbus muttered. 'Each way I look… they all just slip from my grasp.'

That was as dramatic as it was self-pitying, but there was truth in it. He'd raised his *auxilia* from the gutter, and seen them through their first campaign. He'd shown the XII that he still had a future in the Roman army, even without the Legion.

And what had it cost? Only Argias, Bydreth and very nearly Vinculex. Cascana and Merope, too, although it had been their choice, not war's cruel whim, that made it so.

It seemed a rather hollow trade-off, all things considered.

And then of course, there was Aemilia. The longer Orbus had ignored her letters on campaign, the less resolve he had to answer any of them, and he wasn't looking forward to that reunion at all. He hadn't even mentioned the wedding to Sextus, and he didn't feel like ripping open that particular wound now.

'The first time I gathered Optatis' men,' said the Praefector, 'I told them that their previous lives ceased to matter. That whatever their shames and disgraces, this was the taste of a second chance.' His gaze absently went to the window, shutters gently trembling in the evening breeze. 'Perhaps leading them will be mine. If Cascana and I ever see eye-to-eye again, at least.'

'If you're done whining,' Sextus muttered. 'What, then, do you plan to do now?'

'Rebuild the Ironbreakers, first and foremost,' Orbus replied. Yet another impulse choice he was regretting – that ludicrously theatrical name already seemed to be sticking among the cohort, despite his best efforts. Probably just to spite him. 'Finding new recruits will hardly be difficult. Replenish their ranks, and keep them out the way of whoever wishes me ill.'

'The Praetorians?' Sextus raised an eyebrow.

'I was more referring to Thracian,' his brother replied. 'But it's a good point, yes. I doubt any good will come of crossing paths with them again. Or that Sejanus fellow.'

'Fair enough,' Sextus reasoned. 'And what then?'

'Then?' Orbus wrinkled his brow. 'Wait for the next war, I suppose.'

DUSK GAVE WAY to sunset. September nights in Baiae weren't much cooler than the days, something that never did much for Sextus' sleep.

Still, now he found himself with a little time alone, he could properly reflect on the day's events before bed.

His brother was taking his customary walk to Ascanius' gravestone, just as he'd done on his last visit. All in all, it had been nice to see him again, especially now he seemed less of a dead man walking.

Sextus smiled. For now, at least.

He leant back in his chair, pulling open a desk drawer. The source of his bonhomie was revealed – a small, nondescript bag of cured leather, tied at the neck with a string of flax. He knew what lay inside, of course. Not a grand number of *aurei*. But enough. Enough to begin reviving Elysia's fortunes. He'd always known he'd get there. To do so quickly was an unexpected bonus.

And there in the drawer, beside the blessed money, lay the price for this favour.

The letter's seal had already been broken, but Sextus hadn't been born yesterday. That seal was the only thing proving the sender's veracity.

If things went south, that proof might well keep his neck from the hangman's noose.

Sextus reached in, picking up the letter up. By and large, the cooperation it asked for hadn't troubled him too much. Not to the degree he'd thought. Funny, how things turned out in the end.

The seal was made of dried wax, dyed in the style of the sender's heraldic insignia. They were a showy bunch, he supposed, and had every right to flaunt their means.

The seal's imprint showed an eight-legged emblem. A scorpion of jet black, atop a pale white backdrop.

Sextus put the letter back in place, shutting the draw.

And smiled once more.

NIGHT FOUND THE Praefector in his brother's field, right where he always seemed to end up. A little way off, Ascanius' grave stood equally unadorned as last time. No surprises there. The brothers Orbus weren't a sentimental family.

It was another funerary marker he'd come for, this time. One far smaller and less conspicuous. With no inscription or votive markings, you'd hardly know it was there.

Somewhere deep within the ground before it, lay the ashen remains of a young woman, as undisturbed as they'd been from their interment two years past. Strange, how time fails to heal some wounds.

Some holes in your heart were simply there to stay, no matter how hard you tried to fill them.

And his heart had enough holes to spare. His wife. His legion. His comrades in arms.

Merope had been a way to fill the void Caesula had left, albeit far from a perfect fit.

For the space in his soul that the XII had once held... perhaps the Ironbreakers would, in time, grow to fill that too.

Orbus reached within his tunic, fishing out the cold metal *phalerae* that hung around his neck. How easily, he'd gotten used to wearing that mark of office. The steel medallions denoting him as a legion officer felt part of him, as much as the Fulminata's ink had. Each had become a piece of who he was.

Orbus slid the *phalerae* off his neck, giving the headstone one final look. He wasn't sure what he expected to see, but old habits in an old soldier died hard.

'The others are right, Caesula,' he said aloud to the open air. 'I cannot buy back my past. The future is where I must look to now.'

He hurled the *phalerae* out into the field, where they landed some way away in the waist-high grass. There would be no finding them again now, even if he'd wanted to. Not until harvest-time.

'Here we are, at the end of all things.' He turned back, free of the last connection to his old life. 'And now… I can begin again.'

The Ironbreakers will return in Prince of Knaves

ACKNOWLEDGEMENTS

A novel is always more than the sum of its parts, and after eighteen months of nigh-on continuous work I've got quite the litany of gratitude to work through.

A mandatory shoutout must go to my parents, for continuing to support and accept me as their favourite financial burden. And for simply having the faith that locking myself in my bedroom for a year would lead to anything to actually show for it.

Some less generic praise should also go to my own little '*bernium* of test readers; Enrico Manfredi-Haylock, Kester Bond, Nisha Hare, Alice Clarke, Scott Kennard and the Brothers Handa. The editorial advice of John Rickards and Merilyn Davies has also been worth its weight in gold.

My *optio*, Raman Handa, deserves special commendation for god knows how many hours of evaluating, back and forth messaging, listening to the most banal of questions and repeatedly asking '*why not just…*'

Thanks must also go to Ruth Chaloner for the week-in, week-out sanity checks, which probably kept me straight long enough to plough to the end.

I owe a truly extortionate debt to Nik and the whole team at Book Beaver for the truly stunning cover you crafted for me – I certainly know who I'll be coming back to for the rest of the series.

My former tutors, Professors Alison Cooley and Michael Scott, kindly provided me with advice as well as uni lecture material that proved so damn useful... almost makes me wish I'd gone to more of them!

I owe some thanks to various denizens of AuthorTube for their practical wisdom, inspiration and in some cases hilarity – in particular, J.P. Beaubien of *Terrible Writing Advice* and Meg LaTorre of *iWriterly*, and on the BookTube front, Leonie of *The Book Leo*.

A very particular shoutout is reserved for Chlöe Standen, and a chance reunion on the Leamington U1 which led to me giving this whole writing thing another go. Without that bus ride, I sincerely doubt there would be any Ironbreakers. Or anything else that follows them.

And one last little thank you must go to Cigarettes After Sex, for the many hours spent writing while listening to your dulcet tones.

ABOUT THE AUTHOR

Vijay Hare comes from Oxford, and read Classics at the University of Warwick.

Some misguided early career steps, a bout of appallingly poor health and the 2020 global pandemic all left him trapped at home for almost two years, where he begun novel writing as a way to weaponize the ominous-looking gap in his CV.

Outside of writing, he enjoys starring in amateur dramatics, long walks, and the occasional Kopparberg.

Legion That Was is his first novel – and, for the sake of his career prospects, hopefully not his last.

Visit www.vijayharewriter.com to find out more about his upcoming projects.

If you enjoyed this novel, then please consider leaving a review on Amazon and/or Goodreads.

Printed in Great Britain
by Amazon

77280160R00307